HARD RIDE
ACROSS TEXAS

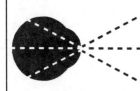

HARD RIDE
ACROSS TEXAS

MICHAEL ZIMMER

THORNDIKE PRESS

A part of Gale, a Cengage Company

GALE
A Cengage Company

Farmington Hills, Mich • San Francisco • New York • Waterville, Maine
Meriden, Conn • Mason, Ohio • Chicago

Copyright © 2018 by Michael Zimmer.
Thorndike Press, a part of Gale, a Cengage Company.

ALL RIGHTS RESERVED
Thorndike Press® Large Print Western.
The text of this Large Print edition is unabridged.
Other aspects of the book may vary from the original edition.
Set in 16 pt. Plantin.

LIBRARY OF CONGRESS CIP DATA ON FILE.
CATALOGUING IN PUBLICATION FOR THIS BOOK
IS AVAILABLE FROM THE LIBRARY OF CONGRESS

ISBN-13: 978-1-4328-4708-1 (hardcover alk. paper)

Published in 2019 by arrangement with Michael Zimmer

Printed in the United States of America
1 2 3 4 5 6 7 23 22 21 20 19

HARD RIDE
ACROSS TEXAS

CHAPTER ONE

On the matter of my killing Henry Kalb, then fleeing to the buffalo grounds of West Texas, I will say this: I was young and naïve in the ways of life outside the shelter of home and family. I lived under my father's roof, and so I obeyed his commands. When, on the eve of Henry's death, he ordered me to leave, I did so without challenge. What resulted afterward is the basis of this narrative.

It was never my intention to kill Henry that night, although I suppose our nation's penitentiaries are filled with men who would offer similar claims. Of those who have since fallen before my guns, I make no apology. Those incidents were matters of survival, thrust before me like unwanted bills or moldy bread in a jail cell. I consider my responses appropriate for the circumstances, their deaths regrettable but strictly of their own making.

Nor will I seek pardon from my colleagues, many of whom will doubtless find themselves unsettled by these confessions. I have a past, as do they; mine is perhaps a bit more unorthodox, but I will claim it in its entirety, warts included. I will add but a single caveat. I am an educator now, and have been for the better part of four decades, but I was a son of the soil in 1877, and spoke as such. To the best of my memory and ability, I will present this account in the vernacular of that distant youth. May the gods of grammar forgive me.

My encounter with Henry Kalb occurred early in the evening of the day the assault charge against him was officially dismissed by Judge Robert Wetzel of Milam County, Texas. Earlier that afternoon my family and I had returned to our farm some miles west of the little town of Shelburn. It didn't take long for me to change out of my good Sunday suit and back into the range clothes I felt most comfortable wearing — sturdy denim trousers and low-heeled boots, a blue cotton shirt of a style I favored at the time, with a shield front, tiny ivory buttons, and black piping at the seams. My hat was a gray felt Pettigrew, wide-brimmed and flat-crowned, darkened around the band from perspiration.

I was sitting alone on the top step to the dogtrot that separated the twin log rooms we called home. My little brother Beau, who was twelve that year, had stayed behind to look after the place in case we were gone overnight. I still recall how he'd fled into the trees across the creek when he saw the looks on our faces upon our return. Bess was down by the chicken coop entertaining Baby Luke with kernels of corn that he'd toss into the pen by the tiny handful, laughing gleefully at the frantic darting and pecking of the hens. Luke was too young at the time to realize anything was amiss, but Bess, though just a few years older, must have sensed the tension, because she stayed at the coop and kept her brother occupied. I'm not sure how much she really understood about what had happened or how it was going to affect our family in the coming weeks and months. I was having a hard enough time myself trying to put it all in perspective. Judging from the terse murmurings coming from the summer kitchen where my pa and ma and sister Ester had retreated on the pretext of fixing supper, I'd say they were also finding the day's unexpected turn of events difficult to comprehend.

Ann Dunford's refusal to testify on my

sister's behalf had caught all of us off guard. At the time, I found her sudden change of heart puzzling, but age and experience has since clarified her decision. The Kalbs had gotten to her, that much was obvious. Or at least they'd gotten to her family. Not with money — the Dunfords had too much integrity for that — but most likely through intimidation. The threat of dragging Ann's name through the quag alongside my sister's must have struck terror into the hearts of both of Ann's parents. I'm sure it would have mine, and I've often wondered what my mother's response would have been had the situation been reversed. I didn't have any doubt about how my father would have reacted, but his was a male's approach, quick and blunt. My mother, I've noticed, generally took the long view.

Judge Wetzel knew what must have happened. You could see it in his face, hear it in the disdain coloring his words as he dismissed Ann as a witness. But his hands were tied. Without corroborating testimony, it was Ester's word against Henry's, and my sister's happy flirtations on the dance floor during Shelburn's annual Harvest Festival the previous week would have risen against her like a mob of brutal accusers.

Everyone at the celebration had noticed

it. Most of them had seemed amused, perhaps recalling their own youthful indiscretions. But Ester's coquetry had turned swiftly against her when she came stumbling out of the shadows later that evening, her hair tousled, a bruise already forming under one eye. A seam on her dress had been torn, exposing nearly an inch of pale shoulder beneath it. Throwing herself into her mother's arms, she'd raggedly sobbed out a story of how Henry Kalb had lured her into the darkness by promising to let her ride his horse. None of us knew until much later that the animal had been stabled all day at the Shelburn Livery on the other side of town.

Henry pleaded innocence, claiming it had been Ester who enticed him into the darkness behind the Masonic Hall where the dance was being held, then thrown herself at him like a common trollop. Ann had been with them — Ester never would have followed Henry alone — but Kurt Dunford had hustled his daughter away that evening before the charges and counter charges could be sorted through. Ann had promised my father the next day that she would testify to what actually happened, how Henry's brother Paul had grabbed her from behind while Henry tried to force himself on Ester.

Although both girls managed to break away, Ester had come out the worse for it, weeping uncontrollably as she ran into the dance in search of her mother, never thinking of the image her disheveled appearance would create, the speculation it might infer. How could she, barely sixteen and thinking herself in love with one of the county's finest? Thinking he felt the same way toward her, I suppose.

The trial, called into session the following Thursday, had been but a sham. Henry and Paul stood before the bench exchanging broad smirks with their friends in the gallery, while their father — fiery old Linus Kalb in his finest suit, broad-brimmed white hat on the table by his side — huddled with his attorney at the defense table. Ann Dunford's complexion had resembled old milk as she approached the witness stand, and her expression was one of impending ruin. Her mother and mine and Ester had wept quietly through it all.

I wonder now if they'd known even then what was about to happen. I certainly hadn't. Neither had my father, that much was evident from the look of utter astonishment on his face when Ann pleaded ignorance of the event. It was as if a shaft had opened up beneath Pa's feet and swallowed him whole.

No one spoke on the way home. Pa drove the buggy with Ma and Ester crowded onto the seat beside him. I rode behind on my dun gelding, Dusty, staying well back and trying to make sense of what had happened. Trying to understand how an upstanding family like the Dunfords — hell, how an entire town — could stand back and allow an innocent girl's reputation to become so sullied.

The trial had been scheduled for eleven o'clock. It was over by noon and we were back home by three, but other than the normal chores associated with life on a frontier farm, we didn't do much for the rest of the day. I milked the cows as the sun dropped behind the trees to the west — normally Ester's responsibility — and Bess and Baby Luke dumped hay into the manger for the horses and our two mules. Then, while the youngsters tossed eared corn to one of our penned sows that was about to farrow, I walked back to the house and dropped down on the top step as exhausted as if I'd been following a plow all day. My parents and Ester were still in the summer kitchen behind the house, the spicy aroma of Ma's good chicken gumbo drifting pleasantly across the yard and through the dogtrot to where I sat hunched forward like an old man. My folks were originally from the lower Sabine River country, and had brought a lot of that culture with them to the Brazos.

Smelling Ma's fragrant stew briefly assuaged the melancholy pressing down on me. Vague memories of my Cajun roots — of cypress cabins and Spanish moss, of old Elmer Taupree's pirogue nearly overflowing with 'gator flats as he glided silently across the still waters of our bayou — temporarily lifted the sense of betrayal I knew we were all feeling. Better times in a better place, or so it seemed to me that late October eve. In fairness, I'd only been four years old when we left the Sabine, the oldest of the seven children Ma and Pa would eventually bring unto the earth.

My gaze drifted across the gently tilted pasture east of the barn to the fenced-off oak tree under which Mickey and Louise had been laid to rest just a few short seasons after our arrival here. Five and six years of age when they passed from the fever. I'd been eight at the time, bedridden for nearly a week with aching muscles and a temperature like flames eating away at me from the inside, although I'd escaped the seizures and internal bleeding that eventually claimed my two siblings. Only Ma and Beau, for reasons unknown, had avoided the plague's embrace entirely.

The Texas frontier was hard on everyone. Even the Kalbs had lost children to the yellow scourge as it swept across the lower Brazos Valley a dozen years before. Their losses had been worse than our own — five children taken by the ravages of yellow jack, and one daughter, barely seven, rendered blind and permanently dull-witted from her extended delirium. Ma speculated their casualties were the result of Linus having brought his family down from the Alabama mountains in the early 1850s, and that from such soft origins they'd lacked the "tougher hide of bayou folk" in combating an epidemic born in the southern swamps.

But I wasn't thinking much about Linus Kalb's losses that evening. I was thinking about Ester's, and the Kalb's second-youngest son, Henry, and how he'd taken advantage of my sister's innocence, and there was a mad stirring in my gut like a thousand angry hornets.

The sky softened as the vibrant colors of sunset drained off into the horizon, while night crept in from the east like a stalking panther. A bobwhite trilled from the woods across the creek, and my jaws clamped tight.

Ester loved the call of those sturdy quail. She could mimic their unique two- and three-toned cries so perfectly she'd often been able to coax them into responding, the pair of them chattering back and forth like old friends. Tonight's halting song brought a fresh burst of sobs from the summer kitchen, and something inside of me seemed to snap so violently I swear I felt it.

Pushing to my feet, I stalked into the south-side cabin where Beau and I shared a curtained-off room in the rear corner. My revolver, one of those older model Colts converted to shoot a .44 Henry rimfire cartridge, sat on top of the wardrobe alongside my belt and holster. I brought them down and strapped the belt around my waist and settled the Colt on my right hip. My Winchester was leaning against the wall next to my bunk and I grabbed that and a box of cartridges off the floor next to it on my way out.

I caught a glimpse of Pa as I exited the cabin. He was sitting on the summer kitchen's stoop with his shoulders angled toward the ground like a mountain's sharp slopes, his gaze fixed on the hard-packed earth in front of his boots. Lord knew where his thoughts were as he listened to Ester's anguished keening from inside.

Keeping the twin cabins between us, I dropped off the edge of the dogtrot and headed for the barn at a jog. I'd corralled Dusty out back that afternoon rather than turn him loose in the big pasture like I'd normally do. Maybe on some level I'd known that I'd soon be returning to Shelburn. I led the gelding inside the barn and hitched him to an iron ring bolted to one of the support posts. Then I ducked into the tack room to fetch my saddle and bridle. When I came back out, Pa was standing at the barn's entrance, propped wearily against its frame. I still remember his single word to me, and especially its unnaturally subdued tone.

"Gage."

Orrin Pardell was a strong man, and he had a voice to match. Neither loud nor overbearing, just solid and confident. The day's events had taken that out of him. Out of all of us in one way or another, I suppose.

Keeping my back to him, I tossed a saddle blanket over the dun's back, then straightened it with my left hand while holding the saddle tight against my right hip. When I was ready, I lifted the rig onto the horse's back and shoved the cinch off the far side.

"It won't do any good," Pa said.

"Are we going to just forget it happened?" I asked, reaching underneath and grabbing the cinch as it swung toward me.

"I don't know," he admitted. "Your mother and I need to talk about it, but she isn't ready to do that yet. She says we have to think about Ester first, and she's right. We all have to, Gage, even you."

That slowed my hand for only a moment. Then stubbornness prevailed and I pulled the cinch up to thread the latigo's tongue through the polished iron ring. "You know what he's doing."

"Henry?"

I nodded rigidly. "He's either in the Alamo or down at the Roost with that bunch of troublemakers he drinks with, and they're laughing about what happened today. Laughing about what happened at the dance last week, too, like it's . . ."

My voice broke and my hands trembled as I pictured Henry and Paul Kalb and the boys they liked to raise hell with — Bill Eisner and the Lapwins and some of the Hennings clan from downriver. Not to mention the usual riffraff that hung out along Shelburn's river road. My jaw set like a chunk of iron; I yanked the cinch tight, then drew the latigo down through its horizontal loop to snug the saddle in place. After a long minute, Pa sighed and pushed away from the door.

"Let me have a couple of minutes to talk with your ma, Gage, then I'll go with you."

"No!" I turned in alarm. "You can't go with me."

"I'm not letting you go by yourself."

"I can handle Henry Kalb."

"It won't be just Henry you'll have to deal with. It'll be the whole damned bunch of 'em, especially if they've been drinking."

"I won't be looking for trouble. I just don't want them saying . . . things about Ester that they don't have any right to say."

"How do you plan to stop them?" he asked gently. "Shoot them?"

"It won't come to that. Henry'll shut up quick if I tell him to."

"What if he doesn't?"

"Then I'll shut him up, but not with a gun. I ain't looking for that kind of trouble, Pa. I promise."

"No one ever is," he said tiredly, then squared his shoulders as if finding a little of his old strength returning. "Wait here while I fetch my rifle and tell your ma where we're going."

"You can't go, Pa."

He looked at me, the defeat I'd seen in his eyes all afternoon vanished. "Just who's

19

going to stop me?"

"Ma, I'd hope."

"I still make the decisions around here."

"I know, but I don't have a wife and kids depending on me. You do. You've got Ma and Ester and Bess and Baby Luke. Beau, too, even if he'd say otherwise."

"Boy, I don't need you telling me what my responsibilities are," Pa said, and his words were as of old, hard as steel.

"You've got this farm to run and a family to raise." I was treading over perilous ground and knew it, but I was also young and bull-headed and determined to be heard. "You can't risk going up against the Kalbs, Pa. You know you can't."

Anger flared briefly in his eyes, then abruptly smothered out. Indecision took its place, a back-and-forth struggle between his obligations as the family patriarch and a primal desire to ride into Shelburn and rip the heads off of Henry and Paul Kalb, and anyone else who might think it funny the way they'd beaten the charges against them, not caring a whit about its cost to others. And not just Ester, although I knew she'd suffer the most before it was over — if it was *ever* over for her — but the Dunfords as well, who would have their own crosses to bear. Especially Ann, after turning her back on her friend.

I thought for a minute Pa would accept the futility of his appetition and give up his decision to ride into Shelburn with me, but I guess in the end it was too much for him to turn his back on. Spinning toward the house, he growled, "Saddle my horse, Gage."

"Pa," I called after him, but he just waved me off, heading for the cabin in that long-legged, determined stride of his.

My right hand curled into a fist, but there was nothing to bash it into. Chafing with irritation, I slipped the bridle over Dusty's head and buckled the throatlatch. The Winchester's scabbard was already fastened under the off-side fender. I slid my long gun inside, then grabbed a halter and lead rope off a peg next to the tack room door and went out back to fetch Pa's chestnut mare, Sally. Being older and spoiled, she came as soon as she saw me approaching the gate.

A plan began to take shape in my mind as I secured the halter. Keeping Sally close on her lead rope, I moved around behind the extra stock — a pair of mules, a seal brown gelding Beau normally rode, and the buggy mare with her colt — and hied the bunch of them through the gate toward the trees. The mules gave me a puzzled look as they exited the corral, but took off in a fine gallop when I popped the end of the lead rope against the jenny's hip. Beau's seal brown and the buggy horse and her colt ran with them, all three snorting happily and kicking up their heels. I smiled in satisfaction as they disappeared into the timber across the creek. They were going to be hard to catch with full dark coming on, and with luck, wouldn't be collared until the next day.

The chestnut was another matter. Too mellow to run far, she probably would have come trotting back to the barn as soon as Pa thought to rattle a grain can with a little shelled corn inside. I'd have to take her with me, at least partway.

I loosened Dusty's halter rope and led both horses outside. Pa wasn't anywhere to be seen. Likely, despite his gruff assertion to the contrary, he'd run into trouble trying to convince Ma that him and me going into town that night was a good idea. Ma was a good, gentle woman, but she was stubborn, too, and wouldn't be easily swayed.

Cramming my foot in the stirrup, I hauled up into the saddle and tapped the gelding's ribs with my heels. I was hoping to make a clean break, but hadn't covered fifty yards at a slow trot when I heard Pa hollering for me to come back or risk a hide-tanning. He was standing in the fading light of the dogtrot, just about smoldering for being so angry. He was going to be madder still when he found out I'd scattered the rest of the stock into the woods.

Figuring I was in it with both feet anyway, I kept riding. I left the chestnut in a clearing a couple of miles down the road, knowing she wouldn't stray until it was time to be fed the next morning. Or until Pa or Beau found her. Beau, if you're wondering, still hadn't showed up. I figured he was out there in the trees somewhere yet, struggling with the same helpless fury the rest of us were battling that day. Looking back, I wish I'd gone with him.

CHAPTER TWO

It was normally a three-hour buggy ride from our place to Shelburn, but with a good road and clear skies I was able to keep Dusty at a lope the whole way, shaving nearly an hour off that time. Even so, it was well past dark when I rode into town, although not overly late.

Shelburn isn't much more than a wide spot in a poorly graveled road today — a dozen homes at most, plus a general store with a gas pump out front and post office drop box beside the cash register — but back in '77 it was a fair-sized town, sprawled across the top of a bluff below old Port Sullivan and overlooking the Brazos River. The main business district and most of the fancier houses sat up high, where an evening breeze out of the west kept the mosquitoes at bay, but there was another section of town we called Lower Shelburn that probably only the old-timers remember today. It sat below the bluff near where the wharf used to be, back when most of that area's cash crops — primarily cotton and sugar cane — were shipped to Galveston by steamboat. Even in '77 you'd still see an occasional paddle wheeler tied up along the Brazos's muddy bank, but most of the crops at that time were being freighted north to Hearne by wagon, then shipped east on the Houston and Texas Central Railway.

A narrow belt of sweet gum trees concealed most of Lower Shelburn from the more respectable element up above, but it was in the seedier part of town that I expected to find the Kalbs. I paused before reining in that direction. There was some kind of an altercation taking place in front of the Dunfords' small brick home a couple of blocks away, three or four individuals milling in the light of a single lantern, while animated voices flowed up the street on the humid air. Although naturally curious, I was still bitter over Ann's betrayal of Ester, and turned away without further investigation. It was one of those small decisions we all make in life, the kind that can change your future forever, like turning right instead of left and getting trampled by a team of runaway horses . . . or meeting the woman you'd eventually marry.

Lower Shelburn was accessed by a narrow thoroughfare with the unimaginative title of River Street, a stubby limb of the town's main artery. While Upper Shelburn boasted a few quiet taverns and a nice hotel with a restaurant off the lobby, River Street was where you'd find the rougher saloons and brothels. The Alamo was the largest of the bunch. It had been a pretty fancy establishment at one time — two stories tall with a broad veranda and an upper deck where the working girls liked to hang out whenever a steamboat docked at the town's hull-battered wharf. Back in the days when paddle wheelers ruled, the whores would strut around up there like vitiated royalty, exposing legs and shoulders and an occasional breast, all the while calling on the stevedores and deckhands to come on in when they were finished and find out how much fun a Shelburn gal could be.

Occasionally, when what we called "decent folks" were aboard a ship, the captain would send one of his crew into the saloons to warn them to keep the doves out of sight until the more genteel class could be transported to Main Street and settled into a proper hotel. That might seem like an odd arrangement today, but it worked just fine for Shelburn, allowing the saloons and brothels to stay in business while the bluff dwellers could pretend the sins they represented didn't exist.

Barely a handful of buildings occupied the Brazos side of River Street. These were mostly rundown and water-stained from earlier floods, shack homes and tiny, one-room businesses where dreams had long ago been swept away. Even this late in the season there were still a few fireflies skimming over the water and playing hide-and-seek in the rushes. The land across the river was broad and flat and rich as gold in the eyes of a farmer, a patchwork of fields running mostly to tan and brown now that the fall harvest was nearly completed.

Figuring the Alamo was my best bet, I reined in that direction. The number of horses hitched in front of the building was a surprise. I wasn't expecting such a large crowd in the middle of the week, although in fairness I didn't usually come into town except on Saturdays.

Henry Kalb's spotted bay was tied out front, easily recognized by the pattern over its rump. Turning in at a tobacco shop a couple of doors down, I dismounted and looped my reins over the hitching rail. Then I just stood there for several minutes, one hand clinging to the cheekpiece of Dusty's bridle while my stomach roiled in doubt. Part of me — a damn *big* part — wanted to climb back into my saddle and go home, but I knew I couldn't. There was trouble brewing for my family inside the Alamo that night, and I figured it was up to me to stomp it out before it grew into something too large to corral.

Even though I didn't have any intention of killing anyone, I knew what I was walking into, so I took a moment to loosen my old Colt in its holster before starting for the saloon.

It was a warm night for late October, and hordes of nocturnal insects were swarming the wall lamps on either side of the saloon's main entrance — clouds thick enough that a smart man would keep his mouth shut and avoid inhaling as he passed through the doors. It wasn't as bad inside, where ropy tatters of lamp and tobacco smoke created an effective smudge, although the smoke was just about as annoying.

For all the patrons crammed around the tables and at the bar, the Alamo seemed unnaturally quiet. It might have been because it was midweek, but even the working girls seemed to be keeping their fake squeals and high-pitched laughter to a minimum. I stopped just inside the swinging double doors to eye the crowd. Henry Kalb wasn't there, but I spotted his brother Paul standing at the far end of the bar with Seth Henning and Bill Eisner.

Shelburn was a small town with few secrets. Everyone in the Alamo must have known what had happened in the courtroom that day. They must have figured they knew why I was there, too, because all of a sudden even the murmur I'd heard upon entering faded into a silence deep enough to swim in. Real slow, I started down the length of the bar. It felt like every eye in the place was fastened on me, waiting to see what I'd do. I hadn't covered more than a dozen paces when the bartender called my name. I jerked to a stop, my scalp crawling.

"Gage," the bartender repeated, then tipped his head to motion me over. Like a damn fool, I went.

"What are you doing in here tonight?" Ed Shiffler inquired in an amiable tone.

"I'm looking for Henry Kalb. Have you seen him?"

"Henry was in here earlier, but he ain't around now. Took off when it got dark. Probably halfway home by now."

"No, his horse is still out front."

"Well, he ain't here now." Ed pulled a bottle and glass off the backbar shelf and set both of them in front of me. "Have a drink, Gage."

"I ain't thirsty."

"That's all right, have a drink anyway." He pulled the cork and poured a couple of fingers into the glass.

Ed's cordialness caught me unprepared. I wasn't a stranger to the Alamo, and had been inside numerous times over the past couple of years, but I always ordered beers. Surely Ed knew that. The idea that he might be up to something did occur to me, but I mostly put it down to his just wanting to avoid a fray. Busted furniture and shattered glass cuts deep into a saloon's profits, even if the brawlers agree to pay for the damages afterward. There's still lost business to consider and hidden expenses cropping up after the fact. I didn't argue with him, though. Maybe it was the extra fortitude the whiskey would provide that I craved, although I think all I really wanted was to postpone having to brace Paul Kalb and his cronies. Accepting the glass, I swallowed down half of it, then waited for the familiar burn.

I said I never drank whiskey in the Alamo, but I wasn't unfamiliar with the stuff. Beau and I would occasionally sneak a little homegrown stuff out of the jug Pa kept hidden in the feed room, a clear, fiery brew that nearly took your breath away on the first swig. But the expected rush of heat up through my sinuses didn't occur that night. Instead what I felt was a slow spreading warmth and a solid little glow in my belly that instantly settled the nerves.

"Better?" Ed asked.

"It doesn't change anything."

"Let it drop," he said, keeping his voice low so that others wouldn't overhear. "Hell, we all know what happened, and ain't no one gonna blame Ester for it."

It kind of bothered me that he knew her name, and didn't seem right that he'd say it aloud in a saloon. Especially one with whores.

"I reckon I'll see it through," I replied stiffly.

"Then at least let it go tonight. Come back when you ain't so mad."

"I don't think what happened today is ever gonna wear off," I said, then pushed away from the bar, leaving my half-empty glass in the middle of it.

Henry's friends hadn't acknowledged my presence until then. Now Bill Eisner and Seth Henning stepped away from the bar, casually moving a few feet to Paul's right. Henning was sporting a cocky grin, but Bill and Paul looked dead serious and more than a little concerned.

"If you're huntin' trouble, Pardell, we'll kindly oblige you," Henning said, and the men standing at the bar between him and me quickly cleared out of the way.

"I'm looking for that yellow jackass you call a friend," I said, loud enough for the entire saloon to hear.

Henning's smug look disappeared. "You'd best watch your tongue, Pardell, 'less you want it snipped off."

"I doubt you've got enough sand for that, Seth," I replied easily, then shifted my gaze to Paul. "Where's your brother?"

"He's around," Paul said quietly.

"Where he is ain't none of your business," Seth added.

"You still here?" I asked, feigning surprise. "I thought I'd heard you scurry off like a mouse."

Brother, the tension after that remark grew strained nearly to the breaking point. I was pushing a lot harder than necessary, and a hell of a lot harder than I'd planned to on the ride in. I can see now that my bravado was just a feeble attempt to keep my own courage bolstered, but it wasn't winning me any favor that night. Henning was about to reply when Bill Eisner reached out and casually dropped a hand over his shoulder.

"Leave it be, Seth."

Henning's lips peeled back to reveal gritted teeth. There wasn't any doubt what he wanted to do, but I guess he respected Eisner too much to buck him. Or maybe he was afraid of him. I know a lot of people were, especially later on when the Eisner gang started robbing trains and banks up in the Indian Nations.

"Yeah, you're right, Bill. If I shot the son of a bitch, I'd have to clean my pistol when I got home, and he ain't worth that much effort." Then he laughed to show he wasn't afraid, and spit on the floor. He and Eisner returned to the bar. Paul swung away as well, putting his back to the room.

"You tell him," I said, my voice carrying. "Tell him I'm looking for him."

Paul flinched like he'd been popped with a whip but kept his eyes on the drink in front of him. The others didn't look around, either. It was Ed Shiffler who broke the charged silence.

"They'll tell him, Gage, and if they don't, I will."

"All right." I took a dragging step backward, my pulse raging. "All right," I repeated more softly, then turned and walked outside on legs as unyielding as fence posts.

I had a lot of mixed feelings churning around inside of me as I walked over to stand beside my horse. Anger and relief and vague disappointment seemed to be vying equally for control of my emotions. Loosening Dusty's reins, I pushed him away from the rail with one hand on his shoulder. As I did, a high-pitched cackle burst from the alley between the Alamo and the tobacco shop. I tried to spin around to face it, but Dusty spooked at the unnerving sound and just about yanked me out of my boots as he backed rapidly into the street. I hung onto the reins, but we came to within a few feet of that sharp drop-off into the Brazos before I got him stopped. Whirling about, my heart sank as Henry Kalb emerged from the blackness of the alley. His revolver was already drawn, though pointed toward the ground.

"What are you lookin' for, Pardell? Trouble?"

"I'm looking for you."

Henry stopped sideways to me, and now his gun was angled toward my feet. "Well, I'd say you sure as hell found me." Then he lifted the revolver and pointed it at my chest.

When I look back on that evening now, I truly believe Henry was just trying to put a scare on me. Regrettably, I had no way of knowing that at the time, and doubt if it would have made any difference. Henry Kalb was leveling down on me with a revolver, and I did what came naturally, drawing my own and firing from the hip. At the Colt's explosion, the dun snorted and jumped sideward, away from the riverbank but still dragging me along with him. By the time I got him quieted and managed to turn back to face the alley, we were in the middle of the wide street, although probably thirty-odd feet down from where we'd been when I pulled the trigger.

Henry was still standing at the alley's mouth. Taut with dread, I thumbed the Colt's hammer back to full cock, expecting to feel the tear of lead through my flesh at any moment. But he just stood there, staring at me like I was some kind of abomination dredged up from the bottom of the river. Then, clumsily, he returned his revolver to its holster, having to try several times before he found the opening. He continued watching me while he did this. Then, with his weapon sheathed, he turned unsteadily toward the saloon. He managed two jerky, stiff-legged strides before his knees buckled, pitching him face-first into the dirt.

Someone shouted from the saloon's entrance. I don't remember now what he said or if I even caught it. I was still numb from the sudden violence, not yet comprehending the full impact of what had happened. The rumble of moving men — of scraping chairs, questioning calls, and thumping heels — spewed from the saloon a couple of seconds before the first wave of gawkers pushed through the doors. The crowd's pace immediately slowed when the men in front noticed me standing in the street with my revolver drawn, a body on the ground not far from where they stood. Pressed from behind, they began to fan out along the portico, the bright colors of the whores' dresses — deep reds and purples and luminous greens — appearing as incongruous as canaries against the work-worn clothing of the men.

Ed Shiffler bulled a path to the front of the throng with Paul Kalb, Bill Eisner, and Seth Henning right behind him. Paul cried out when he spotted his brother and ran to his side, turning him gently to cradle the fallen man's head in his lap.

"Henry!" Paul cried, as if sensing his brother already slipping away from him, from all of us. And in the unnatural silence that followed, we all heard Henry's ragged, gasping reply.

"Oh, God, Paul, he's killed me. Gage Pardell has killed me."

A chill ran up my spine to mushroom across the back of my skull. Those words were seared into my brain that night. They've never faded.

. . . he's killed me. Gage Pardell has killed me.

Then Henry stiffened and Paul wailed in protest. Barely a heartbeat later, Henry's body slumped, and his head lolled gently in his brother's lap.

Seth Henning turned toward me with murder in his eyes. "You son of a bitch," he practically screamed. "You shot him down in cold blood, didn't even give him a chance to pull his gun."

"No, he drew it," I replied, startled by the fire in Henning's accusation. "He drew first."

Seth flung an arm toward the Kalbs. Henry's head and shoulders were locked in Paul's arms, while Paul rocked listlessly in grief. "Like hell he did," Seth retorted. "His gun is still in its holster."

It was, too. I'd watched Henry return it, but how was I ever going to explain that to the men and women gathered outside the Alamo that night? How could I explain it to anyone — Henry's dazed expression and clumsy stabs at the holster, followed by the awkwardness of his gait as he tried to walk away from his own mortality. My own thoughts condemned me: *Why would he re-holster it? Why would he even try?* And I knew with sudden clarity that I could protest Seth Henning's allegation until hell grew cold, and no one would believe me.

Bill Eisner went for his gun, but mine was already out. One of the whores screamed as I brought it up. Several of the men swore, and everyone except Kalb and Henning and Eisner scattered for cover. I slammed a round into the Alamo's front wall, making Eisner duck and his shot go high, winging into the trees across the river. Seth was firing by then, too, and his bullets — those coming closest — were making an odd, whirling sonance as they passed my ears. It was a sound once heard, never forgotten.

Already skittish, Dusty immediately began lunging sideways, snorting and grunting and fighting the bridle. Once again, I was dragged along, hanging onto the reins with one hand while trying to return fire with the other. My shots were all going wide, but they were keeping Eisner and Henning moving, too, and that was to my advantage. Then one of Seth's bullets hit my saddle and Dusty reared and damn near jerked free. I knew then that I had to get out of there. I'd either lose my reins or they'd kill me or my horse if I didn't. Pulling the gelding's head around until it was pointed down the street, I gave a yell and swung into the saddle without using my stirrups. That was all the encouragement Dusty needed. He bolted with his head held high and the bit in his teeth. Bent low over the horn, I let him run.

Chapter Three

It must have been nearly midnight before I got home. I rode up to the house with Pa's chestnut on a lead rope close by my side. There was a lamp burning inside, and I didn't even get my off-side foot out of its stirrup before the front door was flung open and my parents stalked out. Judging from the look on Pa's face, I was in for bad weather, and had I been a few years younger, a whuppin' behind the summer kitchen with a switch off a hackberry tree might have been in the offing. But I guess my expression was telling, because Pa's stride quickly faltered.

"Gage?" Ma said tentatively.

"What happened?" Pa demanded, not yet sure how much hell he wanted to raise about my scattering the stock and taking his mare.

"Henry Kalb drew his gun."

Pa swore and Ma gasped. Ester came to

stand at the door behind them, and I saw Beau at the window, his eyes wide in the amber light.

"Did you shoot him?" Pa asked.

"Yes, sir, I had to."

"Oh, Gage," Ma said quietly, and Ester turned away with a sob.

Pa stepped down off the porch, his expression like something chiseled from stone. "How bad?"

"I'm . . . he's dead."

Pa swore like I'd never known him to, not even when it was just him and me out on the range by ourselves. Then he looked away, his jaw working violently but no more words coming. Ma came slowly to my side, her work-calloused hands latching trap-tight around the calf of my leg. "Are you sure, Gage? Are you really sure?"

Recalling Paul Kalb's anguished lament and the way Henry's body had gone so abruptly slack, I nodded morosely. "He drew first . . ." I began in some half-hearted attempt to justify my actions, but Pa immediately cut me off.

"It doesn't matter," he said, pulling the chestnut's lead rope from my grasp. He put his other hand on Ma's shoulder and eased her back. "Go on inside and get his pack ready."

"Orrin?"

"Go on, Molly." His fingers tightened briefly on her shoulder, and she turned and climbed the steps with her head bowed. Pa gave me a look I couldn't fathom, then jerked his head toward the barn. "Come with me."

I rode down to the barn at Pa's side, then dismounted while he led the chestnut through the barn to the corral out back. By the time he returned, I had a lantern lit and was standing in the entryway with Dusty's reins in my hand. I wanted to unsaddle him and turn him out with the chestnut, but sensed that wasn't going to happen.

"All right," Pa said. "Tell me. I want to hear it all."

I tried to read his voice or the look in his eye, but his face was inscrutable; it was like trying to interpret the thoughts of a cigar store's wooden Indian. I told him everything that had happened. It didn't take long. When I finished, he sighed and walked past me to the barn's entrance, staring toward the road from town that passed our place just a couple of hundred yards to the east.

"Why did he holster his pistol?"

"I don't know."

"It's not a thing you'd expect a mortally wounded man to do."

When I didn't reply, he turned back into the barn.

"This doesn't bode well for you, Gage."

"Yes, sir, I know."

"It's not the law that worries me so much, it's Henry's father. Likely with folks around here, knowing us the way they do and knowing the Kalbs the way they do, you'd get a fair enough trial. Maybe they'd put you behind bars for a spell, and maybe they should. That'd be for a jury to decide. But it wouldn't satisfy Linus. He's gonna want some blood."

"What am I going to do?"

He gave me a sharp look, no doubt having to bite his tongue to keep from pointing out I should have thought of that before riding into Shelburn. Taking a deep breath, he said, "Your ma and I have been talking."

My chin came up in surprise. "You knew this would happen?"

"Gage, I've been dealing with men like Linus Kalb and his boys since before you were born. Of course I knew it was possible. Hell, it was probably likely. Your ma saw it that way, too."

"Pa, I'm . . ."

He raised a hand as if to strike, but I didn't flinch or draw away. "Just don't you goddamn apologize like some whining pup.

I won't stand for that." He lowered his hand. "Your ma and I want you to go to Rattlesnake Springs until I can sort this out. You crawl into those trees, boy, and you stay put. Keep your horse close and saddled, too. You can take along some grain so you don't have to graze him."

I nodded solemnly. Rattlesnake Springs was about twenty miles northwest of our place. We were mostly subsistence farmers in those years, but it was a lazy man who couldn't put together a small herd of beeves with all the mavericks running loose in Texas at that time. With my help, Pa had burned his O-P brand on probably two hundred head that we generally let run loose. Some years earlier — I was probably Beau's age at the time, Ester maybe eight or nine, and Bess hadn't even started walking yet — Pa had taken all of us north to a thicket of short-growth mesquite and thorny scrub that had good water in the middle and open prairies surrounding it. His cows had drifted that way over the winter, and we'd gone to haze them back closer to home, after branding what young stock we could find.

Pa and I rode, and Ma followed along with Ester, Beau, and Bess in the buckboard, carrying enough supplies to make a comfortable camp for the two weeks Pa figured it would take us to gather the herd. Pa and I were setting up a tent for Ma and the youngsters while the women started gathering wood. We'd barely gotten the canvas staked down when Ma's scream came hurtling through the mesquites like something straight out of hell. Pa dropped his corner of the tent and sprinted into the thicket faster than I'd ever seen him move. I was slower, but got there in time to see him helping Ma to the ground. Six-year-old Beau was hopping around waving a stick and shouting at a rattler coiled up next to the trunk of a mesquite, while Ma hollered for him to get away from it and Ester started bawling at all the commotion erupting around her.

I'd grabbed Beau by the arm and yanked him away from the snake and took him over to where Pa was sliding the hem of Ma's dress up past her ankle. The black stockings she wore had been torn just above the top of her shoe, and when Pa pulled it down you could see the twin puncture marks in front of the ankle bone. My mouth went dry at the sight, and I looked helplessly at Pa. He was examining the tiny wounds closely, probing them gently on either side with his thumbs. I remember him asking her if it hurt and her replying that it felt like she'd been stung by a bee. Then he asked her how she felt and she said all right. At that he leaned back, and the expression on his face was like nothing I've ever seen there before or since.

"I don't think it released any venom," he said.

Ma looked just as relieved. "Are you sure?"

"We'll know better in a few minutes, but if it had, we'd likely be seeing signs of it around your ankle by now. You'd be feeling almighty sick and sweating a heap, too."

"It does hurt," she admitted.

Pa nodded his sympathy but didn't reply. Holding her foot gently in his big, work-hardened hands, he continued to focus his attention on her ankle. I've since learned a rattler's strike can feel like you've been whacked with a club, but that they don't always inject their venom. Especially if their reaction is more from being startled than angered. After a bit Pa had me fetch his jug from the buggy and he doctored the tiny cuts with whiskey dabbed on a cloth that he pressed against the wounds. Then we all stood around for another twenty minutes before Pa declared her fit and ordered us back to our chores.

The first thing I did was grab a shovel and kill the snake that bit Ma. I chopped off its head and buried it, then Pa and I made a couple of sweeps through the mesquite looking for more snakes — rattlers or copperheads. We didn't hold any ill feelings toward reptiles in general, we just didn't want something poisonous lurking around where Beau or Bess might get struck.

We killed two more rattlesnakes and buried their heads, then Ma skinned out the bodies and put them in a stew. People say snake tastes like chicken, but I say it doesn't. Snake tastes like snake, and if you've ever eaten it, you'll know what I'm talking about. Personally, I'd rather have a good steak any day.

So yeah, Rattlesnake Springs. Pa and I had been there numerous times since then — Beau too, once he was old enough to start helping with the gather — but Ma never went back. She never went along on any of our other roundups, either.

"Go on up to the house and talk to your ma," Pa said after a stretch of silence. "I'll water Dusty and put some shelled corn in a sack to take along."

"I can water my own horse," I replied, but he just scowled and yanked Dusty's reins out of my hand.

"You do what I tell you, boy," he said, and I knew better than to argue.

Ma was in the front room when I got there, shoving pieces of clothing into the biggest set of saddlebags we had. I paused under the dogtrot roof to watch. When she'd returned to the house after Pa told her to get a pack ready, she'd looked weepy-eyed and somehow broken, but there was a grimness to her face now as she moved about the tiny front room, and no sign of welcome. Ester was standing against the far wall, her eyes still puffy from a day of crying, face pale with fatigue. Beau sat on the floor beside her with his back propped to the hewn log wall, his eyes bright with curiosity.

Standing uncertainly in the doorway, I said, "Ma?"

"Go get what you need from your room," she snapped without looking around.

"Pa wanted me to talk to you."

"Your father wanted you to talk to me earlier, but you didn't. Now you're leaving home in the middle of the night like some . . ."

She didn't finish what she was going to say. I don't guess she needed to. I crossed the dogtrot to the room Beau and I shared and lit a candle on the small table between our bunks. The soft pad of bare flesh on the puncheon floor told me I'd been followed.

"Where you goin', Gage?"

It was Beau, standing in the door with his hands shoved deep in his pockets, his hair mussed from the pillow.

"Looks like I'm going away for a while."

"Where?"

"I don't know," I admitted, then walked over to my bed and started rolling up my blankets. Beau watched silently as I tied them off, then fetched what extras I thought I might need — another box of cartridges that fit both my rifle and revolver, a sturdy camp knife for those chores my Barlow would be too small to handle, the packet of green-headed matches sitting on the table next to the pewter candle holder. I didn't worry about extra clothing, having noticed socks and shirts on the table where Ma was packing my saddlebags, although I did take my heavy wool jacket down off its peg.

I carried it all into the other room where Ma was still shoving a few smaller items into what space was left in the saddlebags. She was quick and rough, and I knew better than to ask what was bothering her. Ester was still standing against the back wall, tears rolling slowly down each cheek. I wanted to tell her not to cry, but knew it was too late for that. Ma was just buckling the flap down over the last bag when Pa came in. He glanced at her, then silently lifted the saddlebags and my bedroll off the table and gave me a jerk of his head. I followed silently. Dusty was standing ground-tied in the front yard. Pa slung the rolled-up blankets across the seat, then lifted the saddlebags over the rear skirt. He threaded the saddle strings up through the bags' brass grommets before adding my bedroll on top and tying it all down.

I stood next to Dusty's head, absently stroking the side of the gelding's face until Pa was finished. Coming up alongside the dun, he said, "Did you tell her goodbye?"

I shook my head. "She ain't talking."

He sighed. "Likely she won't for a few days. We'll just have to ride it out." He stared pointedly. "Me and the others."

"I know you don't want me to say it, but I am sorry. I didn't mean for anyone to get hurt."

"If you didn't want anyone getting hurt, then why in hell did you go into Shelburn looking for Henry Kalb?"

"I don't . . ." I shrugged. "I guess I just wanted to hit him."

"Hit him?"

"Yes, sir. Right in the face and just as hard as I could."

Pa smiled bleakly. "Well, I don't guess I can fault you for that. I'd have liked to have done it myself." Then the smile faded and his voice grew stern. "I meant what I said about staying out of sight, Gage. Linus Kalb is a mean devil, and he's going to want your hide for what you did to his boy."

"What are you going to do?"

"There's no point in me talking to the marshal. He'd be bound by law to lock you up until your arraignment, and that'd just give Kalb time to decide what underhanded trick he wanted to pull. I'll ride over to Cameron in the morning and see if I can get the county sheriff involved." He was quiet a moment, thinking. "Maybe I ought to just go on down to Austin and talk to the state authorities, find someone there who's never heard of Linus Kalb and doesn't give a hoot how much money he pumps into our local politics." Then he looked at me. "I'll sort it out, son. You just stay back in that mesquite until I send word."

I nodded glumly. "All right."

"You'd best get started, Gage."

I glanced over my shoulder. Beau was standing in the shadows of the dogtrot, watching, but Ma and Ester were still inside.

"Give her time," Pa said, then stepped away from Dusty's side. "Be careful, son."

51

Chapter Four

It was all the rest of that night and a couple of hours after sunup before I reached Rattlesnake Springs. I paused some distance away to study the patch of thorny mesquites surrounding a tiny flow of water that never amounted to much, not even after a rainy spell. We'd dammed off the head of the spring as best we could with rocks and sod to create a shallow pool, but what over-flowed was mostly mud, pocked by the tracks of cattle — ours and others' — deer, mustangs, and wild hogs. I might also mention that even though we called it Rattle-snake Springs, there was only that one little seep of water. I couldn't tell you why we always referred to it in the plural.

Outside the ring of trees, the land was open and gently rolling, good graze for cattle but not worth turning with a plow was the opinion of the day, although I know they've been farming that area pretty heavily in recent years.

I rode into the trees and dismounted, and before doing anything else, I checked for snakes. A couple of big browns and a rat snake that probably would have measured all of six feet in length — startling but nonvenomous — were the only unwelcome inhabitants I turned up. A sturdy branch under their midsections was all that was needed to transport them away from the spring.

I didn't make any kind of a formal camp, and I certainly didn't kindle a fire, but I did strip the saddle from Dusty's back and rub him down, regardless of Pa's admonitions. It probably wasn't a very smart move, me being a wanted man and all. I suppose in hindsight, the idea of my being sought by anyone — especially the law — hadn't yet sunk in.

After seeing to my horse, I wandered through the trees in search of who-knows-what, my thoughts occupied with images from the night before — the shocked expression on Henry Kalb's face at the impact of my bullet, and the jerky way he'd reholstered his own revolver before turning toward the saloon's entrance and collapsing. At that point, there in the chaparral, it came to me as a hazily recalled nightmare, something not quite real but impossible to forget. I kept looking south as if expecting Pa to come riding in on his chestnut to tell me it was all a misunderstanding, that Henry wasn't dead after all and I needed to get back home and start on my chores. With the fall harvest in, we were grubbing stumps out of the field behind our house. Pa wanted to increase the size of our sorghum crop the following year, but we still had a long way to go before it was ready for planting.

Pa never showed up, but toward the middle of the afternoon I spotted a couple of horsemen way off to the north, little silhouettes moving steadily westward along the top of a ridge. Despite the distance — I was well back in the trees and probably wouldn't have been visible even if I'd jumped up and down and waved my arms — I instinctively withdrew deeper into the thicket. I could tell they were hunting something. It might have been me, or it just as easily could have been strays. Either way, I didn't want to take any chances.

After the riders had moved on over the horizon, I stepped out from behind the gnarled trunk of a mesquite where I'd taken refuge, rubbing my palms deliberately up and down over my ribs as if trying to dry some imaginary sweat. I think for the first time, my life on the scout was beginning to sink in.

What I wanted to do was saddle Dusty and haul my bones out of there as fast as he could carry me, but common sense held me back. I recalled what Pa had said about going to Austin to try to straighten out the mess I'd put myself — hell, that I'd put my whole family — in. Even on a fast horse, which his chestnut wasn't, it would take him a couple of days to reach the state capital. Figure a day there minimum, then two back, and I swear my stomach gave a little lurch. At best, that meant five days waiting, nearly a week hid out like some rabbit in the weeds, scared every moment for the shadow of a hawk to drop over me.

With my life so joltingly put into perspective, I decided to take stock of my situation. I had enough shelled corn for Dusty for maybe two days, and about the same — cold roast beef, some butter in a little earthenware crock, half a loaf of bread, and some parched corn — for me. Although I could hold Dusty out on grass at night if I had to, I knew I was going to get almighty hungry if I couldn't hunt or build a fire. I've heard of men eating raw snake, and even insects and grubs, but I wasn't looking forward to such rations.

That day passed, then another. I napped off and on, whittled spoons and forks out of mesquite limbs, and about wore a path in the dirt with my aimless ramblings through the trees. It was on my third day in the thicket, about the middle of the afternoon, when I spotted a rider coming out of a draw a couple of miles to the south. After a cautious pause, whoever it was reined toward the Springs. Feeling my heart climbing toward my throat, I slid my Winchester from its scabbard and went to crouch behind a mesquite at the edge of the thicket. Although I couldn't tell who it was, judging from the slenderness of the rider, their leisurely approach, and the small colt trotting alongside, I was hoping it was Beau riding our buggy mare.

I was only partially wrong. It was our mare all right, but it wasn't Beau in the saddle. It was Ester. Watching as she drew closer, I felt a little prickly sensation spread across the back of my neck, and quickly walked over to where I'd left Dusty tethered for the day. I threw my saddle on his back, then booted the Winchester. Ester had already spotted me by the time I finished, and was loping the mare the rest of the way in.

Even as concerned as I was about it being Ester out there instead of Pa or Beau, it was a relief to see her. She slowed to a walk entering the thorny mesquite, and I noticed with a twinge of unease the heavy pack strapped behind the cantle of her saddle. Normally Ester would have greeted me with a shout and a smile, but her expression was as somber as a funeral as she halted the mare some yards away. The colt had stopped at the edge of the trees after spying Dusty and me, his neck sharply arched, ears tipped forward like miniature lance tips as he contemplated this unexpected encounter.

Ester kicked loose of her sidesaddle and dropped nimbly to the ground. "Gage, are you all right?"

"I'm fine," I replied, stepping forward to take the reins from her hands. "Just about busting to know what's been happening, though."

She was looking around at the ground as if recalling her last visit there. "Have you . . . seen any snakes?"

I couldn't help grinning. "Not since I first got here," I replied as I tied the mare's reins to a mesquite limb.

"I'm sorry. It's just that after what happened to Mama that time . . ." She shook her head as if discarding such a trifling concern over rattlesnakes. She was a farm girl, after all, and thoroughly versed in the handling of hoes and clubs when it came to serpents.

"Papa didn't go to Austin right away, like he said he would," Ester said. "He decided to go into Shelburn and talk to Judge Wetzel first. He didn't want to ride all the way to Austin, then have someone there tell him to talk to our local authorities first."

"What did Wetzel say?"

"Nothing Papa said he could latch onto, whatever that means. Papa came home planning to leave for Austin that same afternoon, but Beau saw some men hiding in the trees up on Milford's hill."

"Men?"

Ralph Milford farmed about seventy acres across the road from us. I knew the trees Ester was talking about, a little hilltop copse maybe half a mile from our place.

"Beau said there were five or six of them watching our house with field glasses."

"Who were they?"

"Beau says he didn't recognize them. Papa went to talk to them, but they rode away when he got close. Then they came back almost before Papa got home. Papa says he didn't recognize them, either, but figures they work for Linus Kalb."

My right hand curled tight. I wanted to punch something, slam my fist into just about anything hard enough to knock the frustration out of my system. Keeping my arm rigidly by my side, I said, "What did Pa do?"

"He didn't do anything the rest of the day, but that night he tried to slip out the back way, only he didn't get very far. He says there were men in the trees behind the barn waiting and watching, so he came back. He and Beau sat up all night with rifles, but whoever it was didn't try to come close to the house.

"They were out there all day yesterday, too, then this morning Papa decided to trick them. He rode south, and sure enough, two of the men followed him. When they were out of sight, Beau went down to the barn and saddled Brownie, then tied some burlap sacks filled with hay behind his saddle."

Brownie was the seal brown gelding Beau liked to think of as his own.

"Papa wanted it to look like Beau was taking you some more supplies," Ester added.

"Did they take the bait?"

She nodded excitedly. "They went right after him, though staying back and thinking they were being slick."

"Then you came here?"

"Yes, but I wasn't followed."

"Are you sure? How many men followed Beau?"

"Two."

"But Beau said there was five or six men watching from the Milford place. If two of them followed Pa, then two more followed Beau —"

"I wasn't followed, Gage," she cut in with a faintly perturbed edge to her voice. "I watched behind me the whole way."

I nodded my acceptance of her assurance, although I'll admit I wasn't feeling it. Something kind of quivery was squirming around in my gut, and my gaze kept returning to the grassy draw where I'd first spied her approach.

"Papa says you can't stay here," Ester continued.

With my thoughts on the men watching the house, her words were slow to register. "Huh . . . what?"

"Papa says that if Linus has hired men to look for you, then he probably plans to take care of this himself, without involving the courts. Papa says he thinks Linus is afraid a local jury might not go as hard on you as he'd want, after . . . you know, what happened at the dance."

"Pa wants me to leave?" The astonishment in my voice must have rung out like a church bell.

"He doesn't *want* you to leave," Ester protested. "It's just too dangerous for you to stay."

"Where am I supposed to go?"

"Mama says you're to go find Uncle Abran and stay with him until Papa can get everything sorted out here."

"Abran?"

Abran Bernard Foret was my ma's oldest brother, hailing from the same Cajun neck of the woods as Pa's side of the family, although Uncle Abran had abandoned the bayous of southeast Texas years before Ma and Pa drifted west. He had come to stay with us for a few months back when I was barely knee-high to a short horse, but all I could recall of his visit was a towering giant of a man, a deep bass voice, and a sable beard.

Ester began blinking rapidly as I stared into the middle distance, pondering this unexpected boulder rolled into my path, but try as she might, she couldn't prevent a solitary tear from creeping partway down her cheek. I felt an instant rage at seeing it. Since she was a toddler, I'd hardly ever known Ester to cry. Neither skinned knee nor bee-stung knuckle had ever elicited more than a hissing, indrawn breath. That son of a bitch Henry Kalb had sure taken a lot of the starch out of her, and as much as I regretted his death, at least by my hands, I didn't have any regrets about my going into town to confront him.

"Gage, I'm so sorry."

"Sorry? About what?"

"About everything that's happened, but especially my stupidity in going with Henry that night."

"That wasn't your fault, Ester. It's Henry's fault, and Paul's."

"No, it's mine. If I'd stayed at the dance like I knew I should have, none of this would have happened."

"If I hadn't gone into town the other night, it wouldn't have happened, either."

"But you had to go, didn't you?" Her tears were coming faster now, thin ribbons of moisture tracing each cheek. "You had to protect my honor, never even thinking that I'd already lost it."

"You haven't lost anything, Ester. *Nothing.* Do you understand?"

"I was so stupid, and now you have to go away and I may never see you again."

"It won't be forever, I promise you that. Pa will figure this out, and when he does, I'll come back. You'll see."

"Papa says that even if he can strike a deal

in Austin, you might still have to go to prison for a while."

I didn't have any kind of response to that, although it had been in the back of my mind all along, a nagging certainty that no matter how well Pa "fixed" my problem, I'd still have to stand accountable for Henry Kalb's death. For not the first time since that evening in Shelburn, I mentally cursed Kalb's determination to reholster his revolver. It would be — figuratively, I hoped — the knot in the hangman's noose if I was caught before Pa reached Austin and could negotiate some kind of arrangement to keep my feet on the ground and my neck unstretched.

When I looked up, I was startled to find Ester watching me closely, as if trying to read my thoughts. Forcing a wan smile, I said, "It'll be all right."

"Will it?"

I nodded. "Sure."

"Papa says you shouldn't try to write to us. He says to have Uncle Abran write us, and that Mama will send her letters to him to let you know what's going on. That way the Kalbs can't track you as easily."

"Did either one of them say where Abran was for sure?"

"Not for sure, but Mama's last letter from

him was from Fort Griffin."

That was the way I remembered it, too, him working for some kind of trader near the fort, dealing in buffalo hides, deer skins, and wolf pelts.

Fort Griffin was a military post way the hell out on the frontier, part of a line of forts set up in the late 1860s as a barrier between settled Texas and *Comancheria* — that land the Comanches historically considered their own. Even though I didn't want to leave home in this manner, I can't deny a spark of excitement at the thought of visiting some of our state's wilder regions. I'd never seen a living buffalo, nor many Indians other than those few who used to work on the steamboats that docked at Shelburn from time to time. I almost said something about my going not being such a bad thing after all, but then my gaze shifted to the south and I abruptly stiffened.

"Gage?" Ester turned to look, her brows furrowing. "What is it? Did you see something?"

"No . . . maybe." Then, after a pause, "I'm not sure."

And maybe I wasn't, but I still walked over to where Dusty was standing and tightened his cinch.

"I know I wasn't followed," Ester said,

although without the same level of confidence she'd expressed earlier.

"I want you to go home," I said, lowering the stirrup. "But not the same way you came. Go east for a while, then turn south. Just make sure you get there before dark. Run that mare hard if you have to. The colt will keep up." I hesitated. "Do you have a gun?"

"I've got Mama's Stocking pistol."

"All right. I'm going to follow you a ways, make sure no one's out there."

"Gage, Mama sent some things for you to take along."

Ester walked to the mare's side and I went with her, eyeing the bulky pack behind the cantle. Pulling it off, I discovered a sack bulging with food, another of shelled corn for my horse, and several extra blankets. Gloves, a woolen scarf, and Pa's heavy coat were strapped on top of the load. My hands lingered on the blue duffel coat with its black stripes and red trim. I must have stared at it a long time, until Ester said in an almost apologetic tone, "It's nearly winter, Gage. Mama says it might take a long time for Papa to get everything straightened out so you can come home again."

"Yeah," I replied, then grimly shifted the load from the mare's back to the skirt of

Dusty's saddle. By the time I had everything secured, I noticed Ester's tears had dried, and that her morose expression had been replaced by one of stern conviction.

"You'll be all right," she said. "I know you will."

"Sure," I agreed. "I'll probably be back before our first freeze."

"There's a letter inside with the food, and some money Papa drew out of the bank in Shelburn. Mama wants you to give the letter to Uncle Abran when you find him. The money is for supplies, or whatever else you might need."

"All right. Tell them . . . tell them I said thank you."

She managed a subdued smile, then gave me a quick hug and hurried away. I didn't offer to help her mount. She'd been managing a sidesaddle just fine ever since turning twelve, when Ma put a stop to her riding astride. She'd even helped Pa and me trail a small herd of beeves to a cattle buyer in Cameron a few years before.

I stepped into the dun's saddle. "You go on, Ester," I told her. "I won't be far behind."

"You don't have to come with me."

"I know, just do it."

Her eyes were growing misty again as she

reined away, winding through the trees to leave the thicket on its east side. The colt followed, high-headed and full of sass, snorting and jumping at every little thing and having a high ol' time of it. I lingered awhile, staring toward the distant draw where Ester had first appeared. My scalp was crawling for no good reason that I could detect. I waited until Ester had about a hundred yards on me, then heeled Dusty into the sunlight. As soon as I did a puff of dust appeared at the lip of the arroyo. Seconds later, a pair of horsemen surged into view, and I immediately reached for my rifle.

"Gage!"

Ester was pointing toward the horsemen. I waved in acknowledgment, then motioned for her to keep riding. "I'll draw them off," I shouted.

"Be careful, Gage. I love you." Then she kicked the mare with her free heel and took off at a gallop. The colt whinnied in alarm, then raced after his mama.

I pulled Dusty around to face the approaching horsemen, both of them riding dark horses and wearing light-colored dusters. The one in the lead had a hat of the same pale hue as his coat, its wide brim pushed up tight against the crown. The other wore either a smaller hat or a cap; he was too far away for me to tell at that point. Both were riding low in their saddles, and had their rifles drawn.

I watched their approach anxiously, while Dusty capered and tossed his head. He was sensing danger and eager to run, even though Kalb's gunmen were still well out of rifle range. I wasn't worried about them catching up with Ester, or her getting away. Whoever these men were, they weren't after her. It was my hide they wanted nailed to the side of Linus Kalb's barn — and I intended to make them fight for it.

CHAPTER FIVE

One of the things I noticed right off was that although the two men who had trailed Ester from home were too far away to identify, they were sitting their mounts with a competence you wouldn't ordinarily associate with farmers or other common laborers — folks more accustomed to following a plow or swinging a hammer than riding fast horses.

When Ester told me about the men watching the cabin, then said Pa figured they were some of Linus Kalb's hired help, I'd assumed they were field hands. I know Linus kept several on his place — dirt-poor families and a handful of single men who labored daily to keep Kalb's sprawling plantation running efficiently. Most of them farmed little patches of their own on the fringes of the Kalb farm, sharecroppers whose debt to the old man would likely never be paid off. It was as sorry a business then as it is today, although already well established in the years immediately following the War Between the States.

I didn't know who these men coming after me were, but I was fairly confident by then they weren't farmers. I also doubted they were drovers, which left only one other possibility. Old man Kalb had gone to Lower Shelburn to hire some of the riffraff who liked to hang around the saloons down there. Men like Bill Eisner and the Henning boys, and Don and Jay Lapwin, all of them friends of Henry and Paul Kalb. There would be others to choose from as well, just as deadly if not more so. There always were, if the pay was right.

I waited until those two were within half a mile of the thicket before reining Dusty around and heeling him into a hard gallop. As I'd figured, they both veered off to follow me, leaving Ester free to find her way home unaccosted.

I didn't try to outrun them, but kept moving westward at a steady pace. It was a warm day, and after a couple of hours, the hair along Dusty's neck became dark and ruffled with sweat. His hide would be damp under the saddle, too, although the leggy gelding was still breathing easily, his gait as smooth as flowing silk.

Dusty was five years old the year I left Milam County, a solid, dependable mount that I'd earned with my own sweat by helping Ralph Milford bring in his corn and sorghum over a several-year period. Money was tight in those days, but we had ways of paying off a debt. Ralph's was to offer me a dun gelding on my sixteenth birthday, which I'd accepted with all the enthusiasm of a half-starved cat laying into a fat rat.

What boy wouldn't have?

I named him Dusty because of his color. He was a green-broke two-year-old just in off the western plains, part of a herd of mustangs bound for markets in Louisiana and Arkansas. I couldn't have been happier with him if he'd come to me from the fanciest horse farm in Kentucky. I'd had to rustle up another source of income for my tack, though, finally trading a couple of bales of raccoon and muskrat pelts trapped during the winter for a good used saddle and a bridle with a snaffle bit. Trapping was also how I got my rifle and revolver, if you're wondering.

The hours slid past and I eventually brought Dusty down to a jog. Although half expecting my pursuers to make a sudden push to overtake me, they didn't. They slowed as well, and I didn't know what to make of that. I remember thinking, *Who's leading who, here?* and soon found out. Dusk was creeping across the land when they made their move. In the dimming light, I wasn't sure at first if they were actually advancing on me, which I guess is what they were counting on. That and maybe me being too tired or inexperienced to keep an eye peeled behind me with full dark rolling in.

As soon as I was sure they were closing the gap, I slapped my heels to Dusty's ribs and he took off with a fresh burst of speed that brought a grin to my face. I'd never before pushed the gelding that hard, and I was half-afraid he might not have much left to give, but he ran like a colt, sailing over the plains while the night closed in dark and snug as a heavy quilt. Those two jaspers were still more than a quarter of a mile behind when I finally lost sight of them, and although they were spurring their horses for all they were worth, they weren't gaining anything.

With full dark I brought Dusty back to a jog, then switched directions. I watched over my shoulder for a good long while, listening for pursuit and hearing nothing but the gentle thud of Dusty's hooves and the soft creak of saddle leather. After half an hour or so, I decided I'd probably lost them. I kept my Winchester unsheathed, though, butted to my thigh with my right hand on the rifle's slim wrist, my thumb within easy range of the hammer. I'd chambered a round back at the Springs while waiting for the two men to catch up, and didn't intend to clear it until I was dead certain I was no longer being followed.

I rode on into the night, keeping my pony at a walk now, and angling north-by-northwest. Fort Griffin lay somewhere off in that direction, although I wasn't sure exactly where. I was nineteen that autumn of '77, but I'd never seen a true map of Texas, something that showed how the rivers ran or where the towns and forts and such were located. Sooner or later I was going to have to find someone I could ask directions of, but I'd already decided it might be wiser to hold off until I'd put a couple of days between me and Shelburn.

It was closing in on dawn when we came to a little slough lined with rushes. I watered Dusty first, then rode off a ways and dismounted. After looping the reins above the gelding's neck so he could graze, I hiked back about fifty yards to a low rise. There I settled down with my rifle across my lap to watch and listen. A gentle breeze was nosing through the tall grass, and the steady buzz of tree frogs, cicadas, and katydids from the marshy ground created a nearly unrelenting wall of noise that I found comforting for its familiarity. Like a train whistle and the rattle of boxcars over the rails, they were sounds that could bring a person unaccustomed to them bolt upright in bed, but which seldom disturb the slumber of those who have lived close to them their entire life.

Finally satisfied that I was alone in that rugged land, I went back to where I'd left Dusty and pulled the saddle from his back, the bridle from his head. I hadn't planned to linger when I stopped, but this seemed like a pretty good place to hole up for a few hours — a shallow basin maybe an acre in size, with water on one side and plenty of graze. I figured Dusty could use the rest, and there was no telling what we might encounter on the morrow.

After picketing my horse in the middle of the little bowl, I dug some jerky from my saddlebags and had supper. Then I lay down with my head on the bedroll and almost immediately fell asleep.

The sun was blazing down like a fireplace poker when I awoke. My cheeks were running sweat and my shirt clung damply to my frame. I judged the time must have been right at noon by the way my shadow was huddled directly under me. I sat up in alarm and looked around, but nothing seemed amiss. Dusty was still there, grazing lazily on the end of his picket rope and acting as unconcerned as if he were back in his own pasture. The horizon, what I could see of it, was empty. For that, I was grateful. I hadn't slept well since leaving home, but it surprised me that I could pass out so completely after what I'd been through the day before.

After slaking our thirst at the water's edge, I saddled up and moved on. If I'd been worried about Dusty being stove-up after his long run the day before, I shouldn't have been. He stepped out with a lively stride, eager to be on his way.

I rode west into the afternoon, the country stretching out wide on every side — a vast, rolling prairie under a sky of autumn blue — and in all that time I didn't see another human being. Not even chimney smoke or a far-off patch of tilled soil, although from time to time I did spy cattle in the distance, longhorns as lean and skittish as deer. I'd probably have wondered if I was still in Texas if I hadn't seen cattle. Even there in the southeastern part of the state where I hailed from, they were as plentiful and tough-hided as armadillos.

Although my original intention had been to ride on through that second night, I changed my mind as twilight curdled into dusk. Coming to a creek with a road intersecting it — the first sign of civilization I'd seen all day — I rode down into the bottoms and made camp. After staking Dusty out on deep grass growing next to the stream, I gathered several armfuls of wind-blown limbs for a fire and kindled the first blaze I'd had since leaving home. I'd been craving coffee for days, and soon had my little kettle brewing over a low flame. Supper was parched corn and the last of the jerky Ma had sent along, but I was as content as a fat mare by the time the flames died to coals, sipping my coffee straight from the kettle and savoring every drop. Tobacco was a habit I hadn't developed yet, but I'd learned to like coffee at a tender age, as so many of us did in those years, and I'd surely missed it since Pa sent me into hiding.

There was a light fog hugging the bottoms when I awoke the next morning, along with a chill in the air that reminded me the seasons were changing. I wore my jacket as I broke camp, and gave the damp, gray ashes of my fire a last, longing glance as I rode out of the trees and turned onto the road, westbound and melancholy. I believe that was my first day of real homesickness, although it wouldn't be my last by a long chalk.

The mist burned off soon after leaving the creek bottoms, but the air remained cool, the sky a kind of brilliant blue one sees only during the autumn months in that muggy part of the country. The land around me started to change as well. The day before the country had seemed wide open and unbroken, but now I began to notice increasing signs of civilization — fields left barren after the fall harvest and an occasional farm lane winding off into the distance. There were more trees, too, rambling patches of timber scattered like tiny islands on both sides of the road. It was shortly before noon when I spotted a cabin off in the woods, and even though I'd told myself earlier that I needed several days between me and Shelburn before seeking information, curiosity nearly did to me what it did to the cat.

The cabin wasn't a whole lot bigger than a good-sized corncrib, constructed of rough-hewn oak with a shake roof. The man who came to the door as I rode up looked as gaunt as a wind-rattled scarecrow. He was wearing bibbed overalls and a shirt worn through at both elbows. He was barefoot and hatless, and his wiry gray hair stuck out above a pair of jug ears like moss on a rock. He was holding one of those old converted muzzleloaders from the war, and looked like he knew how to use it.

"Who are ye?" the old-timer demanded in a reedy voice.

"Just a friend," I assured him, hauling up with my left hand while raising my right to show it was empty, and that I wasn't there to cause trouble.

"I know my friends, boy, and ye ain't one of 'em." He leaned forward, his watery old eyes narrowing suspiciously. "Ye ain't Hank Askin's boy, are ye?"

"No, sir," I replied, then hesitated, wondering whether or not I wanted to give him my real name.

"Well," he barked, and I sighed.

"My name is Gage Pardell. I'm on my way to Fort Griffin."

"Griffin? That's an ambitious journey, youngster. Most folks who stop by here are generally headin' someplace closer. Like Austin, or Werner Clark's store."

"Griffin is my goal, but I'm not sure which direction it lies in."

"West and north and another two weeks'll likely get ye close." He tipped his head toward the road. "Clark's is down that away a small piece. Might be someone there'll know more'n me." He chuckled. "Likely ye can count on that."

I thanked him and started to rein away, but stopped when he called my name. "Yes, sir?"

"Watch ye hide goin' into Clark's, son. Kalb's got men in these here parts, and they ain't makin' no bones about wantin' to find ye."

My mouth went cottony and my heart sank toward my belly. "Kalb?" I managed to croak out.

He nodded sagely. "Yeah, figured it was ye. Couple of Kalb's hired turds come through here yesterday lookin' for a boy named Pardell. Claimed he gunned down one of Linus's sons. I tolt 'em I'd keep a hawk's eye peeled for ye, and get word to Kalb if I seen anything, but I won't. Ye can rest easy about that. The Kalbs ain't thought too highly of, even over here to Lampasas County."

"What did these two men look like?"

"Hard-eyed idjits, the both of 'em. Ridin' good horses, though. Bays, they was. One of 'em — the one in the saddle, not the horse

— wore a wide-brimmed planter's hat. The other's was smaller, what we used to call a beehive back during the war. Neither one of 'em looked especially smart, although I don't reckon that'd make 'em any less dangerous."

I took a deep breath while the fingers on my right hand curled slowly into a fist. The old man's description pretty well fit the image I had of the two men who had chased me away from Rattlesnake Springs. I thought I'd lost them that first night, and it worried me that they'd somehow figured out how to circle around in front of me. It was like they knew my route better than I did.

"Friends of yourn?" the old man asked.

"No, but I've seen them before." I took a look around. "You said this is Lampasas County?"

" 'Tis, though ye'll still have some ridin' to do to get shed of Linus Kalb's rifle sights."

"Just how far does Kalb's sights range?"

"I'd say yon side of Hill Country ought to set ye free."

"How far is that?"

"If the weather holds and ye horse don't throw a shoe, figure six or seven days."

"Then another week to Fort Griffin?"

"Thereabouts."

After a pause, I asked a question I'd been dreading for some time. "Is there a reward?"

"They didn't mention any, although if they're bounty men they probably wouldn't. That kind ain't keen on sharin'."

Taking another deep breath, I forced my fingers to relax. "I'm obliged to you, mister."

"It ain't nothin' I wouldn't do for any man got hisself crossways to the Kalbs of the world." Then he tipped his head toward the road as if anxious to see me off. "Be along with yeself, youngster. I've a opossum on the spit, and the smell's tellin' me it needs turnin'."

I nodded and reined away.

"I hate burned opossum," he hollered after me.

"Yes, sir. I don't blame you."

"It's a small one, otherwise I'd invite ye to stay."

"That's all right," I assured him. Twisted half around in my saddle, I watched him scurry back inside. He kind of reminded me of a opossum in the way he moved — a funny old man, but I owe my life to him. I said at the beginning of this narrative that I was young and naïve when I left Milam County. I was about to do some growing up.

CHAPTER SIX

When the old man with the opossum told me about Werner Clark's store, the most I'd pictured was a solitary log trading post out in the middle of nowhere. What I discovered instead was a modest community of a couple of dozen homes, along with a combination roadhouse and stagecoach stop, a tannery with stacks of brindled cowhides piled outside, and a blacksmith shop advertising *Fine rifles and Pistols* on a hand-lettered sign above the door. Probably sixty or more residences scattered up and down the right-hand bank of a pretty little stream shaded by tall oak and elm trees.

Clark's store was the largest structure in sight, and I reined in at one of the hitching rails out front. A small black and white dog had followed me all the way through town, yapping and snapping at Dusty's heels. I could hear kids laughing down by the creek, and the sharp odor of penned hogs drifted along the street on a lazy wind.

I stepped down feeling real cautious about what I might be getting myself into. If the men who had passed the opossum man's cabin the day before had ridden on through, then I'd likely be fine. But if they were still around, I figured the odds were good that I was going to be in deep trouble real soon. I suppose a smarter man than I was in those tender years would have circled wide around the little community and kept riding, but I was getting low on supplies and wanted to re-outfit myself before pushing on. I was also eager to find someone who could direct me to Fort Griffin, where I hoped to locate my Uncle Abran and feel like I had somebody watching my back for a change, rather than struggling against the notion that I was all alone in the world.

Clark's was typical for its time. Canned goods and clothing stacked on tables and shelves, feed and farm supplies in back, fresh vegetables, fine lace, ribbons, and mule shoes, all within easy reach. There was everything a body might need, and a good deal more to satisfy most folks' wants. They didn't have a map of Texas, though. I know because I asked.

After shaking his head to my inquiry, the clerk said, "If you're needing directions, my pappy could help you." He was a stout-built young man not much younger than me, with blond hair, pimples across his chin, and a faintly German accent.

"Who's your pappy?" I asked.

"He owns this store," the clerk replied pridefully.

"Then that's who I need to talk to."

The kid's expression sagged. "Shoot, he ain't here. He went to Austin to see about getting a post office for our town."

That kind of irritated me, although I tried not to let it show. "Is there anyone else nearby who might know the way to Fort Griffin?"

"My Uncle Wilber might have known, but he passed away a year ago last December."

"Hell's fire," I replied, no longer bothering to mask my exasperation. "Is there anyone close by who *ain't* dead that can point me in the right direction?"

"You don't have to get snippy about it," the kid replied petulantly. "Why would anyone want to go somewhere if they didn't know the way?"

Well, hell, that there just banged the goose on the head as far as I was concerned. My fist curled tight. For the first time in a long while I had something handy to punch, but I didn't do it. Struggling to control my temper, I said, "I'll tell you what, why don't I just buy some grub and be on my way. I can ask directions from someone else."

The kid shrugged like he didn't give a damn one way or another. Biting back my irritation, I purchased two tins of sardines, a can of tomatoes, and a dozen crackers, making sure to sort through the drawer carefully for the freshest and least crumbled squares I could find. I also bought a gallon of oats for my horse, then had to fork over the exorbitant price of two dollars for the works. Between high prices and that kid's snooty attitude, I figured it was a good bet theirs was the only store within a couple of days' travel. In my experience, a lack of competition often breeds that type of avarice.

Before our conversation fell apart, I'd asked the kid about a couple of strangers who might have arrived the day before, but he claimed ignorance of any such travelers. I took that to mean my pursuers had either passed on through without stopping, or had taken a different direction before reaching the little hamlet. Feeling relatively safe, I carried my purchases outside cradled in one arm and led my horse down to the river, where I dropped the reins to let him browse. Even though I had those oats for him, I figured to save them for down the trail, where the graze might not be as abundant. Then I plopped down on the bank and opened the sardines. A lot of folks today seem to have an aversion to dining on anything with the head still attached, but we weren't as picky back then. Sardines are a little oily and a whole lot salty, and satisfy a craving for both; plus, they have an oddly pleasing crunch when you bite through their tiny skulls. Crackers toned down the worst aspects of the meal, and the tomatoes afterward, plucked straight from the can after finishing my *entrée,* hit the spot dead center.

I was leaning forward to wash the tomato juice off my fingers when I sensed someone approaching from my left. I turned partway around, more out of curiosity than concern, just in time to witness a cloud of smoke erupting from the muzzle of a rifle not fifty yards away. The slug whirred past the tip of my nose with a little gust of warm air, and I squawked and fell back on my butt half an instant before a second shot roared from the rear corner of Clark's store. That bullet came close, too, zipping over my left shoulder near enough for me to hear the angry hiss of its passage.

I rolled onto my belly while shucking my

Colt. Both men — I recognized the hats right off, one broad-brimmed and pale, the other smaller and darker — fired again, and I sucked my breath sharply as one of the bullets cut a hot trail across the ribs under my right shoulder blade. Although the ground was open around me, I was making a poor target because of the river's gently sloping bank. Still, I knew that wasn't going to be enough to protect me for long. Raising up to my knees, I thrust the Colt forward with both hands on the grips. You might consider the posture unmanly, but I wouldn't care now and I sure as hell didn't care then. I rocked the hammer to full cock, then dropped it with a steady pull on the trigger. My bullet caught the man with the rifle somewhere in his midsection, and he curled over the wound and fell to the ground. My second shot missed its mark as the man at the store's rear corner sprinted toward a woodpile some distance upstream from where I was kneeling, but my third struck him in the thigh and he went down as if clubbed from behind. He was still scrambling desperately for shelter when I jumped to my feet and raced to Dusty's side.

Recalling how I'd barely managed to hang onto the reins in Shelburn, I figured I was damned lucky the horse hadn't bolted from behind Clark's store as soon as the shooting started. I vaulted into the saddle and spun him around and jammed my heels into his ribs, and we took off like it was a Fourth of July horse race, leaving behind a litter of broken crackers, empty tin cans, and Dusty's oats scattered across the riverbank.

There was yelling in the street, dogs setting up a caterwauling, and women shouting for their kids to find shelter, but I didn't hang around to see how it all shook out. Dusty had stood solid against the gunfire, but he was ready to run and I let him have his head. We tore out of that little burg so fast I figure our shadow must have had the devil's own time keeping up. I didn't look back, and I've never had any desire to return.

I rode steadily on through what remained of the afternoon, glancing back every so often for signs of pursuit, but I don't believe anyone came after me. Maybe the townsfolk knew about Kalb, and that those two men were working for him. Or maybe they just didn't want to get involved in affairs that didn't pertain to their own. I was relieved that I wasn't followed, but still veered north, away from the road, as soon as the sun went down.

Maybe I ought to take a moment here and explain a few things. One is that I don't want you thinking I was so hardened by that time that I wasn't affected by what took place behind Werner Clark's mercantile. I was shaken down to my heels. Not from what I did — they'd come after me and I did only what I had to do to survive, and if either of them died of their wounds I wasn't going to lose any sleep over it — but because of how sudden and intense it had been. Like an explosion of violence that probably hadn't lasted for more than a minute or two, yet continued to haunt my dreams for days to come.

The other thing that rattled me was how close I'd come to not making it out of there. That deep burn across my ribs was a constant reminder of how near I'd come. The wound itself wasn't bad. My shirt was ripped but the skin wasn't torn — neither blood nor raw flesh — but it stung like a son of a gun for a week or more, and the scar — finger-length and just about as wide — remains to this day.

There wasn't much of a moon that night, but the skies were clear and the stars as thick as spilled salt. After a time, I came to an east-west running trail and reined onto it. Soon we were winding through an increasingly dense forest, while the hills rose higher and steeper on every side. I didn't stop until well after midnight, and was on the move again before the sun came up. This was the eastern edge of Hill Country, and it was as pretty as a painted picture, especially with the trees changing colors and the sky as blue as the willows on Ma's fancy Sunday china.

I kept riding, pushing doggedly westward. The air remained crisp and cool and the days passed more swiftly than a person on the dodge had a right to expect. Yet for all the pleasantness of the country, I was anxious to get through the Hills. I wanted open land, where I didn't have to imagine bushwhackers atop every ridge. The old opossum hunter's words haunted my thoughts daily.

"Just how far does Kalb's sights range?" I'd asked him.

"I'd say yon side of Hill Country," he'd replied, and when I asked again, *"If the weather holds and ye horse don't throw a shoe, figure six or seven days."*

I kept my eyes peeled, and the only people I saw were those I approached — farmers working their fields for next spring's planting and, once, a solitary shepherd tending a flock of *churro* sheep that probably numbered close to five hundred head. I nodded politely to the farmers and kept riding, but my grub was running low by the fourth day when I spotted that sheep wrangler. A nickel bought me a bowl of mutton stew and a chunk of coarse bread that I ate without dismounting. A couple of days later I came upon a trio of barefoot boys fishing in a quiet pond and asked what they knew of the country to the west.

"Injuns out thataway," the largest of the bunch informed me solemnly. I figured him for eight or nine, skinny and tow-headed and as serious as a snake bite. His face was streaked with grime, his toes calloused.

"What about the country?" I asked. "How far until I get out of these hills?"

"Another two days due west is what my daddy told me. Ain't never been myself, but he was a Ranger before he lost his hand to a goddamnYankee minié ball."

He pronounced it as one word, *goddamnYankee,* I mean. A lot of folks felt the same back then, and I guess a lot of people still do. My pa had been of a mindset to "let it lie" once the shooting was over, and he'd instilled that same mentality in me, although we were both smart enough not to mention it where veterans or their families might congregate. Especially those who'd lost a friend or family member, or maybe a piece of their own flesh, like that boy's daddy.

I bought a pair of largemouth bass for a penny apiece, then tapped Dusty's ribs with my heels. I believe he would have preferred to linger, but there were still a few hours of light left and I wanted to take advantage of it. I fried the bass that night and had one for supper and the other for breakfast. It wasn't the best fish I've ever eaten. It had a faint muddy taste, no doubt exacerbated by my not having any cornmeal to bread it with, but it filled an otherwise empty stomach, and set well throughout the day.

Some forty-eight hours later, true to the boy's words, the hills got lower and the trees started to give way to scrub. The land was dry and rocky, and the air wasn't nearly as humid as it had been east of the Hills. The farms petered out and were replaced by isolated ranches. From a distance, most of them looked like small, family-run outfits, although I passed a couple of larger spreads. Drovers on runty cow ponies and *vaqueros* with their wide sombreros and saddles with horns like small meat platters patrolled the ranges. I made an effort to give these men plenty of room to pass on by, and although my actions likely raised a good deal of suspicion against me, I didn't care. A sheepherder on foot or a bunch of boys with fishing poles didn't pose much of a threat in my opinion, but I didn't feel as charitable toward men on horseback, armed with revolvers.

I might have continued my quest for Fort Griffin without talking to another soul if my food hadn't given out a few days after leaving the Hills. I was fortunate that it did, even if it did cost me a bit of belly discomfort. There'd been plenty of game in the Hills, deer and turkeys and rabbits enough to fill a score of pots, any of which I could have dropped easily with my rifle. But I hadn't *needed* meat then. Now that I did, there wasn't a buck or bunny to be found. That's why when I spotted a column of smoke off to the north, I reluctantly reined toward it.

What I found was a small limestone shack under a cap of woodsmoke. Sheets of meat were draped like saddle blankets over a mesquite rack between the fire and the sky. The two drovers monitoring the flame and drying the meat didn't notice my approach until I stopped some forty yards away and hollered a greeting. They both jumped like they'd been popped on the butt with whips, and the taller of the two made a move toward a rifle leaning against the front wall of the stone shack before the other one called him back. After a pause, the shorter man waved me in.

They were young men, both of them sporting more fuzz than whiskers on their cheeks, making it easy to understand how the term cow*boy* might have originated. Heavy pistols hung at their waists, and their clothing looked ragged and heavily soiled. Uneasy glances passed between them as I rode up. Only the matching brands on their mounts — the same as the one on the green steer hide dumped nearby — offered me any measure of reassurance.

"How do," the kid who'd stayed near the fire commented when I drew rein a few yards away. He had rust-colored hair and freckles like splattered barn paint across the bridge of his nose and over both cheeks. His companion was fence-post slim, with an upper lip protruding the way they sometimes do when a person's teeth are bucked and they're self-conscious about their appearance.

I returned the greeting, then tipped my head toward the meat they were jerking over the fire. "That looks mighty tasty."

"It will be when it's done," the one I'd

already dubbed Rusty agreed. "You hungry?"

"Some," I confessed. Then my stomach rumbled loudly as if in confirmation, which brought a grin to Rusty's lips. "I ran out of food night before last, and ain't seen hide nor hair of anything to shoot since," I added.

"Well, don't go getting no ideas about shooting a Bar-Ten steer," the guy with the poky lip said.

"Aw hell, Glen," Rusty said. "The man's hungry. You know the boss wouldn't say nothing about a stranger filling an empty belly." His eyes narrowed a bit, as if sizing up my intentions. "As long as he doesn't make a habit of it."

"I've likely got some moldy morals," I allowed, "but none that includes stealing another man's property."

"Well, you won't have to face any temptation today," Rusty assured me. "You're welcome to share what we've got."

"Obliged." I stepped down and loosened Dusty's cinch, then pulled the bit from between his teeth and hung the bridle from my saddle horn. The redheaded guy fetched a cast-iron kettle filled with beans from inside the shack and set it close to the fire to rewarm, while I dug a plate and spoon from my saddlebags. And what do you think that red-haired guy's name was? Yeah, damned if it wasn't. Maybe not the name his ma had given him, but Rusty was the brand they'd tagged him with on the Bar-Ten, and no more than to be expected with a face as speckled as his. Neither offered a last name and I didn't give them mine, either. Nor was it necessarily expected in those simpler times.

The drying meat was from a steer that had broken its leg falling into an arroyo the day before. They were jerking the bulk of it, but had fried up a bunch earlier that they'd seasoned with pepper and greasy flour, and had a small mountain of steaks piled atop a nearby rock with a piece of old rag dropped over it to keep the flies away. Along with the pot of beans I already mentioned and some biscuits that weren't quite as hard as stone, but might have been mistaken for such in the dark, it made a semi-palatable meal. I'll admit neither of those boys had the culinary skills of a buzzard, but we were all young and had stomachs tough enough to handle such poor fare. And as pitiful as that meal might have been considered by some, I was more than happy to have a portion of it, and thanked them heartily afterward for their hospitality.

Rusty mentioned a river to the south that

was chancy with quicksand, in case I was heading in that direction, so I told them my destination. It was a good thing I did, too. Had I continued along the course I'd been following, I would have reached the Pacific Ocean before I did Fort Griffin.

After a pleasant conversation of a couple of hours — I hadn't realized until then how lonely I'd become — I pushed on, heading more north than west now, and reached what passed for a town below Fort Griffin less than two days later.

CHAPTER SEVEN

In regard to Fort Griffin, I'll confess I hadn't known what to expect when I began my journey. I remember an old-timer some years back describing the fort as perched on the edge of the frontier like some kind of shabby bird getting ready to take flight. That isn't a bad description of the place, although in my own early ignorance of life outside of Milam County, I'd pictured something quite a bit different. Based on tales I'd heard of earlier days among the Eastern tribes, stockaded walls and watchful sentries were more in line with what I was expecting, with vast herds of bison roaming the plains just over the horizon to the west, and Indians . . . Lord almighty, the Indians. Comanches and Kiowa and Apaches — tribes so fierce and bloodthirsty they'd damn near take your breath away just thinking about them.

Turns out life ain't nearly as colorful as a

kid's imagination. Griffin was only one of my early disappointments. What I'd eventually learn is that the fort on Government Hill was a fairly typical example of a Western military installation. The parade ground was a lot bigger than seemed advisable for protection against attack, and although the buildings were mostly made out of logs or green lumber sturdy enough to withstand a Comanche arrow, there were no outer walls to keep back the savage hordes. There wasn't even a bastion for lookouts. On top of that, I'd learned from my buddies back at the Bar-Ten line shack that the fort was only scantily garrisoned now that the worst of the Indian trouble had been laid to rest.

Something else my cowpuncher friends had enlightened me on was that it wasn't the fort I was in search of, but the town below it called the Flat. Spying the community from a distance, it wasn't hard to figure out the name's inspiration. The land in that region of north central Texas was by and large a gently rolling plain, with good graze for livestock and groves of mesquite and pecan trees along the creeks and rivers. But where the Flat stood, Titans could have played billiards without complaint of warped or tilted surfaces.

From a couple of miles away it looked like

a big city, but when I got closer I realized that what I'd mistaken for buildings were actually piles of buffalo hides stacked eight and ten feet high. There were probably a hundred of them, stiff as oak planks but hardly smelling after having been dried to flint before being hauled into town by the wagonload. The Flat itself was a rough collection of shacks, picket-post buildings, weather-ratted tents, and tiny dugouts burrowed into the nearby bluff. A majority of the structures were businesses catering to the hiders, soldiers, and drovers who frequented the community. There were saloons, cafés and restaurants, stables, brothels and dance halls, dry goods stores, rooming houses, two hotels, and at least one small grocery with a bushel basket of dried peas sitting on a stand next to a front door carved from the stiffened hide of a buffalo with the hair still on.

Only a handful of the buildings were constructed from planed lumber. Keith Tolliver's Hunter's Emporium was one of them. It sat toward the middle of town, across the street from the Bee Hive Saloon and just south of a crowded hide yard.

Not knowing exactly where my Uncle Abran worked, other than that it was supposedly supplying the area's hunters and trappers with merchandise needed for their trade, I figured Tolliver's would be as good a place as any to start my search. Turns out it was an on-the-nose bet. I tied up out front and walked inside and there he was, standing behind a dozen ten-pound ingots of lead while haggling with a bearded hide hunter on the near side of the counter.

The hunter was trying to talk my uncle into dropping the five-cents-a-pound price to three-cents-per, but he wasn't having much luck. Pa always said Abran was a shrewd businessman, and I had a front row viewing of his skills that afternoon. They eventually settled on four cents a pound, but with the stipulation that the store got first whack at any hides the hunter brought in. I figured Tolliver's was going to earn back that penny-a-pound deduction in a few weeks, and maybe a little more for the inconvenience. It was a valuable lesson, and like a lot of my experiences on the wild frontier, it was something that would stand me in good stead as my life unfolded.

I'd hung back to watch Abran and the hunter argue, and even though my uncle hadn't acknowledged my presence, I knew he was aware of me standing there. Leaving a junior clerk to help the hunter fill out the rest of his order, Abran walked down the rear of the counter in my direction. It was obvious he didn't recognize me, but you could tell something was sparking his interest.

"Help you?"

Out of nowhere, a stupid grin I couldn't get rid of split my face nearly in half. "Maybe, if you're interested in saying howdy to kin."

His brow briefly furrowed, then just as quickly relaxed. "Molly's boy!" he exclaimed.

"Yes, sir." I thrust a hand over the counter. "I'm Gage."

A chuckle rose from deep within his chest, as warm as a wool blanket on a chilly night. "Hell and be damned if you ain't." He grasped my hand in a firm shake. "You've grown some, you."

He still had his Cajun accent, though softened some in the years since I'd last seen him. He was shorter than I remembered, too, although still above average in height, and he still had the same lanky gait and long honker of a nose as all of ma's kin. A heavy beard covered a square jaw, and his eyes were as dark as twin shafts bored into the side of a mountain. Tobacco stained his teeth and gums, and I remembered that he'd been a chewer even when he stayed with us. In fact, the only complaint I'd ever heard Ma raise about Abran Foret was his tobacco habit and poor aim.

Couldn't hit a spittoon if he was standing on top of it, was her assessment.

"What brings you out here so far from home, young buck?" Abran was still grinning, but his question quickly wiped the smile off my face. He noticed, and his own expression sobered. "Come on, we'll talk in the back room, you and me."

I followed him around the counter and into a small office with a desk under a solitary glass window frosted with dust, shelves sagging with ledgers. There was a chair at the desk and another beside it, and a badly tarnished spittoon between the two, the floor surrounding it stained a dull tobacco brown. Motioning for me to take the chair next to the desk, he immediately got down to business.

"How much trouble you in, young buck?"

"More than you might want to get involved with."

"Bah! We family, you and me. Tell me now, and don't bridle anything."

So, I told him, and in quite a bit of detail, too. About Henry Kalb and Ester, and then me killing Henry and Henry reholstering his revolver — which brought a doubtful hitch to Abran's brows — and how Pa had sent me into hiding for several days while he tried to set things straight in Shelburn. I told him about the two men who had followed me away from Rattlesnake Springs and how that same pair had tried to waylay me behind Clark's store, and how I'd run from that, too, after which Abran nodded solemnly and told me I'd done right.

"Locked up ain't no place to defend yourself from," he agreed. "Not when a man like Kalb wants you dead."

"Do you know Linus Kalb?"

"Not him personally, but men like him." He shook his head with a menacing growl. "Lots of men out here like that."

"Ma sent along a letter for you to read, but I don't know what's in it. The letter is in my saddlebags."

"That your dun I see you come in on?"

I nodded.

"Not stolen, is it?"

That kind of made me angry. That and recalling the suspicious arch to his brow when I told him about Henry returning his gun to its holster, but I bit off any retort before it could cause further grief.

"That horse is mine, clear and legal," I said. "Ralph Milford gave it to me for helping him on his farm."

"I remember Milford," Abran said, nodding. "A good man, him, but he needs some sons. That old woman he married always looked barren to me." He pushed back in his chair. "My house is on the north side of town, near the creek. You get that dun you're riding and meet me there. Best no one sees you-me together, so ride around to creekside before you come in."

He told me what his place looked like, and that I should tie Dusty off under a grapevine arbor his wife had growing next to the back door.

"You're married?" I asked in surprise.

That was something else Ma liked to fret about, that her older brother hadn't found a wife to take care of him.

Abran grinned sheepishly. "Not like your mama would approve of. That's why I don't tell her, but Rita is a good woman, her. Come along, young buck. I want you two to meet."

We parted company in front of the counter and I went out and climbed into my saddle and rode north to the creek, then along that until I spotted a little three-room picket house with peeling blue trim on the window and a faded yellow door. Chickens pecked in the dust of the side yard. The house sat in the afternoon shade of a gnarled pecan tree, its leaves mostly brown and on the ground by now. The nearest neighbor was a hut with a canvas roof thirty or so yards away.

The vine arbor my uncle had told me about was in about the same shape as the pecan tree, its yellowed leaves mostly fallen, but there were four sturdy posts to hold it up and I tied Dusty to the one in back where he wouldn't be as easily noticed by prying eyes. Then the back door swung open with a bang, and a short, dark-skinned beauty with a round face and fiery eyes stepped outside with a double-barreled shotgun snugged tight to her shoulder. She said something real fast in Spanish, but must have realized from my startled expression I didn't understand what it was. She repeated her instructions in better English than you'd expect from someone with her background, which I'll explain in a few minutes.

"Get back on your horse and get out of here," she said. "Before I pepper your ass with buckshot."

I held up both hands, my left one still gripping Dusty's reins. "Don't shoot, ma'am. I'm a friend of Abran."

"I know all of Abran's friends, and I ain't never seen you before." As low laughter rumbled from the interior of the house, the woman threw an annoyed glance over her shoulder. "What are you snorting at?"

Abran appeared in the door behind her, grinning in my direction.

"You know this one?" she demanded. "Is he telling the truth?"

"That my nephew, Boo. His name is Gage."

"Gage? Molly's son?"

"One and the same, him. Now put that shotgun down. His ass don't need no peppering."

She lowered the weapon, but you could tell she was irritated by the situation.

"Tie up your horse and come inside, young buck. Bring my sister's letter with you."

He and the woman called Rita disappeared into the house while I looped Dusty's reins around the far upright, then searched for Ma's letter. When I found it I also discovered her little money pouch — green-dyed leather with a brass clasp — that she and Pa had sent along. Its sides bulged with greenbacks. I'd half-forgotten it was there, but still wasn't curious enough to see how much they'd sent. Sure as hell they didn't have much. Maybe a couple of hundred dollars deposited in the First Bank of

Shelburn, plus Ma's egg money that she kept hidden in the bottom of the flour bin. I was afraid to speculate on how much they'd taken out for my needs, facing who knew what kind of difficulties of their own because of my stupidity. Still, although I was determined not to spend any of it, it was nice to know it was there in case my situation became dire, and I'll always appreciate them for that sacrifice.

I went inside the house and had a look around. The back room was a kitchen with a small cookstove against the inside wall where it would help heat the front room in winter. There was a table with two chairs, and a wooden spice cabinet with a cutting block on top. A variety of spices and herbs hung from the open rafters, and a painted tin image of the Virgin Mary was nailed to the wall next to the stovepipe. The floor was hard-packed dirt, though recently watered and swept clean. A low door in the south wall revealed an iron-frame bed covered with quilts and a low chest of drawers. A crucifix of dull pewter hung above the headboard, and a Sharps rifle leaned against the wall in the corner. I didn't see Rita's shotgun, and wondered if she was still carrying it.

"In here," my uncle called.

I followed his voice into a front room with a sofa and two upholstered chairs, separated by a small table with a lamp on top. A picture of Christ's crucifixion hung prominently on one wall, probably one of the most gruesome renditions I've ever seen of the final Passion — torn flesh under the thorns, a gaping puncture in the ribs, his side from the rib cage on down covered in an ocean of blood. The sun was setting behind him in streaks of red and gold.

"Come in, young buck. Don't let that picture frighten you."

"It won't scare him if he's taken the Lord into his heart."

Abran shrugged and looked at me. "She puts more faith in religion than I do, but she cooks damned fine. Pretty good in bed, too."

Rita's lips thinned in disapproval, but she held her tongue. I couldn't help wondering about their relationship. I'd deduced from Abran's comment back at Tolliver's that they weren't married in a traditional Catholic ceremony, which is the only kind that would have satisfied Ma. Now I began to wonder if they were hitched at all.

"Sit down, you." Abran tipped his head toward one of the chairs. He and Rita were sharing the sofa. After handing him Ma's

110

letter, I took the seat he'd indicated. "Boo, you fix this boy something to drink while I read his mama's letter."

"Is he so crippled he can't walk out back and dip his own water out of the bucket?" She gave me a glaring look. "It's a damned long walk up here from the creek."

"That's all right," I replied. "I'm not thirsty."

I was, but how the hell was I supposed to respond to a challenge like that?

Abran ignored her rejoinder. He had Ma's letter unfolded on his lap, and began to scowl almost as soon as he started reading. I noticed it was several pages in length, and wondered how much of it was about me. I never did find out. When he was finished, Abran folded the letter and slid it back into its envelope. Then he sat there for the longest time, tapping the edge of the envelope on one knee while he stared at me like he might a stranger. I was starting to worry he was contemplating chasing me out of the house before he finally spoke.

"We have no stable here for your horse, young buck. Take him to Tolliver's. There be a stable behind the store where you keep him. Come back here when you're done, and Rita will fix you something to eat. You look hungry." He gave her a scolding glance.

"And thirsty. You didn't fetch this boy no water, you."

"He can fetch his own damn water. What does that letter say about him?"

"Don't worry none about that letter. Go get him something to eat and drink. I got to get back, before Tolliver sees I'm gone."

"That drunken bastard won't notice anything."

"Mebbe so, that, but I still got to get back." He looked at me. "Bring your gear inside and we fix you a place here to sleep until I decide what to do about this." He tapped his breast, where he'd tucked Ma's letter inside his vest.

"How long is he staying?" Rita demanded.

I guess her resistance to my presence finally got to Abran, because he gave her a withering look and she rose and flounced into the kitchen without further comment.

"An awful lot of mad that one has crammed down inside of her yet," he said in lieu of an apology. "Spanish, her, not Mexican. Her daddy was *hidalgo,* very rich, very pure blood. He was from Spain, and wanted his *niños,* his children, to have an education. Even the girls. He sent Rita to a school in St. Louis, the Academy of Arimathea, where the nuns taught her what she need to know to be a good wife and mother. Then,

112

coming home, her caravan was attacked by Comanches and she was taken. Three years she lived with the Indians, but when she was ransomed by *Comancheros,* her daddy didn't want her no more. She was damaged, he said, her purity tainted."

"He didn't want her!"

I guess in my surprise I let my voice rise a bit too high, because I heard a bang from outside the rear door, followed by an angry utterance in Spanish that I'd later learn was pretty obscene, even for the frontier.

Abran grinned at my discomfort. "A temper that one's got, but she a good woman. I am lucky to have her . . . if she don't slit my throat some night."

I kept my mouth shut, not knowing how to respond to such a statement, or if he was even serious about it. He stood and told me again to bring my gear inside, then stable my horse behind the store.

"Tolliver," he added, "is getting drunk somewhere along Griffin Avenue and probably won't be in no more today. That means I won't get back until after the last customer leave tonight." He smiled wryly. "Try not to make Rita too mad."

"It seems like my being here is already doing that."

He nodded somberly. "Makes your job all

the harder, certain damn sure, that." Then he plucked his hat from a nail in the wall beside the front door and left the house.

I exited through the back door and was relieved when I didn't see Rita. I figured she'd likely taken off so she wouldn't have to fix me any grub, or dip up a cup of water for my thirst. I was grateful for the reprieve. After taking my bedroll and saddlebags inside, I mounted and rode back toward the center of town. It was getting pretty late in the afternoon, and the shadows were stretched tall and thin to the east. Griffin Avenue was the Flat's main street. It was fairly hopping with wagons and men on horseback or afoot. There were a few women, but not many, and a lot of the men were drunk; others were seeing to their business, either re-outfitting for the range or selling what they'd brought in — hides or horses or pelts.

I didn't know it then, but the Flat had only two or three hundred regular residents. The rest were largely transients, swelling the town's population at times to well over 1500 souls. I'd guess about half that many were in town on the day I arrived. There was a bull train parked down by Collins Creek and probably twenty-five or thirty hunting outfits camped west of town. The hitching rails in front of the various businesses, especially the saloons, were jam-packed with saddle horses.

Most of the men I saw didn't pay me a lick of attention, and the few who did offered only a cursory glance, like you would anyone you passed on the street. It wasn't until I started to dismount in front of Tolliver's that I spotted a couple of jaspers who seemed to be taking an inordinate amount of interest in what I was doing. A little prickle of unease skipped across the back of my neck, making me want to reach up and feel for some kind of crawly critter invading my collar. It also reminded me of sitting ingenuously on the creek bank behind Clark's store, eating crackers and sardines and very nearly getting my head blown off because of my inattention. I might be slow on occasion, but I ain't often dumb twice, so when I swung down in front of Tolliver's that day, it was with my right hand already on the grips of my old converted Army revolver. I even wrapped Dusty's reins around the hitching rail with my left hand.

The men staring so intently in my direction had been standing in front of the Bee Hive Saloon. Now they started across the street toward me, spreading out a little as they drew closer, and my grip tightened on the Colt. They were strangers and fairly nondescript save for the bright yellow neckerchief snugged up against the Adam's apple of the fellow on my left. I had no reason to believe they knew who I was, but when they got closer and spotted Pa's O-P brand on Dusty's hip, the man with the yellow scarf hollered, "That's him, sure as hell," and reached for his revolver.

That other fellow had been watching me and not paying any attention to my horse. You could tell his partner's exclamation startled him, putting him a beat behind in going for his pistol. I was fortunate in having a suspicious mind, and had my Colt leveled about as quick as the man with the scarf. We both fired at nearly the same instant, but my bullet flew truer than his, and caught him square. His went low, tugging at the outside seam of my pants' leg like a shy child wanting your attention.

I swung smoothly to the other man just as he pointed one of those big Smith and Wesson Americans my way, and snapped off my second round without aiming. He lurched and stumbled to one side, but kept trying to bring his Smith to bear, so I shot him again and he dropped to his knees before learning forward with his head in the dust. The guy with the yellow scarf was also on the ground, writhing slowly with both hands clasped in front of him, blood spurting red as strawberry wine from between his fingers.

I didn't hear the guy coming up behind me, didn't even know he was there until I felt something hard poking into the flesh above my kidneys. A deep-throated rumble ordered me to drop my pistol or by God get blown to hell and gone. I glanced around far enough to see he was holding a single-barreled shotgun with the hammer rolled all the way back, and knew better than to argue. My Colt hit the ground, and I was about to tell him my actions had been in self-defense when I saw the scarred stock of that shotgun swinging toward my head in a short, vicious arc.

Chapter Eight

It ain't a lie when I said it was like pitch had been smeared across my eyes when I came to. For a long time — ten minutes or more — I lay there without moving, the only sound the thunder of my own heartbeat. My mind was an utter blank. I couldn't have told you where I was or why. I couldn't have even given you my name. But after a bit, my vision started to clear, my eyes to roam, and that's when I spotted a rectangular piece of gray off to one side and came to understand it was a window. By focusing on that dim chunk of light and telling myself what it was and what it meant, my scattered memory gradually regrouped. Up to and including that hellacious swipe taken at my cranium with a shotgun butt.

I took a long, deep breath, and damn near gagged as the odors of old urine, vomit, and who knew what else filled my sinuses. Running my fingers across the back of my skull produced a cool, tacky substance that had oozed from my scalp to mat my hair. A lump under the laceration felt like a fried egg turned to stone had been slipped unbroken under the flesh.

I don't remember being much of a curser in my youth, not like I am today, but I do recall the sharp expletive that rushed through my lips when I rolled onto my side. That and a total blackness that seemed to take a quick swoop downward, then rose again as if deciding I'd had enough. I swore once more, though softer this time, and closed my eyes to wait out the dizziness.

With my nose scant inches from the floor, I caught a whiff of earth and realized I was lying on a dirt floor rather than in a bunk. After the pain began to subside, I kind of wobbled to my feet. Even then I had to lean against a wall for a few minutes to keep from keeling over. Eventually I was able to shuffle to the window and take a peek outside, but my line of sight was restricted by several dozen mounds of buffalo hides. There were neither lights nor movement in front of me, although I could hear a banjo playing off in the distance, along with coarse laughter and the shrieks of women, all of it as faint as a summer memory. The fresh air helped though, and when I turned away and spotted a door in the opposite wall, I was able to walk to it without fear of passing out.

The door was locked — no surprise in that. A slot maybe six inches high and ten across had been hacked into the wood at eye level. On the other side was a room as small as my own cramped cage. In the murky light spilling through a window in the far wall I could make out a chair and a table with a lamp on it. An empty ammunition box filled with paperwork sat on the corner, and my hat hung on a peg attached to the wall behind the table. I couldn't tell if the floor was dirt or wood, but figured the former. I stood there a few minutes staring and thinking, then went back to the corner where I'd awakened and lay down again.

It was light when I next opened my eyes, a predawn gray with a definite chill to it, although not overly uncomfortable. The rattle of harness chain and the heavy thud of hooves drifted in through the window, but the raucous sounds of celebration from the night before had faded to a few low curses as men lined out their teams somewhere nearby.

I sat up and looked around. My quarters were tight and Spartan, consisting of a waste bucket and a couple of ragged wool blankets heaped in one corner. The floor was uneven dirt, as I'd surmised the night before, the walls hewed logs. The chinking was coming loose in a few places, although not nearly enough for me to slip through. It was a cell, sure enough, though a piss-poor one by just about anyone's standards. Rising, I moved to the window for another peek outside, but the view wasn't any better than it had been the night before — stacks of flint hides and trampled grass, a couple of big Murphy freight wagons parked at the far side of the hide yard. To my left I could make out a corner of the bluff where the fort lay, although I couldn't see any buildings. There were no bars on the window, but as with the loose chinking, the gap was far too small to shimmy through. After another couple of minutes, I went back to the corner where I'd spent the night and sat down with my back to the wall.

The sun still wasn't yet up when the front door opened in the other room. I stood and walked over to see who it was. The sight wasn't encouraging. A man I'd never seen before, heavy-gutted and slow-moving, somewhere on the shady side of fifty. His hair under a rough wool cap with a leather brim looked as stiff as a boar's bristles, and a stubble of several days furred all three of his chins. He glared when he spotted me at the slot.

"You're awake, huh?"

"I'm standing here, ain't I?"

"A goddamn wiseacre, too. Ain't that just my luck?" He came over and glanced inside, then wrinkled his nose. "I ain't cleaning that mess up."

"It ain't mine. You should've cleaned it up before putting me in here."

"It wasn't me put you here, it was Max."

"Who's Max?"

He looked at me like he was trying to decide if I was hoorawing him. Deciding I must be new to the town, he said, "Max Jennison is the deputy. He's in charge when the marshal ain't here, which he ain't."

"Who are you?"

"I'm the poor sumbitch gonna bring you your meals till the marshal gets back. He's in Jacksboro right now on business."

"I didn't know Griffin had a marshal."

"It don't, but the Flat does. Bill Gilson has the office now, although I'd be surprised if he don't soon give it up for something that pays better. This town doesn't have a dime's worth of respect for the law, and it pays accordingly."

"What's your name?"

"Inquisitive little fart, ain't cha? My name is Foster, not that it changes your situation any."

"Just what is my situation?"

He laughed hard enough to make his belly jiggle under a shirt worn thin and gray. "You, bub, are nose deep in a barrel full of shit."

I guess it was okay that someone found my predicament amusing, but I sure didn't. I continued on with the game, however. "Why am I locked up?"

"You ain't the sharpest knife in the drawer, are you? Why do you think you're locked up?"

"If it's because of those two men I shot, they were the ones who came after me."

"Yeah, they sure did, didn't they? But here's the thing, me and Max know who those boys are. Or who they were, before you laid 'em low. Chip Moore and Lee Walker were bounty hunters, both of 'em tough nuts to crack, but you did it. That makes me and Max real curious about who you are and why they were gunning for you."

The turnkey's words sent a chill spiraling through me. I'd been worried all along that Linus Kalb might put a bounty out for my return — dead or alive, knowing that son of a bitch. Now it looked like my worst fear had been realized.

"I'd guess they mistook me for someone else," I bluffed. "If there's a bounty on my head, I haven't heard about it."

That wasn't a one hundred percent lie, although it was pretty close. I could tell Foster wasn't having it. I probably wouldn't have either, had the boot been on the other foot, but I was going to give it my best, and intended to do so right up until they dropped a noose around my neck.

I don't know if you've picked up on this yet, but that naïvety I'd left home with was starting to wear down in spots. Like with my little lies to Foster, and spotting Moore and Walker right off. At some point since leaving Clark's store I guess I'd accepted that if I was going to survive against the kind of men Kalb was likely to send after me, I was going to have to shed my green real quick, like a snake wiggling free of its old skin.

A shadow passed in front of the street-side window and the door swung inward. An old woman — she must have been in her late sixties — wearing a dusty brown dress and calico bonnet came in toting a small tin bucket and a rag-capped mason jar filled with what smelled like coffee. Foster stepped back from the cell door and tipped his cap polite as you please. "Morning Mrs. Pickerel."

"Morning, Van." She set the jar and pail on the table, then came over to have a look at the prisoner — what little she could see of me through that tiny slot, which I reckon was mostly eyeballs and brows and the bridge of my nose. "Catch yourself a mean one, did you?" she asked the turnkey.

"He fancies himself as such, but Max snubbed him down yesterday without much trouble. He'll get snubbed even tighter when the marshal gets back."

She kind of cackled like you'd imagine a witch might, bent over her bubbling cauldron of dark brew. "I hope you like beans, Mr. Man Killer," she said.

"Oh, he will," Foster promised. "If not for breakfast, then surely by suppertime."

The woman laughed again, her wrinkled face crinkling with delight. Foster offered her an IOU for the grub, but she turned him down. "I'll collect my money when Bill gets back," she promised, moving toward the door. "You watch this one, Van. He's liable to skinny out that little hole and scurry away."

"I'll watch him, Mrs. Pickerel," the turnkey promised with a friendly grin, but as soon as she was out the door, his expression turned to stone. "Don't you go getting' no fancy notions about what she said, bub. Been more'n one nose-picking jackass thought he could bust out of our little jail, but it ain't been done yet. That might be dirt under your feet, but there's enough hard rock under it you'd need dynamite to bust through."

"I'm not going anywhere until the marshal gets back and we can get this mistake straightened out," I replied, kind of astonishing myself with how my lies were becoming quicker and smoother.

Foster snorted like a bug had flown up his nose. "Yeah, I've heard that one before, too."

He went over to the table to have a look at the beans and coffee, as if maybe contemplating a second breakfast for himself. Then he picked them up one in each hand and brought them over, slipping the little bucket through first, then the coffee. A spoon was fasted to the vessel's bail with miller's twine, and there was a hunk of bread floating on top of the beans.

"I'll be back later to fetch the empties, then I'll march your ass out to the privy. Don't make a mess in here, bub, because you're going to live with it if you do."

So that was that, I thought, watching him leave and using a padlock to secure the front door. I took my meal over to the corner and slid down with my back to the wall. The smell inside the cell hadn't abated any, so I suppose I was getting used to it. Besides, the aroma of that coffee was making my mouth water. The beans weren't half bad, either, although a little on the mushy side. I used the bread to swipe the bucket after I'd finished, then cleaned up what I'd missed with a finger. Foster came back as promised to take my utensils, then escorted me to a single-holer to the side of the jail. The entire journey there and back was made at the muzzle of the same single-barreled shotgun Max had used to put me inside to begin with.

Sadly, that twice a day trip to the privy was the highlight of my stay at what passed for the Flat's little hoosegow, and my hard luck if I needed to use it at any other time. Van Foster's main employment was working for one of the local horse traders. Although he'd occasionally look in on me throughout the day, the deputy who actually arrested me, Max Jennison, never came around at all.

As time passed I began to worry that Uncle Abran might have given up on me. I told myself he probably didn't want to get involved with a killer, especially if it meant going against friends and business associates. Or maybe he'd decided I wasn't worth helping. For that matter, how long had it been since he'd last laid eyes on me — twelve or fifteen years at least? Hell, if you think about it, I was practically a stranger.

I was also doing a lot of worrying about Kalb's men — those two here at the Flat and the two back at Clark's. Ester had mentioned half a dozen men skulking in the trees atop Ralph Milford's hill, keeping an eye on our farm with field glasses. I kept thinking about those two yet unaccounted for, and wondering how Chip Moore and Lee Walker had come to be waiting here at Fort Griffin for me to show up. Were Moore and Walker part of the original six, or had Kalb loosened even more hounds on my trail?

That was the line of my thinking as I sat on the dirt in my little cage, and why the low but catlike screech of nails being pried from wood at the jail's front door in the middle of my third night's residency there sent an almost electrical surge coursing through my frame. I sprang to my feet, eyes darting for some kind of weapon, but my only defense would have to be my fists, painfully inadequate against a couple of armed toughs. Determined to do my best, I took up a position in the middle of the cell and braced myself for what was to come. I'll admit Abran's thick Cajun accent caught me by surprise. I'd expected help from that quarter to come in the form of bail or an attorney.

"You in there, young buck?"

I exhaled loudly and moved to the door. "I was beginning to think you'd given up on me."

"Not yet I don't." He came over to finger the padlock on its hasp. "There a key to this thing, Gage?"

"Not here, not that I've seen. Foster takes his key with him when he leaves."

Abran muttered something under his breath, then slid a short pry bar behind the lock and pulled back slowly, as if that might somehow lessen the protest of the wood. Unfortunately, its shrill cry quickly filled the cell. "Ah, you *fils putain,*" he scolded softly. "You would tell the world I am here, yes?"

"It wasn't that loud," I said.

He gave me a disgruntled glance. "Lie to the law, never to your own."

Humiliation warmed my face as Abran readjusted his pry bar. Loud music played in the distance, and laughter, catcalls, and the occasional pop of gunfire filled the sky above the Flat, but the area immediately surrounding the jail was dark and quiet. If anyone was passing too close when the hasp broke, they'd likely hear it easily.

"Now," Abran said, knuckles turning pale on the heavy bar. "We make a grand noise, then will be over." He raised his eyes to mine and grinned. "Reminds me of when I was your age, young buck, and the hell me and *mon amis* liked to raise." Then he leaned back, face scrunched, teeth clenched, and the wood gave a final squawk to release its grip on the hasp. I stepped quickly into the front room and Abran punched me lightly on the shoulder. "Where are your guns and saddle?"

"I haven't seen them," I replied as I grabbed my hat off the wall rack. "Either Foster or Jennison must have taken them."

"Probably Jennison. Probably try to sell them." He shook his head. "Lot of people think Jennison should be the one locked up, but that don't matter tonight. Come on, let's get out of here, you-me, while we can."

We stepped outside and turned north, away from the howls and hollering of the saloons and whorehouses farther down the street. Keeping to the shadows as much as possible made it a twenty-minute hike back to Abran's house on the edge of town. A candle burned in a pewter holder on the kitchen table; its light guttered to near extinction as we entered. Rita stood in the parlor door fully dressed, her expression a mixture of anxiety and relief. Relief won out by a wide margin when she spied Abran crowding in close behind me.

"Were you seen?" she asked, coming into the kitchen.

"Not by nobody," he assured her, then placed a firm hand on my shoulder. "In here," he said, and guided me into the dark front room. "Boo, get this boy something decent to drink, then some solid food."

"No beans," I added, and Abran's teeth shone briefly in the dim light from the kitchen.

"County pays Cloris Pickerel twenty-five cents a meal, but it don't tell her what to fix. Beans be cheap."

"She makes a decent pot of coffee, but the rest was wanting."

He motioned to the sofa. "Sit down, we got to palaver some, you-me." He took a seat across the room where he could face me in the dim light. "That Moore fella, he dead. Foster tell you that?"

I nodded.

"That other one be just about dead, too."

"Just about? Foster said I'd killed both of them."

"Likely you did. He was pretty close, last I heard. Army doc come down off the Hill to have a look, said his future ain't promising." He shook his head. "Damn me, Gage, what are you trying to do, kill off half the state?"

"I'm trying to stay out of trouble."

Abran guffawed. "Damn poor job you doing. Killed that boy back to Shelburn, then another here, and probably that Walker fella too. Three men, and you barely shaving yet. You call that staying out of trouble?"

"Five," I corrected quietly.

He scowled. "Five?"

I'd already told him about Clark's store and the two men who'd tried to waylay me behind it. What I hadn't mentioned, for reasons I wasn't quite sure of myself at the time, was the bullets I'd put into both of them. I told him now, and added that I'd probably killed at least one of them for sure, and maybe both. Expecting anger when I finished, Abran instead got a funny, almost perplexed look on his face. Then he laughed and leaned back in his seat.

"Damn me for a fuzzy-headed woodpecker, boy. Who taught you shoot a pistol gun like that?"

"Nobody."

"Nobody! Nobody, hell. Folks still be talking about how quick you skinned that piece in front of Tolliver's. Shot them boys good, and they be professionals, them two." He shook his head in distaste. "Goddamn bounty hunter, the both of them." Then he looked at me and the humor slid off his face. "You practice some maybe, eh?"

"No, sir, I just do it. I don't think about it, and I don't practice. It just seems like every time it's happened, it's been so fast I haven't had time to think, so I pull and shoot."

A grin the size of a small arroyo split Abran's bearded face. "Whoeee, boy. Just pull and shoot? That's some, that."

I stared back without speaking, not sure how to take his unexpected praise.

"Gage, you be one mighty hell roarer, but now you in mighty big trouble." He was silent a moment, staring at the floor. I could hear Rita in the other room gently rattling her pots and pans. Finally, Abran said, "We got to get you out of town. They going know you didn't escape on your own, not with them locks pulled like that. They start asking around, and real soon someone is gonna remember you coming into Tolliver's that first time. You can bet your hide someone seen you riding up behind this house, too. Won't take long, after that, and Max Jennison going to figure out where you hied off to." His brows rose in question. "You tell them your name?"

"No, sir, I didn't tell them anything, and they never asked. Never asked my name or where I was from or what I was doing here. Foster called me bub when he called me anything, but mostly he brought my food and took me to the outhouse, then left as quick as he could."

Abran snorted. "Yeah, that sound like the law on the Flat. They probably figure you'd lie, was they to ask. Bill Gilson was here, it be different, but Jennison and Foster have other jobs that keep them busy."

"If I can get to my horse and tack, I can leave right away."

"You going to have to forget that horse, young buck. Jennison got it in with a herd belongs to that trader man Foster works for, and trader man keeps armed guards watching his stock. Has to, otherwise he lose them all to thieves and scallywags." He raised his hand with the tips of his fingers lightly touching, then quickly spread them wide. "Poof, like that."

"I've got to have my horse."

"Forget that horse," Abran replied

brusquely.

But I had no intention of forgetting Dusty. In my mind I was reliving all the miles we'd traveled together. Not just coming out here, but around Milam County. He was my first horse and I'd spent a lot of time working with him, and as crazy as it might sound, I considered us friends. The thought of losing him was hitting me low and hard.

"What for the long face?" Abran demanded of me, but Rita knew. She was standing in the door to the kitchen with a plate in one hand and a cup in the other, and for the first time I saw a softening of her expression when she looked at me.

"You need to do what your uncle says, Gage. You can always buy another horse, but if Kalb catches you, you won't live long enough to say *adios* to that dun."

"Maybe you could buy him," I said hopefully, thinking of the pouch in my saddlebags with the money my folks had sent along. Plus I had nearly twelve dollars of my own hidden inside my jacket. But Abran was already shaking his head.

"Rita-me, we got no need for a horse, and the trader man would know that. So would Jennison. Besides, I already got an idea how to get you away from here."

"Without Dusty?"

"Damn me, boy, you got to forget that horse. Your saddle and guns, too." He pulled a watch from his vest pocket, tipping it so that the light from the kitchen played across its face. "I got to go tell a man he got a deal. You stay here with Boo, and try not to make her mad."

"What kind of a deal?"

"A deal that take too long to explain, but that is going to get your ass off the Flat without you riding out in a pine box or with your hands manacled." He jerked his head toward the kitchen. "Go on now, both of you. I be back soon." He went to the door and grabbed his hat and a suit coat off a peg. A revolver hung from its trigger guard next to them, and he took that too, thumbing the gate open and spinning the cylinder to make sure it was loaded. Then he ducked outside and closed the door gently behind him.

CHAPTER NINE

"Come on, Gage," Rita said after Abran was gone. "Your uncle has a plan, but we're running out of time."

I followed her into the kitchen. She set the plate and cup on the table and motioned for me to dig in. It looked pretty tasty after a three-day diet of beans and black coffee, and didn't disappoint. There was roast kid with gravy, green beans, fried potatoes, and fresh biscuits. The coffee might not have been as good as Mrs. Pickerel's, but it was more enjoyable to drink it sitting at a table instead of on a dirt floor smelling of someone else's piss.

Rita was at the spice cabinet pulling down various jars and roots, chopping a little of this and adding a smidge of that, then mixing it all together in a wooden bowl that she'd poured a little black coffee into. I didn't pay her much mind, lost as I was in schemes to steal Dusty back, since buying him didn't seem to be an option.

When I was done eating, Rita came over with the bowl of brown paste she'd been working on. I frowned when she sat it on the table, and she laughed.

"Don't worry, I'm not going to make you eat it."

"It looks like it would set up hard in the belly, for a fact."

"It's a dye," she told me. "We're going to turn you into a Mexican." She dipped a wooden spoon into the bowl and brought out a tiny bit. "Roll up your sleeve. I want to see what it looks like."

"Wait a minute," I protested, pushing back in my chair. "What do you mean, make me a Mexican?"

"It was your uncle's idea, but I'm the one who told him about it. I learned it studying botany."

I think I might have asked her what a botany was, still being fairly uneducated in those years, and she explained the field and how she'd studied it where she'd gone to school in St. Louis.

"We used the dyes on fabric, but if you weren't careful and got some on your skin, it could take several weeks for it to wear off. One of the girls, as white as new bone china, put some on her face to try to match my shade." Her gaze hardened in the capering light. "They beat her pretty bad for it, too. The nuns at the Academy of Arimathea were convinced the darker a girl's skin, the more prone she'd be to mischief. That was their word for becoming too familiar with boys." She abruptly shook her head as if breaking loose of whatever memories had momentarily gripped her. Laughing curtly, she said, "They would have peed in their habits if they'd been with me in *Comancheria.*"

I sat there with my mouth clamped shut and didn't utter a word. Not even when she tipped my face back and started rubbing that paste onto my cheeks. Rita didn't say any more either, and concentrated on the chore at hand. Her lips were drawn thin, and I recalled what Uncle Abran had said about her the first time I met her.

She's got a lot of mad crammed down inside of her yet.

I got smeared real good, all over my face and upper chest and the back of my neck and up both arms past my biceps. She rubbed it in with a rag, pressing hard to avoid streaking. Then she stepped back and wiped sweat from her forehead with the back of her wrist. After a moment's scrutiny, she suddenly smiled. "Damn me, young buck, that don't look half bad."

Both of us laughed at her mimicking of my uncle's accent.

"Now we need to add a darker dye to your hair."

"My hair?"

"It's got to be black, Gage. Yours is brown."

"Will it wear off?"

"It'll grow out. You can cut it off then if you want to."

She brought a bowl of black paste over and tipped my head forward, then muttered a soft imprecation and set the bowl on the table.

"Who did this?" she asked, running her fingers lightly over the blood-matted hair and still-tender flesh on the back of my head.

"Max Jennison hit me with a shotgun."

"Someday somebody is going to kill that son of a bitch," she murmured, then went to get a wet rag to clean the scabbed wound as best she could.

Rita must have worked a good three hours that night to transform me from a mixed-blood Cajun — Pa had a good deal of German on his daddy's side of the family — to *Mexicano*. When she was finished, she stepped back to appraise her creation with a critical eye.

"It looks good," she decided.

"You reckon I'll pass for Mexican?"

"No, not Mexican. Your features are too European for that."

I still recall how I admired listening to her musings that night, the range of her vocabulary that could run circles around mine. "European" and "botany" were words I'd never heard before. When I look back on my life, I think it was being around Rita that started me thinking about furthering my own education someday.

After being dismissed, I slipped outside to get away from the lingering odors of the dyes. Judging from the sliver of moon hanging in the western sky like a set of cocked steer horns, it must have been close to dawn. If Abran wanted me off the Flat before my escape was discovered, we were going to have to hurry.

When I went back inside, Rita was gone. I found her in the cramped bedroom, lying fully clothed on her side. I could tell from the way she tensed up that she was awake and aware of my watching her. I turned away without speaking. There was a half cup of coffee left in the pot from the night before, faintly warm but bitter as alkaline. I poured it into my cup anyway, then sat at the kitchen table to await Abran's return.

I must have been more keyed up than I realized, because when the front door opened in the parlor I jumped out of my chair and whirled around with my fists cocked. Abran chuckled when he saw me through the inner doorway.

"Jumpy like a cat, you."

"Yeah," I breathed, lowering my arms.

Rita came out of the bedroom. You could tell she hadn't been asleep, either.

"Is it done?"

Abran nodded and shut the door, then came into the kitchen with a bundle tucked under one arm, forcing me to back across the room until the candlelight reached my face. "A damn fine job, Boo," he said approvingly, after studying my features for a moment.

"Like a *criollo.*"

"I think so, yeah."

"What's a *criollo*?"

"A Spaniard of pure blood," Rita said.

"Pure blood?"

"I am *criolla,*" she said tersely. "The child I left behind in *Comancheria* is not."

Abran put a hand gently on her shoulder, but she shrugged it off and turned away. Sighing, he walked over to the table and unfurled the bundle he'd been carrying across the top of it. I saw a dirty gray sombrero and a wool blanket with a hole cut in •the middle for a man's head; there was also a coarsely woven blue shirt and worn buckskin trousers. A revolver in a belted holster was partially hidden under the poncho. For a second I thought it might be my Colt, but it wasn't.

"A bullwhacker ain't gonna be carry him no fancy six-gun, Gage," Abran said as if reading my mind.

"Bullwhacker?"

"You know how?"

"I've never driven a team of oxen in my life."

"When Bob Jolley asks, you don't tell him that, okay. I already told him you can handle a bull team."

"Is that what I'm supposed to be, a Mexican bullwhacker?"

"A *boyero.*"

"*Boyero?*"

"You have much to learn, young buck, and the best way to do that is keep your mouth like this." He pressed his lips tightly together, and I nodded that I understood. But I wasn't on the trail yet, and I still had a lot of questions I wanted answered.

"Just what kind of plan do you have for me?"

"Bob Jolley a friend, him. Got a trading post maybe ten days west of here, to supply the hiders and haul in their skins for a cut of the profit."

"Does he know who I am?"

"He knows you can take care of yourself. I told him you worked hard and was honest, not someone to leave him short-handed if the trail gets tough, or try to steal him blind when he not looking. That was all he cared to know."

"He's going to know I'm a liar the first time I try to yoke a team of oxen."

Abran laughed. "It ain't so hard a thing to figure out, young buck. Just watch what the others do, then do the same. Now go and change, become a *boyero*, and I will have Boo burn your old clothes."

I hated to think about doing that — anyone who grew up poor would — but I'll be the first to admit I'd left home wearing a noticeable outfit — a bib-front shirt with ivory buttons and black piping, and light-colored denim trousers. Van Foster might not have asked me for something so simple as my name, but he'd surely remember the clothes I was wearing.

Gathering up the shirt and pants Abran had set on the table, I took them into the front room and changed in the dark. The

Mexican clothing fit well enough, and I was glad to keep my old boots. When I went back into the kitchen, Abran smiled pleased as punch.

"Try the sombrero," he said.

"I got a hat," I reminded him.

"You wear the sombrero until you ain't being chased no more. Now put it on, see it fits."

I did, and it did. The hat wasn't as big as some I'd seen, neither as tall, for which I was grateful, nor as far reaching with its brim. It was stained and smelled of smoke from hovering over trailside campfires, and had a brass-studded leather band and leather strings underneath that I could snug up under my chin in a high wind to keep it from sailing off. Then my eyes strayed toward the table.

"A Joslyn," Abran said, pulling the revolver from its crudely stitched holster and placing it in my hand. "Forty-four caliber." He dug a paper-wrapped package from his coat pocket and set that on the table next to the gun belt. "Some cleaning supplies here, extra caps and powder and ball, a mold to cast your own bullets if you run out. Also, there is a belt pouch, but you will have to sew on a new strap. Bob is carrying several tons of lead in his wagons, plenty of powder, too. He will sell you what you need if you ask, then deduct what you owe from your wages when you reach his post."

My chest grew tight and my throat seemed to constrict behind my tongue. I turned the Joslyn slowly in my hands, examining it from every angle. It was a percussion model from the late war, a five-shot side-hammer revolver with partially checkered grips, a knurled cylinder pin that extracted from the rear, and a flat iron butt plate — a far cry from my old Colt Army in looks and quality.

"Bob is going to be here soon," Abran went on. "His wagons pull out two days ago, but one of his *boyeros* got hisself hurt, and now Bob needs another man, another *boyero.*" He nodded toward the gun belt. "Try that on, see how it feels."

I buckled the belt around my waist and was once again surprised by the near perfect fit. As with the sombrero, shirt, and trousers, my uncle obviously had a keen eye for sizes, likely developed over years of selling not just shooting supplies, but also clothing for the range.

"What about my rifle?" I asked as I holstered the revolver.

"Your Winchester be gone, young buck, like your horse and saddle. Max Jennison is going to sell it, along with everything else he took off you." He smiled with something like sympathy, the first hint of it I'd seen from him. "You be mad about that all you want, but don't start thinking you can do anything about it. Go out on the buffalo range with Bob and stay there until I send word it safe to come back."

"How long is that going to be?"

"You know well as me, Gage."

Meaning neither one of us had any idea what my future held, other than that I was soon going to be spending my days staring at the east end of a westbound cow, all of us heading for buffalo country.

CHAPTER TEN

Bob Jolley showed up before first light. He was a short man in his mid- to late-forties with a potbelly, bowed legs, and bushy sideburns. Abran kept the introductions brief, then Bob explained my duties — bullwhacking a twin-wagon outfit pulled by eight head of oxen — for a flat sum of fifty dollars, payable at the end of the trail. I asked how long it would take to reach his trading post and Jolley told me a week to ten days, oxen being notoriously slow. Then he asked if I was interested in the position. I promptly replied that I was.

"He will make a damn fine hand, this one," Abran said, clamping a hand to the top of my shoulder.

"He had better," Jolley replied. "Otherwise I'll cut him loose and find another." He looked at me. "Grab you stuff, Pardell, and meet me in front of Tolliver's Emporium in ten minutes."

Ten minutes doesn't seem like a lot of time for goodbyes, but it turned out we didn't have all that much to say. Abran shook my hand and wished me luck. I tried to thank Rita for her efforts with my disguise, but she waved me off and retreated to the kitchen as if dismissing an errand boy. My gear — what remained of it — sat in the corner next to the sofa. I tucked the bedroll under my right arm and carried the saddlebags in my left hand.

"I ain't coming with you, Gage," Abran said as he walked me to the front door. "It be best if you just disappear."

"I appreciate all you've done."

"You be family, young buck. I could do no less." Then he slapped me lightly on the shoulder, grinned a farewell, and propelled me through the door. Thirty seconds later the candlelight inside the small picket-post house blinked out and I stood alone in the darkness.

It wasn't much of a hike to Tolliver's. Bob Jolley was waiting for me out front with a couple of mules — one a tall gray with a saddle already outfitted with bags and bedroll and a scabbard from which protruded the stock of a long-barrel rifle. The second was a smaller bay, a jenny with what they call a blue nose, which was basically just the darker hair around the muzzle. She was wearing an old Dragoon saddle with the pommel and cantle jutting both fore and aft like some kind of Viking battleship. It wasn't pretty and it sure as hell wasn't comfortable, but I'll bet it was cheap.

Jolley saw me coming and was already astride his mule when I arrived. Nodding to the jenny, he said, "Strap your gear in place, Pardell. The train's already two days out. I hope to catch up to it before nightfall."

Jolley and I were going to be traveling a whole lot faster on our mounts than an ox-drawn wagon could ever hope to, so two days out with a team of bulls probably didn't equal more than twenty or twenty-five miles. Maybe less, if the country was hilly or gouged with arroyos.

I strapped my bags and bedroll behind the cantle, then stepped into the saddle. The jenny flicked her ears a couple of times, but I told her to keep her opinions to herself and any planned shenanigans in the wings. I'm not saying she understood me word for word, but she recognized from the tone of my voice that I wasn't going to be buffaloed. I might not have known much about driving oxen, but I'd been handling mules since I was eight years old.

It was still dark when Bob and I rode away

from the Flat, but there were lights coming on in some of the houses, and fires being kindled in a few of the hunters' camps down along the creek. The jailhouse window was still dark, though, and I was relieved we were getting out of there before Van Foster showed up to discover my absence.

We pushed on into the day, alternating between a slow jog and a walk. About ten miles west of Griffin, the country began to change again, as it had after leaving the Hills, segueing into a land of wide, shallow valleys and low hills. Rocky outcroppings jutted from the ridges like broken teeth, and the flora turned as bristly as a hog's chin whiskers. In places tracts of prickly pear twenty yards across forced our trail to meander north or south, but for the most part we kept to a straight westerly course. The sky was wide open and deep blue, with only a few vagrant clouds to obscure the sun, their black bellies offering promises of rain that never materialized. The shade felt good as they passed, though, always welcomed, and always too brief.

We camped that night along a shallow stream. I kind of expected Jolley to be riled by our not catching up to the train, but he seemed more pleased than anything. Happy,

I suppose, that the outfit was making good time.

We were in the saddle again by first light. Jolley didn't talk much, and I took my cue from him. He impressed me with the respect he paid to the country we passed through, as if he recognized its dangers and was ready to face anything it might throw at him, be it weather, bandits, or wildlife.

It was just shy of noon when we came in sight of the train, strung out across a wide meadow with the oxen turned loose to graze. Jolley pulled up on the rim of the little valley where the train was nooning and I stopped at his side, leaning forward with both hands braced against the top of the goose-necked saddle horn, half standing in my stirrups to ease the strain on my aching thighs. I'd crossed a big chunk of Texas on the back of a horse and hardly complained, but a day and a half in the cradle of that Dragoon monstrosity had nearly done me in.

Although I figured Jolley would be happy that we'd caught up, his darkening expression told me otherwise. I was learning, though, and kept my mouth shut as we put our mules over the edge and started down toward the valley floor.

I don't know if you've ever seen a big

freight outfit, but it's a sight to stick in your mind. The wagons themselves were massive. Built of seasoned oak to withstand the rigors of the trail, their low canvas covers towered twelve feet above the ground, and at six feet or more, the rear wheels were taller than most men. Each vehicle was capable of carrying nearly six thousand pounds of freight, and with two wagons to a hitch, pulled in tandem by eight yoke of cattle — sixteen head altogether — that amounted to between five and six tons of goods for each team. I counted eight wagons, which meant four separate outfits.

The word *oxen* is something of a misnomer. Hearing it used the way we did, you might be inclined to think we were referring to a specific breed of cattle. The reality is that what we called oxen was generally no more than what was available at the time. Steers as a rule — the male of the species have more pulling strength than the female — and generally beef, rather than dairy cattle. In our case, Texas being Texas, the herd I saw grazing below us was mostly longhorns.

When we got down off the bluff, Jolley reined his mule toward the lead wagon. I followed along without question. Our destination was a small fire where several men lounged in the vehicle's shade. As we drew near, a wiry guy under a broad-brimmed hat pushed up off the ground and walked out to meet us. Whatever he'd done to earn the boss's ire, it was evident by his expression he was already aware of it. I had to wait a few minutes before I figured out what the trouble was.

Pulling up a few yards away, the boss said, "Tellis."

"Mr. Jolley."

"What's wrong with the circumstances here?" Jolley asked, waving a hand toward the line of freighters stretched out behind him.

"I reckon you'd say they're spread too far apart."

"You *reckon*?"

Tellis sighed and glanced behind him at the men beside the fire, slowly climbing to their feet. Several of them were still holding coffee cups in their hand. "Yoke up, boys, we're pulling out."

After the bullwhackers had taken off to fetch their grazing cattle, Jolley leaned forward over his saddle horn. "If I had not just returned from Fort Griffin with another hire, I'd cut you loose here and now, Tellis. One more example of such slack judgment, and I'll do it anyway. Is that understood?"

"Yes, sir, it is."

"Very well." He twisted partway around in his saddle and motioned me up. "This is Gage Pardell," he said. "I've hired him to replace Thompson. Pardell, this is Ralph Tellis. For the time being, he's my wagon master. Whether he stays in that position remains to be seen. In the meantime, you'll take your orders from him. Understood?"

"Yes, sir."

"Very well. Tellis, show Pardell his team. I want these wagons rolling within the quarter hour."

"Yes, sir," Tellis replied, but he was speaking to Jolley's back, the boss having already ridden off to check the creek crossing. Tellis turned a critical eye on me. "How much experience do you have driving bulls, Pardell?"

Figuring honesty might be my best bet, I said, "Probably not as much as Mr. Jolley thinks."

Tellis grinned at that. "Well, at least you're not a bullshitter." He held out his hand. "My friends call me Tell. You can, too. Come on, I'll introduce you to your stock."

After unsaddling my little mule and turning her loose for the wrangler to deal with, I hauled my gear back to a pair of wagons at the rear of the column. Tell said to heave my stuff in over the tailgate, rather than scale the dozen or so feet to the top and drop it inside. I left the Dragoon saddle up by the fire, and never did find out what happened to it, although burning it would have been a blessing to the next man who needed a rig.

With my gear stowed, I came around to the front of the wagons, where Tellis was lining up the eight hardwood yokes lying on the ground in front of it. I watched as the bay mule was driven to the rear of the caravan to join a mixed cavvy of mules and oxen, watched over by a young Mexican boy who couldn't have been more than sixteen. These were spare cattle, in case one of the oxen became ill or died, and mules Jolley intended to sell to hunters once we reached his trading post.

I liked Ralph Tellis right away. He was lanky and easygoing, and it quickly became evident he knew how to run a freight outfit, even if it wasn't with the military-like precision Bob Jolley might have preferred. Tell was probably in his thirties, with a scruffy beard shot through with early gray and dark eyes under heavy brows. He led me to the cattle and pointed out my teams. They were typical longhorns, most of them brindled in white, sorrel, and black, with their horns sawed off to within a few inches of their skulls — and don't go thinking that's some kind of torture, because it isn't, no more than clipping your fingernails or cutting your hair, being composed of more or less the same substance. I no longer recollect all their names, but I do remember the leaders were called Pacer and Buff. The former was a light-colored steer with a wary manner, his partner shorter and fatter — the sole female in my hitch — and constantly rubbing her neck up against me when I dropped the yoke in place, as if wanting to have the hollows behind her ears or crown scratched. She was an old girl and fairly spoiled, but that suited me just fine.

Yoking a team of oxen turned out to be a lot less complicated than fitting harness to a mule. It helped that as soon as Tellis and I brought in the first pair, the rest started wandering in on their own. Our trio of milk cows back home had been the same way. Every morning and evening, as reliable as a five-dollar watch, they'd come in off the pasture without fetching, and as soon as the barn gate was opened they'd tromp into their respective stalls where a double handful of shelled corn or oats, depending on the season, would be waiting for them. Even if they finished early, which the last one to

157

be milked almost always did, they wouldn't back away from the feed trough until Ester gave them a gentle slap on the hip to let them know they were dismissed.

By the time I got Pacer and Buff yoked, the rest of the team was already standing in place. All I had to do was ease the yoke over their necks, slip the bows up from underneath, then pin them in place. A center chain ran up the axis of the hitch from the tongue, fastening to heavy iron rings in the middle of each beam — and that was it. I was lucky I was able to begin my short career as a bullwhacker with well-disciplined oxen, though. Some years later I watched a couple of teamsters working with a pair of shorthorns fresh in off the range, and those two steers damn near killed themselves and the men working with them before the morning was through.

Even though things went fairly smoothly, I was still the last one yoked and ready to roll. Tellis had taken off to saddle his horse, but he returned soon enough to watch my struggles. Bob Jolley was there, too, and I could tell he was already questioning my abilities. There was a bullwhacker's whip — sixteen feet of tightly braided leather at the end of a four-foot wooden shaft of Osage orange — in a bracket behind the left front wheel. When I was finished, Tell rode over and pulled it out without dismounting, then heeled his horse over to where I stood sweating beside my wheelers and handed it to me.

"Just keep an eye on them, Pardell," he said, keeping his voice low so that Jolley wouldn't overhear. "They shouldn't cause you any trouble." Then he jogged his horse back to the head of the column, and his command to *"Roll 'em out!"* soon rang down the line.

I heard the pop of a couple of whips, but kept mine shouldered like a soldier marching off to war with his musket. When the trail wagon in front of me rocked into motion, both Pacer and Buff leaned into their yokes, and the rest of the team dug in and pulled out. And me? Hell, at that point I was just along for the hike.

We crossed the creek — I was able to jump it without even getting my heels wet — and rattled up the far side and out onto the open plain. Way off in the distance I could see a low mountain range. Or maybe "mountain" is too generous a description. It was definitely a wrinkle on the skyline, though, rising above the surrounding land-scape like the broken spine of a wolf. The way we were angled, I surmised they would be our destination for the night, but when the sun started to settle into the horizon, those craggy ridges didn't look a bit closer than they had at noon. I was getting my first inkling of unfiltered distance, out there where the sky seemed endless and the air was thin and dry.

The light was growing soft when we arrived at another small creek as lacking in water as the former — just little pools scattered up and down the bed, their surfaces skittery with water-walkers. Tellis ordered our wagons into a crude circle, then came back to where my oxen had halted of their own accord. I looked ahead for Bob Jolley, but he was nowhere to be seen.

Reining up nearby, Tellis said, "How'd it go today, Pardell?"

"No trouble."

"You inherited a seasoned team. Keep doing what you're doing, and as long as we don't run into bad weather or get caught up in a buffalo stampede, you should be fine."

"Where's Mr. Jolley?"

"He went on ahead."

"To his store?"

"You can never tell with him. He might be back later tonight, or we might not see him again until we get there."

"Where's there?"

"Place called Deep Creek, fifteen or so miles north of its junction with Big Sulphur Creek. Big Sulphur is a tributary of the Colorado River."

He might as well have said it was halfway between Mars and the moon; I still hadn't laid eyes on a Texas map.

My blank expression brought a grin to his face. "Another week," he clarified, and I nodded my thanks. Lifting a hand in farewell, he rode off to take care of whatever business a wagon boss needed to take care of in an evening.

Meanwhile, I looked after my oxen, starting up front with Pacer and Buff and working my way back along the line. It didn't take long to unyoke. I spent a few minutes checking each animal for fresh cuts or scraped hair where the heavy yokes had laid across the top of their necks, but they all looked fit as brand-new fiddles. The Mexican kid I mentioned earlier came through and rounded them up and drove them toward water, while I laid out the center chain and yoke beams for the morning hookup, trying to stay busy because I didn't know what else to do.

It wasn't long before a couple of bullwhackers came up and introduced themselves. Andy Brenner was a sandy-haired man in his late twenties, wearing patched overalls, a ripped shirt, and brogans that looked like they were ready to fall apart. His hat was of the slouch variety, lacking a band but with a turkey feather poked through the felt on the left side. Roy Potter was stocky and dark-complexioned, with a thick black beard that reminded me of a bird's nest and a brooding gaze. It was Brenner who invited me to join their fire that evening, which I gratefully accepted.

"We'll meet down yonder," Brenner added, tipping his head toward a copse of trees bordering the creek. "Jolley furnishes the kettle, but bring your own plate and such if you've got it."

I promised to meet them creekside as soon as I fetched it from my trailer, which is what we called the second wagon in our hitch. Feeling better about my situation, I went around to the rear wagon and started climbing the tailgate. There were no handholds, but plenty of rope to keep the canvas tight over its low hoops — imagine a covered wagon, but with bows only a couple of feet high to allow access — and I used those to shinny up to the top. I was halfway inside when I gave a startled yelp and damn near lost my footing. Scurrying backward out of the wagon, I kicked free and dropped clumsily to the ground, where I lost my balance and rolled back on my butt. Raucous laughter greeted my clumsy descent, and I scrambled to my feet to find the whole crew standing around with wide grins on full display. I'd been set up, for a fact.

"Is that your idea of funny?" I demanded hotly, brushing off the seat of my pants.

"It ain't what I'd look for if a town was handy, but it'll do for the middle of nowhere," Brenner replied, then started laughing anew.

Ralph Tellis had ridden up in the middle of all this and must have quickly figured out what had happened. Fighting his own smile, he said, "Don't fret too much, Pardell. You couldn't have known he was in there."

Jerking my thumb toward the wagon, I said, "Who is he?"

"Homer Thompson. He's the man you were hired to replace."

"Is he dead?"

"I haven't seen him since the noon stop," Tell admitted. "Does he look dead?"

I shrugged and muttered something about not getting close enough to tell, which brought up another burst of laughter.

Still smiling, Tell said, "All right, boys, you've had your fun with the new man. Let's get back to work. Andy, crawl in there and see if Thompson is still alive. If he is, let's get him out here where he can have some fresh air."

"What if he ain't?" Brenner asked.

"Then he'll still need to come out so we can bury him, you just won't have to be as careful getting him to the ground."

Tell rode away and Andy Brenner gave me a friendly punch to the shoulder as he passed me on the way to my trailer. "You're all right, kid," he allowed, but I knew better than to think I'd passed any kind of final test with this outfit. I was going to need to be on my toes.

CHAPTER ELEVEN

Homer Thompson wasn't dead, but his time on earth was obviously winding down. I carried him in my trail wagon for two more days before he cashed in his chips. If he ever regained consciousness, it wasn't when I was around. I couldn't speak for what happened while we were on the move.

Uncle Abran had told me I'd been hired to replace an injured man, whom I'd assumed had come back to the Flat with Bob Jolley. As it turned out, Thompson hadn't been injured, at least not as far as anyone knew. According to Tellis at the supper fire that first night, no one could say what had happened to Thompson. He was fine one night before crawling into his blankets, and just never woke up the next day. It was Tell's opinion, and mine now that I'm older and hopefully a little wiser, that some internal organ had gone bad on him. Had maybe been going bad for a while and he just hadn't mentioned it. We buried him beside the trail, then covered his grave with stones to keep the scavengers away. Bob Jolley wasn't there, apparently having ridden on ahead to his trading post, but Tell oversaw the interment. Since no one knew if Thompson had family anywhere, Tell said there wasn't any point in putting up a marker.

"He'll be fine here, and better buried than a lot of men I've seen die on the trail."

A couple of men muttered an "Amen" to that, and Tell called it good. Back at the wagons he pulled Thompson's war bag and bedroll out of my trailer and laid everything out on the ground. He added what had been taken from the dead man's pockets and what he'd normally carried on his person — a Remington revolver and hunting knife, a Spencer carbine in a scabbard, his hat, boots, and a coat and vest. He asked if anyone had any claim to what was there, but no one stepped forward.

"Good enough," he said, and started rummaging through the dead man's gear. That may seem kind of morbid, but as I've said before, it was a hard land, and not a soul there didn't know the same fate awaited their own death along the trail. Myself included after that evening.

Thompson had close to eighty dollars on

him that Tell split evenly among the bull-whackers. I took my share silently and shoved it in my pocket without counting it. Then he told the men to sort through what was left for whatever they wanted, and to toss the rest. All except for the carbine. Tell took that and told the men he was giving it to me.

"Pardell is the only one here without a long gun, and he could well need it before we reach Jolley." Noting my puzzlement, he continued, "They're saying the Comanches are on the prowl again, Gage. Word is they're moving south, looking for trouble."

A shiver ran down my spine, and I remember thinking how I'd once felt excited by the prospect of visiting the frontier. The actual experience wasn't comparing favorably to my imagination. Keeping those thoughts to myself, I quietly accepted the Spencer, along with a pouch containing some cleaning gear and about thirty rounds of 56-.50 ammunition.

There wasn't much light remaining that evening when the wrangler, still out on the grazing grounds with the cattle, shouted a warning. We all jumped to our feet and moved back out of the lambent firelight. Ten minutes later a voice hailed us from the dusk.

"Hello the wagons."

Ralph Tellis stepped forward. "Who is it, and how many are you?"

"Deputy Max Jennison from Fort Griffin, with three others."

"Come on in slow," Tellis told them.

I stayed where I was, tucked safely between my lead and tail wagons with the Spencer clutched tightly in both hands, the Joslyn like a small anvil at my waist. Instinct screamed for me to get out of there, to find that bay mule I'd joined the train with and take off for parts unknown. Fortunately, logic kept a firm rein on my panic, and as Jennison and his men rode up to the fire I stepped out of the shadows along with the rest of the crew, although staying to the rear of the pack where I wouldn't be as easily noticed.

Jennison pulled up but didn't dismount. It was the first time I'd seen him since that single, brief glimpse right before he rapped the back of my head with his shotgun. He was bigger than I remembered, middle-aged and going to a gut, although there was nothing soft about his expression. His posse, I noticed, looked younger and leaner. Meaner, too, if that was possible. He and Tell exchanged greetings, and Tell invited them down off their horses.

"Coffee's hot, and there's grub to share if you're hungry."

"No, thank you, Mr. Tellis, but we can't tarry. I'm looking for an escaped prisoner I believe to be on foot. We couldn't find him on the Flat, and there's no trace of him going east. I thought maybe he'd hitched a ride with your train."

Tell calmly shook his head. No one glanced my way, for which I was grateful.

"What did this escaped prisoner of yours do?"

"He killed two men."

A look of surprise came over Tell's face. "Are you talking about that kid who killed Moore and Walker?"

"That's the one," Jennison confirmed. He was speaking to Tell, but his gaze was sweeping the camp, lingering briefly on each of us. My pulse quickened when his eyes came to me, but after a few seconds they moved on without recognition.

Sweet Rita's magic paste was working!

"These all your men?"

"I've got a Mexican kid watching the herd."

"The one I'm looking for is a white man, young and kind of caved in at the belly like he ain't been eating regular. Got a cagey look about him, too."

Tell shook his head. "That's not Pedro. He's been with the outfit nearly as long as I have, and as far as I know he's never killed anyone."

"Anyone else pass this way? Maybe a man on a horse, or another wagon?"

"Haven't seen another soul since leaving the Flat."

Jennison sighed and glanced at his men. "Looks like it's been a wild goose chase, boys."

One of the posse members chuckled. "A dollar a day is a dollar a day, whether we find him or not."

Jennison shot the man an angry look, then swung back to Tell. "We'll be heading back now, Mr. Tellis. I appreciate your time."

"You're welcome to stay the night if you'd like."

"No, thank you, but we'd best be riding. It's my intention to find that kid before he gets too far away." Then he reined his horse around and rode back into the night, heading east toward Fort Griffin. The posseman who'd made the remark about not caring whether or not they found me was the last to leave the firelight, after casting a longing glance at the coffeepot. When they were gone, the men returned slowly to the fire, all except for Tell, who motioned me aside.

We walked out onto the prairie a ways.

"They didn't mention a name," Tell said casually, after we'd moved out of earshot.

"They never asked for a name."

"Then it was you?"

I stopped to face him, forcing him to stop as well. "Is that going to be a problem?"

"No. I'd wager half the men out here are running from something. If they weren't, they'd be back where living wasn't so dangerous." A smile crossed his face, barely discernible in the starlight. "I've spent a night or two in the Flat's hoosegow myself, and it was lax by most standards. I'll say it was to your advantage that no one asked your name, though. If the regular marshal had been there, he damn sure would've."

"Bill Gilson?"

"Yeah. Gilson is a good man. It serves Jennison right that you got away."

"Why?"

"Because he wants Gilson's job, and intends to run for it the next election. Meanwhile, he likes to act like he's hard snot and not easy to chip. Not against anyone who's willing to tell him to stuff sand, mind you, but to drunks and those he can catch unaware."

I told him about Jennison coming up behind me and slamming his shotgun into my skull after I'd already dropped my pistol.

"That's Jennison," Tell agreed with derision.

"I appreciate you not pointing me out when he was here."

"It was none of my business, Pardell. Besides, I need a man to handle Thompson's team, and you're him." Then he walked off. After a couple of minutes, I followed him back to the wagons.

It was another six days to Bob Jolley's trading post on the east bank of Deep Creek. We spotted the line of trees shortly after the noon halt, but didn't reach the post itself until late afternoon. It wasn't until we guided our wagons down off the dusty plain onto the bottomland along the creek that I got my first good look at what was already being referred to as Jolley, Texas, in all its ramshackle glory.

The trading post sat back in the trees like a giant clump of mud dropped from the heavens. Hailing from East Texas as I did, I'd never seen a true adobe building until coming to the Flat below Fort Griffin, and those had been little more than shacks. This was large and sprawling and as impressive as hell, like a fortress with its tiny windows set high in the thick walls and a massive front door that looked like it could withstand a cannonball. If offered a choice of where to hole up during an Indian attack — either here at Jolley's or within the scattered huts of Fort Griffin — I'd choose the trading post hands down.

Although the post was a fairly recent addition to the area, there was already a small settlement running north of the store, scattered among the cottonwoods flanking the creek. A lot of those buildings looked like residences . . . sort of. None of them were solidly made. Many were little more than threadbare tents and crude wickiups thrown together, often with poorer hides thrown over the top to shed the rain. Of the sturdier structures, I saw a saloon sheltered inside a picket-post shack with a crude drawing of a foaming beer mug nailed to the wall beside the door, and a barn of slab lumber downstream from the post with corrals on two sides and the words *Jolley Livery* painted above the wide double doors. Other buildings lacked signage, but seemed to carry merchandise to appeal to the hunters and drifters who frequented the community — rifles and knives displayed in dirty windows, used clothing, dented cookware, and twenty-pound sacks of beans sitting beside open doors.

All this I noticed in passing. Then Ralph Tellis led the caravan through a gate behind the trading post and motioned the lead wagon toward the rear of a sprawling wagon yard surrounded by an adobe wall a good six feet high. There was a loading dock behind the store, and row after row of dried buffalo hides lining the inside of the far wall, probably several thousand skins all together.

We halted our wagons in a rough side-by-side formation, set the brakes, then quietly set about unyoking our teams. An old guy with a badly hunched spine came in on foot to gather the oxen and drive them toward a larger enclosure to the south. Two others on horseback separated the mules from the cattle, including the jenny I'd ridden away from the Flat on, and herded them back through the gate toward fresh grass downstream from the post. As I came around to the rear of my trail wagon, I spotted Bob Jolley standing on the loading dock, keeping an eye on the proceedings while talking with Tell, who'd halted his mount at the edge of the platform. I couldn't hear what they were saying, but felt a moment's unease when the gazes of both men came to rest on me. Tell spoke again and Jolley shrugged and replied, then both men looked away and I exhaled softly.

"Need a drink, Pardell?"

It was Andy Brenner approaching from his own outfit, an eager grin shining out from under his slouch hat, and I nodded acceptance of the offer. Although the crew had never become overly friendly toward me, after that first evening and my unexpected discovery of Homer Thompson lying unconscious in my trailer, they hadn't attempted any further pranks. I suspected some of that might have been a result of Max Jennison's visit. Although the deputy hadn't mentioned me by name, everyone seemed to know I was the one he was looking for. Which meant I was also the one who'd bested Chip Moore and Lee Walker in front of Tolliver's Emporium with a six-shooter; it was the kind of reputation that marked a man, not often for the good.

"What about our pay?" I asked Andy as we made our way around the front of the trading post to where Roy Potter and Loomis Tucker were waiting for us.

I've already described Potter and Brenner, but I don't believe I've mentioned Tucker. He was the fourth bullwhacker in our crew, a tall Negro with a broad nose and curly black hair he kept cut short. Loomis had grown up on a cotton plantation somewhere in Alabama, working the fields from dawn to dusk just about every day since he was a waif. He liked to say he came west looking for freedom, but judging from both expression and mood, it didn't appear that he'd found it yet.

"We ain't likely to get paid until tomorrow," Andy confided.

Loomis grunted affirmation. "Old man Jolley won't shell out any money 'til he's inventoried the wagons," he added.

Andy laughed. "Our last trip out, a barrel of whiskey near the back of the load evaporated nearly a third of its contents. Fortunately, we were able to save most of it with our cups."

"But Mr. Jolley didn't believe you?" I asked.

"Ain't no mister to his name, Pardell," Roy Potter said sourly. "The goods are delivered and we ain't working for him no more. That makes Jolley just another son of a bitch, far as I'm concerned."

"Ol' Roy here is carrying a fair-sized chip on his shoulder where Jolley is concerned," Andy told me, then slapped Potter's back between his shoulder blades, raising a small cloud of pale dust in the process. "What he needs is a drink." Then Andy looked at Tucker and winked. "And ol' Loomis is

176

buying."

"Like hell I'm buying," Loomis fired back, and Andy cackled happily.

There was no boardwalk along the street, nor really even much of a street, just a meandering track created by wagons coming in off the buffalo ranges or following the trail between the little settlement of Jolley and points east. The saloon I mentioned earlier was our first stop. It looked small from the street and felt that way inside, too, cramped and uncomfortable. There were no windows, just a bar along the right-hand side of the room — the sideboards from a wagon laid across a couple of empty barrels — and a trio of tables with mismatched chairs on the other side. The floor was dirt, the ceiling low, sagging toward the middle. A long shelf nailed to the wall behind the bar was lined with a variety of bottles, crocks, and canning jars filled with a clear-looking liquid I recognized as home-squeezed corn liquor.

The place was all but empty when we walked in, just the bartender sitting on a stool against the rear wall. He rose and ambled along the sober side of the bar at our arrival. Andy called him Bannon, but although they exchanged greetings by name, they didn't seem particularly friendly. Andy ordered whiskeys all around, and after dropping a silver dollar on the bar, Bannon brought out a bottle and four badly smeared glasses and set them up in front of us. I noticed as he poured there was a fly floating on top of the liquor, either dead or drunk. The fly spilled into Roy's drink, but he picked it out with his fingers and flicked it over his shoulder.

"Gentlemen," Andy said, raising his glass as if in a salute, "here's to the end of the trail and a well-earned spree."

"I ain't gonna argue with that," Potter agreed emphatically, while Loomis muttered something under his breath that I didn't catch and I offered my own half-hearted, "Here, here," before taking a sip.

Although hot as blazes, Bannon's whiskey was no worse than some of the stuff Pa kept hidden in the feed room back home. I took a second, larger swallow, then braced myself as the heat flowed through my limbs and set my nose to running. I bought the next round, Roy the third. I figured Loomis would catch the fourth, but he said he had to water the weeds out back, and quickly slipped out the rear door. Andy laughed when he was gone.

"What?"

"He ain't coming back."

"Why not?"

" 'Cause he's as tight as a Dutchman's ass, that's why," Roy chimed in.

"He's done this before," Andy furthered. "Ol' Loomis is as honest as a blind preacher and he doesn't shirk his duties on the trail, either, but he's been dirt poor most of his life, the kind of poor that puts its mark on a man. He won't be back, and I'd bet the next drink on that."

I took Andy up on his offer and we gave it a bit, but he was right and Loomis didn't return. That was all right, and I bought the next round without complaint. After that Andy splurged for a bottle and we moved to one of the tables. The light inside, already gloomy, grew even more sullen as the sun sank. It was damn near like a cavern inside before Bannon lit a couple of lanterns and hung them from hooks above each end of the bar. We had the place to ourselves for a while, but as the evening progressed, more men began to wander in and the room seemed to shrink accordingly. Finally having enough, I stood and moved the Joslyn around on my hip.

"Where you goin', Pardell?" Andy asked.

"I need some fresh air."

"Hell, amigo, if you need fresh air, that means you ain't drank enough."

"Let 'im go," Roy growled.

"I'll see you tomorrow," I said to Andy, then wormed through the crowd to the front door.

It felt good to get outside, away from the hot press of bodies, but the chill in the air caught me off guard. Although the sun was down, there was still enough light in the sky to find my way back to Jolley's. The hike there proved difficult, though. I guess I'd drank more than I realized, because the ground seemed to be playing tricks with my eyes, either rising up too soon to smack the bottom of my feet, or unexpectedly dropping away. I remember cursing the earth a time or two for its trickery, too far along at that point to make the connection between the alcohol flowing through my veins and the uneven terrain.

I went around back of the trading post and retrieved my gear from the wagon, then took it over and set it out of the way at the far end of the loading dock. After digging my old hat from the pack, I punched it back into shape as best I could and put it on. Feeling more genuine than I had since putting that damned sombrero on back on the Flat, I walked over to enter the trading post through the rear door. It took a moment to figure out I was in the warehouse, and even longer before I found the door to the main room. I should have realized sooner that the lamp burning in its wall bracket was close to the door, but I didn't — just one more example of the whiskey's chicanery on my senses. I wasn't so drunk I didn't recognize Bob Jolley's anger when he spotted me coming through the warehouse door. He buzzed over like a hornet on target, and I swear there were tiny bolts of lightning flashing in his eyes.

"What were you doing back there, Pardell?"

"Getting my stuff."

"From the storeroom?"

"Out of the wagon."

He hesitated. "Where's Tellis?"

"Ain't seen him," I replied, trying without much success to stifle a whiskey belch. Jolley made a face and backed up a step.

"Drunk already?" he said scornfully.

I was starting to feel peeved by his demeanor. "Hey, I did my job, Mr. Jolley. I want my money."

"You'll be paid tomorrow afternoon after I've inventoried the wagons. Come back then. In the meantime, stay out of my warehouse."

I froze there for a moment, and the fingers of my right hand curled as tight and hard as an oak knot. After all I'd been through the last several weeks, I realized my patience was starting to wear in spots. There was a part of me that wanted to slam my fist into Bob Jolley's face for his impertinence. I'm glad now that I didn't do it. Instead I stalked clumsily out the front door, into the cool darkness of the rutted street. It wasn't until then that I remembered the gear I'd left on the loading dock. I briefly considered storming back through the store to retrieve it, then decided I'd probably caused myself enough trouble with my demand to be paid that night, when I already knew none of us were going to receive our wages until the next day.

Feeling oddly quelled, I walked around back and got my stuff, then carried it down along the creek. There were probably a dozen or more camps scattered up and down the stream, nearly all of them belonging to buffalo hunters in off the range — shooters and skinners and camp tenders alike. Finding a quiet spot not too far away — with neither horse nor wagon to consider, my needs were few — I dropped my saddlebags in the grass, then unrolled my blankets beside them. No longer on Jolley's payroll, I was on my own as far as rustling up a meal was concerned. Had I felt up to it, I would have hiked back into town to find a restaurant or store where I could buy some supplies, but the whiskey I'd downed at Bannon's was pulling me toward my bedroll, and I no longer had the will to resist.

CHAPTER TWELVE

I've already mentioned how Beau and I used to sneak sips out of Pa's jug of corn liquor back home, but that night in Bannon's was the most I'd ever drank at one setting, and it knocked my lights out for fair. The sun was already well up when I groggily opened my eyes the next morning, the first time I'd slept past its rising in more years than I cared to remember. I slid my blankets back and rolled over and pushed to my feet like a cow coming up from an afternoon of cud chewing — meaning butt-first and grunting from the effort.

I was still dressed, right down to boots and gun belt, although my hat had fallen off during the night. I stared at it a moment, trying to remember what had become of the sombrero Uncle Abran had given me, then shrugged it off and carefully stooped to pick up my old flat-brimmed Pettigrew, then glanced around to check my surroundings. I don't know when they'd come in or how they'd found me, but Roy Potter, Andy Brenner, and Loomis Tucker were all wrapped in their blankets nearby.

I climbed the bench above the stream and turned north, away from Jolley's. Turns out that little settlement there along Deep Creek was bigger than I'd at first realized, primarily because it ran with the creek, rather than spreading outward from the trading post like spokes on a wheel. In addition to Bob's trading post, the livery, and Bannon's Saloon, I soon discovered a boot and shoe repair shop housed inside a faded canvas tent, a gunsmith in a dugout burrowed into the bank on the west side of the creek, a hotel — well, maybe more of a fleabox, but beds to rent, nonetheless — two small restaurants, a wagon repair shop, and a laundry run by a one-eyed Mexican and his wife.

There were hiders camped in every direction, wagons and mules and hired men sitting around their breakfast fires, all of them staring at me as I passed like I was some kind of preacher looking for souls to rescue from perdition. And not one of them, I might add, looked especially eager for that kind of deliverance. I suppose they felt as I did in those early years, and were waiting for a more age-appropriate time to embrace salvation.

The settlement ended abruptly where Deep Creek made a sharp bend to the east, and beyond which the timber abruptly played out. On my way back to camp, I stopped at the larger of the two eating establishments, Cathay's Café. It had a wood floor and front wall, but canvas tentage elsewhere. Meals were served at a long table with benches along either side. The fare was simple and uninspiring. I ordered fried buffalo steak — the first I ever sampled of the species — and fried potatoes. It came with a biscuit on the side and that great staple of the frontier, beans. The coffee was bitter but hot, and included a thin film of color floating on top, although it all went down easy enough. No doubt my last solid meal having been nearly twenty-four hours earlier, with nothing in between but stale water and raw whiskey, helped enhance its flavor.

As I exited the restaurant, I noticed an unusual assemblage rolling down the street toward me. Out front was a stout, well-dressed man probably in his forties, with dark hair and a beard flecked with gray, leading the tiny caravan from the saddle of a fine bay mare. Following him was a mud wagon with the curtains rolled up, its three bench seats crowded with women of a type I knew best from the Alamo Saloon in Shelburn. The stripped-down coach was pulled by a two-horse hitch driven by a wizened old coot wearing range clothes. Behind the coach came a high-sided farm wagon with a flat canvas cover, its driver a woman who didn't appear to be any older than I was. Bringing up the rear was a Conestoga pulled by six massive gray horses, a broad-shouldered Negro in dove-colored trousers, a bright red vest, and bowler hat handling the lines. The stub of a cigar jutted from one corner of his mouth like a smoking chimney knocked askew from its brackets. Taken as a whole, it was the damnedest spectacle I'd seen up to that point in my life, and I had to stop and watch.

The heavyset guy on the bay gave me a surly scowl as he rode past, but didn't otherwise acknowledge my presence, and the old guy driving the coach ignored me altogether, but the same couldn't be said of the women inside, several of whom leaned forward with undisguised interest when I was spotted standing alongside the road like a jug-headed bumpkin. One of the women, chubby and blond and wearing a low-cut dress made from some kind of flimsy material, poked her head out the window. Her heavy breasts crushed up against the frame reminded me of a pair of down-filled pillows, and I'll admit the thought of placing my head between them and burrowing in for the winter brought a grin to my face.

"Hi-ya, sweet pea," the blonde greeted lustily.

"Ma'am," I automatically replied, which I think only augmented the appearance of a yokel.

Laughing like she'd just taught a monkey how to tip its hat, she glanced over her shoulder at the others. "By God, they grow 'em polite out here, girls," she declared loudly — she reminded me of the kind of woman who never spoke softly or acted timid. "Maybe this ain't going to be as uncivilized as I'd feared."

The woman sitting next to her said, "He's barely full-growed yet, Big Star. I bet he ain't even been broke to harness yet."

Flashing me a cheek-to-cheek grin, Star said, "Come on over to Amos's later on, sweet pea. I'll raise your spirits and trim your wick, all on the same coin." Then she pulled her head back inside the coach, leaving me standing there feeling like an oaf.

The flat-topped wagon was next, and the gal driving it looked about as much like Big

Star as the moon did to a heap of cow dung. She had auburn hair pulled back under a gingham bonnet and a pale blue dress that clung to her bony frame like lost hope. Our eyes met briefly as she passed, and the image I took from that brief encounter was one of fear or dread, assuming there's ever any real difference between the two. She didn't speak, and in fact barely glanced my way, then she was gone, disappearing behind the rocking bed of her wagon as if a door had been pulled closed behind her.

As the Conestoga pulled even with me, the Negro handling the lines stopped his team with a bass-toned *whoa,* then leaned forward to prop his elbows on his knees. His gaze narrowed as he studied me. "You look like you know how to swing a sledge-hammer, sonny. You want a job?"

"What kind of job?"

"We got us a big ol' tent to set up before noon if we want to be open for business before sundown. You want to help with the raising, I'll see you get a free trip to heaven on top of Big Star."

"Are you her boss?"

"Naw, that'd be Mr. Amos Montgomery, sitting that fine bay hoss up there, but I'm authorized to speak for him in matters of pitching tents and setting up the bar."

"Is that what you're bringing in, a saloon?"

"What we are bringing in is class, sonny. Mr. Montgomery furnishes only the best for his guests, fine liquor or accommodating women of the highest order." He grinned, revealing surprisingly small teeth for such a large man, like twin rows of dried corn still on the cob. "What about it? You interested?"

I hesitated, although I already knew I wouldn't do it. That auburn-haired gal with the scared eyes, though . . . she intrigued me.

"I'll think about it," I replied.

"You do that," he said, straightening and flapping his lines along the rumps of his two wheelers. "Hup there, you ornery brutes." He gave me an appraising glance as his team started forward. "Don't think too long, sonny."

I didn't reply, but I didn't turn away either, and the Negro with the tiny teeth laughed and turned back to face the swishing tails of his six big grays. I watched until I saw them turn off toward the creek, and recalled seeing a shallow spot there earlier where the hunters forded their wagons coming in from the western ranges. They'd set up somewhere on the other side of the creek, I surmised, and no doubt start drawing customers away from the businesses surrounding Jolley's trading post. I decided I'd check it out myself after I'd been paid, but as a customer, not a laborer looking for a free hump.

Only Loomis was awake when I got back to what passed as our camp. He was sitting next to the creek, staring morosely into its shallow waters, and acted like he didn't even hear me. I left him to his thoughts as I rolled up my blankets and dumped them on top of my saddlebags. The Spencer in its scabbard and the shooting bag of extra cartridges leaned against the trunk of the cottonwood I'd spent the night under. I left it there and went down to sit on the bank a few feet from Loomis. Although the days were still warm with autumn, there was a wind picking up out of the northwest that swayed the branches overhead, loosening little showers of dried leaves that fell with a soft clatter. After a bit, Roy Potter rolled out of his blankets. Standing on the bank downstream from us — although still upstream from a lot of other businesses and camps — he unbuttoned his fly and peed into the creek. The sound of Roy urinating finally brought Loomis out of his rumination. He looked at Potter, then at me, and shook his head. I shrugged in reply. I guess neither of us approved of peeing into someone else's drinking water. When he finished, Potter buttoned his fly, then trudged up the bank to the road and disappeared in the direction of Bannon's Saloon without having uttered a word.

"Ol' Potter takes some getting used to," a voice spoke from the mound of blankets where Andy Brenner's slouch hat sat on top of his war bag. "He ain't a bad sort, otherwise."

"I wouldn't want to turn my back on him of a dark night," Loomis replied distantly, without looking around.

"No," Andy agreed with a short laugh. "I wouldn't either, and I do believe I might be his best friend."

"His only friend, most like."

"That could be, Loomis, that could well be." Andy sat up, and the wool blanket that had been pulled over his head piled up around his waist. He glanced around as if unaware of his surroundings. Considering how much he'd drank the night before, I figured that might well be the case.

"Jolley send word about our pay yet?"

"Not yet," I replied.

"Well, he'd damn well better fork it over soon. I'm down to my last two bits."

"The old man'd probably spot you to a meal," Loomis said, meaning Bob Jolley.

"The old man can kiss my hairy hind end," Andy replied, although without the venom I'd heard in Roy's voice the day before. Andy threw his blankets back and pulled on his old shoes, adjusting the leather laces so that the knots he'd tied in them wouldn't catch at the brogan's eyelets. I'd swear he was the worst-dressed man on Deep Creek, but he seemed as unmindful of his ragged clothing as Potter had been of the downstream camps.

"What are you boys going to do when you get paid?" I asked.

Andy laughed and said he intended to buy another bottle of Bannon's cheap whiskey.

"Hair of the wolf that bit me," he added slyly. "Then I gotta make up my mind whether I want breakfast first, or a woman."

I told him about the Montgomery outfit, and the black man's offer for assistance in setting up the traveling brothel's tent.

"That don't sound like much of a deal to me," Andy replied. "Five dollars labor for a two-dollar whore."

"Where you going to find a job 'round here pays five dollars to set up a tent?" Loomis asked.

"I wouldn't do it for any less," Andy said.

"What about you, Loomis?" I asked. "What're your plans?"

"I'm going back to Fort Griffin, if I can hire on with the old man's train."

"What train?"

"Jolley's gonna send them wagons back to Jacksboro loaded with hides," Andy said.

"Who's driving them?"

"Who knows." Andy shrugged. "They're Jolley's wagons. He might hire us to take 'em back, or he might bring on a whole new crew. You can never tell with him."

"I'm going," Loomis said determinedly, as if the matter had already been decided. "Going all the way to Jacksboro, and maybe on past that if I can. Be more jobs in that direction, especially with winter coming on."

"We probably all will," Andy added, then looked at me. "You, too, if you want to."

Having a job with winter coming on was tempting, but I couldn't risk going back through the Flat, couldn't count on my ruse working a second time against Max Jennison.

"We'll know soon enough," Andy said. "Tell is gonna talk to him after they inventory the wagons."

It seemed like a good deal for the others, and I was already starting to feel some melancholy at losing the few acquaintances I had, but things didn't work out the way Andy expected. Tell showed up later that afternoon, spotting us beside the creek and sliding down the incline to join us.

"What's news, boys?" he said, coming to a halt between Andy and me.

"I'd say you're the man who has that to share," Andy replied, and Loomis stood and came over to where I'd kindled a small fire, more for comfort's sake than heat or to fix a meal. A camp ain't a camp without a fire to gather around.

"I've got your pay," Tell said, pulling a wad of cash from his pocket and waving it above his shoulder.

The pay was mighty good for teamster wages — fifty bucks apiece for less than two weeks labor — although Loomis pointed out that Jolley had been hard-pressed to put together a crew for the outward journey.

"No one's wanting to get caught so far out this close to winter," he said.

"That helped," Tell agreed, dividing the stack of bills into four piles and handing one each to me, Andy, and Loomis. "Where's Potter?" he asked.

"Bannon's, unless he found a jug somewhere closer," Andy said.

Tell shoved the remaining wad of cash into his pocket. "Tell him I've got his wages, next time you see him." Then he looked at Loomis. "Bad news for you, Loomis."

The black man's eyes narrowed suspiciously. "What kind of bad news?"

"The old man ain't hiring for the return trip this time."

"The hell you say?"

"Claims there's too many men wanting to go back before the weather gets bad. He told me to pass the word that anyone wants to drive an outfit for him, he'll furnish food and protection against the Comanches, but that's it."

"He's just throwing that Comanche talk out there to scare folks," Loomis said. "The Comanches are already holing up on the reservation for the winter. Won't have to worry about them again until spring rolls around."

"I don't doubt you're right, but Jolley still says he ain't paying a salary for anyone wanting to go back. Our options are thin, boys. We either stay here and hope to find work, or go back to Griffin and the Flat, or maybe on to Jacksboro."

I glanced at Loomis. His disappointment was obvious, as was his bitterness, but Jolley had him, had all of them, over a barrel if they were serious about returning.

"You said *our* options were thin," I reminded Tell. "Aren't you still working for him?"

"Nope, the son of a bitch fired me."

"Fired you," Andy exclaimed. "Why? You've been working for him for a couple of seasons now."

"A year and a half, just about," Tell agreed. Then he looked at me and laughed. "You can thank Gage here for getting my hind end fired, although it's a fact the old man was getting more and more irritated with me."

"How'd I get you fired?"

"I was supposed to be watching the wagons and the rear dock last night," he replied. "When you slipped in the back way, the old man got mad as hell about it. He came outside and caught me sitting on a stack of hides shooting the bull with a couple of friends, and had himself a fine ol' conniption. I was about ready to quit the old fool anyway, but after we got the wagons unloaded this morning and the inventory all checked out with the invoices, he took me into his office and told me I was fired."

"He fired you, *then* asked you to pay us off?" I found that thoroughly confusing, although the others didn't seem overly surprised by it.

"You've got to understand, ol' Bob doesn't care what happens to you boys now that his merchandise has been delivered," Tell said.

197

"It's your good fortune I'm an honest man, otherwise I could have been halfway back to the Flat before anyone realized what'd happened."

"That old man is a son of a bitch from the roots up," Andy declared earnestly.

"Ain't many who'd argue with you about that," Tell agreed. "But you watch and see, Jolley'll own half this county before he croaks."

"He might croak faster than he expects if he keeps holding folks' toes to the fire like he does." Andy glanced at Loomis. "That change your plans any, Tucker?"

Loomis thought about it for a moment, then shook his head. "No, it don't. I got no urge to stick out a winter on the buffalo range. I reckon I'll go on and drive an outfit for the old man, even if I won't get paid for it. It'll be the last time I work for him, though."

"Last time a lot of folks will, word gets out what he's doing," Tell predicted. "What about you, Pardell? You going back to the Flat, or are you staying out here?"

"I'm staying, but I'm going to have to find some kind of work if I want to eat regular."

Tell nodded. "Brenner?"

"Like I told the boys earlier, a bottle of whiskey and a fat whore."

"And after that?"

A wicked grin split Andy's face. "Why, I'll crawl out of her bed and have myself a fine Christmas morning breakfast, Tell."

We shared a laugh at that, then agreed we'd keep our eyes and ears open for some kind of employment for the four of us — meaning me and Tell and Andy and Roy, since Loomis seemed determined to go back with Jolley's next eastbound wagon train. Then we split up. I returned to Jolley's, wanting more ammunition for my revolver, or a better gun if they had one I could afford. I was examining a .44 Remington when Bob spotted me at the counter and came over.

"Come into my office when you're done, Pardell," he instructed, and I nodded, perplexed, but told him I'd be there.

I didn't buy the Remington. It was forty dollars — frontier prices I suppose, and twice what I'd have had to pay in Milam County. Plus I'd gotten used to having a rifle and revolver that shot the same ammunition. In my case that had been a Colt Army conversion and a 2nd Model Henry rifle, both lost to Max Jennison back on the Flat. I made up my mind there in Jolley's that my next purchases would be a Winchester and handgun shooting .44-40, an updated and more powerful cartridge than the Henry round.

Leaving the clerk to return the handgun to its place in the glass counter, I made my way to the rear of the store and knocked on the door to Jolley's office.

"Who is it?" a gruff voice demanded.

"Gage Pardell."

"Come in, Pardell."

I entered a more spacious office than I would have anticipated, considering our remote location. A heavy braided rug covered most of the oak flooring, and a small but ornately carved rolltop desk, chambered with pigeon holes, sat against the wall. There was a small iron safe on rollers, several wooden file cabinets, and a small cast-iron stove tucked into the far corner, its stovepipe disappearing through a tin collar in the ceiling before exiting above the trading post's flat adobe roof. And damn if there wasn't a framed map of Texas hanging on the wall opposite Jolley's desk, probably five-foot square and the different counties shaded in subtle colors. I'll tell you, it was all I could do not to walk over and have a long look.

"Sit down," Jolley said, waving toward a ladder-back chair next to his desk. He spun around in his own wooden swivel chair, and a faint grin tugged at the corners of his mouth. "You're starting to fade, Pardell."

"Sir?"

"I said you're starting to fade." He tapped his cheek with a forefinger, and I instantly understood what he meant. Rita had warned me the dye she'd applied to my skin would begin to dissolve within a few weeks. Maybe all the sweat I'd poured down my face on the long hike here from Fort Griffin had hastened the process.

Jolley's grin broadened. "I knew you weren't a Mexican the first time I saw you."

"But you hired me anyway?"

He shrugged. "Why not? Abran said you were a hard worker and honest, and that's all I needed to know. Then this morning Tellis told me about the posse that caught up with the train, and who they were looking for. It didn't take long to figure it out after that."

"Did Tellis tell you why the law is looking for me?"

"He said you were the kid who gunned down Lee Walker and Chip Moore in front of Keith Tolliver's Emporium. Is that true?"

After an uncertain pause, I acknowledged that it was.

"I heard about it. They said it was a fair fight, and that you beat both of them fair and square."

"I wasn't looking for trouble."

"And I'm not looking for a troublemaker, but I could use a man who's good with a pistol, and if you outgunned Moore and Walker, then I'd say you're more than handy with one."

"I wouldn't say I'm handy. Mostly I've been lucky, which is something I don't want to push too far."

Jolley chuckled amiably, but I could tell from his expression the conversation wasn't going in the direction he wanted it to. "Most folks I've known live more on luck than skill. Only a few of us use our skills to make our luck. I'd say you're a part of that latter group, Gage. You make your own luck. I could use a man like that, someone to . . . let's say handle problems that come up around here from time to time. The pay will be good, and meals and a room are included."

It was an intriguing offer, but what I was remembering was the way Jolley had treated me the night before, when I'd wandered into his store from the warehouse. Standing, I said, "I reckon not, Mr. Jolley, although I appreciate the offer."

"Would a hundred dollars a month change your mind, Gage?"

"No, sir, it wouldn't." I'd taken my hat off upon entering Jolley's office. I put it back on and turned toward the door. My eyes grazed the Texas map as I crossed the room, but I knew I wouldn't be looking at it anytime soon.

"You're making a mistake, Pardell," Jolley called after me, but I kept walking. Out the door and through the store, the sound of my boots on the plank floor like thunder in my ears. I didn't breathe deeply again until I reached the street and turned toward our little camp along the creek. Even then, the hair across the back of my neck continued to stir uneasily.

Chapter Thirteen

There was no one around when I reached the camp, but everyone's gear was still there, stacked in little piles under the same cottonwood tree where I'd left my own bedroll and saddlebags, so I wasn't worried they'd taken off. Not that I needed them, but it had been nice having people I knew and felt like I could trust to talk to, maybe bum a nickel off of if I needed a beer, or buy a drink for them if they asked. It had been a long, lonely ride across Texas, and I was discovering — to my surprise — that I possessed a somewhat gregarious disposition.

Still feeling the effects of Bannon's whiskey from the night before, I lay down with my head on my bedroll and almost immediately drifted off to sleep. The wind had been acting finicky all day, blowing first one way and then another, but when I woke up a couple of hours later it was coming steadily out of the north, with a bite like an angry bulldog. Shivering, I sat up and drew the Mexican poncho from my gear and pulled it on over my head. It helped, but I knew I'd need to dig out my jacket if it got much colder. There was a change coming. You couldn't see it yet, but you could feel it, hanging out there heavy and ominous.

Fearing rain, I used the oilcloth from my bedroll to cover my gear, then climbed up the bank to the road and headed for Bannon's. It seemed more likely I'd find the others there than anywhere else, and sure enough, as soon as I walked in, I spotted Tell sitting at the middle table with a tall, broad-shouldered man dressed like a hunter in sturdy wool trousers and a flannel shirt. The tall guy was wearing a cartridge belt around his waist that held a dozen or more rounds of some large rifle caliber, along with a revolver and heavy Bowie knife. Blond hair fell over his shoulders in back, and his mustache reminded me of the hand broom my ma used to sweep ashes off the hearth back home. Although his dress seemed typical for the region, there was something about his demeanor that made him stand out. When Tell spotted me at the door, he waved me over.

"Gage, this is Jim Scurlock," Tell said,

sweeping a hand toward the hunter. "And this," he continued without pause, bringing his hand back in my direction, "is the man I was telling you about, Gage Pardell."

"Mr. Pardell," Scurlock said amiably, reaching across the table to shake my hand. "A pleasure to meet you."

I nodded and returned the greeting.

Motioning to an empty chair, Scurlock said, "Please, join us. Our mutual friend here has intimated you might be in search of employment."

"I might be," I replied, pulling the chair back and sitting. "Are you hiring?"

"Perhaps. I've just recently arrived in Texas from Dakota Territory, where I've been hunting bison the past two winters." He hesitated at my puzzled expression, then smiled in concession. "My apologies, Mr. Pardell. I hunted buffalo. Bison is a term I picked up during my tenure as a student in Manchester."

"Manchester?" I repeated.

"In England, two hundred miles, I should say, northwest of London. Are you familiar with the Isle?"

"No more so than I am with Dakota Territory," I replied, and was glad when he let the subject drop.

"The Dakota winters are brutal," he

continued, "which is why I decided to move my operation south. Not that I anticipate balmy temperatures here, mind you, but perhaps milder weather and snow that can be measured in inches rather than feet."

"Winters are rough here," Tell warned him.

"Probably not like Dakota, though," I added. I'd seen an artist's sketch of a Dakota winter on a Missouri River outpost in a *Harper's Weekly* some years back, and had been daunted by the bleakness of the scene.

Scurlock smiled as if in appreciation of my remark. "Very true. Unfortunately, my northern crew wasn't responsive to my offer to bring them south, so I now find myself in need of new hands. Mr. Tellis has about convinced me he is a hunter of some renown locally, and that he can furnish me with a suitable corps of skinners and camp tenders, as well."

"What I've got in mind," Tell cut in before I could respond, "was Andy and Roy as skinners, and you to look after the camp and the hides we bring in."

"Your primary responsibility would be to look after the hides," Scurlock emphasized. "They will need regular care, turning them periodically until the skin is fully dried, and keeping them free from bugs and other scavengers. You'll also guard the wagons and livestock not in use against thieves, so proficiency with a firearm is a must, since you will be alone most of the day."

"Gage can handle a gun well enough," Tell said with a grin I found vaguely disquieting.

"Splendid," Scurlock beamed. "Of course, you'll also be charged with a number of the more mundane chores around the camp."

I think I might have sighed at that. "You mean doing the cooking?"

"Surely it isn't that odious of a chore?"

Not being entirely certain what the word *odious* meant, I merely shrugged and replied, "I reckon a job's a job, although I noticed you haven't mentioned what it pays, or how long we'll be out."

"Wages are a dollar a day and found, and I anticipate being out for at least two, and possibly three months, before returning to any form of civilized society. Or here," he added wryly.

"Jolley ain't overly civilized yet, although I've seen worse," Tell said.

"It will be considerably more polished than the region I've recently scouted."

"Where's that?" I asked.

"Several days north of here with wagons, along the Double Mountain Fork of the

Brazos River and north of the McKenzie Hills."

I almost laughed when I heard that. All these weeks of travel, all my adventures, and where was I going to end up? On a fork of the same river I'd left nearly six weeks before. It made me wonder if, come the spring runoff, I couldn't make a raft and float it all the way downstream to the Brazos River dock at Shelburn.

"What about it, Mr. Pardell? Are you interested?"

Bob Jolley had asked nearly the same question back on the Flat. So had the Negro who'd just that morning offered me a job raising a tent for Montgomery's whores on the other side of Deep Creek. It took about the same amount of time to make my decision regarding Scurlock's offer.

"Looks like you've hired yourself a camp tender, Mr. Scurlock."

"Excellent!" Scurlock's voice boomed across the room, causing a couple of hiders at the bar to look our way. Scurlock and I shook hands a second time to seal the deal, then he motioned to the bartender. "Another glass, my good man," he called.

The hiders were still looking at us, one with a brow cocked as if searching his memory. I turned my back to them and waited until the bartender brought a glass over, setting it in front of me and walking away without comment. No one mentioned the thick smears as Scurlock filled it to just below the brim, pouring from a bottle labeled *Fine Kentucky Bourbon*.

"To success, gentlemen," Scurlock said, and I took a sip of the best whiskey I'd ever had. It made me wonder if he'd purchased the bottle there, or brought it with him from elsewhere. It was sure as hell better than what we'd been drinking the night before.

Moving on, Scurlock said, "I've contracted with Bob Jolley to pick up my hides in the field. That way we won't have to concern ourselves with transporting our harvest to market. It will also allow us more time in the field, with less trekking between the Double Mountain and Jolley Town."

Jolley Town — that goes to show you how fast a community can start to take root in those early years. Scurlock went on for several more minutes, with Tell now and again trying to butt in with some comment to show off his skill as a hunter. For me, Tell's main accomplishment that day was to convince me of the wisdom of something Pa used to say to us kids on a regular basis: *Keep your mouth shut if you ain't got nothing worthwhile to say.*

I drained my first glass and poured another, and after a while the conversation began to flow through one ear and out the other, like a stream of words warmed over the glow of Scurlock's good bourbon. It occurred to me at some point in there that my die was cast for the next few months, and that the questions I'd been mulling over regarding my future, and especially Bob Jolley's offer to "handle problems that come up around here from time to time," had been settled.

There was still a third of a bottle left when Scurlock whacked the cork and slid what remained into the side pocket of his coat. "Where might we find these other two gentlemen you mentioned?" he asked Tell.

"I reckon they're around somewhere." He glanced at me. "Any ideas, Gage?"

"There was another outfit pulled in this morning," I said, then briefly described my encounter with Montgomery's whores, outside Cathay's Café. "She called the place Amos's."

"Amos Montgomery?" Tell sat up a little straighter in his chair. "Yeah, I've been to Amos's place a time or two, back in Jacksboro. I'd heard he was gonna open a whorehouse on the Flat, but it sounds like he's decided to try his luck farther west instead."

"Might that be an establishment to capture the interest of the gentlemen you've recommended as skinners?"

"Hell, I reckon," Tell said, laughing. "Why don't I go roust those boys into the open before they wear themselves out? I can ask if they're interested in skinning buff while I'm at it."

Although Scurlock's lips thinned in something like distaste, he still nodded assent. "As long as all of you realize this will be your last frolic until our return in the spring. I'll not tolerate the shirking of one's duty once we're in the field." He was speaking to Tell, but looked at me to make sure I understood his proclamation extended across the board.

"You won't have no problem with us," Tell assured him. "But we're fresh in off the trail ourselves, and need to blow off a little steam before setting out for the buffalo ranges."

"Very well," Scurlock conceded. "Have your fun tonight, but I'll expect everyone to be assembled and ready to commence at first light tomorrow."

"We'll be there," Tell said, shoving to his feet with unforeseen eagerness.

Scurlock and I watched him wind his way through the growing crowd to the door, then the Englishman turned to me. "What about you, Mr. Pardell? Will you be joining the others at Montgomery's?"

"Maybe later. What kind of chores do you have that need to be done today?"

A mixed look of surprise and appreciation crossed Scurlock's face. Then he smiled warmly and stood up. "The list is extensive, though hardly intimidating with the two of us working together. I've purchased a pair of sturdy wagons and the teams to pull them from Mr. Jolley. The wagons are parked behind his post now, ready to be loaded. Shall we begin?"

I downed what remained of my drink in a single swallow, then rose and wiped my lips with my sleeve. "Let's get to it," I said.

We spent the rest of that day behind Jolley's trading post, securing supplies into the wagons. One of them was a small Studebaker he planned to use to haul hides into camp, the other was a larger John Deere farm wagon carrying the heavier items we'd need on the range. Although Scurlock wasn't extravagant in his purchases, he wasn't overly frugal, either. The stuff he bought was of a decent quality, built to last — like the six cases of Sheffield skinning knives and a foot-trundled sharpening wheel with an iron seat. There were a dozen palm-sized grinding stones as well, each in its own little leather pouch, and a couple of slim steels the skinners would carry on their belts to keep their knives sharp in the field. Scurlock had brought his rifles with him from Dakota, a pair of Sharps in .44-77 caliber, along with all the paraphernalia — dies and punches and such — to reload in the field. For ammunition, he purchased three hundred pounds of lead in ten-pound ingots, five thousand primers, a case of felt patches for wads, and a hundred pounds of powder in twenty-pound kegs. Grub would be simple but plentiful — two hundred pounds of potatoes, another two hundred of beans, sixty pounds of coffee in ten-pound cloth bags, and one hundred pounds of flour. He included some side pork for the trip, but assured me we'd be eating buffalo once we reached the area he'd chosen to hunt.

In addition to these staples there was salt, pepper, several bottles of hot sauce, sugar, tea, and a bunch of extras such as molasses and hard candy. There were also medicines like codeine, laudanum, Mustang liniment, and a green salve I was familiar with from the farm. We'd use it to treat cuts and bot wounds on the livestock, and Ma would apply it to any scrapes or bee stings us kids might acquire.

That's just a partial list. There was a lot of

other stuff, like a Dutch oven for biscuits and a kettle for beans, a couple of frying pans and a coffeepot, shovels and axes, a bucksaw, extra rope, nails and iron shoes for the horses and mules . . . you get the idea. Jim Scurlock was a forward-looking man who liked to be prepared, and for that I was grateful. Anyone would be, going where we were bound.

The sun had dropped into its own pool of rust by the time we finished, and my breath was forming thin, vaporous clouds with every exhalation. The chill was penetrating, especially where I'd sweated, and I was soon wishing I'd dug my jacket from my war bag that afternoon, instead of Abran's poncho.

Scurlock's newly purchased mules — four to a wagon — were brought in and harnessed, then with Jim taking the lead in the Studebaker and me following behind with the John Deere, we wheeled out of Jolley's rear lot to follow the rutted street north along the creek. I stopped off at my old camp long enough to grab my gear, then climbed back into the seat and clucked my team after the Studebaker's retreating tailgate. We crossed Deep Creek in shadows so thick I couldn't see the water, only hear it as my mules splashed through to the other side. On the west bank Scurlock turned north to follow the tree line. A couple of hundred yards in the opposite direction I could see scores of lights surrounding a large tent, and heard a woman's high-pitched, girlish squeal, like a street barker's promise, above the rattle of the Deere's running gears and the creak of harness. It brought to mind Big Star's promise that afternoon to "trim my wick," and my face turned warm from the memory.

Jim Scurlock had already set up a camp half a mile or so north of the Deep Creek ford, close enough to the growing settlement of Jolley for protection if he needed it, far enough away that the water was fresh, the grass still largely ungrazed. There was a small wedge tent set up in front of a recently dug fire pit, and a couple of horses — one a leggy gray that was Scurlock's saddle mount, the other a stocky little bay he'd used to carry supplies on his recent scouting trip — on picket ropes west of the camp. Scurlock stopped his team in front of the tent and set the brake, and I did the same. Coming back to where I'd dropped to the ground next to the Deere's front wheel, he said, "Everything appears undisturbed."

"You're lucky no one's crabbed off with your horses," I remarked.

"I quite agree, Mr. Pardell, and I'm

relieved that I now have someone here to watch over the camp when I'm gone."

We unhitched in the dark and stowed the harness under the wagons in case of rain. Although the skies were still clear, the wind hadn't abated and the feel of moisture in the air was undeniable.

I led the mules down to the creek two at a time to drink, while Scurlock kindled a fire and started the evening meal. Afterward, my belly filled with beans and fatback, I stretched out on my side to stare into the wind-tattered flames. Pulling a pipe and tobacco pouch from inside his jacket, Scurlock quietly packed the bowl. Keeping his eyes on the task, he said, "I must confess, your reputation intrigues me, Mr. Pardell."

"I didn't know I had a reputation."

"Both Mr. Tellis and Mr. Jolley seem to think that you do, apparently enough of one that the latter attempted to hire you for a city marshal's job."

"I've got no reputation, Mr. Scurlock. I got into a scrape back on the Flat that some people are making out to be bigger than it really was."

"Then you are not a shootist?"

"No, sir, I'm not. I'd also appreciate it if you'd stop calling me Mr. Pardell."

"Very well, Gage. Now, I need one more

217

favor of you before we can consider the evening complete. I need to be certain Mr. Tellis has been able to hire the men he promised. Unfortunately, I've no urge to visit the Montgomery establishment myself, and I wondered if you would feel up to the task?"

"You want me to find Andy and Roy and ask if they'll skin for you?"

Scurlock pulled a burning twig from the fire, then paused with it halfway to his pipe. "If you don't mind," he said, then touched the tiny flame to his tobacco.

I stood and brushed myself off. "Nope, I don't mind a'tall."

He nodded but didn't reply until he had the pipe glowing to his satisfaction. "Very well, then." He tossed the twig back into the fire. "And while you're there, I suppose it would be prudent to take a moment or two for your own needs. Do you have sufficient funds?"

I stood there a moment, staring down at the Englishman's guileless expression. Then I smiled and said, "Yes, sir, Mr. Scurlock, I believe I have enough, if it comes to that."

"Splendid, then I shall see all four of you first thing in the morning."

"Before that, I imagine," I replied as I turned away from the fire. Scurlock stopped me before I was out of the firelight.

"One final thought, Gage. Perhaps it would make our time together somewhat easier to digest if we would all dispense with the formalities of Mr. this and Mr. that. My name is Jim. I'll answer to it at any time."

I grinned. "That sounds like a fair enough plan," I agreed, then continued on my way.

CHAPTER FOURTEEN

Amos's large tent saloon was packed when I got there, leaving me to wonder if there was anyone left in Jolley Town other than a few irate storeowners and the indigent. I'd wager Bannon was none too thrilled with this fresh competition, not that I felt much sympathy for the guy after the tonsil varnish he pawned off on us the other night.

Amos's tent was of the marquee variety, with red trim on its scalloped fringe and batwing doors framed into the entrance. There was plenty of lantern light both inside and out, and the happy cries of the women — real or feigned, I couldn't say — created shrill but regular interruptions to the otherwise masculine din of the establishment. Almost overwhelmed by the cacophony of laughter and voices was the music of a crude orchestra playing somewhere inside. I recognized a banjo and squeezebox, and what I thought might be some kind of wind instrument like a bugle. There were probably thirty or more men standing around outside the entrance when I got there, with at least twice that many horses hobbled or staked out nearby. I wound through the crowd and went inside.

The saloon itself took up only half the space of the marquee. The bar ran across the rear, with the old man I'd seen driving the mud wagon behind it, hustling to keep up with the demand for drinks. He had on a clean white shirt with garters on the sleeves, and what hair he had left had been slicked down tight to his scalp with some kind of tonic. The black man who'd offered me a turn with Big Star in exchange for my help setting up the tent was standing to the left of the bar with a fierce scowl imprinted across his face, guarding the entrance to the cribs in back like it was a government mint. He was still wearing his garish outfit from that morning, the brilliant maroon of his vest standing out among the rough-dressed hiders like a canary within a murder of crows. A heavy wooden club dangling by a leather thong from the wrist of his right arm left no doubt regarding his authority over the whores' stalls.

Montgomery was nowhere in sight, nor was the auburn-haired gal who'd driven the flat-topped wagon, but Big Star was there in all her glittering glory. She had her back to the bar, elbows propped on top in a way that threw her massive breasts front and center to the dozen or so admirers surrounding her, their eyes fixed on her deep cleavage nearly popping out of the top of a low-cut dress the color of fresh-spilled blood. Her smile reminded me of a spotlight on a stage, the gawkers like so many moths drawn to the flame. There was a mirror in the backbar. In its reflection, I could see a sheen of sweat along Star's naked spine; a similar glaze lined her upper lip.

Andy and Roy were sitting at one of the tables, engaged in conversation with several men I'd never seen before. Tell wasn't in sight, and I wondered if he'd returned to Jolley Town to look for Scurlock, or if he was still in back with one of the whores. I went over to the table, and Andy shouted a welcome when he saw me.

"Pull up a chair, Gage. Modine here was telling us about the Comanche trouble they had last summer."

"Comanche?" I echoed skeptically.

"Jus' a little band, must've slipped off the reservation," replied the bearded hider on Andy's left. "Caught us flat-footed along the Colorado River."

"Anyone hurt?" I asked, glancing around for a chair and not finding anything that was unoccupied.

"None 'cept Orson Seavers, if you count a bullet in the brisket and losing your topknot hurt."

"I'd say that counts," I replied soberly. "How many Comanches were there?"

"Didn't see 'em myself, but from the tracks we figure five or six bucks."

"Might'a been a small bunch, but it was deadly enough to put Seavers under," another hide man asserted.

"Where was this?" I asked.

"Maybe fifty miles southwest of here," Modine replied.

"Not so very far from where Scurlock wants to take us," Andy added gravely.

"Jim's got his sights set on country northwest of here," I amended. "Plus, with winter coming on, most of the roving bands will be back to the reservation by now."

Roy's face scrunched up in a scowl. "When'd you become such an expert on Comanches, Pardell?"

"I didn't say I was an expert, I'm just telling you where Jim plans to hunt, and it ain't nowhere near the Colorado."

"So it's Jim now, huh?"

Andy chuckled and clamped a hand over

Roy's shoulder. "Don't mind Potter, Gage. He gets cranky when he's in his cups, and he's been drinking steady since noon."

Roy rolled his shoulder out from under Andy's palm. "Lay off, Brenner," he warned.

Speaking to Andy, I said, "Jim wants to know if you two are coming with us."

"Yeah, we've already told Tell we'd throw in with you boys."

"He's camped about a half mile north of here, this side of Deep Creek. Two wagons and a small wedge tent. You can't miss it. He wants to pull out at first light."

"Scurlock can go to hell," Roy growled.

"Damn, Roy, haul in your reins," Andy chided. "The man's offering us a job, not a bucket of horseshit."

"Will you be there?" I asked, still speaking to Andy.

"We'll be there." He looked at Roy and grinned. "Ol' Potter here might not be awake, but we can throw him in back of one of the wagons until he sobers up."

"Ain't nobody throwin' me anywhere," Roy assured them. "Not 'less he wants his head busted open."

Andy was still grinning widely at Roy's antagonistic mood, as were the others. I didn't know why, and wasn't sure I wanted to. Telling Andy I'd see him in the morning,

I walked over to the bar and ordered a beer. The barman had barely set a foaming mug in front of me when I heard a whoop from several feet away and looked around to find Big Star steaming toward me like a locomotive through a snowbank.

"Well, hell's bell, if it ain't my good friend, sweet pea. Howdy, honey."

Stifling a curse, I swung around to meet her head-on. "I didn't know we were such good friends," I said.

"Well, let's just say I'm friendly with everyone." She came up close — too close — and pushed a breast against my arm. Affecting a remorseful expression, she said, "Noah said he offered you a job helpin' set up, but that you turned him down. It wasn't nothing I said, was it, honey?"

"No," I lied smoothly. "I had to help load some wagons for the range."

She smiled. "I figured as much. That damn nigger said you was afraid of me, but I knew that couldn't be the case." She pressed in a little tighter. "Fact is, I told him not an hour ago I'd bet you'd be in to see me tonight . . . soon as you got those wagons loaded. I said you'd be well-nigh salivatin' to spend a little time with ol' Star. Course, now you'll have to pay."

She was speaking loudly, for the crowd,

and I was aware of several men sitting at nearby tables, and others along the bar to either side, watching with a kind of hungry anticipation, half-starved for some new excitement. I was also mindful of Big Star's motives in wanting to stir up a little trouble, to draw more attention her way, as if the scooped neckline of her brightly colored dress wasn't enough.

"That sounds tempting," I replied. "But I'll need to finish my beer first."

Star's eyes hardened to flint. "You can finish that beer in back with me, sweet pea . . . if you ain't afraid."

I don't know what came over me then. Sure as hell it wasn't the way I'd been brought up to treat women, no matter what their occupation. But I was suddenly fed up, and not just with Big Star's bullshit either, but with the whole goddamn fiasco of the last few weeks that had put me out here on the Texas frontier like some lost pup afraid to howl for attracting too much attention to itself. It was like the evening I killed Henry Kalb, but before that, sitting in the dogtrot listening to Ester's sobs and something inside just snapping. With my right fist curled tight as stone, I said in an eerily calm voice, "Why don't you back off a few paces, Star."

"Sonny," she started to bluster, but I straightened to my full height to glare down into her bloodshot eyes.

"Enough," I said, my tone as sharp as a fresh-honed skinning knife.

Star took a backward step and her eyes widened. She took a moment to study me up and down, as if to gauge the bite behind my bark, and whatever attractiveness she might have possessed vanished behind the anger in her face, the venom in her words.

"I got friends here, mister," she said. "Good friends." She jerked a thumb toward the Negro she'd called Noah. "All I got to do is wiggle my little finger and he'll be over here to swat you down like a bug."

"Call him," I challenged tautly. "Either call him over here, or get away from me."

"You jackass," she hissed, then glanced around at the men watching. They were a sober lot now, their eagerness to be entertained dissipated by the threat of violence. They just weren't yet certain which direction it would come from — me, or the black man at the end of the bar, staring our way with sinister intensity.

I waited without speaking, until Star turned her head and spat on the trampled grass that served as the floor.

"I'd finish that drink, then haul your ass

outta here," she told me. " 'Fore I forget I'm a lady." Then she turned away with a steam-engine-like huff and set sail for the other side of the saloon.

At my elbow, a slight man with a cocked eye chuckled. "That's puttin' 'em in their place."

"Just who the hell are you?" I snarled, and he shrugged and turned away. I took my beer and walked to the side wall of the tent. If I hadn't already paid for it, I would have left immediately. A few minutes later, the bearded hide hunter who'd lost his friend to the Comanches on the Colorado River sidled close.

"I'd watch that one," he said, tipping his head toward Noah. "Montgomery doesn't want it to get around, but he and Big Star are married."

"Who? Montgomery, or Noah?"

"The nigger. Montgomery doesn't want that spread around because some men don't shine to the idea of a black man wedding a white woman." He shrugged. "Not that folks out here much give a damn, but you never know." He held out a hand. "I'm Aaron Modine."

I shook reluctantly, my hackles still raised after my run-in with Big Star. "How do you know about those two?" I asked.

"Heard about it in Jacksboro. Couldn't say whether or not it's true, but judging from the look he's giving you, I'd say it's possible. Either way, he's a mean son of a gun, and takes his job seriously."

I glanced Noah's way, and sure enough his gaze was still locked on me like a tick on a hound's ear. I stared back for a moment, but Noah wouldn't look away and I didn't have the energy for such schoolyard games.

"Will you be going back out soon?" I asked Modine, just to make conversation.

"Yeah, soon enough."

"Which direction?"

"South again. Roy Potter might not think so, but I figure you're right about those Comanches heading back to Indian Territory for the winter."

"You ought to come north with us, in case I'm wrong. We could watch one another's backs."

"No, we've got a nice little spot and the hunting has been good. We'll stay where we are until the shaggies move on." He gave me a curious look. "How long have you been partnered with those two?"

"Andy and Roy? Not even two weeks, why?"

"No reason," Modine replied, shrugging. "I've heard some stories about Roy, is all."

"What kind of stories?"

He was quiet a moment. "Nothing specific. I'd keep an eye on Roy, though."

"Why?" I repeated, and Modine turned his gaze to mine.

"Because I'm a cautious man," he said unflinchingly, then changed the conversation by asking about Jim Scurlock and his experience.

I told him what I knew, which wasn't much, then Modine told me how he'd gotten into hunting buffalo after he lost his farm to the bank in eastern Kansas. From there we moved on to hunting buffalo in general, with me doing more listening than talking, trying to absorb as much information as I could. After a while Modine's partner came over and the two of them moseyed toward the bar. I stayed where I was and finished my beer. Andy and Roy were still at the same table where I'd found them, and looked to have gotten up a card game with some other hunters. I thought about what Modine had said about Potter. There was no denying Roy's behavior had changed since leaving behind the responsibilities of his job, but I didn't know what to attribute that to. Was it his unemployment? Some kind of deeper resentment toward Bob Jolley that I wasn't aware of? Or was it as I'd originally assumed, the steady diet of whiskey he'd been consuming since our arrival?

I finished my beer without coming to any solid conclusion and took my mug back to the bar. I was on my way out the door when I noticed a couple of men coming inside. Both were heavily armed and unsmiling. One wore a dark hat with a snakeskin band, the other had a silver concho sewed on the outside of his holster. They paused and their eyes moved over me and a nervous prickle stirred the hairs of my scalp. It was the same feeling I'd gotten back at Tolliver's Emporium, just before Lee Walker and Chip Moore started across the street toward me. The nearest one, with the concho, started to speak, but the other guy put a hand on his back and gave him a gentle shove toward the bar. I passed them without slowing down, but stopped once I was outside, swallowed by the press of hide men standing in the cool night air. The pair inside had moved on to the bar, but they were staring back now with a piercing concentration. Shivering, I turned away from the saloon and strode swiftly back to camp.

CHAPTER FIFTEEN

I kept a wary eye out that night for unwanted visitors, and spread my blankets on the prairie well away from the wagons, but the hours passed uneventfully. By first light I had my bedroll stowed away in the John Deere, the Spencer in its scabbard fastened to the footboard where it would be easy to reach in case it was needed.

Tell and the others were there as promised, although looking quite a bit worse for wear. Roy sat by the fire, staring into the dying embers and speaking to no one, while Jim and I brought the mules in and hitched them to the wagons. Tell had the same horse he'd ridden while bossing Bob Jolley's train out from Fort Griffin, a sorrel mare with a narrow snip down its nose. I'd figured the animal belonged to Jolley, but Tell assured me it was his own.

"If I hadn't furnished my own outfit, that cheap son of a bitch would have had me riding a mule with that Dragoon saddle he put you in," Tell said, standing nearby with a steaming cup of coffee in one gloved hand.

"You made a wise choice," I replied solemnly.

"Damn right, I did. If I'd had to straddle that rig all the way from the Flat, I wouldn't have been partying with Belle all night."

I paused with a trace strap partially unrolled. "Do you know those women who work for Montgomery?"

"Not all of 'em, but a few." He gave a short bark of laughter. "Some better than others."

"Do you know the woman who drove that flat-topped wagon?"

"I don't know who was driving what, but if it was a gal, I'd wager it was Jenny Heflin."

"Skinny, with kind of reddish-brown hair, looked scared."

"That's Jenny all right, and she probably was scared. Amos has her helping out in back, keeping the whores in line and doing whatever cooking and cleaning needs to be done."

"What's she afraid of?"

"Amos, would be my guess. Most whorehouses expect the girls to take care of themselves, but Jenny doesn't want to whore, so she tags along without pay, just meals and what cast-off clothes she picks up along the way. Oh, and a place to sleep where she doesn't have to worry about fighting off some stranger trying to take advantage of her. Trouble is, Amos wants her on her back. Says she'd make more money that way, and he wouldn't be out any more than he already is. He won't force her, though. At least not yet, according to Belle."

"What do you mean, not yet?"

After shrugging nonchalantly and taking a sip of coffee, he said, "Belle says a couple of girls stayed back on the Flat, and Montgomery is short-handed for the demand. He's been pushing Jenny to change her mind. I reckon sooner or later she'll either have to do it, or find some other job. That'll be tough in a place like Jolley Town." Then he grinned. "You ain't gone soft on that gal, have you, Gage?"

"Me? Naw. Hell, I've never even talked to her. I just saw them coming in yesterday, and noticed how out of place she seemed."

"Well, give it another couple of months and you won't be able to pick her out of the herd," he predicted, then dumped what remained of his coffee into the grass and headed back to the fire.

The rain that had been threatening since yesterday afternoon continued to hold off as we got underway, but the wind strengthened with the rising sun. It was like I had a sparring partner with me there on the Deere's high seat. I tugged my hat down tight and buttoned my jacket all the way to the neck. I kept the poncho handy, too, and by late morning I pulled it on over my jacket as the first sweeping veils of icy rain began to fall. Coming in from the north, it struck the mules square in the face and turned them balky.

Andy Brenner was handling the Studebaker's lines, with Roy Potter curled up in back. We figured he was sleeping off his drunk from the night before, and didn't know until we made camp that first night that he'd brought along a quart bottle of Old Crow, and had been nipping on it all day. It was Jim Scurlock who found him. When Roy didn't show himself after we stopped, Jim went around back and hauled him out. Roy was swaying like rubber in the mauling wind, and Scurlock gave him a shove that probably wouldn't have cost Roy more than a step backward if he'd been sober. The way he was, he ended up on his butt in the wet grass, head swiveling back and forth as if wondering who jerked the ground out from under him.

Grabbing Roy by the collar, Jim yanked him to his feet, then damn near chewed the hide off him for being drunk on the job. Roy took it silently, unless you happened to glance into his eyes. Those two dark orbs were speaking volumes.

Afterward, Jim told Roy to start gathering firewood, and to not stop until he was "relieved of duty." That was military jargon, which Jim would drift into from time to time, although he never admitted to serving in the Queen's army, or any other nation's.

It stopped raining during the night, but was still cold when we rolled out of our blankets the next morning. Roy was still there, which kind of surprised me. I wouldn't have been surprised at his sloping off during the night and returning to Jolley. We didn't bother with a fire — you could tell that angered Roy, after all the work he'd done hauling in wood the night before — but, instead, slapped slices of side pork between layers of biscuits and ate on the trail. Jim and Tell rode up front on their horses. Roy sat with Andy on the Studebaker's seat, hunched and miserable after his long drunk. I brought up the rear with Jim's packhorse tied behind the Deere, trudging along with its head lowered as if feeling abandoned.

It was another three days to the spot Jim had picked out for our camp, a little flat set amongst rolling hills. Grass was plentiful, and there were mesquite thickets scattered up and down the banks of a winding stream that bordered the narrow plain on the east. Jim guided us to one of the bigger groves near the center of the valley and motioned toward a clearing back among the trees.

"We'll set up in there," he explained as Andy and I halted our wagons before him. "Andy and Roy will raise the tent and start gathering wood. Gage, I want you to begin building several drying racks. We won't be able to harvest all the meat, but we'll take as many tongues as we can, and dry some of the better choices for the coming winter. Tell and I shall reconnoiter the perimeter for Indian sign. I don't expect to find any, but it's wise to know who your neighbors are."

I nodded and climbed down and un-hitched my mules, and after taking them to water, hobbled and turned them loose. We set up the wall tent Jim had purchased from Jolley, then Andy started unloading the wagons while Roy went after firewood and I made my way downstream looking for suitable timber to construct a series of drying racks. The light was fading before Jim returned to announce the land to the west seemingly free of hostiles.

"The buffalo are plentiful, though," he stated, and there was an odd hitch to his voice, an underlying agitation in his movements as he hauled his reload stuff out of the Studebaker and began setting up in front of the tent.

Tell came in shortly after dark with a similar report — no sign of human habitation, but small herds of buffalo in just about every direction.

"We'll have good hunting for a while," he predicted. "But the others'll find us sooner or later."

"What others?" Jim asked, looking up from where he was examining a row of already formed brass.

"Hunters," Tell said. "Buffalo are getting scarce in these parts. We've got a good spot here, but other outfits will start showing up in time."

"Be damned to that," Jim responded indignantly. "This is our range. I'll not tolerate others poaching it or disturbing our herds."

Tell was standing beside his mount, hitched to the Deere's rear wheel as he loosened his cinch to remove the saddle. He paused with rig pulled half off. "You ain't gonna have any say in that, Mr. Scurlock."

Tell still referred to Scurlock as *mister,* as did Andy and Roy. As far as I knew, I was the only one Jim had given permission to call him by his first name, although I hadn't yet done it, at least not since leaving Jolley. I guess part of that was because the others didn't. It wouldn't be until some years later that I realized Scurlock had given me leave to do so because I'd shown more responsibility in hanging around that first day to help him load his wagons, rather than taking off for Montgomery's saloon like a bullet out of a gun barrel. Tell had a point about other hunters finding us, though. No matter what Jim thought, he wasn't going to keep hiders off this range. He just hadn't realized that yet.

We spent the next day finishing up around the camp, Andy and Roy gathering and cutting enough firewood to last us a month, while I finished constructing about twenty feet of low scaffolding to dry the meat the hunters would bring in. As soon as that was finished, Jim set me to fashioning stakes out of mesquite limbs. When I asked how many he wanted, his reply was that even if I whittled day and night until Christmas, I wouldn't have enough. It seemed an optimistic outlook, but who was I to argue? I knew older men back in Shelburn who would sit on a porch and whittle all day for nothing, and here I was getting paid seven dollars a week for the same relaxing occupation.

Jim went out on our third day in camp, and within the hour I heard the distant boom of his Sharps. It rang out thirty or forty more times before midday, then Andy and Roy hitched up the smaller Studebaker and drove out toward the killing grounds. Tell, meanwhile, saddled up and rode east, but I only heard his rifle once, and when he returned that night it was without tongue, meat, or hide. Jim, on the other hand, came in at sunset, his eyes bright with excitement.

"Be ready, Gage," he advised me as he dismounted. "You'll be staking hides until your knuckles ache as soon as Brenner and Potter arrive."

"You must've had a good hunt."

"It portends well for the future," he agreed with a knobby laugh, and I vowed once again, as I had after talking with Rita back on the Flat, that I'd someday get a real education. One where words like *portend* didn't fall uselessly to the ground at my feet because I didn't know what to do with them.

It was after midnight before Andy and Roy

showed up with their wagon nearly buried beneath a load of green hides. Skins fresh off a carcass like a buffalo can weigh anywhere from fifty to eighty pounds, depending on the animal's size and sex. That equaled roughly a ton of unprocessed leather and hair, and a tribute to the Studebaker Brothers Manufacturing Company that the axles didn't splinter under such a cumbersome load — especially considering the kind of terrain they had to cross.

Staking out buffalo hides was a lot more work than I'd expected, having only handled deer, hog, and cow hides in the past. We dragged the skins out of the wagon and across the wet grass and spread them out hair-side down, then cut little slits — twenty or so on the smaller hides, up to thirty for a bull — around the edges, before hammering the mesquite stakes I'd whittled into the rain-softened earth to keep them stretched flat and taut. If the skies ever cleared up, the sun would dry the skins to what we called flints, turning the inner side pale and stiff, though making the hide considerably lighter.

It was nearly dawn before we finished, Andy and Roy having stayed to help. I was sore and stiff and chilled to the bone as we trudged back to the fire. I'd started a big pot of coffee the night before that was still warm, although bitter. The biscuits and beans left over from supper were cold, but we ate them anyway, then crawled into our blankets and quickly dropped off to sleep. Jim and Tell were up at dawn, and Jim kicked Andy and Roy awake to tell them which direction he'd be hunting in so the two could come looking for them around midmorning. Neither man mentioned that they'd barely crawled into bed. A hunter's life was a hard one — feast or famine, with little in between — and Jim intended to gorge while the hunting was good.

Tell, I noticed, didn't say anything, but he didn't act particularly pleased with the way the trip was turning out. As for me, I withheld judgment, and didn't grumble when Scurlock told me to have a better supper prepared when he got back that evening than the one I'd served the night before.

"Slop fit more for swine than human consumption," was his review of the previous evening's fare.

I still hadn't called him Jim, and resolved that morning that I never would.

We continued on that way for another two weeks, Scurlock bringing in anywhere from half a dozen to fifteen hides per day, while Tell did lucky to harvest a third of that. You could tell Scurlock was growing irritated with his poorer showing, even though he was bringing in enough hides on his own that we weren't hurting. Sure as hell he was keeping his crew busy. My days ran from "can to can't," meaning *can see* to *too dark to see,* with most of it spent either turning hides or looking after the fire and cooking. Any spare time I had was spent whittling new stakes to keep up with the growing demand of Scurlock's rifles.

Buffalo are migratory animals, and it wasn't long before we had to move camp to keep up with the shifting herds. Andy and Roy drove the wagons, while Jim left me behind to dry the hides that weren't ready to be stacked. One of my duties that I haven't mentioned yet was to brand each hide with the letters RJ, which stood for Robert Jolley, Bob having already agreed to purchase Scurlock's hides on the range for three dollars apiece. Scurlock could have gotten a lot more for them if he'd hauled them in himself, but he was more interested in the hunt. As time passed, I began to realize he was a little *too* invested in the stalking and killing.

Jim left me his packhorse and panniers with enough supplies to last me a couple of weeks, along with a letter wrapped in an oilcloth wallet to pass along to whoever Jolley sent out to pick up the hides. I was to keep his old wedge tent for shelter, while he took along the larger wall tent they would all sleep in if it rained or snowed.

"We'll be moving north and a little west," he informed me the morning they pulled out. "Our tracks should be easy to follow. Be sure to count the hides as they're loaded onto Jolley's wagons, and bring me the signed invoice." After I told him I would, he said, "Are you nervous about being left alone out here, Gage?"

"No, sir," I replied.

"Good, there's nothing to be afraid of, and you're well-armed against predators." He grunted. "The two-legged species, although you'll need to watch out for wolves and coyotes, as well."

I knew it wasn't *my* skin Scurlock was thinking of, but those still pegged out on the drying grounds. With all of the free meat available, it wasn't likely a coyote would waste much time gnawing on a piece of iron-tough hide, although you could never be certain what any animal would do — no matter how many legs it had.

I'll tell you what, I was a lonely man when those wagons pulled out. I stood there beside my little fire and watched as they grew small in the distance, then finally disappeared over the horizon. I'd told Scurlock I wasn't afraid, and I wasn't — not much, anyway, those tales of Comanche raiders notwithstanding — but as I'd learned on my long ride across Texas, I preferred company close by. Even if it was just a farmer in the next field.

CHAPTER SIXTEEN

I was eight days by my lonesome before Jolley's crew showed up — six big Schuttlers with the sideboards and tailgates removed, each pulled by a ten-horse hitch. A small trail wagon carrying camp and personal items was hitched to the rear of the last wagon in line. The train was led by a short, stocky man with a black beard and a patch over his left eye, and when he got close I saw he was also missing his left arm just below the elbow. He ordered the train toward the flat ground west of camp, then reined his mount in my direction. I waited next to the fire. He pulled up about ten yards out.

"Howdy," he called. "I'm looking for the Jim Scurlock outfit."

"You've found it."

"Good," he replied with an easy grin, then dismounted and led his horse forward. "I'm Harry Brooks, one of Bob Jolley's foremen."

With his reins draped over the stub of his left forearm, he reached out with his right to shake hands.

"I'm Gage Pardell. Pleased to meet you." Then, after a pause, "You said *one* of Jolley's foremen?"

"He's got several to manage his various enterprises. My task is to gather the hides Mr. Jolley has contracted for, and take them back to the post. There's another man who guides his supply trains, and a third who manages the trading post itself. Mr. Jolley travels back and forth between his post and either Fort Griffin or Jacksboro."

"I didn't know his company was that big."

"That big and getting bigger."

I didn't ask who had taken over Ralph Tellis's old job of guiding the supply trains between Griffin and Jolley.

Tipping his head toward the fire, Harry said, "You mind if me and my boys shared your camp tonight? We can start loading hides today, and probably pull out again first thing in the morning."

"You'd be more than welcome," I replied, feeling damn near starved for fresh conversation.

Harry turned toward the train and made a broad, sweeping motion with his right hand, and the wagons jolted into motion. I watched as they formed a rough circle, more to keep the livestock inside after dark, I suspect, than from any fear of Indian attack.

Motioning toward my coffeepot — the small one, Scurlock had taken the larger pot with him — Harry said, "Is that fresh?"

"Not much," I allowed, "but it ain't more than a week old, either."

"Week-old coffee is better than no coffee, far as I'm concerned." He pulled a dented tin cup from his saddlebags, then went over and sat down cross-legged by the fire. I poured for both of us, then flopped down opposite him. Pulling the collar of a heavy mackinaw coat closer around his neck, he said, "My bones have been telling me it's going to snow soon."

"Are your bones fairly honest?"

"More often than not." He took a sip, then smacked his lips with a smile. "I was expecting worse." Then his expression sobered. "Where's Scurlock?"

"He took the rest of the crew on to fresh grounds."

"And left you here to watch over these hides?"

"Yes, sir." I pulled my shooting bag closer. The wallet Jim had given me was inside, and I handed it over. After scanning the letter, Harry refolded it and handed it back. "That looks fine, Gage. What we'll do is give my boys a short break, then start loading the wagons. You and I will stand between them and the stacks and count each hide as it passes. Does that sound fair to you?"

I nodded that it did.

"Good. About how many hides do you have here?"

"Mr. Scurlock counted them twice before pulling out. He says there's one hundred and twenty-one skins altogether."

"Did you count them?"

"Yes, sir. One twenty-one is what I got, too."

"Fair enough. That'll make it easier, although we'll still count them together and make it official." Rising, he walked over to where his horse was standing ground-tied and extracted a number of envelopes from the pommel bag fastened to the saddle's near side. "These are some documents Mr. Jolley sent along for Scurlock." He smiled and winked as he eased back to the ground across from me. "I also serve as a mail carrier for these parts . . . unofficially, of course." He handed the bundled envelopes over. "You can pass them along for me. There are also some letters in there addressed to you, care of some guy named

Foret, from Fort Griffin."

I took the letters and quickly ruffled through the batch, separating mine from Scurlock's and tossing Scurlock's aside until I could stow them somewhere safe. There were three, one with a return address from Uncle Abran, and two that included only my name and *Fort Griffin, Texas* in the middle of the envelope. I recognized Ma's handwriting, and couldn't stop a grin from forming on my lips. I think my hands were damn near trembling with eagerness to tear open those last two envelopes and find out what was going on at home.

Chuckling at my impatience, Harry drained what remained of his coffee in two long swallows, then shook out the dredges and pushed to his feet. "I'll be with my crew," he said. "Come over after you've read your letters and we'll get started on those hides."

"Yes, sir," I replied distractedly, already tearing open the top envelope.

It was from Ma, all right, written in her chicken-scratch script that made it hard to decipher. I won't go into everything she said, but there was quite a bit of fretting about my having enough warm clothes with winter coming on, and what I needed to eat to remain healthy. I had to smile at that. I doubt if she would have thought too highly of my current diet of beans, biscuits, and buffalo.

A couple of things she said stood out, though, and my expression soon turned grim. She explained how Pa hadn't had any luck so far with the law, and that Linus Kalb remained determined to see me returned to Shelburn to stand trial for Henry's death, *or otherwise pay the balance for it,* which I took to mean the men he'd sent after me. She also stated that Pa had tried to get the venue changed to Austin, and when that failed, to the county seat at Cameron. The trouble, Ma asserted, was that Linus had hired an attorney who was fighting Pa's every effort, and although she didn't say it, or need to, I knew our family couldn't afford a lawyer.

The other thing she said that worried me was just a passing remark: *Your brothers and sisters are doing well, although Ester seems to be suffering from a malady of spirits.*

Nowadays they call that depression, but I knew what she was talking about. Ester was still blaming herself for what happened at the Harvest Festival, and especially for what occurred afterward — my killing Henry Kalb, then fleeing to the buffalo ranges like a common horse thief.

I folded the letter and returned it to its envelope, then just sat there staring into the lowering flames until I heard Harry Brooks hailing me from the wagons. Yanked from my reveries, I stood and tossed my letters and Scurlock's inside the tent where the wind wouldn't skate off with them, then hiked out to where we'd stacked the dried buffalo hides on the south side of the staking grounds. Harry's half dozen teamsters were standing around the rear wheel of the first wagon, shoulders hunched to the cold, hands thrust deep into the pockets of their heavy coats. I nodded to the men one by one, but stopped short when I realized I knew one of them.

"Pedro!"

Pedro Morales grinned big as you please. "Hello, Mr. Pardell. I'll bet you didn't think you would see me again."

"No, I didn't. I thought you'd still be with Jolley's supply train."

Pedro, if you don't recall, was the wrangler on Jolley's supply train when we came out from Fort Griffin, the Mexican kid I'd turned my bay mule over to, and who herded the extra stock along behind the wagons.

"I go where Mr. Jolley sends me," Pedro replied, and Harry added, "We were short a man this trip, and since Mr. Jolley wasn't sending any loose stock back to Fort Griffin, we snagged him. I hope we can keep him, too. He knows horses and mules as well as any man I've ever met."

"*Sí,* horses I know. People . . ." He shrugged elaborately.

I smiled in agreement; yeah, I knew. We shook hands, and I'll admit I was genuinely happy to see a familiar face. Harry introduced me to the rest of the crew, then ordered them to get busy. Four of the men started dragging our dried-stiff hides off the stacks and over to the wagons, where the other two laid them in place, then tromped them down tight. Harry and I stood off to one side to watch. It took several hours to get the last hide packed and the load tied off. When it was done, the men gathered around as Harry and I compared notes. Our counts came up identical and in agreement with what Scurlock and I had tallied earlier — one hundred and twenty-one hides. Harry signed a paper acknowledging the count and handed it to me, and I did the same with a second sheet for him. Then we shook hands, and our business was completed.

Glancing skyward, Harry said, "It's getting on toward dark, boys, and Gage has graciously invited us to share his camp tonight. Floyd, you and Pedro and Gimp drive the horses down to the creek and let them drink their fill. Davis, you're handling the skillets tonight."

"The hell! I cooked grub t'other night," an older man who looked like he'd been through a wringer more than once in his life replied.

"I know, but you're the best biscuit slinger we've got, and young Gage here deserves a decent meal." He grinned. "Chipper up, Davis, at least the fire's already lit and there's plenty of wood."

Davis grumbled under his breath as he slogged toward the trail wagon. The others scattered to their chores, while Harry and I walked back to the fire. I headed for one of the nearly empty meat racks to bring down the last of the buffalo meat Scurlock had left for me, but the wagon boss called me back.

"We've got beef, Gage. I'm guessing you could use something with a little fat in it, after a few weeks of eating buffalo."

"I won't argue with that," I agreed, and came back to add more wood to the fire.

Harry sat down and reached for the pot to pour himself a fresh cup, his movements sure and confident. I was amazed by his mobility, not just in something so mundane as filling a cup of coffee, but in handling paperwork in a gusting wind, or unsaddling and hobbling his horse while I read Ma's letter. I never heard how he'd lost his eye and forearm, but assumed it had been during the late hostilities with the North. The South was flush with such men, mangled limbs and breasts filled with bitterness, gazes hardened by the unfairness of their fate. Yet Harry seemed to lack any such animosity, and his cheerfulness seemed almost contagious.

The others gradually came in and took seats around the fire, while darkness closed in from every side. A couple of men started talking between themselves. At first I didn't pay them any heed, but you know how you can tune out a conversation until a certain word — like your name, or maybe the town where you were born — pops up and your ear immediately latches onto it? We all have a few of those. One of mine, and I imagine this held true for a lot of Texans in those days, was the word *Comanche.* When the guy said it, my head immediately snapped up. I didn't try to pretend I wasn't listening, either.

"There couldn't have been too many," one of the men said.

"You don't know that," his partner argued. "There could've been a hundred of 'em."

Glancing up from where he was slicing potatoes into a greased skillet, Davis mumbled, "We don't know there was any, not for sure and certain."

"What are you talking about?" I asked.

Harry Brooks raised his gaze above the rim of his cup and shook his head. Lowering the little mug away from his lips, he said, "There's a rumor floating around some of the camps that a war party has slipped off the reservation and is raiding in this direction."

"The rumor is they killed a couple of hunters up on the Canadian," the first man continued. "Cut 'em up pretty bad, too."

"There hasn't been any confirmation of that," Harry reminded him.

"What the hell kind of confirmation do you need?" he demanded.

"I'd like to hear it from someone with firsthand information," Harry replied. "Someone who's actually *seen* something."

"Where Comanches are concerned, I tend to believe what I hear. That way, if I'm wrong, I still got my scalp, but if I'm right, my odds are better for being ready."

"I'm not arguing with that," Harry conceded. "But we aren't going to abandon our responsibilities because of a rumor, either." He looked at me. "Mr. Jolley has contracts with seven other camps, besides Scurlock's. We first heard about the possibility of a Comanche raid from a camp we visited two days ago, Tim Ferguson's outfit."

"I've heard of Ferguson," I said. "I've never met him."

"He seems like a level-headed sort, and wasn't panicking about it. He just wanted to pass the word along, which I appreciate. You might want to do the same with Scurlock."

"I will," I promised.

After that the conversation moved on to other topics. I sat and listened in and occasionally added a comment, and by and by Davis announced that the meal was ready for anyone interested. We all naturally were, hard work and cold weather being a handy combination for building appetites, and I've got to admit Harry Brooks was dead-on-target in his assessment of Davis's prowess with a skillet. That was probably the best meal I'd had since leaving home, and I'm not sure it wouldn't have given Ma's reputation as a cook a run for its money. I don't know why Davis was wandering around the buffalo ranges hauling hides for a man like Bob Jolley, instead of working for some fine restaurant or in a millionaire's private kitchen. I can only assume it was for the same reason many of us were out there, straining our guts with hard labor; because we were hiding from something, or someone.

I ate more than I should have, and leaned back afterward to ease the pressure on my belly. While Floyd and Gimp took care of the dirty dishes, most of the others headed for their blankets. Finally, only Harry and Pedro and I remained, feet extended toward the flames, clouds building up overhead and slowly masking the stars. Eventually Harry bid me goodnight, leaving only Pedro. Since he and I had already reminisced about our limited "old times," I assumed he had something else on his mind. Once Harry was out of the picture, it didn't take long for him to get to the point.

"I remember when that deputy came into our camp," he said.

"Jennison?"

Pedro nodded. *"Sí.* And I remember how hard you tried to look *Mexicano."* He lightly touched one cheek with a finger, and I knew he was referring to the dye Rita had applied to my flesh, long since faded away.

"I had my reasons," I replied.

"Sí, I know that, too. In Jolley, before we

left, there were two men who say they are looking for someone. The way they described him, I think maybe it's you."

I sighed, staring into the fire as I recalled the two hard cases I'd passed as I left Amos Montgomery's saloon. "What did they look like?" I asked rhetorically.

"Average, except when you look into their eyes. Then they look . . . mean. Very mean."

"Was one of them wearing a black hat with some kind of snakeskin band, the other with a concho on his holster?"

"*Sí*. Seamus Thornton wears the snakeskin on his hat. The other, with the concho, is Wade Adams."

"I've never heard of them."

"I haven't either, but I think maybe they've heard of you, and are eager to find you."

"Do they know where I am?"

"I think so. The African called Noah, who watches over Montgomery's whores, told them where you went."

A little shiver of . . . what? Fear, maybe? . . . coursed through my veins. "What did they do?"

"Nothing," Pedro replied. "They are waiting. I think they are waiting for you to return, rather than come out here looking for you when there is so much country to search."

That was a relief, although a small one.

"I wanted you to know," Pedro said, putting his hands on his knees and preparing to rise.

"I appreciate it."

"*De nada,* my friend. A lot of people in Texas still remember the Alamo, and do not look kindly on my people. I appreciate it when others look past Santa Anna's sins and treat me as a person. You did that."

"The others did, too," I reminded him.

"And I would do the same for them." He grinned. "Besides, it isn't much, this little warning, but I hope you can use it."

"I can," I assured him.

"Good, then I will go and find my blankets, because we will pull out early tomorrow, as soon as there is enough light to see where we are going."

"Good luck, Pedro."

"And to you, *amigo.*"

And with that, he was gone. Although grateful for the news, I didn't know yet what I'd do with it.

Alone by the fire, I crawled into the wedge tent long enough to retrieve the two letters from my family that I hadn't had time to read. I opened Ma's second letter first, but there wasn't much new in it. Although neither of her missives was dated, it was obvious this was the first she'd sent me, relating how Pa hadn't had any luck with the local authorities, or those in Austin.

Whereas Ma's letters had included admonitions to remain safe and dry and not to shirk my prayers, Abran's cut straight to the bone.

Young Buck. B Gilson is back from jacksburo and will press no charge against you for the incident with Moor and walker Max Jennyson is talking bad abaout you but wants the job of marshall so is trying to make a example of you. But that is going Nowhere, and is not expected to However you should know two men came threw looking for a man of your descripshion wanted for murder in east texas, and it is considered likely you are that man. these men are called Thornton and Adams, and are considered dangerous company in their part of texas near Austen. you should be careful of them, and pass them by at every opportuneity. No news from your mother. best of Luck, Abran.

I'd smiled at Ma's cramped penmanship, but in comparison, Uncle Abran's made hers appear as if it had been produced by a typewriter. Her spelling was considerably better, too, which oddly made me longingly recall Rita and her obvious education. I returned Abran's letter to its envelope, then sat there staring into the coals until they were covered with gray ash, and the cold wind drove me into the shelter of my little tent. Homesickness had been an ongoing malady ever since leaving Milam County, but some nights were harder than others. That night there alone, with Ma's words and Uncle Abran's alive in my mind, almost like I could hear them speaking, was one of the worst, and I don't mind admitting I had to struggle not to let a few tears escape my eyes.

CHAPTER SEVENTEEN

True to Pedro's words, Harry Brooks had his outfit hitched up and ready to roll by first light. I stood next to the dead ashes of my fire and watched them pull out, my hands thrust deep into the pockets of the blue and black duffel coat Pa had sent along, its collar turned up against the chill. The wind had eased up overnight, but the clouds had thickened into a deep, angry gray. I remembered Harry's prediction, based on his aching joints, that there was snow in our near future. My guess that morning was that it was nearing our doorstep.

With the wagons gone, I brought the packhorse in and broke camp. The slimness of the panniers once I had them strapped in place was worrisome. If you've noticed that I haven't mentioned a mount for me to ride, you've been observant. Not that having to hoof it shank's mare was all that uncommon. A lot of people think everyone rode everywhere in those days, and there's a certain amount of truth to that, but there are always exceptions, and spotting a man trudging along with a packhorse, or even carrying his personal belongings on his back, wasn't all that uncommon either. Although I would have preferred a saddle horse, and specifically my horse, Dusty, which Max Jennison had stolen from me back on the Flat, I was out of luck in that regard. So, it was off on foot I went, striking out in the same direction Jim and the boys had taken when they left me a little over a week before.

The wagon tracks were easy to follow, especially the heavier print of the John Deere. Since the trail led more westerly than I'd been led to believe it would, I was grateful for the deep impressions in the sod. The clouds troubled me, though. They seemed to drop lower as the morning progressed, and by noon my fears came true. It began to snow, tiny little flakes that swirled up under my hat brim on the breeze, peppering my cheeks and latching onto my eyebrows. It had been cold long enough that the snow wasn't melting, either, and I feared I'd lose the trail if it got too deep.

By the time dusk forced me to start looking for a place to spend the night, the snow was like a white sheet spread over the hills, although the wagon tracks were still visible. They were there the next morning when I struck out, too, but within an hour of leaving camp the wind died completely and the snow started to fall in earnest, the flakes larger and wetter than the day before, coming down around me with a soft hiss. I took my bearings as best I could as the horizon closed down to within a few hundred yards, then plunged stubbornly onward.

I had no idea where I was when the light started to fade that second day. Concerned about spending the night out in the open with no water for my horse or wood for a fire, I damn near whooped for joy when I spotted a small grove of trees lining a meandering creek.

When the snow continued into the third day, I decided to stay where I was, rather than risk overshooting Scurlock's camp and hiking all the way to Santa Fe. There was plenty of water under the ice in the creek, and more firewood than I could burn in a month, and even though my food supplies were running low, I had my Spencer and could always hunt.

The snow continued to fall until well into the afternoon of the fourth day before finally stopping, the clouds clearing out almost immediately afterward. I felt kind of like a badger emerging from its den as I crawled out of my tent. The sun seemed unusually brilliant after so many days of murkiness, and the cold set my nose to dripping. I climbed the nearest hill hoping to catch a glimpse of smoke, or better yet, a hunter's camp, but the land appeared desolate to my eye, although beautiful in its own rugged way. Cliffs tinged with red, dappled with the deep green of cedars, and lines of mesquite following the streambeds in the valleys. This was *Comancheria,* the heartland of a once vast and dangerous territory claimed by the Comanche Nation. Although the Southern Tribes were mostly confined to reservations now, I knew it was still a perilous country, where roaming bands of marauders — red and white — wouldn't hesitate to attack a solitary individual leading a packhorse loaded with who-knew-what. The fact that I was afoot would only be an added incentive, a sign of easier prey.

I hiked back down the hill to break camp. Although the tracks of Scurlock's two wagons were buried under a fresh blanket of white, I'd noticed a low pass between a couple of hills to the northwest, the general direction Jim had told me he intended to go, and I decided I'd make for that and see what was on the other side. If I didn't locate *someone's* camp by then, I'd need to decide if I wanted to keep wandering the plains like a vagabond, or make my way back to Jolley.

It was a six-hour trek through snow sometimes eight to ten inches deep — yeah, I know that's not much to some folks, but I was from Milam County, and it was a chunk and a half to me — to reach the trail leading through the pass. I took a breather at the bottom of the slope, one arm hanging over the packhorse's withers to ease my aching calves and half-frozen toes. There was a tin of mink oil in the bottom of my nearside pannier that I'd put off digging out because I didn't want to lose so much time. The way my feet were feeling, I knew I'd made a bad decision. If you're wearing leather footwear — boots, shoes, or moccasins — you have to keep them well greased in wet weather, especially the seams.

Right at that moment all I wanted to do was make camp and kindle a fire, but wood was just about nonexistent as far as I could tell, and with clear skies overhead, I knew the temperature would plummet as soon as the sun went down. Figuring I didn't have much of a choice, I kept going, breaking trail through the deepening drifts while the packhorse followed close behind. On top I paused again, and my hopes soared when I spotted a column of smoke scrawled across the pale blue slate of winter sky. I didn't know whose camp sat beneath it, nor did I care. With a hoarse cheer, I turned to the packhorse and said, "We're goin' in, boy. If it's a Comanche camp, you'll be a Comanche pony by morning, and I'll probably be dead, but at least my feet will be warm."

Well, it wasn't an Indian encampment I stumbled into, but it wasn't Scurlock's outfit, either. The head man's name was Emmet Strobel, a blocky German out of Fredericksburg, Texas. He was there with his brother-in-law and two sons, hunting buffalo for both the hides and meat.

"A little money for to spend in the spring," he told me in his heavy German accent.

I asked if he'd had good hunting, all the while edging closer to the fire where the rest of his clan were standing. Nobody had their guns drawn when I came in, but they all looked wary and capable.

"Pretty cold you are, huh?"

"I haven't felt my toes since the other side of that pass yonder," I replied, jerking a thumb over my shoulder in the direction of the low pass several miles east of Strobel's camp.

You could just about see the guardedness drain out of his face. "*Yah,* you come on over to the fire, we get you warmed up some, no?"

"*Yah!*" I agreed, and didn't resist when the brother-in-law stepped forward to take the packhorse's lead rope.

They fed me a stew thick with buffalo, corn, carrots, and some kind of squash that settled on my empty stomach like a pile of warm coals. I'd toed my boots off after sitting down and propped them up close enough to the fire to aid in their drying, but not so close it might damage the leather. My socks were hung up beside them and immediately started to steam as the heat chased the wetness from the wool. I didn't have any other shoes, but I did have another pair of socks that I pulled on before thrusting both feet toward the fire. After wolfing down two bowls of Strobel's good stew, I leaned back with a cup of coffee laced with whiskey from the brother-in-law's packs and I told them my story. As luck would have it, Strobel had already locked horns with Scurlock. I started to sit up in alarm, but the big German chuckled and motioned me back.

"A prickly one, your Scurlock, but plenty

of buffalo there is to hunt, and plenty of country to hunt them in."

"Did he give you any trouble?" I asked.

"*Nein.* A little perturbed he was, but he cooled off when I told him we would hunt in a different direction."

"Which way's his camp?"

Strobel tipped his head to the southwest. "Maybe by horseback, half a day."

"How far on foot?"

"All day," he allowed, "but we won't let you so far to walk with wet boots." He looked at his brother-in-law. "Karl, tomorrow you will take Mr. Pardell to the Scurlock camp, no?"

Karl nodded that he would. "We'll get an early start. You'll be ready?"

"I'll be ready whenever you say," I agreed.

"Good, then I think I will turn in." He stood and yawned and said goodnight, then made his way to one of the wagons, where I could see a bedroll beneath it, already unfurled on top of a buffalo hide to protect it from the damp earth.

Emmet Strobel's claim that he hadn't taken offense at Scurlock's harsh treatment worried me some — a lot of men I met out there would have simmered over it, and maybe considered some kind of revenge, if not on Jim, then on one of his men — but I awoke the next morning intact and unblemished, and after a hearty breakfast of oatmeal and buffalo steaks, Karl brought in and saddled a couple of horses while I readied my pack animal. After thanking the family for its kind generosity, we started out with Karl in the lead and me bringing up the rear with the packhorse in tow. Strobel had estimated a half-day's ride to Scurlock's camp, but it was still an hour or so before noon when we came in sight of it, tucked in among a grove of cottonwood and hackberry trees as snug as fleas on a dog's butt. Karl reined up about a quarter of a mile away, and I rode up beside him.

"This is as far as I go," he announced.

"What? Why? Come on in and have some coffee, at least."

"No, your boss made it plain we aren't welcome in his camp."

"I'm saying you are," I countered firmly, but Karl only grinned at my blunt determination.

"I believe you, Gage, but it isn't your friendship I'm turning my back on. It's your boss's attitude. He is spoiling for a fight, that one, and so are the others."

"The others?" For a moment, I didn't know what he was taking about. Then it dawned on me, and I nodded slowly.

"You know who I talk about, then?" he said.

"If you mean Roy Potter, I guess I've seen it coming for a spell."

"I don't know their names, only what I saw." He held his hand out, palm up, and I knew it wasn't to shake my paw. Dismounting, I handed him the reins to my horse. "You are a good man, Gage Pardell. I wish you luck."

"I appreciate your help," I replied, then stepped away as he pulled his horse around and started for his own camp.

Although the temperature was still somewhere below freezing, the sun was out and doing its job, and the snow on top was beginning to melt. It made for slick footing, and I took my time negotiating the long slope into the camp. A ribbon of smoke curling into the sky told me someone was nearby, but I didn't see a soul, nor did I see any hides staked out on the gently tilted hillside south of camp. It wasn't until I was within a hundred yards of the John Deere wagon that a man stepped out from behind a tree with a rifle held firmly in both hands. My heart gave a little skip, but I kept on. Back in the shadows like he was, I couldn't make out who it was. Evidently, he hadn't identified me in my heavy duffel coat either

— I hadn't worn it until recently — although he should have recognized Scurlock's packhorse.

When I got closer, I saw it was Ralph Tellis standing next to the cottonwood's broad trunk with his heavy-barreled Remington single-shot. He was wearing a bulky green coat, and had replaced his Stetson with a plaid cap with earflaps. I shouted a howdy and he waved, but didn't speak until I walked into the camp.

"Damn, boy, I'm glad you found us," Tell said, leaning his rifle against the cottonwood and stepping forward. "We were beginning to think you'd gotten lost."

"Not hardly," I lied, but after relating my adventures since leaving our old camp on the Double Mountain Fork, he saw through it.

"It was Emmet Strobel who saved my bacon," I added.

"Strobel . . . yeah, I've met him. He seems like a good man."

"He doesn't hold the same opinion of Jim."

"No, he and Jim butted heads about ten days ago. Strobel was hunting grounds Scurlock claimed as his own."

"His own? What right does he have to do that?"

273

"Not a lick, but he's bullheaded, and getting more so all the time. It's our good fortune Strobel is an easygoing man, otherwise there could have been gunplay."

"Where's Scurlock now?"

Tell barked a short, sour laugh. "Shooting buffalo, where else?"

Glancing at the empty slope south of camp, I said, "Then where are the hides?"

"Back yonder." Tell nodded toward the trees flanking the camp on the north and west sides. "We ain't staked 'em out yet. Scurlock says it's cold enough now that we don't have to. He's got over a hundred hides stacked up in there, froze stiff as an oak floor. He says we'll wait until the snow begins to melt before we worry about staking 'em out."

Peering into the trees behind Tell, I spotted the low stacks, covered with snow and looking like squared-off headstones in a deserted cemetery.

"Scurlock's got Roy and Andy with him to do the skinning. He's kept me here to watch the camp. I think he's afraid someone'll slip in and steal his hides." He shook his head in disgust. "The crazy bastard, thinking a few dozen hides'd be as easy to walk off with as a sack of gold."

"Karl seems to think there's trouble brewing here."

"Karl's a smart man," Tell replied. "Scurlock and Potter have been butting heads pretty regular the past week or so, and Andy's starting to slide into the fray on Roy's side."

"What are they arguing about?"

"What ain't they arguing about?" He stepped forward to lift the packhorse's lead rope from my hand, as Karl had done the night before. "Go get yourself something to eat, Gage. You look about done in. I'll take care of Poky."

"Poky? Is that his name?"

"Yeah, what have you been calling him?"

"Horse," I replied, then slipped my Spencer in its scabbard and my saddlebags from the off-side pannier and walked over to the fire. Tell was right, I was dog-tired after my long trek across the high Texas plains, and my feet were still chilled to the core. Plopping down in front of the fire and finally being able to warm myself without worrying about the future — the immediate future, in any case — was like sitting down after a big Thanksgiving feast. By the time Tell got back from caring for Poky, my eyelids were drooping.

It was midafternoon before Jim Scurlock showed up, kicking his horse into a lope when he spotted his packhorse grazing on the end of a picket rope in front of the Deere. He had a big grin plastered across his face, and damn near leaped from the saddle as he slid his mount to a stop. I stood uncertainly as he strode forward to clasp my hand in both of his, taken aback by his enthusiasm.

"Bloody hell, Gage, we thought you'd gone under! Glad you didn't." He took a moment to eye me up and down. "You don't look much worse for wear. Did you have any trouble finding us?"

Again, I related my experiences after leaving our first camp. I'd do it one more time, later that afternoon when Andy and Roy clattered in on the Studebaker with another eleven hides. It was edging onto full dark by the time we got the green pelts laid out in the trees behind the camp. We wouldn't stack them one atop the other until they were frozen, otherwise we'd have a few hundred pounds of buffalo skins welded into one solid lump by the frosty weather.

It didn't become evident that the mood of the camp had changed dramatically until after supper that evening. Although Jim tried to keep the conversation rolling by focusing more on my arrival and the news I'd brought with me from Harry Brooks, the others weren't joining in. Not even Andy Brenner, who'd always been so outgoing. It wasn't until I mentioned the rumor of a Comanche war party that Roy Potter raised his head with any interest, although he didn't say anything at first.

"That seems unlikely," Jim replied after I'd finished.

"That was Harry's opinion, too," I said.

"It's too damn cold for Indians to be out raiding," Tell added, then chuckled without humor. "They've got more sense than your average hider."

"They've families to think of," Jim said.

"Comanches don't give a shit about their families," Roy chimed in.

"I'd argue that assertion," Jim responded, so quickly it almost seemed like he'd been waiting for Roy to speak.

"That's 'cause you didn't grow up around 'em," Roy said. "Those of us who are Texas-born have a better understanding of how them savages think."

"Savage is a relative term, wouldn't you say?" Jim replied mildly. He had lit his pipe after pouring a second cup of coffee, and was puffing it calmly with one eye half-closed against the thin coil of smoke toying with his left eye.

"What's that mean . . . *relative*?" Roy

demanded suspiciously. "Comanches ain't no relatives of mine."

Jim's smile was coldly condescending, and it dawned on me that he was baiting Roy, trying to get a rise out of him.

"Relative means in relation to," Jim said. "It has nothing to do with family ties, nor the attitudes of the indigenous population."

You could see the puzzlement on Roy's face, with Scurlock's words hanging before him like insults he didn't quite grasp. Even Andy appeared uncomfortable with the exchange, until Tell thankfully changed the subject.

"Do you want me to start shooting again tomorrow, Mr. Scurlock?"

After a pause, Jim nodded thoughtfully. "Yes, I believe that might be best, now that Gage has returned to watch over the camp." He looked at me and smiled. "What do you say, young man? Are you ready to resume your responsibilities?"

"Yes, sir," I replied.

"Perhaps you could start by burying this mess and fixing us something more palatable for breakfast tomorrow." Then, without warning, one booted foot shot out to send the kettle of mushy beans and tough meat spinning across the ground.

"Hey," Roy shouted, scrambling to one

side as the fire-darkened kettle and its spilled fare skittered past him.

I froze; we all did. Roy was on his feet, standing hunched forward and ready to fight, and I would have sworn he was going to pull his pistol. I glanced at Scurlock, whose gaze was locked tightly on Roy's. The funny thing was, Jim hadn't moved, hadn't even flinched after returning his boot to its niche under his thigh. If Roy decided to pull down on him, I didn't see how Jim stood a chance in hell of surviving. But Roy didn't, and that surprised me almost as much as Scurlock nearly kicking the kettle into the man's lap. It was as if Scurlock knew Roy wouldn't do anything, when everyone else would have bet a month's wages he would.

"Sit down, Mr. Potter," Scurlock said after an extended pause.

"No."

Jim moved the pipe from his mouth with his left hand, and now his right hand slid a couple of inches closer to the butt of his revolver. "Please, do," he said. "I have more to say regarding our hunt tomorrow."

Roy's movements were as jerky as a marionette's as he returned to the fire and sat down.

Turning to Tell, Scurlock said, "I've been hunting to the southwest, but the bison are becoming skittish as the small herds I've shot into mingle with other bunches. I want you to go north tomorrow, then make a sweep to the west. I'll go due west, then swing north. We should rendezvous somewhere close to a sharp ridge running west to east by early afternoon, unless of course we've run into a sizable herd that fails to take flight."

"You mean get a stand?"

"Precisely, although I'd be satisfied if you managed to shoot even one or two head."

Tell's face reddened in the pulsating light of the fire. Jim looked at Roy, then shifted his attention to Andy. "You'll follow me in the small wagon, of course, and pick up whatever skins I leave for you."

"All right," Andy replied flatly.

"Excellent. Now I suggest we all turn in. Tomorrow promises warmer weather, if I'm reading our breezes correctly. It will make the trails slushy and travel difficult." He took a moment to knock the dottle from his pipe, then rose and made his way to the tent.

Someone whispered, "You son of a bitch," and I looked around to see who it was, and was surprised as hell when I realized it was Andy.

CHAPTER EIGHTEEN

We seemed to settle into an uneasy alliance over the next couple of weeks. As often as not, Roy would keep his distance from the fire at night, coming in only long enough to fill his cup and plate before wandering off into the darkness to eat alone. Those evenings seemed to amuse Scurlock to no end. Without a doubt, it was he who held sway over our after-dinner conversations, whether Roy was there or not. Although Jim often included me in some of his discourses, he was standoffish with the others.

It took a few days to piece together why he seemed more accepting of me, but I finally figured out it was because, on the day he hired us back in Jolley, I was the only one who'd hung around to help him load his wagons. Tell, if you recall, had taken off as soon as he learned Amos Montgomery was setting up his tent saloon across Deep Creek.

Scurlock's ill will toward Andy apparently stemmed from that evening, when Andy elected to stay at Montgomery's instead of returning to camp with me, although what the hell it mattered at that point is beyond me. As far as his excessive animosity toward Roy, that was a mystery to all of us — especially Roy.

On the surface, everything seemed calm enough. We'd roll out of our blankets before first light in the morning and dig into our assigned tasks without complaint, but we all knew the peace wouldn't last. It was like an expensive lamp perched on the edge of a table. Sooner or later, you knew something would jolt it over the side. Two weeks after my return, it happened.

The weather had continued cold, with brief periods of snow between days of sun but no real warmth. We were still stacking our hides back in the trees, waiting for the snow to melt before we hauled them out and pegged them down to dry. My labors had eased considerably because of this — flipping hides so that neither side remained on the ground too long had taken up a large part of my days — but I was still in charge of the camp, which included not only fixing the meals, but cleaning up afterward. I'd been down to the creek with a bucket and an ax, the latter to bust through the ice, and missed the beginning of the argument, but I could tell something was up as soon as I got back. Jim was watching Roy like he would a rabid dog, while Roy glared back with murder in his eyes. Tell's gaze was moving worriedly between them, while Andy sat leaning slightly forward as if thinking he should do something but not knowing what it was.

"What's going on?" I whispered as I lowered myself and my bucket down next to Tell.

"This . . . this son of —" Roy sputtered.

"Careful, Potter," Scurlock cautioned.

"Careful, my ass. That's the stupidest goddamn thing I've ever heard."

I glanced at Tell, but he only shook his head.

"What's crazy?" I asked.

"That the world is moving," Roy said.

"Surely you are not so uneducated as to believe the sun revolves around the earth, are you?" Jim asked.

"Then what's that I see coming up in the east every morning? It sure as hell ain't the moon."

"It's the earth, concluding its daily orbit." A smile flitted briefly across Scurlock's lips. "It spins, as well."

"What spins?" Roy asked suspiciously.

"The earth. It spins like a child's top. Scientific journals estimate its speed at the equator at approximately 24,000 miles every day, hence twenty-four hours in a day . . . more or less."

Roy's nostrils flared. "That's a goddamn lie, just like that gravy shit you were spitting out a couple of weeks ago."

"Gravity," Jim corrected with a look of weary resignation. He turned to me. "You've heard of gravity, haven't you, Gage?"

"I've heard of it, I'm not exactly sure what it means."

"It's all related," Jim replied, then quickly held up a hand to stave off a retort from Roy. "*Not* in a familial sense," he added.

"Not in any sense," Roy replied stubbornly.

"Oh, but there you are mistaken, my foul-smelling friend."

Roy half rose, his eyes blazing, body nearly trembling with rage. I braced myself for what had to come — guns, fists, or knives. But then Roy did the unexpected, and eased back to his seat with a spurious grin.

"What'd you expect?" he taunted Scurlock. "Us lowly skinners being the children of monkeys."

That was from a discussion several evenings earlier, with Scurlock taking Darwin's side in the argument over evolution. Jim's contention was that Darwinism in fact *didn't* support the belief that humans were descended from apes, as Potter and so many others took his thesis to mean, but that ape and man had derived from a common nucleus, before developing their own separate lineages. Although Jim had tried to elicit my support in the debate, I'd pleaded ignorance on the subject, and a desire to remain outside the fray.

Gravity was another point of contention that had flared up around the fire some nights back. Although I was curious about the theory, I didn't anticipate covering much new ground that evening. You could tell from the way Roy was leaning forward so eagerly that he'd come up with some fresh arguments of his own.

"You ever see a bucking horse start to spin, Scurlock?"

"*Mister* Scurlock. I am still your employer."

"You ever see one?" Roy persisted, keeping his nose to the scent. "You don't get throwed toward the center when you lose your seat. You get throwed out."

"And down," Scurlock amended. "That, my friend, is gravity."

"That, my friend, is getting bucked off and hitting the ground. Hell's bells, if we were traveling as fast as you claim, a man'd find himself in the next county between losing his saddle and hitting grass."

"Seems like if we were moving as fast as you say, Mr. Scurlock, we'd all get throwed clean off the planet," Andy added tentatively. "I reckon the lucky ones might grab onto something like the moon, but the rest of us would go bouncing off into stars."

"Oh, no," Roy sneered. "Not anymore. Now, before this Isaac Newton fella discovered gravity, that might've happened. Hell, before he got whopped on the head with an apple, we were all just floating along over the earth like angels, or magpies. Didn't even need boots. Ain't that right, *Mister* Scurlock?"

Jim's head tipped back in hearty laughter. "No, that's not what I said, although it's one of the more colorful interpretations of Newton's Law of Gravity that I've heard. To put it in more simplistic terms that you might understand, Sir Isaac Newton's discovery of gravity was no different than, say, Columbus's discovery of the Americas. The land mass we inhabit today has always been here, Potter, as has the fauna we're so accustomed to . . . the red man, the panther, bison, that you still quaintly refer to as buffalo, despite my efforts to clarify its correct classification. Christopher Columbus merely discovered its existence, as Newton did with gravity. He made us aware of its presence, as Columbus did with the New World, and as I dare say you might *not,* if you ever discover the uses of a bar of soap and some hot water."

Lordy, but Scurlock was pushing him hard that night. Roy jerked as if stung, and I recall my own head coming up sharply. Roy's sanitation was a subject Scurlock seemed to come back to time and again, although he stunk no worse than any of us — Jim included. Pushing to his feet, Roy stalked into the darkness beyond the wagons, a string of curses trailing behind him like black smoke from a locomotive's stack.

"Hell, Mr. Scurlock, it's winter," Tell said quietly. "I reckon we're all pretty ripe by now. Hard not to be, handling green hides and raw meat day after day. But it just ain't practical to take a bath when you'd have to break ice to reach water."

"I am aware of our situation, Mr. Tellis, but Potter's stench is of a deeper nature. It is the kind that emanates from a decaying soul."

"How do you figure that?" Andy demanded.

"Experience, Mr. Brenner. I've seen his kind before, served alongside them on two continents. My God, man, can't you smell it?"

"I don't smell nothing coming off of him that I don't smell off of you, or any of the rest of us."

Scurlock looked at me. "What about you, Gage? Can't you sense the man's weaknesses, his cowardice?"

I shook my head. "He's always been snappish, but I've never seen him shy away from work."

"I've never seen any evidence of cowardness, either," Tell said. "And I've worked with the man since early last summer."

"Then, gentlemen, you have never stood beside his kind in the face of lancers."

"Lancers?" I echoed, but in the silence that followed, it quickly became apparent Scurlock had no intention of clarifying either his opinion of Roy or his choice of words.

Rising, he said, "Goodnight, gentlemen. I would suggest you not spend too much time trying to analyze my opinion of Mr. Potter's character. As long as I am in charge, I shall run this camp as I think best, and that includes guarding against our weakest link."

With that he turned and walked away. Not a one of us spoke until he entered his tent and lit the lantern that he kept inside — and here I guess I should explain that Scurlock was the only one of us who used that big tent regularly anymore. The rest of us slept outdoors, either under the shelter of a couple of primitive lean-tos covered with buffalo hides if the weather promised more snow, or close to the fire if the skies were clear and cold.

We sat there in silence for a good long while after that, before Andy said to me, "Has Scurlock ever told you what army he served in, Gage?"

"No."

"Me, neither, but he sure acts like he was a tom turkey somewhere. Figures he is here, too."

"I reckon he is here," Tell said. "He's the one paying our wages."

"Well, he's gonna get his feathers plucked if he keeps digging his spurs into Roy's flanks."

"Roy's put up with it for this long, he can last another month or so," Tell replied. "Next time one of Bob Jolley's hide-hauling crews finds us, Roy can ride back with them if that's what he wants to do."

Andy was silent a moment, his expression

CHAPTER NINETEEN

I don't know when Christmas fell that winter of 1877, but we figured it was several weeks behind us when a switch in the direction of the wind brought a welcome relief from the cold northern zephyrs that had been pummeling us. Almost immediately, the warmer breezes started chewing on the blanket of snow that had covered the ground for so long. You could feel the moisture on the breeze flowing up from the Gulf of Mexico, but the skies remained clear, without even a hint of rain.

The snow turned slushy and difficult to walk through, but was mostly gone within twenty-four hours; only a few patches lingered, cowering like fugitives in the deeper shadows and north-facing arroyos. Although the ground in camp turned muddy, out on the plains the deep-rooted grasses allowed the wagons unencumbered passage along the ridgetops. It was a different story with the creeks, where the sudden melt quickly transformed their sandy beds into fast-flowing currents filled with debris.

Scurlock hunted through it all, scouting out creek crossings where he had to, then railing at the skinners to follow where he led. I swear the man seemed possessed. In looking back, I've often wondered whether it was money that drove him so relentlessly, or if it might have been something more visceral.

With warmer temperatures and bare ground, I began pulling hides off the stacks back in the trees and dragging them out to the staking ground south of camp. I pegged them flesh-side-up first, to allow the warming rays of the sun to work its magic on the pale, fatty tissue, although because of the lingering dampness in the soil, I had to move and flip them regularly to prevent rot.

The bad blood between Scurlock and Potter continued like the breaking of a slow surf, spiking for a while, then abruptly waning when Roy had enough of his employer's abuse and retreated into the lean-to he shared with Andy. In the evenings after retiring to our own shelter, Tell and I would discuss the growing animosity between the two men.

"It's like the son of a bitch woke up one

morning and just decided to make his life a living hell," he said, staring at the shelter's crude ceiling.

As for Scurlock, he more often than not seemed merely amused by our puzzled looks and Roy's heated reactions to his constant prodding. If he worried that someday he might push Roy too far, it never showed.

If I remember right, we had five or six days of decent weather, with highs in the sixties at least, and lows that never quite reached freezing, although I suspect they came close. Then, as we knew it would, the wind shifted to the northwest, bringing with it the scent of the unexplored — of high plains and distant mountains, and storms filled with ice and cold. We pushed on into the face of it. Light snow fell off and on for two days. Then a blizzard, what we called a blue norther, came sweeping down over the rugged Texas plains. Confronted by its fury, Scurlock called a halt to his hunting. For thirty-some hours, the storm hammered our little camp. It flattened the tent first, forcing Scurlock to take shelter under the Deere's flapping canvas cover, burrowed under so many buffalo hides you wouldn't have known he was there if not for him occasionally poking his head out to glare at the snow flying horizontally across the wagon's small rear opening.

Tell and I huddled in our flimsy hut like chicks in a roost, wrapped in every blanket, hide, robe, and piece of clothing we could lay our hands on. We had food and water under the blankets with us to keep them from freezing, and as crass as this might sound, an empty coffee tin between us that we urinated in, rather than expose any part of our flesh to the elements. If not to occasionally check on our stock, I doubt if we would have ever left the lean-to. And then the shrieking wind calmed as if someone had shut a door somewhere to the north. The change was immediately noticeable, but so unexpected it took us a moment to realize what had happened. After a minute, Tell whispered, "Do you hear that?"

"Yeah, I hear it," I replied, oblivious to the irony of his question and my response — what we were hearing after a day and a half of crazed howling was nothing more than blessed silence.

We laid there a moment longer. Then I reached out to lift a corner of the heavy robe we were using as a door. An icy chill ducked inside, but it lacked the teeth afforded by the wind. Outside, the air seemed calm, and sunshine bathed the land.

"What do you think?" I asked.

"I think I'd better duck out back real quick, otherwise I'm gonna fill this pee bucket with something a whole lot worse than piss."

"Go," I said, and pushed the robe back and up, over a shoulder of the lean-to, to open the door completely.

Tell scurried outside and disappeared into the trees behind the wagons. I emerged more slowly, blinking at the eye-stabbing brightness. The sky was mostly clear, with just some tattered clouds far to the south, hurrying after the rest of the storm. Drifts three feet deep swooped gracefully away from the wagon wheels and woodpile, while in other places the ground had been swept nearly bare by the wind.

The fire was out, but it wouldn't take long to kindle a fresh blaze. I did that while Roy went to check on the horses and mules. By the time Tell returned from the woods, I had a fire going and Andy was using an ax to chop pieces of buffalo off a shoulder propped against a nearby tree, the meat hoared with frost and nearly as hard as stone. When Roy came back, he stopped in front of the fire, holding his hands out to its warmth while staring at the wagon where we knew Scurlock had retreated after losing his tent.

"What do you think?" he asked softly.

"Maybe he froze to death," Andy suggested, also in a low voice.

"I doubt it," Roy replied glumly.

Then, before anyone could speak, a shot rolled in from the north, far off but traveling clearly in the brittle air. A thump from the Deere was quickly followed by a curse. Half a minute later, Jim Scurlock dropped to the ground behind the wagon. He looked like hell, to be honest. Bewhiskered and red-eyed, his face haggard with weariness, hair like an abandoned bird's nest fallen to earth. His gaze moved over the crew, then he took a step forward and his hand slid up to grasp the revolver holstered at his side, making me wonder if he'd even removed it during the storm.

"Where did that rifle shot come from?"

Tell tipped his head in the direction of the report. "Sounded like it might've been a few miles away," he said. "Sound carries in this kind of cold."

"Carried or not, this is my range. I won't have others hunting it."

Tell and I exchanged glances. No one man owned the buffalo ranges. Hiders were free to roam where they pleased, and if another outfit was already there, it was just plain tough luck for them. If Scurlock had been hunting as long as he claimed, he should have known that. Or maybe he did, and just didn't care.

"Gage, you and Tell saddle your horses. Andy, saddle mine." He glanced at Roy, and I thought for a moment he was going to bark out a few more commands. Then a look of utter disdain crossed his face and he stalked to his collapsed tent and began searching under the snow for the flap.

Roy's lips thinned to two cold, hard lines. Then he also walked away. Tell, Andy, and I walked out to where the livestock was pawing at the snow for grass. My horse, in case you're wondering, was the pack animal Scurlock had left with me at our first camp, the little bay gelding called Poky. There was no extra saddle, and I had to make do with a blanket thrown over the gelding's back, then cinched down with a girth strap from one of the harnesses for the mules. When we got back to camp I dug my revolver and carbine from the lean-to, strapping the Joslyn around the outside of my heavy coat and slipping the Spencer's scabbard strap over my shoulder with the shooting bag that held its extra ammunition. Jim and Tell were both much better armed than I was — Colt revolvers and heavy rifles booted under the fenders of their saddles. Scurlock's eyes were like two icy scabs as he studied the men he intended to leave behind — Andy standing expectantly nearby, Roy staring sullenly into the flames of the campfire.

"This could be hunters crowding my range, or it could be Indians or hide thieves. If anyone shows up while we're gone, keep your guns on them until I get back. And if anyone does get the jump on you and steals anything out of this camp, go ahead and hang yourselves from the tallest tree you can find. If you don't, you can count on it that I will."

His gaze cut across to where Tell and I sat our horses.

"All right, men, let's ride!"

He spoke with an authority that displaced any lingering doubt I might have had regarding some kind of past military experience. Wheeling his mount, he set off at a brisk canter, his spine erect, head thrown back as if posing for a painting. His troops left a lot to be desired, especially the one bringing up the rear, riding atop a shaggy packhorse with his scabbard bouncing against his back with every forward leap of his cob. There was no enthusiasm in my soul for what we were doing, even though I recognized a partial need for it. Someone was nearby, and we did need to know whether it was friend or foe. But I already had a pretty good idea who it was. When the shooting resumed fifteen minutes after leaving camp, I felt certain of it.

It didn't take long to find the source of the gunfire. Topping a rise a few miles out, I spotted a small wagon near the bottom of the slope. A copper-toned sorrel was tied to the wagon box, and a pair of mules waited patiently in harness. Two men lounged nearby, one of them smoking a pipe. Maybe a half mile farther on, a hunter was crawling slowly toward a group of seven or eight buffalo, staying low and using patches of prickly pear and sprays of yucca to mask his approach.

My lips parted slightly in wonder. Other buffalo were visible in the distance, little herds of half a dozen to twenty or more animals in each one, but probably several hundred of these tiny bunches scattered over the gently rolling hills and low bluffs, stretching out as far as the eye could see. This might sound odd considering my occupation the last couple of months, but up until that day I'd never seen a living buffalo. Lord God, they were beautiful. The epitome of power and grace, no matter how awkward their appearance that day as they used their massive heads to sweep away the snow for the rich grass underneath. Their hoglike grunts floated above the land, as much a part of it as the wind and rain.

Closer, I saw a dead animal, its hide already removed, its carcass a pale mound that contrasted oddly with the snowy earth surrounding it, like a wad of sputum on a clean floor. Only its unskinned head remained pure to the land, cocked at an angle as if puzzling over something confusing — perhaps its own demise, I speculated absently. My gaze returned to the hunter, making his way through the spotty clumps of cactus on his hands and knees, his broad hind end in dark woolen trousers like a target against the white background.

"Stubble jumpers," Scurlock grated without bothering to hide his disgust.

It was an expression, one of many, that Westerners used to describe farmers. Scurlock apparently didn't realize that, despite Pa's small herd of Texas longhorns, it was mostly toiling in the soil that kept our small Milam County homestead afloat. Not that he would have cared.

"It's that German we ran into a few weeks ago," Tell said, then glanced at me.

"Emmet Strobel," I added.

Scurlock glanced irritably over his shoulder at us, although I couldn't say whether it

300

was our familiarity with the other outfit or our speaking in the ranks that bothered him most.

"Then he's already been warned once," Scurlock stated.

"Hell, Mr. Scurlock, none of us owns this land," Tell said reasonably. "Strobel is as free to hunt it as we are."

"Then he had better be ready to defend that claim." Scurlock looked at me. "What about you, Gage? Are you as soft on defending what's yours as your chum here appears to be?"

"It's not that," I replied. "It's just that I don't see this land as mine, or yours. Seems like it belongs to all of us."

"It belongs to Texas," Tell interjected, then tipped his head toward me. "Gage here is a Texan, born and raised. I'm not. I was born in Indiana. Didn't come out here until sixty-eight."

He let the rest hang in the bitter air, but his implication was clear. Scurlock was the newcomer here. Hell, even the Strobels owned land in Fredericksburg.

"This is open land," Scurlock replied stonily. "It belongs to whoever is powerful enough to hold it. I claim this range, and I claim the bison that graze on it. You men work for me, and you'll back me up, whether

301

you agree with my interpretation or not. Is that understood?"

Tell looked at me as if he'd just swallowed something he shouldn't have. I stared back at Scurlock, my mind racing.

"I asked if that is understood."

My gaze shifted to the buckboard. We'd been spotted. The two men at the wagon were standing and looking our way, and they were each holding a long gun. I couldn't tell from where we were if they were rifles or shotguns.

"Yeah," Tell said finally, in defeat.

Scurlock fixed his eyes on me. "Mr. Pardell, your answer, sir."

"Let's go see what they have to say first," I replied.

"I want an answer, Pardell."

"I know you do," I acknowledged, then guided my horse around Scurlock's gray and rode toward the wagon. Off in the distance I saw where Emmet Strobel had abandoned his stalk and was quickly returning. The buffalo he'd been closing in on watched his departure vigilantly, ready to take flight at the slightest hint of danger.

I kept Poky to a walk, my seat being a lot more precarious than if I'd had a saddle. Scurlock wasted no time in pushing to the head of what I suppose he considered his "column" of troopers. Tell brought up the rear, no more enthused about what I suspect we both feared might happen than I was.

We got there a few minutes before Emmet did, reining up in a short arc facing the south side of the wagon. Karl and Alfonso, Emmet's oldest son, stood on the other side of it. Karl was holding an old Enfield muzzleloader and Alfonso had a double-barreled shotgun. Both men carried revolvers at their waists. They eyed me silently, no doubt recalling my last visit to their camp and wondering where I stood now. Although there was no welcome in their gazes, there was no open hostility, either. They were wary, but curious.

Emmet strode up shortly afterward, and to his credit he was carrying his Sharps canted over his left shoulder like a fishing pole, its breech dropped, chamber empty. I noticed he also had his right hand resting on his revolver's grips. He wasn't wanting trouble — the rifle told me that — but he wouldn't back down from it, either, and that's what his handgun was saying.

"Good mornin', gentlemen," he greeted cheerily.

Scurlock didn't beat around the bush. "You're trespassing on my hunting grounds, Strobel. We've had this conversation before, and I told you then what would happen if you returned."

"Well now, Mr. Scurlock, I'm afraid I didn't see your no trespassin' sign. Maybe the wind took it down." His gaze shifted to me and he nodded cordially. "Good morning to you, Mr. Pardell."

"Good morning, Mr. Strobel. I'm glad to see you survived the norther."

"She was a beaut, wasn't she?" He chuckled. "Like to blew my wagons off their wheels."

"Goddamnit, we didn't come here on a social call," Scurlock said. "You're shooting my buffalo, Strobel. Worse, your shooting is going to scare away the other bunches."

Without taking his eyes off Scurlock, Strobel said, "Look behind me, friend Scurlock. I believe enough buffalo there is to satisfy both our needs, and no reason to think my rifle would spook the critters any more than yours would."

"You're missing the point," Jim replied, leaning forward in his saddle.

"I don't believe I am," Emmet replied. "I came here to hunt, Mr. Scurlock, and hunt I'll do, and only the good Lord in Heaven will stop me from it."

"God can't be everywhere," Scurlock replied coldly as he reached for his revolver, but Emmet beat him to the punch. Jim blinked at the swiftness of the German's draw, as if not expecting such speed from a man of his stocky structure and unhurried speech and mannerisms.

"I disagree with you, sir, but the point is one I won't argue, either. I came to hunt, and I intend to stay."

"You will rue this day, Strobel."

"If it's stopping me you have in mind, then let us be about it here and now. I won't tolerate idle threats of retaliation. It disagrees with my digestion."

"My threats are not idle, and they aren't threats. It's a promise I'm making to you, and time will see it fulfilled."

"*Ach nein,* Scurlock! We will settle this now, by *Gott,* or you'll ride away and leave me to my business, and you mind your own."

Scurlock stared into the muzzle of Strobel's revolver for what seemed like a full minute, worrying me that even though he'd already lost the play, he might still try to beat the German, and likely get the rest of us killed with him.

"Mr. Scurlock," I said gently. "There's plenty of buffalo around. We don't need these."

Scurlock glared at me, his eyes burning

with a wild fury. "Now you've turned on me too, Pardell?"

That puzzled me, as I hadn't been aware of anyone "turning" on him. Shaking my head, I said, "No, sir, I ain't, but there's no reason to shoot one another over a few buffalo, especially when there are enough hides out there . . ." I nodded toward the scattered herds spread across the horizon ". . . to keep us all in skins for the next six months."

"The lad speaks the truth, Scurlock," Strobel said. He was standing firm, short legs spread, planted as solid as posts in the ground, and his revolver was unwavering. "Me and my lads'll be heading home in another few weeks, anyway. After that, the rest'll be yours to harvest as you see fit."

Scurlock leaned back and sucked in a deep breath. He was staring at Strobel with what appeared to be pure hatred, his jaw grinding back and forth like tiny millstones. But he didn't speak, and after a moment he jerked his horse around and drove his heels into its sides. The gray grunted and leaped forward, and Scurlock kicked it once more, putting it into a run.

Tell gave me a startled glance, then wheeled his own horse around and took off after Scurlock. Poky snorted and threw his head up, but I held him back. Looking at Strobel, I said, "You did well."

After a moment's pause, he replied, "And what response would yours have been, Gage Pardell, if Scurlock had pushed the matter into gunplay? Would you have sided with him, or moved out of the way?"

I sat there a long time, considering the question. Then I replied as honestly as I knew how.

"I don't know," I said, and my answer scared me more than I cared to admit.

Chapter Twenty

Something had to give. We couldn't continue the way we were. In the days following our encounter with Emmet Strobel, Scurlock's rage became a blaze that threatened to encompass everyone — hell, it was encompassing everyone now. And maybe me more than ever, considering my traitorous behavior on the range with Strobel. Only Roy Potter suffered Scurlock's anger more than I did, and I could tell he was starting to crumble under the load.

"We gotta do something," Roy said one morning as I helped him back a pair of mules up to the Studebaker. Hitching and unhitching were about the only time he and I had to talk anymore. Not that we were becoming friends. More like comrades in arms against a common enemy.

"We can quit," I said.

"He's already told me if I quit, I won't get paid."

I paused with one of the hames lifted halfway over the nearside mule's head. "When did he say that?"

"A few weeks ago. The man thinks he owns us, Gage, and it's beginning to feel like he does."

"Well, he can't do that," I replied, but I could tell from the look on Roy's face that he'd heard the uncertainty in my words.

"That son of a bitch can do whatever he wants, unless we're willing to stop him."

"If you can figure out how to do that, I'd like to hear it."

After a moment's silence, Roy said, "There're ways. Have you seen that big trunk of his?"

As a matter of fact, I had. Scurlock had never made any attempt to hide its presence in the camp.

"What about it?" I asked.

"He keeps it locked."

"Maybe he's got something inside he wants to keep private."

"I'll tell you what I think he's got in there . . . money."

I hesitated, the leather traces curled in my gloved hands. "What if he does?" I asked.

"I'm just sayin', if he thinks he's not gonna pay us, he's mistaken. I been talking with Andy about it, too."

"About what?" I asked, although by that point I had a pretty good idea what he was leading up to.

"Quitting, going back to Jolley, or maybe on to Fort Griffin."

"And paying ourselves?"

"I ain't leavin' without what's owed me."

"Don't expect me to help you steal it."

"It wouldn't be stealing, not if we only take what we're owed."

I could understand his reasoning, I really could, but taking anything by force or in secrecy was stepping way too close to the edge of larceny for my comfort. I shook out the smooth leather trace, then threaded it through what we called the lazy strap, that loop used to keep the traces from sagging too near the animal's rear hooves, just in front of where it's fastened to the tugs.

"Well?" he said, awaiting my answer.

"No."

"So, you're gonna let him ride your ass straight into the ground?"

"I'm going to keep on doing what I was hired to do."

"We weren't hired to take this kind of bullshit. Hell, Gage, you gotta know the man ain't right in his head."

That brought me up short. It was an argument I hadn't considered, although I knew there were men who'd come back from the war who never seemed quite able to fit in afterward. It was like they'd seen too much, or couldn't get some of the memories out of their minds. I reckoned if Scurlock actually had been a military commander, as we'd all speculated, then maybe that would account for his increasing instability. I also figured it could make him dangerous to cross. Still, no matter what the man's mental state, it didn't, and never would in my opinion, excuse theft, and I told Roy that.

"All right," he said quietly, and when I straightened I saw that he was looking right at me with a flat, cold expression. Then his gaze moved past the mule's hip to where the tug was hanging nearly a foot off the still-frozen ground. "You finished?"

"Yeah." I stepped back as Roy came alongside the wagon. He called to Andy, telling him he was ready to pull out, then climbed into the seat and straightened the lines in his fists. "Are you okay, Roy?"

He looked at me as one might a stranger. "Gonna be," he replied. Then Andy came over and climbed up the front wheel to Roy's side. Scurlock and Tell rode up, Jim with his Sharps resting across his saddle-bows.

"We'll be hunting maybe five degrees south of due west today, boys. Don't be far behind when I start shooting."

"Where do you want me?" Tell asked.

"I want you moving out due west from here. We'll see what we can find, but if the land is shot out, we'll move north." He fixed me with a hard stare. "Right over the top of anyone who tries to stand in our way."

He meant Emmet Strobel and his crew. We all knew it, but no one said anything. We hadn't heard any shooting from that direction in several days, and I was hoping the stocky German had moved on.

Without being told to do so, Roy shook his lines out along the mules' backs and took off at a brisk trot. Almost automatically, Jim and Tell heeled their mounts after the wagon. I stood where I was, watching them ride away and thinking about what Roy had said about collecting his wages . . . one way or another. I felt uneasy, but didn't know what I could do about it. I walked back to the fire to get some dough rising and beans soaking for the evening's meal. After that I took the bucksaw back into the trees and cut some more firewood into suitable lengths. We were starting to run short of dead stuff, and I figured if we didn't move camp to a new location soon, I was going to have to start wandering the hills like some sodbuster's wife, looking for buffalo chips to burn our meals over.

Around midmorning I heard shooting way off to the west. First a solitary report, then half an hour later a string of maybe eight or ten slow shots. I didn't think anything of it at the time. I'd gotten to a point by then where I could identify the two rifles by their sound; Scurlock's Sharps had a deeper, more resonant note, like the rumble of distant thunder, while Tell's rolling block seemed to arrive in camp with a tapering growl. What I was hearing that morning was the echo of Scurlock's rifle, the shots coming several minutes apart as he carefully picked out his targets and dropped them one after the other. Jim was proud of his shooting, and the fact that over half the buffalo he shot were one-shot kills, whereas Tell generally took two, and sometimes three, to bring one of the big brutes down permanently. It was naturally something Scurlock liked to bring up from time to time, to make sure nobody forgot who was the curliest wolf in the pack.

It was about an hour later and I'd just come in with another armload of wood that I'd dumped close to the fire when my ears caught the rapid pounding of hooves. Traveling like that announced trouble in any situation, and I wasted no time sliding my revolver around where I could get to it in a hurry. Grabbing the Spencer and shooting bag with its extra ammunition, I hustled over to the John Deere. If it was a shooting scrape coming my way, I'd quick crawl inside the wagon box where I'd have some elevation, not to mention heavy sideboards and thick buffalo hides I could hunker down behind.

A few minutes later I spotted a pair of horses coming in from the west. I recognized Jim's tall gray and Tell's equally leggy sorrel right away. I also recognized Andy Brenner astride the sorrel by the deep burgundy of his mackinaw. A second glance confirmed that Roy Potter was riding Scurlock's gray.

They hammered into camp without slowing until they were almost on top of the fire. Andy hauled back on his reins first, his horse throwing dirt and half-frozen chunks of mud into the flames. Leaping from Scurlock's gray, Roy led the animal over to where I was standing and looped the reins through the Deere's spokes.

"Best grab your horse, Gage," he said excitedly.

"What happened?"

"Comanches got Tell and Scurlock. They

damn near got me and Andy, too."

I looked — who wouldn't? — but the rolling plains to the west were empty. It was no more than I expected. Andy was over by the edge of the mesquites, where he'd loosened the halter rope from the saddle's bindings to better secure Tell's sorrel.

"Is that right?" I asked him.

Andy paused. His gaze darted briefly to Roy, then came back to me. "That's right, and we'd better scramble quick, before they show up here."

"How many were there?"

Again that quick shifting of his gaze, then he shook his head. "I didn't see 'em, but Roy says there were at least a dozen."

"Could've been more than that," Roy added.

"Or less?" I asked.

Already striding across the camp toward Scurlock's wall tent, Roy jerked to an abrupt halt. "More, less, it doesn't matter. Me'n Andy are heading for Jolley as fast as them two nags can carry us. If you're smart, you'll come with us, but it's your decision." Then he continued on his way.

"Did you see them?" I asked Andy. "Jim and Tell, I mean."

"I saw them," Andy said, then hesitated. "I saw Scurlock, anyway. Roy said Tell went over the side of a bluff, but that he's dead, too. I'd stayed behind to skin a bull Scurlock shot earlier, and wasn't there when the Comanches jumped 'em."

"How far away were you?"

"Probably a mile or so. Close enough to hear the shooting, too far away in those hills to see anything."

Roy had already disappeared into Scurlock's tent. Now he poked his head out. "Get the mules, Andy. We'll take them with us."

"Wait a minute," I protested.

"No, there ain't no waiting to it. We're getting out of here quick as we can. If you want to stay behind and become wolf bait, that's up to you, but there's no point letting any Comanch' have those mules."

Roy ducked back into the tent before I could reply, and Andy took off for where I'd picketed the extra mules downstream.

"Where are the two mules you had with you?" I called after Andy.

His step seemed to catch, then he pushed on. "I reckon the Comanches got 'em."

"They took the mules but left the horses?"

A violent crash from inside the tent nearly drowned out my words. Roy probably didn't hear them, but I suspect Andy did. He didn't stop or acknowledge them, though. I walked over to the fire, standing with my back to the trees so that when Andy returned and Roy emerged from the tent, I'd have both of them in front of me. Not that I knew what I planned to do. I felt certain at least Roy was lying, but I didn't have any proof of it. And what could I do if I did? At that moment, what seemed most important was keeping my own hide intact.

Andy came back with four of the six mules left in camp — two lead ropes in each hand — and tied them to the Deere's wheels. Before he had the last rope knotted, Roy popped out of the tent with a huge grin splitting his face. He held a flat tin box above his head.

"Got it!"

"Got what?" I asked.

"Our money. Come on and grab your share."

"That ain't our money."

"Yeah, then whose is it?"

"It belongs to Mr. Scurlock."

The triumphant look on Roy's face seemed to crumble, peeling away to reveal an angry visage and a dangerous glint to his narrowed eyes. "*Mister* Scurlock? That jackass son of a bitch is dead, Pardell. Get that hammered into your skull. These are our wages now, and we're taking it all. The mules, too." He lowered the box and shifted it to his left hand, freeing his right, which hovered close to his revolver.

"Come on, Roy," Andy said placatingly. "Gage is just confused, like we were when it first happened."

"I ain't never been confused about this money."

"Well, Gage is, but he doesn't mean no harm. Why don't you pack us some grub to take along, while I go bring in the other mules." He looked at me. "You too, Gage. Get Poky, and let's all three of us get outta here."

After a long pause, I shook my head. "No, I think I'll stay."

Andy's surprised, "Stay?" and Roy's disgruntled, "Damned fool kid!" came at me from both sides and at the same instant, the words kind of stumbling over one another in the process. Andy followed up with, "Gage, you'll be dead before nightfall if those Comanches come this way."

"I'll risk it," I said.

"It's your call, Pardell, but we're taking the mules," Roy said. "That bay horse, too."

"No, not Poky."

"Yeah, Poky. We ain't leaving behind anything that'd help a goddamn redskin."

I shifted around to face Roy, Andy quartered behind me maybe thirty feet away. I was gambling he wouldn't involve himself in whatever was about to happen between Roy and me, and hoped I'd read him right.

"Poky stays," I said flatly, then let the Spencer I'd been holding by the forearm slide down my hand until I gripped it at the wrist, my thumb firm on the carbine's side hammer. Although the muzzle was still pointed toward the ground, the implication was clear enough. Andy spoke first.

"Let him have the horse, Roy."

"It ain't his decision to make," I said.

I could see doubt rising in Roy's face, and for the first time realized there were benefits to a reputation as a gunman. What had happened on the Flat last fall when I killed Chip Moore and Lee Walker was serving me well there on the buffalo range.

"What's one more horse matter?" Andy asked.

"All right." A taut smile played across Roy's face. He held the tin box up where we could all see it. "But this stays with me'n Andy. Ain't that right, Pardell?"

After a second's hesitation, I shrugged. "It ain't mine. If you steal it, it'll be from Jim Scurlock or his heirs."

Roy gave Andy an uncertain look.

"His kin," Andy explained.

"What if he ain't got no kin?"

"Then I reckon it belongs to whoever finds it," Andy replied, and Roy's smile stretched toward his ears.

"You got anything else to say, Pardell?"

I shook my head.

Maybe you think I should have put a stop to their theft. Maybe you figure if I was any kind of a real man, I'd have called a halt to their proposed flight. Or that I should have insisted on an investigation into what really happened to Jim Scurlock and Ralph Tellis. To anyone who feels that way, I'll say this: Those are easy assumptions to embrace from the comfort of an easy chair. I also say this, and I say it without qualm: I don't believe for one minute your decision would have been any different, any *nobler,* than my own. My life was on the line out there, from Roy if not from both of them, and my sole concern was to hang onto it until they were gone.

Roy studied me a moment longer, then nodded his satisfaction.

"Get those other two mules," he told Andy, and Andy took off looking relieved.

After pegging me with a final contemptuous glance, Roy tucked the flat box inside his shirt and started putting together food for the long ride back to Jolley. He worked fast and efficiently, but never took his eyes off me for more than a few seconds at a time. I was careful not to make any sudden or unnecessary moves, but I didn't lower my guard or the Spencer, and I kept my thumb on the hammer the whole time I stood there, my finger resting lightly on the trigger.

It took only minutes to prepare for the trail. Andy put the harness on the mules to keep the expensive leather rigging with them, but didn't hitch the animals together. Roy crammed their saddlebags with food and extra ammunition, then strapped his and Andy's bedrolls behind their respective mounts. When they were ready, Roy climbed into the gray's saddle and rode a little ways out onto the sloping plain south of camp. That was the first time I noticed he had Jim's Sharps in the scabbard under his right leg, his own Winchester tied behind the saddle. The boot on Tell's sorrel was empty, and I wondered what had happened to his Remington.

Andy pulled himself on deck, then gave me a final, worried look as he straightened his reins along the sorrel's neck. "You sure you don't want to come with us, Gage?"

"I'm sure."

He glanced at Roy, then back to me, and I

thought for a minute he was going to say something else.

Then Roy called, "Let's ride, Andy. We ain't got all day."

Andy nodded and swallowed, his demeanor that of someone saying *adios* to a man dying of some horrible disease. "Good luck, Gage."

"I think you'll need it more than I will, Andy."

My response seemed to puzzle him, and I wondered again just how much he knew about what had really happened on the range that morning with Jim and Tell. Touching his hat brim, he muttered a final goodbye, then rode over to loosen the halter ropes on the mules, before hazing them toward where Roy waited. They headed southeast, toward Jolley, the mules in a tight bunch before them. I watched until they disappeared over the rim of the hill, and even then didn't fully relax.

CHAPTER TWENTY-ONE

I found Scurlock first. It wasn't hard. Following the tracks of the two running horses led me to the Studebaker, parked at the bottom of a shallow draw maybe six miles out. The mules weren't anywhere to be seen, and when I got close, I saw that the harness had been cut, after which the mules had either been led away or had spooked and run off. The ground here, away from the constant traffic surrounding camp, was still frozen hard. It had also been swept clear of snow by the wind. I couldn't tell much from the tracks. To my unskilled eye they were little more than shallow indentations and sharp scuff marks in the brittle grass.

Jim lay on his back near the top of a nearby rise. I rode up but didn't dismount to check if he was dead. I didn't need to. The degree of violence done to his body was chilling. He'd been scalped, his flesh mutilated. Half-frozen blood was splashed everywhere, and that gave me pause. I hadn't noticed anything on Roy's clothing that would account for this much gore. Judging from the way Scurlock looked, if Roy had done the butchering, he should have been coated in it.

A shiver crawled up my spine as I studied the land around me, but it appeared empty as far as the eye could see. Five dead and unskinned buffalo lay scattered across the slope on the far side of the rise, about two hundred yards away, and I wondered why Comanches would pass up such a prize without at least taking the choicer cuts of meat.

There was no sign of Tell anywhere.

Recalling what Scurlock had told Tell that morning about hunting north of his location, I set off in that direction, staying on top of the rise where I could see, although admittedly wary of being seen, too. I'd pretty much dismissed Roy's claim of a war party earlier — and didn't quite believe it even then — but I'll admit my conviction had been seriously shaken after viewing Scurlock's corpse.

I came to a canyon a few miles north of where I'd found Jim, and turned west to ride along its southern rim. The canyon deepened quickly, with sheer sides fifteen to twenty feet deep, and that much again of scree. The bottom was narrow and winding, with a little stream meandering down its center that was frozen over. Thirty minutes later I spotted an unusual smear of color near the bottom of the nearside cliff and hauled up with a sinking sensation in my breast. Although I couldn't make out what it was, the color matched the deep green of Tell's heavy winter coat.

The canyon's wall was too steep to ride to the bottom, but there was a cleft in the rim not far away where I could climb down. After dismounting and hobbling Poky with the end of his own halter rope, I made my way carefully into the canyon. It took awhile with the scarp as broken as it was, although I don't suppose that mattered to Tell. There was a bullet hole high in his left shoulder, entering through the back and coming out close to the base of his neck. I couldn't tell whether or not the wound itself would have been fatal, but the fall obviously had been, with the entire right side of his head caved in on a rock no bigger around than a large man's fist.

For the first time in a long while, I felt a wave of hopelessness wash over me. I sat there for probably close to an hour with my carbine across my lap, staring at the canyon's north wall while a cold wind flowing eastward ruffled the hem of my duffel coat and played with the brim of my hat. Tell had been a good friend, better than any other I'd made since leaving the Flat, and I felt his loss keenly. Yet I couldn't sit there grieving forever.

Finally, shaking my head in much the same way a dog will shake his after sticking his nose too deep into the water trough, I forced myself to look around for a place to bury him. My options were few with the ground frozen and no pick or shovel on hand, but I eventually found a niche in the canyon's south wall that suited my purpose. I checked his pockets for anything that might identify a family somewhere, but discovered only his pipe and tobacco and some loose change, not even two bits worth.

Although I replaced the smoking paraphernalia, I kept the change and, after some debate, his Colt revolver. I felt bad taking it — especially after my little tirade against Roy and Andy for stealing from Scurlock — and resolved to try to locate a family to forward his possession to when I got back to the settlements.

After dragging Tell inside as gently as possible, I covered the entrance with stones to keep the scavengers away, then stood back to examine my work. It wasn't much, but it was the best I could do under the circumstances.

Returning to the cleft I'd followed into the canyon, I made my way back to the top. As I clambered onto level ground, my toe caught on a piece of jutting stone and dumped me face-first to the cold ground. I laid there a moment, cursing more violently than the fall justified, then started to push to my feet. As I did, I heard a distant boom, spied a puff of smoke several hundred yards to the south, and instinctively threw myself backward a scant second before a heavy chunk of lead tugged at the collar of my coat.

I hit the ground at the edge of the cleft, and momentum took me on over the edge. I might have plunged all the way to the bottom if I hadn't reached out at the last second to grab onto the small protuberance that had tripped me going up.

I quickly shifted around to press my back against the canyon's wall. My breath was coming fast and hard, my pulse slamming wildly through my veins. The Spencer was still on top of the bluff where I'd dropped it, along with Tell's holstered Colt. Although I still had the Joslyn, it was a poor weapon in my opinion, wanting in both accuracy and dependability. On top of that, it wouldn't be much use against a long-range rifle like a Sharps or rolling block.

For a while I just sat there listening to the thumping of my heart. I didn't know what to do. Poking my head up for a look-see didn't seem prudent under the circumstances. That shot had come from a long ways off, and if its target had been my head, it had come too damned close to believe it had been fired by anyone other than a marksman.

I gave it fifteen minutes or so, then cautiously raised my head until my eyes were level with the top of the bluff. Almost instantly I spotted a second puff of gun smoke, the bullet whacking solidly into the ground no more than a foot in front of my nose, showering me with bits of grass and frozen sod as I ducked out of sight. Whoever was watching me had to be using some kind of spyglass or rifle scope; nobody was that eagle-eyed, not from nearly four hundred yards away.

After a bit, I edged down off the canyon wall and found a place to hole up in the rocks along the bottom of the cliff. I didn't know who was out there or why they wanted me dead, but someone sure as hell did, and I decided my best bet for survival was to stay out of sight until nightfall.

Time passed with the speed of a slug crawling over a rock. The temperature seemed to turn cooler and the wind picked up. I kept glancing at what little I could see of the sky above the canyon's wall, wondering if there was a storm brewing out there somewhere, and how bad it would be. Although I'd made it through more than one snowy night on my own so far that winter, I'd never done it without adequate food and shelter. If another blue norther was rolling in that afternoon, I was going to be in deep trouble. Not that there was anything I could do about it. I was stuck down here as surely as if chained to a ten-ton boulder.

Not surprisingly, my thoughts were monopolized with speculation regarding my ambusher's identity. Although Roy Potter seemed the most likely candidate, I didn't think he owned a pair of field glasses, and I knew Jim didn't have a scope on his rifle. I thought about the men Linus Kalb had sent after me, especially the two Pedro Morales had told me were waiting in Jolley for my return. Had they grown weary of the wait? Or had someone given them my approximate location? I'll tell you, for a kid not yet out of his teens, I seemed to have an inordinate number of men who wanted to see me dead.

It was still a couple of hours shy of sunset when I heard another shot. Although undoubtedly fired from a great distance away, the unexpectedness of it gave me a start. I raised my head to have a look around, but there was nothing to see. Then what must have happened hit me like the solid kick of a mule's rear hooves, and I scrambled out of my hideout and back up through that narrow cleft. I slowed at the top, figuring whoever was out there would be expecting me to stick my head up. On the other hand, I needed to know if what I suspected was true. Finally, taking my hat off and shoving it under my chest, I peeked over the top. A curse rolled up my throat like bile when I saw Poky lying flat on his side, his head thrown back in death, tongue flopped out on the snowy grass like a dead trout.

I sank back out of sight, half nauseated by the senselessness of the animal's death, and by all the death I'd seen that day. Not just Scurlock's and Tell's, but the carnage of the hide hunters as well — all that meat wasted. But what we were doing to the bison herds was only a flutter that day. It was Poky's death that bothered me most. Why had the shooter done that? Why kill a horse after waiting for me for so long?

Then, when I turned to start back down the side of the canyon's wall, I had my answer. Off to the northwest, hidden from view from below, stood a solid mass of black clouds, pushing a thousand or more feet into the sky, the air between it and the earth tinged a sickly green. Even as I watched, a gust of wind swept down the canyon, flattening the tall meadow grass along the stream, rattling the branches of the few mesquites that grew there. Earlier that day I'd feared another storm might be on its way. Here was confirmation, as undeniable as the aches in an old woman's hips.

I think my heart might have dropped a few inches in my chest as I hurried down off the cliff. My little hideaway within the canyon's scree might have been enough to conceal me from a gunman's view, but it was going to be woefully inadequate against what nature had rolling my way. I needed something far more substantial, and already had an idea what it would be. Even so, I hesitated on the canyon's floor. My gaze roamed in a near panic as I searched for something better, something not quite so macabre, but when nothing presented itself and a fresh blast of frigid wind whistled gale-like through the gorge, I knew I had no choice. With rising dread, I turned toward Tell's stony tomb.

It took only a few minutes to pull enough rocks away from the entrance to crawl inside. I tried not to disturb Tell's body as I reached back out through the opening to haul several small stones inside with me. Then I closed off the entrance as best I could from within. Without mud for mortar there was no way I could seal the shelter completely, nor did I want to, but the reprieve from the wind was immediately noticeable, and I knew the cramped space would soon warm up, if only marginally, from my own body heat.

The little cubbyhole was not quite three feet high and two deep, but it was a good six feet long, with a gentle slant that had allowed me to place Tell in it with his head slightly elevated. I'd put him on his back, with his arms folded over his chest and a bandana covering his face. His body had grown stiff in the hours since, either from rigor mortis or the falling temperatures. I figured the latter, not that it made any difference. Desperation can make a man do things he'd never consider otherwise, and that was where I was that day, with a bad storm rapidly approaching and no wood for a fire. When another blast of icy wind slammed up against the tiny grotto, I grimly unbuttoned Tell's coat and pried it from his shoulders and off his arms; the woolen scarf around his neck and plaid wool cap with the earflaps were easier to remove.

With Tell's cap on my head and the earflaps tied under my chin, the scarf wrapped snugly around my face and neck, and his heavy winter coat covering my feet and lower legs, I felt marginally secure. After tucking my gloved hands under my arms, I settled back to wait out the storm. It was a bad one. Maybe not as severe as the blue norther that had raided our camp the week before, ripping Scurlock's tent from its moorings and keeping the rest of us buried under blankets and hides until it passed, but deadly enough that I would have hated to have been stranded out in it without some kind of refuge. The wind howled all night, and blowing snow soon filled the cracks and crevices around the rocks stacked between the crypt and the elements, adding an additional layer of protection from the cold. Even with the temperature dropping well below freezing, I stayed moderately warm. Hungry and thirsty and uncomfortable as hell with uneven stone for my bed, but alive, and that always counts for a lot.

I must have dozed off at some point,

because when I next glanced at the grotto's entrance I noticed squiggly white lines shining through the snow caught between the rocks. I stared a moment longer, then stiffly wiggled free of my wrappings and pushed one of the top stones out of place. On my knees, I peered out at a brilliantly white world, the skies clear and blue and the wind died to a bare murmur. Although the scene appeared remotely idyllic, I hadn't forgotten who I'd spent the night with, or what had happened to my horse on top of the canyon's wall, so when I wormed out of my hole it was with my eyes moving swiftly, the Joslyn gripped firmly in an ungloved hand.

Moving warily to the canyon's floor, I scanned the rims to my right and left for any sign of the man who'd shot at me yesterday, but there was no sign of the intruder, no hint that I wasn't the only soul left alive in that part of Texas. I took a moment to study the cleft I'd already scaled twice. The snow collected in the gap looked heavy and treacherous, and wasn't likely to melt off any time soon. If not for Tell's Colt and my Spencer still lying on top under its polar blanket, I might have followed the canyon to its mouth to avoid the climb. But I wouldn't leave them behind, not out here where a reliable firearm could mean the difference between life and death.

Returning to the niche, I covered Tell's frozen corpse with his coat, although I kept the scarf and wool cap with its flaps still tied under my chin, then closed the opening for what I hoped would be the last time. Satisfied that I'd done the best I could for him, I resolutely tackled the steep gap to the canyon's rim. Easing my head over the top, I eyed the distant knob where I'd spotted the gun smoke the day before. Nothing happened, nor did I expect it to. Whoever had been shooting at me was probably long gone, and likely figured I would be, too, without a horse and a winter storm catching me miles from the shelter of camp.

I found the Spencer buried under four inches of fresh-fallen snow. Tell's Peacemaker lay beside it, still in its holster. I cleaned off both weapons as best I could with a finger, then walked over to brush the snow from Poky's hide and pulled the blanket from beneath the surcingle. I draped that over my shoulders, paused long enough to briefly consider taking part of the haunch for a meal — I hadn't eaten anything in damn near twenty-four hours — but decided I'd wait until I got back to camp, confirming the truth of the old adage to never give a name to any critter you might someday have to eat.

It was noon before I reached the valley overlooking our camp and spotted a column of smoke hanging in the still air above it. Although I felt some trepidation, I didn't have much choice but to keep walking. Soon enough, a man on horseback came out of the trees and headed my way. At about the same time I spotted the shapes of several wagons parked on the far side of the mesquite grove. I swung the Spencer up so that I was holding it in both hands, ready to snap it to my shoulder if necessary, but then I recognized the man in the saddle and lowered the carbine in relief.

"*Hola,* Gage!"

I waved with my free hand. "Pedro."

Pedro Morales brought his horse — Harry Brooks's mount — to a stop a few yards away, smiling like he was genuinely glad to see me.

"Are you lost, *amigo?*"

I replied that I wasn't, and something about my expression or tone of voice must have registered, because his smile quickly faded.

"Trouble?"

"Some," I admitted.

Pedro heeled his mount closer, kicking a foot free of the stirrup and reaching down to offer me a hand up. I took it gladly. I was bone-weary tired and my feet felt like blocks of ice inside of my boots. When I was astride, Pedro reined back toward camp, warning me to hang on before kicking the horse to a canter.

Harry Brooks was standing beside the fire with a cup of coffee in hand. The others were there too — Floyd and Gimp and the old-timer called Davis, who was alternating his attention between a deep-sided skillet and a cast-iron griddle. The rich aroma of frying bacon and flapjacks and fresh coffee immediately set my mouth to watering.

"Mr. Pardell," Harry greeted as I slid off the horse's side and Pedro walked it away.

"Mr. Brooks," I returned, then acknowledged the others with nods and "howdies."

There was an air of wisdom about Harry Brooks. Or maybe it was just the look of an experienced frontiersman. Whatever its source, he didn't seem to need me to tell him all was not right within the Scurlock camp. So when he asked, I told him, everything I knew and what I suspected, too. During the telling, Davis poured me a cup of coffee, but didn't interrupt and quietly went back to his chores as soon as I accepted it. When I finally shut up, Harry whistled softly.

"Those are some weighty accusations, Gage. Can you back them up?"

"No, sir. All I have is what I told you, plus a gut feeling that it wasn't Indians."

"The rumors of Comanche raiders are still floating around the camps, but no one I've talked to has actually seen anything." Floyd started to speak, but Harry held up a hand to cut him off. "We're watchful, we're all watchful." Here he turned to peg Floyd with a hard stare. "But we haven't *seen* anything to suggest there's a raiding party out here."

Floyd looked like he wanted to argue the point, and I recalled he'd reacted similarly the first time I met him, but it seemed odd to me that if there was a war party in the area, no one had encountered it yet. I might not have known about it, but surely Harry would have, traveling between the various camps like he did.

Bringing the subject back to my own situation, Harry said, "This is serious business, Gage. You know as well as I do there's no law out here other than our own. When something like this happens, it becomes the responsibility of those involved to take up the cause for justice."

There was a lot of truth to what he said. You might ask about the U.S. Army or Texas Rangers, or even a United States Marshal, but you could have poked a stick under any rock within a hundred miles of our camp that day and not turned up a single servant of the law. Whoever had killed Jim Scurlock and Ralph Tellis needed to be brought to heel, but it was going to have to be one of our own who did it — if possible. I add that because we all had other duties as well, and Harry's was to gather hides for his boss and deliver them back to Jolley's trading post on Deep Creek.

After a long, speculative silence, Harry said, "What are your plans, Gage?"

"It seems to me I'm at the mercy of others. I've got enough food to last me through the winter, but no horse to leave on, and I'm not inclined to hike out on my own. I've been caught afoot in two snowstorms already this winter. A third might just do me in."

"Nobody's suggesting you try to walk out, but you do have choices . . . besides sitting here and waiting for warm weather."

I tipped my chin up in question.

"You can come back with us," Harry said. "I've one more outfit to locate, but after we pick up their hides, we'll be heading on into Jolley. We should be there in a couple of weeks, barring trouble."

"What about Mr. Scurlock's stuff?"

"With your say-so, we'll take what hides he's already harvested, then hook his wagons on behind ours. They won't add too much weight, and you can settle up with the disposition of Scurlock's inventory with Mr. Jolley."

"Me? Why me?"

"Because as long as Scurlock doesn't have any outstanding debts, or family, what's left will belong to you."

That caught me by surprise. "Ain't that stealing?" I blurted.

Harry laughed. So did some of the others.

"Would you feel better if we left everything out here to rot?" Davis asked.

"No, but . . ." My words trailed off.

"If no family can be located, and there's no reason to believe you killed Scurlock for your own benefit . . . and I've seen *nothing* to indicate that . . . then you'd be considered the surviving partner of the venture and entitled to whatever's left."

I didn't reply. The truth is, I didn't know what to say or how I felt about it. Yet on reflection I knew he was right. We'd done basically the same thing when Homer Thompson died along the trail between Fort Griffin and Jolley Town. That was how I'd ended up with my Spencer carbine, not to mention Tell's Colt.

Taking a deep breath, I said, "All right, but first I want to bury Mr. Scurlock. Tell's taken care of, but Jim's still out there, free pickings for any buzzard or coyote that comes along."

"Fair enough," Harry agreed, then told Floyd and Gimp to bring in a couple of mules. "You can ride one," he told me, "and fetch Scurlock back with the other. Meanwhile, the rest of us will start loading hides. I want to be ready to pull out of here first thing in the morning."

CHAPTER TWENTY-TWO

We buried Jim Scurlock in the mesquites behind the camp. Harry called the others in from their labors, spoke a few words over the grave, then had Pedro and me fill it in. Afterward, I fashioned a wooden cross from the stack of firewood I'd cut the day before. If someone wanted to bring the remains back for burying in a proper cemetery, the cross would mark the spot. If not, the wood would succumb in time, and Jim's body would likely be lost forever.

After supper that night, Pedro and I broke down the Scurlock camp, splitting the gear between the John Deere and Studebaker wagons. It was while we were folding the wall tent that I learned Harry and his crew had most recently come from Emmet Strobel's camp, and that it was Tim Ferguson's outfit they needed to find next.

"The hunters tell us where they think they will be," Pedro explained as he handed me an unopened case of knives to stow under the Studebaker's seat, "but we never know where we will find them. They go where the buffalo go, and the buffalo . . ." He made a quick motion with his fingers. ". . . they go where the notion takes them."

"They're notional creatures, for a fact," I agreed absently, although the truth was, after nearly three months on the buffalo ranges, I'd only seen those scattered bunches from a distance. At the time, it had seemed a shame I'd never shot a buffalo myself. I've got to admit I'm kind of glad now that I didn't.

We found Ferguson's outfit four days later, well south of the Scurlock camp. Tim Ferguson was a burly Irishman with a ruddy complexion and curly red hair. He looked to be in his late twenties, and ramrodded a crew of seven — including two other hunters. The staking grounds east of his camp looked like ten acres of shaggy brown carpet, and it took his men and ours all day to load them into Jolley's big Schuttler wagons. We spent the evening there, flopped around a pair of campfires like half-empty sacks of grain, all of us exhausted following the grueling day of labor.

After supper, Harry and Tim rose and walked away from the camp. Catching my eye, Harry motioned for me to join them. Out of hearing of the others, Harry said, "I was telling Tim here of your problems, Gage, and came to find out he knows of your Mr. Scurlock."

"I knew him in the Dakotas," Ferguson elaborated, then paused uncertainly until Harry gave him a nudge with his elbow.

"Tell him, Fergie. He has a right to know."

"Sure, and I wouldn't want to be speakin' ill of the man, but 'tis God's own truth we didn't see eye to eye."

"What was the problem?" I asked.

"We hunted the same range two years runnin', along the headwaters of the Heart River southwest of Bismarck. The problem is . . . was, Scurlock thought he owned the damned range."

Harry and I exchanged a glance. After a pause, Ferguson went on.

"He was a teacher, you know?"

"Scurlock?"

Ferguson smiled briefly at the surprise in my voice. "That he was, back in New York state, though they ran him out for strappin' a lad nearly to the bone."

"Jesus," Harry muttered. I guess he was hearing this for the first time, as well.

"What'd he do? The boy, I mean."

"That I couldn't tell you, though I doubt

it warranted havin' the hide near flayed from his back. 'Twas one of my men who told me this, from a village near where the incident occurred. I wasn't inclined to believe him at first, but as I came to know Scurlock, my opinion changed.

"Before near killin' the child, he was a major in the war with one of New York's infantry units, though I couldn't tell you which one. Accordin' to my skinner, he was a mean one there, too, cruel and condescending to any and all below his own rank."

"He told us he was an Englishman, from somewhere called Manchester," I said.

"Sure, and he had the accent for it, though not pure to the bone," Ferguson replied. "My skinner from New York said Scurlock was born in the States, then sent to England as a lad after getting into some kind of trouble at home. He claims when Scurlock came back to New York, 'twas with a dark cloud shadowin' his teaching credentials, although the details of the scandal were never made clear." He paused, a bushy red eyebrow rising in a near perfect arch over one faded blue eye. "I'd love to know why he left Manchester, and if he was run out of England as he was Dakota Territory."

"He was run out of Dakota?"

"That he was. What did he tell you?"

"He said he got tired of the hard winters."

Ferguson clucked his tongue in disdain. "He thought himself an important man, for sure, but was little more than a sham and a liar in my book. He was a brutal man as well, says those who worked for him, and though he promised them he'd mend his ways, they wouldn't have it. Talk's a pence for a pound, as they say, and Scurlock's reputation was already set and solid. They told him to leave the territory or they'd see his bones molderin' on the prairies before the next full moon, and I believe they'd've done it, too. I reckon Scurlock believed 'em as well, for he left soon after."

"So he was run out of Dakota," Harry mused.

"He was, and by his own crew. That much I know for certain, as I was there when they give him the boot. I didn't know he'd come to Texas until we were both already on the range, though."

"Why did you leave, Mr. Ferguson?"

"The Dakotas?" He chuckled. "I left in July of last year, bucko, not quite three weeks after the Custer massacre, but it wasn't the weather that scared me south. It was the Sioux, on the loose and riled right grand after the Bighorn fight. The word in Bismarck was that the Comanches and

Kiowas were already penned. Of course, with Scurlock and Tellis dead, I'm not so sure."

"They're penned," Harry stated firmly, looking at me in a way that said he shared my views about who'd killed Tell and Scurlock.

"Let's hope you're right," Ferguson replied. "As for Scurlock, well, God's his judge now."

We'd come to a stop well out on the now-empty staking grounds, the silhouettes of the men around the twin campfires in camp etched sharply against the flames.

"I wanted you to hear this from someone who knew Scurlock personally," Harry said to me.

"I appreciate it."

To Ferguson, Harry added, "Gage has been having some doubts about who owns what's left of Scurlock's outfit."

"I was wondering if Mr. Scurlock had any kin that you knew of," I asked Ferguson.

"None a'tall, at least not in the states. I couldn't say who or what he left behind in Manchester."

"Your best bet, Gage, is to forget Scurlock and accept what's legitimately yours now," Harry said.

" 'Tis sound advice he's giving you there,

Gage," Ferguson said.

"You can send a letter to his hometown in New York," Harry added. "You can even put an advertisement in the Manchester newspaper, if that'd make you feel better, but I wouldn't count on learning much."

I told them I wanted to think about it, and that seemed to satisfy them. The conversation moved on in directions I had no interest in after that, and I eventually walked back to the fires alone.

If Harry was hoping knowledge of Scurlock's history might harden my views toward the man and his fate . . . well, he was right. But that didn't mean I could forget what had happened out there. It wasn't just Jim Scurlock who had been killed. It was Tell, and it had come damn close to being me, too. There was a debt I still needed to collect on, and it occurred to me I had one to pay myself yet — back in Milam County.

CHAPTER TWENTY-THREE

It was another six days after leaving Ferguson's outfit before we rolled into Jolley Town. The weather had warmed up considerably in that time, melting the snow from the plains and filling the streams with runoff. Deep Creek was running high and furious as we approached its west bank, and crossing at the ford I'd used last November would have been out of the question. Apparently Bob Jolley had already realized that if he was going to preserve his connection to the hunters, he was going to have to come up with a means of crossing the stream while it was in flood. His solution was a bridge south of the trading post that, not inconsequentially, also managed to bypass the numerous businesses that had sprung up north of the post last summer.

Harry Brooks guided his wagons into the hide yard behind Jolley's store, lining them up side by side in an almost military formation. His men immediately began unhitching and caring for their horses, while Harry came over to where I was helping Pedro and told me to come with him.

"I need to report to Mr. Jolley, and I think he'll be interested in hearing what you have to say about Scurlock and Tellis."

I nodded and shook hands with Pedro and told him I'd buy him a drink later that evening if he was available.

"Sure, I'll be around," he said.

Harry and I entered the store through the warehouse. At the counter a young, bespectacled clerk I'd never seen before informed us that Jolley was in his office. I followed as far as the door. Noticing my hesitation, Harry frowned.

"Something wrong, Gage?"

"No," I replied, deciding not to tell him about my last visit here, and Jolley's annoyance with me for turning down his offer of a peacekeeping job.

Harry nodded and knocked, and Jolley's voice came through the door as commanding as always.

"Who is it?"

"Harry Brooks, Mr. Jolley."

"Come in."

We entered and Jolley's gaze immediately locked on mine. I don't think he recognized me at first, with my range-worn clothes and long hair flowing down over my collar in back and a beard as woolly as a buffalo's. Then something must have jelled, because a crooked smile lifted one corner of his mouth. "Pardell, right?" he said.

"Yes, sir."

He chuckled. "You've changed considerably."

"Yes, sir, I suppose so."

Glancing at Harry, he said, "How did the two of you come to be traveling together?"

"Something I felt you should know first off," Harry said, then motioned me forward.

Jolley studied me closely for a moment, then invited Harry and me to sit down. "Just what is it Mr. Brooks thinks I need to know, Pardell?"

So I told him the story, all of it, and it took a lot longer than I would have anticipated. I guess even then I had a habit of dwelling too much on details that may or may not have been pertinent to the narrative. To his credit, Jolley never rushed me, and only interrupted a time or two to have me clarify something he didn't fully understand. I felt almost drained by the time I finished, and leaned back wearily in my chair. Jolley looked at Harry then, and Harry filled him in on what he knew of the situation, which included some extra information he'd picked up from both Emmet Strobel and Tim Ferguson that I was unaware of. When he was done, Jolley took a moment to stare at the floor, tapping his fingers idly against his desktop. Finally, he looked up, and his fingers stopped their soft drumming.

"A couple of men came through here two weeks ago, leading several mules. They bought some food from one of those little pissant shops north of here, then left the same day for Griffin. It seemed odd at the time that they didn't spend the night, but it was none of my business . . . then or now."

"Do you remember what they looked like?" I asked.

"I didn't even see them," Jolley replied. "You might ask up the street. I'm sure someone there can answer your question."

"Which store did they stop at?"

"I couldn't tell you that, either." He was acting kind of put out by my questions, and I wondered if it was the time I was consuming, or the thought of the dozen or so little stores that had set up around his trading post that was irritating him. He turned to Harry, "How was your trip?"

"It was a good run, but we didn't have to leave any hides behind this time."

Jolley frowned, and I knew from an earlier conversation with Harry that on their first trip, there had been so many hides he wasn't able to bring them all in.

Looking at me, Jolley said, "What are your intentions, Mr. Pardell? Would you be interested in taking out your own outfit?"

I'd have the supplies for it, that was sure. Despite the number of hides Scurlock and Tell had taken, there was still plenty of ammunition and supplies left in the wagons. I could put together a smaller outfit if I wanted to, with just myself and one or two others — Pedro's grinning face flashed briefly before my eyes — but after some thought, I shook my head no.

"I've got business back east," I said. "And I want to find Brenner and Potter, if they aren't too far ahead."

"Considering Scurlock's reputation and from what you've told me, I wonder if his death is worth avenging."

"It's not Scurlock's death I'm thinking about. It's Tell's, and shooting my horse to leave me stranded in a blizzard. If Roy Potter is the one who did it, then I've got a bone to pick with him."

"For what it's worth, there's been no official word of hostiles leaving the reservation. I'm doubtful either Scurlock or Tellis's deaths can be laid at the feet of Indians. On the other hand, there is no shortage of hard cases roaming the buffalo ranges, thieves and killers alike. The men you're looking for don't necessarily have to be Potter or Brenner."

"I won't act hastily," I assured him. "I suspect Roy would lie to me and not think anything of it, but Andy, if I could get him alone, he'd talk. I feel pretty sure about that."

Jolley nodded. "What of the gear, then, the wagons and whatever supplies you have left?"

"I guess I need to sell them."

"It would be advisable," Jolley agreed.

"Gage is having a hard time accepting that it all belongs to him now," Harry interjected. "He thinks it's too close to stealing."

Jolley smiled. "A commendable attitude, although hardly realistic. I'll put the word out to see if anyone has knowledge of family for either man. If someone is located, I can send word to your Uncle Abran. In the meantime, I'd suggest you consider the wagons and everything else yours. The mules, too, if you can catch up with Brenner and Potter."

"Would you be interested in buying it?" I asked.

"You could probably get a better price than I'd offer if you sold them individually. If I buy your goods, it will be with the intention of making a profit."

"I've got no problems with that," I told him.

"Very well then. Mr. Brooks, would you examine the merchandise and make a recommendation for a fair price?"

Harry nodded. "Be glad to."

Straightening in his chair, Jolley tugged at the lapels of his vest in a way that informed me our conversation was ended. "Mr. Pardell, would you excuse us? Mr. Brooks and I have other business to discuss."

I stood and thanked Bob Jolley for his help, then took my leave. Harry found me sitting on the loading dock out back sometime afterward, eating peaches straight from the can like I was starving, which I guess maybe I was — at least for something besides beans and buffalo. It took us a couple of hours to go through all the gear and supplies left over from our interrupted hunt. Then Harry took his recommendations in to Jolley. Thirty minutes later, I left the trading post with two hundred dollars in cash and a note for another twelve hundred, payable from the National Bank in Jacksboro. I remember thinking at the time that robbery paid well, as I still wasn't able to look at that money as entirely mine.

It was March 2nd, 1878. I hadn't known that until I saw the date on the check. I might have guessed it to be earlier, as cold as it had been. I didn't have any idea what date Scurlock hired me on, but figured it was probably sometime in late November. Based on that, I decided I'd worked approximately ninety-five days. At a dollar a day wages, that was ninety-five bucks I stuffed in my pocket. The rest I stowed deep in my saddlebags, under the little dyed-green leather purse my parents had sent along for my use — money I'd yet to dip into, or even count.

Before leaving Jolley's, I bought a whole new wardrobe from the skin out, including a pair of low-heeled boots and a hat with a flat crown and a pencil-curled brim. I kept the Spencer and Tell's Colt, and bought extra ammunition for both. Then, with my purchases tucked under my arm, I went off in search of clean water to bathe in. I was anticipating having to make do with a horse trough or some quiet eddy along the creek, but discovered a bathhouse north of Jolley's post run by a Mexican named Santos. A dollar for hot water seemed excessive until I considered the alternative. After that I forked over the money and enjoyed my first thorough scrubbing since leaving home last fall. I had to admit the water was pretty murky by the time I finished, littered with the curly brown hairs of the buffalo hides I'd staked out, and more than a few drowned lice. Santos sold a concoction guaranteed to keep the tiny critters away — fifty cents for a one-time application — but he swore by its effectiveness, and being relatively clean for the first time in months, I decided it was worth the gamble. I don't know how well it would have worked if I'd gone back to the buffalo ranges, but I know I wasn't bothered by vermin during the rest of my stay in Jolley.

It was after dark by the time I left Santos's canvas-roofed business. The air was chilly, the sky frosted with stars. Still toting my belongings on my shoulder, I went in search of a meal and a place to bunk down for the night. My plan was to buy a horse first thing in the morning, then head back to Fort Griffin, where I hoped to catch up with Potter and Brenner.

Cathay's Café was still open, and the menu had changed for the better since my last visit. Where once only tough frontier fare had been available, there were now pork chops and applesauce, peeled tomatoes and steamed fruits, along with flapjacks and eggs. I skipped the eggs — they were a dollar apiece and hard to come by, there being only three laying hens in the whole town according to my waiter — but I ordered double helpings of applesauce and peaches sprinkled liberally with sugar and cinnamon. I hadn't noticed it before that evening, but I must have been half starved for fruits, because I couldn't seem to get enough of them. I believe I would have paid an extra dollar for some cabbage or fresh onions, and just thinking about one of Ma's rhubarb pies set my mouth to watering 'til I damn near drowned.

I was sated to the point of discomfort by the time I pushed away from the table. I asked the waiter about a place to stay, but my options appeared few and poor.

"They's a guy down the road has a place, but I believe I'd be skeered to close my eyes there, for fear somebody's slit my throat just to rifle my pockets for a smoke."

"Anyplace else?"

He shook his head. "Give 'er another year is what my boss says, and we'll have a regular hotel with glass winders, but right now, Jolley is wanting of such luxuries."

I thanked him for his help and tipped him a penny, which he gratefully accepted, then made my way back to the spot along Deep Creek where Roy and Andy and Tell and I had camped last fall. I figured I'd be safe enough there from any cutthroat who might have heard about my selling Scurlock's outfit to Bob Jolley, but with the creek running so high, there was a good six inches of icy water covering the ashes of last year's fire.

Chilled and tired, I returned to Jolley's. The doors to the post were closed, the gate around back locked against thieves, but there was a veranda out front and I crawled under there and crammed my gear up tight against the foundation. If I'd have been smart I would have stayed there myself. Instead I decided to walk back into town and look for Pedro. Wanting to get an early start in the morning, I was afraid if I waited, I wouldn't see him again.

Bannon's Saloon was nearly empty when I stepped inside. The bartender glanced up at my entrance, then threw a curse after me when I left without buying anything. I tried a couple more places, then crossed the bridge to the west bank and hoofed it to Montgomery's. If Bannon's had looked dark and forlorn in the deep shadows under the trees, the same sure couldn't be said for Amos's. There were a couple of dozen saddled horses hitched to new railings out front, and a pair of lanterns hanging from poles to either side of the main entrance for customers to find their way. Unlike my last visit, there were no groups of men clustered outside. It was too cold for that, but you could feel the warmth emanating from the tent's open entrance from ten feet away, mingled with the sharp odors of sweat, tobacco, alcohol, horses, and mules. Those, and the pungent aroma of death, carried by the hiders like an outer layer of skin.

It was crowded inside, noisy with laughter and hoarse shouting and an incessant flow of conversation. A banjo played somewhere on the far side of the saloon, and I recalled that last fall there had been a squeezebox as well. Smoke hung in tatters from the ceiling, and the floor under my feet was still knobby and uneven, although no longer covered with trampled buffalo grass. It was solid dirt now, packed down hard as concrete. I paused at the entrance but didn't see anyone I knew. Not that I was likely to. I knew very few people in Jolley. Besides, Pedro and the rest of Harry's crew could have been buried somewhere within that solid mass of humanity and I'd never know it without something to mark their location.

The grizzled oldster who had tended bar

last year had been replaced by a couple of younger men who were sweating buckets in their attempt to keep up with the demand. I heard the voices of women, too, although I couldn't see any from where I stood just inside the entrance. I wondered if the whore called Big Star was still there. After our last encounter, I would have been happy if we never crossed paths again, although I wouldn't let it keep me away.

Easing through the crowd to the bar, I ordered a whiskey and a beer, intending to drink the former first, then take my time chasing it with the latter. I downed the shot fast, and was surprised by its lack of harshness. I was going to have to talk to Pa when I got home, and urge him to look for a different source for his whiskey. Either that or start buying my own jug. I guess after what I'd been through in recent months, there wouldn't be much he could say if I wanted to keep a bottle somewhere in my room.

Standing with my back to the bar, I studied the noisy mob with a satisfied grin. I've never been a big fan of saloons, but I admit I like to be around people. Horse people or farmers and ranchers, mechanics or blacksmiths or carpenters. Anywhere that working men gathered to talk and exchange ideas, or just shoot the breeze. Even later in my life, as an elementary teacher first, then as a professor at the university level, I've always preferred the company of men and women who toiled at physical labor for a living. Their views were always more visceral than those who lived lives cloaked in academia, or the shadowy lives of business executives and politicians. Among men and women whose hands grow gnarled with time, I feel closer to the pulse of the nation as a whole.

Standing at the bar, I saw a lot more women, all of a type Big Star would have felt at home with, although I still hadn't spotted the chesty blonde anywhere. Loud and gaudy in their colorful attire, skirts ending just below the knees and scooped necklines that exposed cleavage on those who had it, and a bony plane of pale flesh for the ones who didn't. Decorations in their hair were common, dyed feathers or brightly colored bows, pins with glass rubies or fake diamonds. One in particular stood out, not so much for the frippery of her garments, but for the lackluster way she wore them. She was thin to the point of frailness, her exposed flesh as white as fresh-fallen snow, and her auburn hair was piled high atop her head to reveal more of her neck and bare shoulders. There was something familiar about her, yet oddly out of place in that raucous environment. It took a moment to place her, and even then I was only able to do it because our gazes met briefly across the room. Then hers darted away and her lips drew thin. I struggled a moment for a name, then recalled Tell giving it to me on the morning we'd pulled out for the buffalo ranges.

Jenny Heflin.

He'd also told me Amos Montgomery was eager for her to start whoring for her wages, although she had been able to resist his efforts at that time. From the way she was dressed, it seemed she'd finally relented. Or maybe Amos had called her hand and she hadn't had a choice in the matter. Life is hard all the way around, but it's especially tough on women like Jenny Heflin, mouse-timid and wanting only to stay out of the light and avoid trouble.

Jenny disappeared back into the crowd and I took another sip of beer. Soon my concentration was caught up eavesdropping on a couple of hide men arguing the merits of the under-lever modifications some gunsmith up in Denver was making to the Remington buffalo rifle so many hunters preferred. With my attention focused elsewhere, Jenny caught me by surprise when she reappeared a couple of minutes later, tugging shyly on my sleeve. I spun around with a scowl, and she shrank back as if expecting to be struck.

"What," I said with more curtness than needed, especially when none was warranted.

"Nothing," she said — the word more read on her lips than heard — and started to walk away.

I grabbed her arm and she flinched again.

"You're hurting me."

"I'm sorry. I didn't mean to." I lowered my hand. "You surprised me."

"I didn't mean to do that."

She started to turn away again, and I said, "Jenny?"

She stopped and looked at me as if searching my face for some clue to my identity. "Do you know me?" she asked, then got a panicky look in her eyes. "Where are you from? Not Tennessee?"

"No, ma'am, I'm from Milam County, in East Texas."

She sighed, and I'd swear her shoulders sagged an inch or so. "I thought maybe you were someone Johnny knew."

"Johnny?"

"My . . . someone I used to know. Before he died."

"I don't believe I've ever known anyone named Johnny."

"No, it ain't likely you knew him, not if you ain't from Tennessee." She took a deep breath, then squared her thin shoulders. "You wanna come in back?"

"Come in back for what?" I asked stupidly, then felt my face turn hot as the implication of her offer sank in.

Jenny's cheeks reddened as well. "Look, you wanna come with me or not? It don't matter to me, but I ain't gonna be made sport of, either."

I started to tell her I wasn't trying to mock her, but the man standing behind me — the one who'd insisted the Remington rifles were fine as they were, and didn't need some hayseed gunsmith messing around with them — laughed loudly and said, "I believe that's exactly what this young colt's wantin', darlin'," he said, clamping a hand roughly atop my shoulder. He was a large man, built like the trunk of an ancient oak, and his grip dug into my flesh.

Jenny's face turned an even deeper shade of pink. "Then if that's what he's after, I'll be needin' to see the color of his coin first."

"There ya go, hoss," Remington said, giving me a friendly shove forward, hard enough that I bumped into Jenny's chest and forced her back a step.

"Get your hand off me," I snapped, rolling my shoulder out from under the larger man's grasp.

Although half-expecting him to take offense, he laughed instead and raised both hands in a gesture of surrender. "Hey, you're on your own then, hoss. I was just tryin' to help."

I looked at Jenny but didn't know what to say. It wasn't like we were old friends. Hell, I'd only seen her once before, and that several months earlier. That night in Amos's was the first time I'd even talked to her, but there was no doubt our chance encounter had gotten off to an ugly start. I stared a moment longer, then uncomfortably turned away, as tongue-tied as any jack-legged rube.

"What's the matter, mister?" Jenny demanded, thrusting her chin forward like a tiny fist she wanted to shake in my face. "Ain't I good enough for you?" Then she did something I'd never expected, not from her or any of the other whores who worked there. She dug down into her bodice and slipped both breasts free of the satiny fabric of her dress, then took her hands away to let them stand there, jutting toward the ceiling at cockeyed angles above the gown's tight neckline. "You want 'em, mister? You wanna feel 'em first, see if they's good enough for your grubby paws?" She pushed her chest forward. "Go ahead, they don't bite."

A roar of laughter erupted around me, all of it at my expense, I'm sure. Remington's grin was like a row of crooked piano keys under the bush of his mustache, and his partner was saying something about how I looked like I was choking on a hunk of buffalo steak.

"Hurry up and slap him on the back, Asa," he cried, "before the damn fool passes out."

I heard similar statements from others, but paid them no mind. "Lady," I said huskily, "I ain't your enemy, and you don't have to prove anything to me."

"I ain't provin' nothing to you or nobody."

Tears were streaming down her cheeks, and her nose had started to run. My gaze dropped involuntarily to her erect nipples, taut in their exposure, then moved quickly away.

"You dirty, stinkin' buffalo skinner," she grated, then pushed past me, shoving her breasts back into her dress, her sobs as she disappeared into the crowd still audible above the clamor of the packed saloon.

At my shoulder, Remington said, "Looks

like you're outta luck tonight, hoss."

I told him where to put his opinion, but he only laughed and turned away. Swinging back to face the bar, I stared glumly at the wavering mob of patrons, framed neatly in the backbar mirror. As I did, I spotted Pedro walking into the saloon with that happy grin of his on full display. He must have seen me at the same time, because he immediately waved and started in my direction. Despite my droopy mood, a lopsided smile crept across my face, and my melancholy began to recede. But when I came around to greet Pedro, I found him stopped almost in mid-stride, his smile vanished, his gaze fixed to my right. Looking in that direction, I saw a man approaching me with his revolver already half-drawn. He hesitated when he realized I'd spotted him. Then his demeanor hardened and he took another step forward, sliding his revolver smoothly from its holster. It was in that instant, recognizing the single, silver concho affixed to the tooled leather of his gun belt, that I realized who he was. I'd passed him and his partner last fall, coming into Montgomery's just as I was leaving, but it was Pedro Morales who had identified them for me, out on the range where I'd waited alone for Jolley's crew to come collect Scurlock's hides.

. . . two men who say they are looking for someone. The way they described him, I think maybe it's you . . . Seamus Thornton wears the snakeskin on his hat. The other, with the concho, is Wade Adams . . .

Adams.

With everything that had happened in recent weeks, Linus Kalb seemed another lifetime now, like a story read in a book when I was a kid, or a tale told campside by some stranger passing through.

All that flashed through my mind in the time it took Adams to draw his revolver. I was already reaching for mine, but knew there was no way in hell I was going to get it out in time. From somewhere far off I heard shouts and a woman's scream, sensed pandemonium breaking out around me, as surreal as a man named Kalb wanting to see me dead. Adams's gun leveled on me and I instinctively braced for the impact, even as I continued hauling on my own weapon. Then Remington stepped away from the bar just as Adams fired, the column of gray powder smoke, fiery orange sparks, and spitting lead colliding into him like a runaway team slamming into a brick wall. The big hide hunter stiffened, his eyes growing wide as the gun smoke curled around him in a ghostly embrace. He took a staggering step backward, and I moved past him and fired, my bullet catching Adams square in the chest.

"Gage!"

I whirled and thumbed the Colt's hammer back. Pedro stood twenty feet away, staring to my left, and I came around that way and spotted Seamus Thornton in his black hat with its snakeskin band and his revolver with its own smoky blossom of spent powder and lead. A blow like somebody walloping me in the ribs with a wooden maul drove the air from my lungs, and my shoulders slammed into the bar on my way to the floor.

I landed on my back, sprawled across Remington's legs, and for a moment all I could do was stare at the smoke-filtered canvas overhead. As my senses returned, I raised my right hand and saw that it was empty, the Colt having scurried off to who knew where. Thornton was coming closer, half running with his gun lined up on the bridge of my nose, and I rolled onto my right side, off of Remington's legs, and raised my left hand as if I thought I could swat the bullet away before it reached my skull. I heard the shot and felt its sizzling burn in both hand and shoulder, and was knocked back across Remington's legs. A deafening roar filled the room, and at the far end of a long black tunnel I saw Seamus Thornton skid to a stop, his legs flying out from under him. Then the tunnel closed, and I was left alone in darkness.

CHAPTER TWENTY-FOUR

It was still dark when I opened my eyes. I lay without moving, listening to the pounding of my heart. The silence surrounding me after the din of the saloon — the yelling and screams and gunfire — seemed almost palpable, like I could reach out and grab a handful and toss it in the air like a ball.

I was only mildly curious about where I was or how I'd gotten there. What mostly had my attention, after the stillness, was a dull, all-over ache. That and a sourness in my mouth that made me think of rising bile. The thought brought a shudder to my frame, the shudder releasing little spikes of pain that quickly scattered toward my extremities. I felt . . . strange, muddled and detached, and when a low groan crawled through the shadows nearby, it took several seconds to realize the sound had come from my own parched lips. Then something rustled in the darkness, and I became instantly alert.

"Gage?"

When I didn't answer, a match flared. Its sudden brightness caused me to wince and close my eyes. Even that small movement hurt.

"Gage, are you awake?"

My reply was like a gate swinging on rusty hinges, no words, just the sound. The light moved to the wick of a candle set in the wall behind me. In its glow, Pedro's cheeks gleamed like polished copper. He moved over to peer down at me, his brows knitted with concern.

"How do you feel?" he asked.

I thought about it a moment, then said, "Not so good."

Smiling, he said, "I don't doubt it. How much do you remember from last night?"

Last night?

"I was shot . . ." I said, then glanced at him for confirmation.

He nodded. "Seamus Thornton shot you."

"Seamus Thornton," I breathed. Yeah, one of Kalb's men. "How bad is —"

My words choked off abruptly, lodging firmly in the desiccated gorge of my throat. I hacked violently, but it refused to loosen. Pedro leaned briefly out of the light. When he returned he was holding a canteen made from a hollowed gourd wrapped in rawhide for strength. He poured water into a tin cup and held the cup to my lips. The rim was cool, the water surprisingly clear and sweet tasting when so many streams were running thick with silt. I swallowed greedily, and when he pulled it away, I made a half-hearted grab for it with my right hand.

"More," I gasped.

"Not yet." He corked the gourd and set it aside, then touched my forehead to check for fever.

"Am I going to live?" I asked, only half-joking.

"I hope so. You were going to ask earlier about how bad you were shot, weren't you?"

"Yeah. Do I want to know?"

"You were hit three times, once in the hand and then in the shoulder, maybe from the same bullet. You were also shot in the side. You have a busted rib, and there may be more damage on the inside. We don't know that yet."

"We? Who's we?"

"Harry Brooks and me."

"Ain't there a doctor nearby?"

"Closest one is the army doc at Fort Griffin, but that's a two-hundred-mile trip there and back. Harry says the doc probably wouldn't come out here for just one patient. I don't know that he'd work on a civilian, either, although he might . . . if we could get you to Griffin. The problem is, Harry thinks if we tried to haul you that far in a wagon, you'd probably die from all the jostling. He says your best bet is to wait it out here."

"Here?" My gaze roamed briefly over what I could see of my surroundings. There was a lot of dirt, and the odor of uncured hides permeated the air.

"You're in a dugout south of Mr. Jolley's store. We carried you here before patching you up because there were too many drunks in Amos's trying to help."

"Sweet Lord," I breathed, then looked at Pedro. "You say you patched me up?"

He nodded.

"Then you saw the wound in my side?"

"I saw it," he confirmed gravely. "We picked out as many pieces of bone as we could find, then rinsed it out with whiskey. Harry says that'll help keep infection from setting in. I've been giving you small doses of laudanum for the pain."

Laudanum. That explained the disagreeable taste in my mouth. I slid my right hand up to push the blanket off my chest, but the exercise proved too strenuous.

"I'm weak," I said, as much to myself as

375

to Pedro. My eyes rolled. I tried to bring them back, although without much success.

"You've got a fever, you're real hot."

"I feel hot," I said, but the words seemed to jumble up as they exited my lips, so I wasn't sure if Pedro knew I was agreeing with him.

I don't recollect closing my eyes, but when I opened them again I could clearly make out my surroundings by the light coming in around a loose-fitting door. It was a dugout, as Pedro had said, maybe ten feet wide and eight deep, with sod bricks for the front wall and a rectangular piece of flint hide propped against the entrance instead of a real door. The furnishings were meager. There was a twenty-gallon molasses keg with several broken staves for a table, a lidless gunpowder crate for a drawer, and some odds and ends of clothing heaped in a rear corner. A niche had been hacked into two of the walls with candles set inside them to provide light without getting in the way or being knocked over. The gourd canteen sat against the far wall, but the tin cup was within reach, filled nearly to its brim with water.

Pedro wasn't there. I wondered if he'd given up and moved on, or if Jolley had ordered him back onto the range to gather more hides. The fever was still burning within me, and my limbs felt frail and uncertain, although this time when I tried to push the blanket away, I was at least able to get it down around my waist. My chest, as pale as freshly kneaded dough, contrasted vividly with the purplish hues radiating out from under the bandages covering my ribs. I stared solemnly at the wrappings, at the bright red seepage of blood staining the cloth, then gently lay back and closed my eyes.

I fell asleep again, although not for long. Pain drew me from my slumber. Like a famished rat, it gnawed at my left hand and shoulder, burrowed deep under my ribs; its breath was hot and moist, and sweat poured from my body in winding rills. Memories of the yellow jack that had swept through Milam County in my youth stirred in the back of my mind. I remembered my siblings, Mickey and Louise, and my mother's tears and my father's anger as the fever carried them away.

Sleep, or maybe it was unconsciousness, claimed me once more. Images both real and fanciful darted through my mind. Although some were pleasant, most weren't. Henry Kalb was there. So was Linus, standing in the entrance of the Kalbs' massive stone-walled barn, fashioning a noose out of a hay rope as thick as my wrist. In another I watched stampeding buffalo racing past me on two sides, while I stood rigidly as if on an island in the middle of a surging brown river, feeling the hot wind of their passage on my face.

The light was fading toward dusk when I next awoke. Thirst augered my throat. When I turned my head to check the location of the water cup, I spotted a figure sitting quietly against the opposite wall, knees drawn up, arms wrapped tightly around them. In the dugout's shadowy interior I thought it was Pedro, and I said, "You're back," in a raspy voice.

There was no answer at first, and for a second I wondered if I'd actually awakened, or if I was still threading my way through old memories and hallucinations. Then the figure moved. It leaned forward to reach for the cup, and I grunted in recognition.

"What are you doing here?"

She stopped, Jenny Heflin did, and shot me a hateful look. "You want some water, or do you wanna argue? It don't make me no never mind."

When I swallowed, it felt like broken glass sliding down my throat. "I want some water," I said.

She crabbed forward and picked up the

cup, then looked at me like she didn't know what to do with it. I pictured her throwing it in my face. Instead she got a hand under the back of my head and lifted it almost tenderly. I drank it empty in three deep swallows. She filled it again and I drained that one just as swiftly.

"You ain't been drinking enough," she told me in a kind of scolding tone as she returned my head to the rolled-up piece of hide that served as my pillow.

"Give me more," I said.

"I'll give you more in a couple of minutes. I don't want you pukin' it up by puttin' too much down on a empty gut." She shook her head. "Your skin feels like a old boot that ain't been oiled in years." She moved back to her place against the wall. "Why'd them two jaspers want to kill you?"

"Didn't Pedro tell you?"

"He didn't tell me nothin', 'cept that you'd pay me a dollar a day 'til you was well. Is that true? You'll pay me to look after you?"

"If I have to."

"I ain't doin' it for free, and Pedro's gotta go back out with Harry Brooks tomorrow to fetch more hides for Jolley."

So that's why she was here. Well, Pedro had a job to do, and what he'd done for me so far was more than I had a right to expect. If a dollar a day was what he'd promised Jenny to look after me until I was back on my feet, then that's what I'd have to pay. I couldn't help wondering why he'd chosen her, though. Didn't he know what had passed between us that night, right before my world exploded in gunfire?

"I don't have the money with me," I said.

Her head came up as if smelling something odorous. "Where is it?"

For a moment, I couldn't remember what I'd done with it. Then I did, and swore softly. "It's safe," I said, although I wasn't sure I believed it. "I'll have Pedro bring it in before he leaves."

"He'll likely be back soon. He's helpin' Brooks load up supplies now."

"Did he leave any of that laudanum around?"

Her brows wiggled a moment in thought. "Yeah, I think he did." She leaned over to poke around in the old powder crate, finally drawing out a pint bottle with the image of a rising sun on the label. "Is this it?"

"What does it say?"

Her eyes flashed, then cautiously relaxed. "I can't see, it's too dark in here."

Can't read is more like it, I thought, but for

once was smart enough to keep my mouth shut.

"Hold it over here," I said.

She leaned closer, arm outstretched. The word LAUDANUM in blue print was easy to read, but the instructions weren't. Jenny was right, it was getting dark inside the dugout. I reached out with my right hand to accept the bottle, but couldn't move my left to remove the cork.

"You been shot in that hand. Didn't Pedro tell you?"

I damn near smiled at that. Jenny was still sitting on fight, but I don't believe she could have raised a serious argument out of me with block and tackle.

"He told me," I replied, handing it back. "Pull that cork, would you?"

She took the bottle and yanked the cork and handed it back. I took an experimental sip, then grimaced at the taste.

"You gotta swaller more'n that," she said. "What you took there wouldn't take the ouch off a mouse with a stubbed toe."

The trouble was, I didn't know how much of the stuff Pedro had been dribbling down my gullet while I lay unconscious. I was afraid to take too much, recalling tales of its misuse during the yellow jack epidemic. On the other hand, it was true what I'd consumed so far hadn't made much of a dent in my various aches. I was wanting immediate results, craving that dreamy state where the hurt didn't go away so much as it became easier to ignore.

"Take a big swig," Jenny urged.

After a brief hesitation, I did as instructed, and she nodded approvingly and lifted the bottle from my fingers. Returning the cork to its neck, she placed it back in the crate.

"That oughter do it," she opined.

It did, too. I sucked in a deep breath and closed my eyes against the suddenly wavering walls of the soddy.

"Hang onto the horn, Pardell," Jenny said humorously. "It'll smooth out in a bit or two."

I didn't have a reply for her, and couldn't have grabbed a saddle horn if she dangled one six inches above my nose. The last thing I remember thinking, right before sliding off the edge of the earth into darkness, was: *That was probably too much.*

When I came to, Pedro was there. So was Jenny, shed of her flimsy whore's garb and wearing a modest dress of blue gingham. They were eating from a small kettle, and when they saw that I was awake, Pedro scooted closely.

"How are you feeling?" he asked.

"Cotton-headed," I replied.

"Jenny said you drank too much laudanum. You need to go easy on that stuff. A big enough swallow could kill you."

I glanced past Pedro's shoulder to where Jenny was innocently examining a stitch in her skirt.

"Are you hungry?" Pedro asked.

"Yeah, I think so."

"You should be. You haven't eaten anything in two days."

"Two days?"

Pedro nodded soberly. "You've been kind of loopy the last couple of days, too. Not that you shouldn't be, but you need to start eating, and you need to drink more water, too." He made a motion toward the kettle beside his knee. "I've got some stew here if you want to try it, or I can spoon up some broth if you'd rather go that way."

"No, I'll try the stew," I said, but when I tried to rise, I couldn't do it.

"Let me help," Pedro said, moving around behind me where he could get his hands under my arms. With his assistance, I was able to sit up, then swing around until my back was propped against the wall. I brought my left hand up to where I could see it for the first time, although even that small effort demanded its price in pain. The hand

383

was swathed in bandages from wrist to fingertip, like a cotton ball attached to the end of my arm. The cloth was stained dark with dirt from the floor, then pink with blood. Holding it up in front of me, I wouldn't have been surprised to find the entire thing swarming with hornets, its burn was so hot.

"You ready for that stew now?" Pedro asked.

"Not yet," I said, and gently lowered my hand to my lap.

"You gonna puke?" Jenny asked imprudently.

I was kind of wondering the same thing myself, but didn't say it. Leaning my head back against the dirt wall, I closed my eyes.

"He's gonna puke," Jenny predicted, her skirts rustling as she scuttled out of the line of fire.

"Naw, he's not going to puke," Pedro replied. He felt my forehead, then clucked his tongue. "He's still got a fever, though. Sweating bad, too."

"It's a wonder he can, no more than he's drunk," Jenny said.

"We'll give him a couple of minutes, then see if he can hold down some water."

I felt like telling them I was still there, a human being no matter how banged up the exterior, and not some sick hog in need of doctoring, but it seemed like too much effort. Not to mention being half afraid to move for fear of igniting more pain.

I won't describe every little detail of my recovery. Suffice it to say, it was slow, as you might expect. Mostly, it was drudgery. I slept, ate a little, drank as much as I could stomach, then slept some more. Before it was over I went through two pints of laudanum, and the only reason I didn't polish off more was because Jenny wouldn't buy it for me.

"Don't need you turnin' into no tarhead," was the reasoning behind her stinginess.

It would have been an easy addiction to fall into. I can see that now, and I'm glad Jenny was so bullheaded about it, but the laudanum did make the pain easier to deal with. As far as my drinking water, she was steadfast in her determination that I get enough. More than enough, in my opinion, to the point I once batted her hand away and accused her of trying to drown me.

"It'd make my job easier if I was to drown you," was her feisty reply. "Now shut up and drink this, dangit."

The only incident of note occurred two or three days after Pedro pulled out for the buffalo ranges with Harry Brooks and his crew. I'd been complaining for some time how my thumb ached, and she kept telling me it didn't.

"I ought to know what hurts and what doesn't," I finally exploded.

She gave me a hard look. "Your shoulder hurts and your ribs hurt, but your thumb don't."

I should have put it together then, but didn't.

Watching my face, she made a sound of annoyance and reached across to lift my left hand out of the shadows next to the dugout's wall and place it atop my stomach.

"What are you doing?"

"I'm gonna change that wrapping."

"You changed it a couple of days ago."

"Yeah, I'm gonna change it again, and maybe shut you up once'n for all."

"No," I said, and tried to pull it away.

Jenny grabbed my wrist, her grip as strong as any teamster's.

"I ain't debatin' this with you," she said, then pulled a patch knife from somewhere on her person and began cutting into the cloth. I laid my head back and closed my eyes, the way I'd done no matter which dressing she was changing, but she wouldn't allow it this time. "No, sir," she said adamantly, flicking a finger against the damaged appendage so that my eyes jerked open. "You stay awake, mister. I want you seein' this."

It took only seconds to peel the stained cloth away from my hand. She held it up, my elbow resting in the dirt at my side so that I had to peer down across my chest and the wrappings over my ribs to see it. My heart sank at the sight.

"It's gone," I whispered.

" 'Bout as gone as any thumb I've ever seen," she agreed, her fingers gentle as she turned my hand for me to see it all. "Bullet took it off clean as snot, all but a little flap on the underside. Pedro says it was just about perfect to pull over the stub and sew the wound closed."

"Pedro did it?"

"Him and Harry. 'Course, Harry didn't do any of the actual stitchin'."

No, he wouldn't have, I reflected, having lost much of his entire left arm, along with an eye, long before I met him. Harry Brooks wouldn't feel much sympathy for my predicament, but that didn't matter. Within minutes, I was feeling plenty sorry for myself.

"Where is it?" I asked.

"Your thumb? I ain't got nary a idee. Likely got ground into the floor back to

Amos's, assumin' some hound didn't sneak in and grab it."

"What happened?"

"What happened when?"

"That night in Amos's. It's still kind of hazy to me."

"A couple men tried to kill you is what happened. You killed the first one after he killed that hider got in the way of his shooting, but the second fellow plugged you. Twice, I reckon. I didn't see it personal, but Noah did — you remember Noah, don't cha?"

"The Negro?"

"Nigger Noah's his name, least that's what we call him. He watches the door to the cribs in back and keeps the customers in line. Carries him a sawed-off shotgun, which increases his authority a whole bunch, lemme tell you."

"I remember him," I said impatiently.

"Yeah, well Noah was comin' in to put a stop to the ruckus you was causin', first with me and then with them two jaspers wantin' to kill you. He said he was gonna shoot you, 'til he saw you was already down, holding your hand up like you was beggin' that jasper not to shoot. Noah says it was real clear he wasn't gonna stop, so Noah shot him, instead."

"Is he dead?"

Jenny laughed. "I reckon. Noah gave him both barrels of buck from a twelve-gauge. Near about cut him in two." A thoughtful expression came over her face. "They's some folks sayin' you killed a couple of men back to Fort Griffin. Is that true?"

"It's true. The same thing happened there. Two men came at me, wanting to kill me."

Thinking back to Clark's store, I realized nearly the same scenario had played out there. It made me wonder how much longer my luck could hold out.

"You a outlaw, Pardell?"

"No."

"Somebody just wants you dead real bad, is that it?"

"Pretty much. I shot his son in self-defense, but he wants to believe it was murder."

"And you say it wasn't?"

"That's what I say." I looked at her, curious. "Do you believe me?"

She was quiet a moment, thinking. Then she said, "What I believe is that as soon as you're able, you oughter fork a horse and hightail it outta these parts. If that jasper from Milam County has already sent four men after you, sooner or later he's gonna send more."

"I think you're right, but I'm not going to run any farther. As soon as I can ride, I'm going back and settle this once and for all."

"You a fool, Pardell? Or are you just wantin' to get yourself killed?"

"I don't intend to spend the rest of my life wondering who'll come after me next, or if I'll be ready for them when they do."

"Oh, there ain't no doubt somebody'll come, but you going back to face that crazy old man wants you dead ain't exactly tack-sharp, either."

I shook my head and looked away. There was no point in arguing with her. My mind was made up. Before the ambush there in Montgomery's, all I'd wanted to do was clear my name. Now I wanted vengeance, and the only place I was going to find it was back home in Milam County.

CHAPTER TWENTY-FIVE

It was another week before I ventured outside, hobbling into the bright sunshine like a ninety-year-old malcontent. My shoulders were hunched under my duffel coat, my hips damn near ossified from disuse. I couldn't see or hear the waters of Deep Creek from where I stood, which implied they were starting to recede. The hills surrounding us were still winter-brown, the breeze sharp enough to shave with, but the snow was gone. Even those stubborn little patches hiding among the trees had finally given up and moved on.

Jenny came out to stand at my side, watching expectantly as if waiting for me to keel over. Her opinion seemed to confirm it. "You look kinda peaked. You ain't gettin' ready to heave your breakfast, are you?"

"I must be a real disappointment to you," I replied. "You've been waiting for me to puke ever since you got here, but I ain't done it yet, have I?"

She grinned. "The day ain't done, either. You reckon you can walk a ways?"

"How far?"

"Out to the road'n back'd be a good start. Sooner you get your strength built up, the sooner you can pay me and I can be off."

"I didn't know you were that anxious to get back to Amos's?"

Lips drawn taut, she said, "I ain't goin' back there, not ever."

"Good."

"You damn right it's good." She looked away, jaws rigidly clenched.

Jenny's curse, simple as it was, caught me unawares. In looking back, it occurred to me I'd never heard her curse before. Not even at Amos's, the night she spilled her breasts out of her dress for the whole saloon to see.

"Who are you mad at?" I asked quietly, and expecting her to say it was me, I was surprised when she named Amos Montgomery.

"Him, and them others, too," she continued resentfully. "Thinkin' I ain't nothin' but a dumb farmer's wife with nowhere else to turn, and them women there of the lowest sort."

"It seems —" I started to say, then bit the

sentence off before I could finish it.

"It seems what?" she challenged. "That I ain't no better?"

"I didn't say that."

"You was thinking it though, wasn't you?"

I almost denied her accusation, then decided I didn't want to lie to her. "It doesn't matter what I was thinking," I said, then took a hesitant step forward to cut off any further accusations.

The road that ran between the bridge on the south side of Jolley and the north end of the little settlement where Deep Creek made its sharp bend to the east couldn't have been more than forty feet from the soddy's entrance, but I was sweating like a squeezed sponge by the time I got back. Jenny had remained standing next to the hide door with her arms crossed tightly under her breasts, still obviously angry about my tacit indictment of her choice of occupation. I can't say I blamed her. Who was I to judge anyone, fleeing from an East Texas murder warrant, a string of dead and wounded lying in my wake, another man's money in my pocket?

I hobbled on past without even glancing her way, ducking through the dugout's low door and nearly collapsing onto the pile of buffalo skins that had been my bed for over a week now. I'd felt pretty good going outside, but was hurting just about everywhere by the time I got back. My shoulder never did give me much trouble. The bullet had cut a chunk of flesh out of my hide between the point of my shoulder and the bottom of my neck, and had it been my only wound I'm sure I would have thought it horrible, but it paled real fast in comparison with my rib and hand.

After a while Jenny came in and took a seat on the far side of the dugout, her expression no less stormy than it had been outside. Frankly, it was growing wearisome.

"Look, I ain't your enemy," I told her.

She gave me a sharp look, as if waiting for me to say more. When I didn't, her muscles seemed to relax a bit. "You said that before."

"I did? When?"

"Back to Amos's, that night you seen me there. Right before you was shot."

"Ah, well, that night is still kind of fuzzy, but it's the truth."

"I figure it probably is," she conceded after a moment's reflection. "That's why I said I'd do it when Pedro asked me to come look after you while he was gone."

"That and the money."

"Yeah, that and the money," she retorted acerbically.

"Woman, I believe you are the shortest-tempered human being I've ever known."

"You ain't been so easy to put up with yourself, Pardell."

"Christ," I muttered in exasperation, then closed my eyes and eased my left hand down on my stomach. Now that the pain was becoming more bearable, I found there were positions I felt more comfortable in. For my hand, raising straight up on my elbow was best, although hard to maintain when I was fighting sleep, and that hike to the road and back had taken a lot of the starch out of me. Resting my wrist across my stomach was second best. I wasn't as apt to bump it against the sod wall that way, as I was with it stretched out along my side.

"What are you gonna do, once you're on your feet again?" Jenny asked.

"I told you the other day, I'm going home."

"To that Milam County you keep talkin' about, like it's God's own paradise?"

"That's the place," I replied drowsily.

"You owe me eleven dollars, Pardell. You know that, don't cha?"

"I know it."

"It'll be more'n that 'fore you're on your feet for good and don't need me watchin' over you all the time."

"I know that, too." I twisted around to look at her, sitting against the far wall. "Do you want me to pay you now? Is that what you're asking?"

After a long silence, she softly said, "I want you to take me with you."

That got my attention. "To Milam County?"

"I don't care a hoot about Milam County, or anyplace else in Texas. I just want to get shut of Jolley, go someplace where a woman whose man has died gets a chance to live a decent life."

"I don't know that I'd want that responsibility," I replied.

I don't know why, but for some reason I felt aggravated by her request. Especially thinking about all the guff I'd put up with from her the past week or so.

"What responsibility?" Jenny fired back. "It's been me taking care of you, mister, not t'other way around." Then she snorted. "Shoo, you can't even take care of yourself yet."

I sighed and wiggled my shoulders deeper into the hide's fur. Despite my aggrieved mood, I could sense sleep inching ever closer, pressing down on my eyelids, preparing to drag me under.

"Let me think about it," I muttered.

"You do that," she replied sarcastically, then added something else, but I was too far gone by then to catch it.

It was the third week of March before I started to feel human again. Not fully recovered, but at least able to make my way around town without feeling like I was tugging a locomotive along behind me on a rope. Then one afternoon after finishing a quiet beer in Bannon's, I walked down the road to Bob Jolley's trading post and bought supplies for my return to Fort Griffin. Although I didn't think I'd made a decision on whether or not I'd take Jenny with me, the fact that I got twice as much food as I'd need seemed to imply that somewhere in the deeper recesses of my mind, I had. I guess I just hadn't acknowledged it to myself yet.

Leaving my purchases at the trading post to be picked up later, I hiked to the Jolley Livery to inquire about buying a couple of horses, along with the tack I'd need. The liveryman was a middle-aged man with a thick beard and broad shoulders who looked like he could have lifted a mule if he was so inclined. Although his selection of riding stock was limited, my needs were few, and I ended up acquiring a pair of wiry mustangs he assured me were as gentle as lambs. I told him I'd take them as long as he saddled them and bucked them out the first morning. After a nervous laugh and quick denial that there would be any need for that, he lowered his head and promised to have someone on hand to do it.

"When are you going to want them?" he asked.

I hadn't considered a departure date. Hell, I'd viewed just making my purchases a good first step. Now I knew I'd either have to leave soon, or count on paying for boarding — a two-dollar-a-day per horse expenditure, according to a sign nailed to the stable's front wall.

"I'll be back to pick them up first thing in the morning," I replied, and he nodded and said he'd be there.

I was paying a hundred dollars for the two mounts, but that included saddles, bridles, ropes, and everything that went with them. I handed the liveryman a double eagle and told him he'd get the rest when I picked the horses up the next morning. He naturally protested, but I said I was serious about wanting someone else to take the wild and woolly out of those mounts before we began our journey. Withholding funds was my way of assuring he'd have a man there to do the job.

When I got back to the dugout, Jenny was sitting out front with a kettle of stew hanging from a green limb sloped above a fire. She looked up as I approached, her expression indecipherable. I guess mine wasn't.

"If you want something better, go grab that rifle of yours and shoot it. See if you can't rustle up a turnip or some green beans while you're at it. I'm as sick of this as you are."

"Be ready to ride tomorrow," was my curt reply. "I'm taking you with me."

Her head jerked up and her jaw dropped, and I swear I saw something akin to joy flash in her eyes. It didn't last long, but it told me she was capable of happiness, if she'd only lower her guard once in a while.

"Where'd you get a horse?"

"I bought them, two of them."

"You ain't sportin' me, are you, Pardell?"

"I ain't sporting you. I bought some supplies from Jolley and a couple of horses from the livery. We'll pick them both up tomorrow morning, then be on our way to Fort Griffin. I've got family there I need to see, but after that I'm heading for home."

"What about me?"

"You can do what you want."

She looked away, shaking her head as if in disbelief. "I'm gonna get outta here. I didn't think I ever would." Then she turned back, doubt swimming in her eyes. "I . . . I got something I gotta tell you, Pardell. You might want to change your mind about taking me along after you hear it."

"It ain't likely."

"Maybe," she said, then self-consciously licked her upper lip. "Amos, he knows I'm here."

"I figured he would. It ain't been a secret, as far as I'm aware."

"What you don't know is that he expects me to come back after you're better."

"Tell him you won't."

"It ain't gonna be that easy. Amos has wanted me workin' the cribs ever since Fanny died."

"Fanny?"

"She was one of the girls came out here with us. Back to Jacksboro, I was kind of a helper, you know? I'd cook and mend clothes and look after anyone who took ill. It was generally me that took care of the stock, too, after we left Jacksboro. But not all the girls wanted to come out this far. A few stayed behind, and a couple more dropped off at the Flat, so Amos has been short on . . . on doves, I guess'd be the polite way of sayin' it. Then the weather turned and Fanny got pneumonia and passed last December. That was when Amos told me I had to start earnin' my keep or get out. I looked for another job, but —" Her voice turned suddenly bitter, her eyes moist. "Oh, they was some wanted to put me to work, all right. Doin' the same blasted thing Amos wanted, but I told 'em I wouldn't, that I'd rather be dead. The thing is, when things got bad, when that norther blew through in January, I was near 'bout outta hope. I . . ." She lowered her eyes and blinked rapidly. "I didn't wanna die, Pardell. I said I'd rather be dead than turn to what Amos wanted, but when it came time, I turned weak and gave in."

"You lived," I replied tautly. "Nobility's just a pretty word when your life is on the line, and survival's an instinct in all of us, whether we want to think it's there or not."

Jenny sniffed, then wiped her nose on her sleeve. "Well, there it is, and it sure ain't noble, but I never liked it. When Pedro came into the saloon askin' around for someone to look after you 'til you was healed, I told him I'd do it. Amos raised a fuss, but he didn't stop me. He's got peculiar ways, though. He came to where I was gatherin' up my clothes and such and told me how he'd allow my lookin' after you, but that I'd have to pay him half of what I earned, and come back to work for him as quick as you was able to fend for yourself."

"He doesn't sound so much peculiar as he does a first-rate jackass," I said.

"That might be, but the thing is, he means it. He knows I could'a been makin' ten dollars a night workin' the cribs, but he let me come here anyway. He ain't gonna let me just leave, though."

"I don't see where he's got much choice. You don't owe him anything, do you?"

"He'll say I do. He'll claim he kept me on all those months after Johnny . . . my husband, died, and that I owe him for that."

"But you were working for him the whole time."

"It won't matter," she said in a voice I'd never heard her use before — tiny, like a helpless child.

"Let me handle Amos."

"I'm not sure you can." She looked at me, and sniffed once more. "Besides, it ain't your problem to deal with. It's mine, and I will. I just don't yet know how."

"Maybe you're wrong. Maybe you've been away long enough he'll just say to hell with it and let you go."

"You don't know Amos Montgomery,

Pardell. He doesn't let things go, 'less it's his decision. Trouble is, he's already said I gotta come back, and he won't back off from that."

Stepping up closer to the fire, I eased down cross-legged opposite her and nodded to the stew bubbling in the kettle. "Let's not worry about Montgomery tonight. Let's eat supper, then get ready to pull out at first light tomorrow. If he wants to come after us, we'll deal with it then."

"So you'll take me with you, even knowin' what's to come?"

I nodded. "I'm tired of running, Jenny, and I'm tired of hiding. I won't do it anymore. No matter what the consequences."

CHAPTER TWENTY-SIX

Strangely enough, those two horses — a buckskin for me and a bay for Jenny — didn't buck nearly as much as I'd expected after watching them in the corral the day before. The liveryman had some scrawny Mexican wrangler peel the rough off them, but all he managed to pry out of the buckskin was a few crowhops and a disgruntled snort or two. The bay was even more disappointing in his view, and he apologized for their poor spirit as he handed me the reins. I didn't tell him that gentle suited me just fine, and that I wasn't looking to run races.

We rode back to Jolley's and got the supplies I'd purchased the day before and packed them in our saddlebags. I was wearing Tell's Peacemaker around my waist — having to take the belt in two full notches to get it to fit after my long convalescence — and had the Spencer booted under my right stirrup strap. Its extra cartridges, still carried in Homer Thompson's old leather shooting pouch, hung off my saddle horn since my shoulder was still too tender to take its weight.

I found the Joslyn near the bottom of my left-side bag and slid it from its holster. It was still loaded, although I'd removed the percussion cap from under the hammer on the fifth chamber before stowing it away. The holster was plain leather in poor condition, although I'd done what I could over the winter to repair the damage by rubbing mink oil into the body, then working the stiff leather with my fingers until some pliability was returned. The belt was equally disappointing, stretched and curled, the stitching frayed. But it was a weapon, and the few times I'd shot it, it had functioned adequately. Glancing across the seat of my saddle to where Jenny was tightening the strings on her bedroll, I said, "Why don't you take this," and held the revolver toward her.

She gave me a suspicious look — nothing new there. I believe she'd peek under her blankets for the boogeyman even if she was sleeping flat on the ground — then cautiously reached out to take it.

"You sure?"

"You know how it works?"

"Of course I know how it works."

"Then, yeah, I'm sure. It's not the most accurate gun I've ever owned, but it's better than a stick. Just remember it shoots low. If someone comes after you, wait until they're close, then aim for the head. If you're lucky, you'll hit 'em in the chest."

"Sounds like a cheap gun."

"If you don't like it, I'm sure one of Bob Jolley's clerks can sell you a better one."

She gave me a dirty look, probably deserved now that I look back on it, then took her coat off and strapped the belt around her waist. I knew she was slim, but I didn't realize how skinny she was until she had to wrap the belt twice around her waist before buckling it. She pulled her coat back on. Its hem reached nearly to her knees, hiding gun and holster alike. Handing her a little belt pouch with a broken strap, I said, "Here are some extra cartridges. They're paper, but quicker to reload than loose powder and balls. There a half tin of percussion caps in there, too."

"Obliged," she said grudgingly, accepting the palm-sized pouch and dropping it in her coat pocket. "I can pay you for this, too . . . soon as I get to Griffin and find myself a decent job."

Bob Jolley wasn't around when we left his

little settlement there along Deep Creek, but I left a note with his clerk for Pedro Morales thanking him for his kindness, along with a ten-dollar coin to cover whatever expenses I'd cost him for food and bandages and such. At the top of the ridge east of town I hauled up for a backwards glance, wondering about the community's future. I couldn't have known how short-lived it would be, but I reckon if we could see into the forthcoming, we'd all be rich, and scared shitless.

It was more damp than cold as we rode out of sight of Jolley Town. A steady breeze was humming out of the south, and the clouds were as gray as pencil smudges. The smell of moisture on the air implied precipitation in the offing. I was personally hoping for rain rather than snow, but would have preferred that whatever was coming in missed us altogether. My fractured rib was sore enough that I'd flinch if I sneezed unexpectedly, or even twist my body too abruptly in one direction or another, and my thumb ached like there was a dull knife probing deep into the razed joint. I was using my left hand to hold the reins — it didn't feel natural to do otherwise — and after a while I learned to thread them between my fingers in a way that allowed my forefinger to do what my thumb used to. In the coming years, I'd have to modify any number of habits to adapt for my missing digit, and I can't say it slowed me down, other than when I accidently bumped it against something hard and was reminded that the tenderness there was never going to totally go away.

We kept our horses to a walk, and Jenny, I noticed, kept glancing behind her as if expecting Amos Montgomery to come galloping over the horizon at any moment. If left to her preference, I'm sure we would have done our share of galloping that day, but I wouldn't allow it.

"It's a long way to Fort Griffin, and even farther to Milam County," I told her when we stopped at noon to rest our mounts. "I don't intend to wear our horses to a frazzle the first day out."

Her response was a sullen look and a view of her back as she slid the Joslyn from its holster. Taking a cap from her bullet pouch, she pressed it over the nipple of that fifth chamber. I started to tell her to be sure and keep the hammer at half cock, or better yet, to let it down between chambers, but she beat me to it. She hadn't been lying when she said she knew how to use a revolver.

Keeping our horses to a walk, we made

only twenty or so miles that first day. Coming to a little creek just as the light was starting to fade, I made the decision that we'd stop there for the night. Jenny gave the land behind us another worried inspection, then wordlessly dismounted and handed me her reins. While I took care of the horses, she gathered what wood she could find along the stream's banks and kindled a fire. By the time I got back she had coffee boiling in a two-pint enamelware pot and was slicing strips of dried buffalo meat into a pot. She scowled as I came up.

"If you're gonna start grumblin' about my cookin', you can take over the chore yourself."

I smiled, mostly to annoy her, and said, "Why, I'm gonna miss your stews when we part ways, Miss Jenny."

She gave me an ambiguous look but didn't reply. It took only a few minutes to add some beans she'd soaked the day before and wrinkled carrots to the mix. I didn't complain — Jenny was making do with what we had — but I suspect I'd stretched the truth almost to breaking when I told her I'd miss her stews. Her cooking wasn't bad, it was the sameness of the fare that was tiresome.

The rain caught up with us that night, a fine drizzle that had me burrowing deeper into my blankets, grateful for the oilcloth they were cocooned in. By dawn it was cold enough that we could see our breath, and we were both feeling out of sorts as we dined on a comfortless breakfast of cold stew and creek water. The rain stopped while we were eating, but I wasn't betting on an extended reprieve, not with the clouds low enough they seemed to be snagging on cactus as they slid across the ridgetops.

I was lifting my saddle onto the buckskin's back when a shot rang out, sounding like the flat slap of an oak plank on a stack of lumber. The bullet plowed into the sandy soil between my feet, and I wasn't inclined to assume it was a stray shot or a miss. I turned far enough around to see Amos Montgomery standing on the creek's far bank with a pistol in his hand. A thin curl of powder smoke trickled from its muzzle. Jenny looked like she'd been turned to stone, crouched next to the creek where she'd been scrubbing on the stew kettle with sand. To her credit she didn't scream, but she sure looked sickly; had our situation not been so serious, I might have asked if she was going to puke.

"I thought we had an agreement," Amos called from where he was standing partially hidden in the creekside scrub. He was talking to Jenny, but neither of us answered. I let my gaze move slowly along the stream for sign of an accomplice, but Amos was apparently alone.

I straightened my saddle on the buckskin's back but didn't reach for the cinch. Turning warily, both hands out where the saloon owner could see them, I said, "She's coming with me."

"No, she isn't," he replied, keeping his eyes on Jenny.

"I don't owe you nothin'," Jenny cried. She stood and angrily threw the kettle onto the ground at her feet. "You don't own me, Amos Montgomery. You don't!"

"Didn't say I did," he replied mildly. "But I do disagree with your assessment of what's owed."

"I've paid you back, ever' cent of it."

"Not by my reckoning, precious."

"I ain't your precious!"

"Of course you are. All my girls are precious to me."

I'd thought his attention was focused entirely on Jenny, but when I edged my hand toward my revolver, he spoke sharp.

"Have a healthy caution there, sir. I suspect you've been duped into believing you are rescuing a maiden, and I have no criticism for your honest mistake, but my opinion can be changed with a brash response on your part."

"I ain't naturally brash, but like I said, Jenny's decided to come with me."

"Ah, gallantry. How droll." He smiled real smug, like folks do when they think they're smarter than they really are. I didn't understand it then, mind you, but when I got older and looked back on the incident, I saw it for what it was — a little man with a larger than average vocabulary, though somewhat ragged in its usage. He did have us at a disadvantage, though, and I suspect we all knew that.

"I would suggest you drop your pistol, sir," he said to me.

Jenny gave me a desperate look, but I'm damned if I knew what she expected me to do. Montgomery had already demonstrated who was in charge with that bullet he put into the dirt at my feet.

"Now, Mr. Pardell."

"You know my name?"

"I won't be distracted by questions, sir, nor suffer any delaying tactics. Drop your piece or face the consequences."

My mind was racing, but I didn't see any way out of it, and having been recently stung by another man's bullets, I wasn't eager to repeat the process. It's been said that most men will back away from a knife quicker than they will a firearm, even though the gun is usually more lethal. That's because most men have felt a blade's nip in one form or another, while far fewer have suffered the effects of a gunshot. I believe that to be true. Gritting my teeth in frustration, I gingerly lifted the Colt from its holster and tossed it into some tall grass nearby.

"And now you, precious. I do believe that is a revolver creating that bulge under your coat, however faint the rise. My apologies if I am mistaken."

Jenny glared at him until he cocked his revolver, the metallic ratcheting of the sear dropping into its internal notch as chilling as the sudden whirl of a buzz tail at your ankle.

"Please, don't try anything foolish, dear Jenny. I wish you no harm, but I will not hesitate to end your life if the need arises."

"You son of a —"

She stopped, her jaws moving back and forth as if grinding corn. Even under those conditions, she refused to utter a curse. I kind of admired her for that, and I could tell it amused Montgomery.

"Ever the angel," he proclaimed. "Now loosen your coat and drop whatever weapon you have sheltered within."

Jenny practically yanked the buttons off the heavy outer garment as she opened her coat to reveal the holstered Joslyn underneath. She unbuckled the gun belt and let it fall limply around her feet, then angrily kicked it away.

"Bless you," Montgomery said, sounding genuinely relieved. "Now, Mr. Pardell, would you mind completing the chore I interrupted." He tipped his head toward the buckskin. "Saddle the horse, sir, and Miss Jenny and I will depart your company."

"This is my horse," I said. "They both are."

Sighing, Montgomery pulled a leather pouch from his pocket and wiggled a couple of fingers inside, all the while keeping his revolver trained on the camp, his eyes shifting smoothly between Jenny to me. He dug several gold coins from the pouch and tossed them underhanded across the creek. They glinted in the gray dawn like flakes of sunlight scattered at my feet. "I didn't count it, but there should be thirty dollars there, more or less. That seems more than adequate for the condition of your mount."

"I just gave a hundred dollars for these two horses, plus the tack."

"Then you were fairly taken, sir. They are

worth thirty at the extreme, the tack perhaps another five. Unfortunately, I'll have to owe you the five, as what I've already paid is all I brought with me. However, I assure you my word is as good as the gold at your feet, and dare say some would insist it's better."

"I don't doubt that, but I think I'll keep both horses."

The calm demeanor of the saloon owner's face seemed to crack a little at the edges. "I won't dicker, Mr. Pardell. Thirty is lavish under these circumstances. I suggest you accept it, as the consequences could be dire."

"Why don't you shut up, you bowlegged banty," Jenny said resignedly. The look she gave me was of complete disappointment. "Obliged for the effort, Pardell, but it looks like I'm going back."

"Maybe I'll come with you."

"No," she said. "You go on home to Milam County. This ain't none of your affair."

"Truer words were never spoken," Montgomery seconded, his grin returning as bright as ever.

"No, I'm coming with you." I looked at Montgomery. "I'm going to finish saddling my horse now. I'm trusting you not to shoot me in the back while it's turned."

And there went that smile, flying off his face like a loose tooth hitched to a slamming doorknob. Before he could work up a comment, I turned away and reached under the buckskin for the dangling cinch. Meanwhile, Jenny went back to scrubbing the stew kettle, while Montgomery stayed where he was, looking kind of confused by this unexpected development. I readied Jenny's bay next, then helped her pack up. When we were done, I looked at Montgomery and tipped my head toward the discarded Colt.

"I'm gonna go get my pistol. It's too expensive to just leave."

"I believe I prefer it where it is."

"I don't doubt that you do, but like I said, I ain't leaving it behind."

"What about my gun?" Jenny asked.

"You both seem to be under the misconception that you have a say in the matter," Montgomery replied in annoyance.

"Then you come down here and get it," I said. "You can carry it back to Jolley for me, if that's your pleasure." '

"You weary me, sir." Then, making a shooing-away motion with his revolver, he told me to back off. -

I did as instructed, glancing briefly at Jenny and noticing how she was staring back intently. I think we both sensed that if an

416

opportunity to escape was going to present itself that day, it would be within the next few minutes. I obviously didn't know in what form that would appear, but I was determined to be ready when it happened.

Montgomery made his way down off the bank, skirting cactus and shin oak as far as the water's edge. Eyeing the ankle-deep waters of the little spring creek, I thought for a minute he might refuse to cross for fear of getting his boots wet. Then with a look of aversion, he stepped into the purling water. I waited until he was close to the near bank, less than a yard from Jenny's side, then took a long step toward my Colt. As soon as I did Montgomery brought his pistol to bear.

"Don't try it, Pardell," he warned, and Jenny moved a step closer, calling, "Gage, don't!"

She was standing at Montgomery's side when she cried my name, and I saw him suddenly stiffen and his eyes grow wide. He looked at her as if puzzled. She met his gaze calmly, at the same time reaching out to gently lower his arm, the one holding his revolver. He tried to say something, but all that came out was a bloody mist, sprayed from between crimsoned teeth. Then his knees gave out and he fell forward onto his face, his toes still in the creek. Jenny stared at him for a moment, then reached down and pulled her patch knife from between his ribs. Her expression when she looked at me was like something carved from granite. Then she turned away and went to the creek and stooped to wash the blood from the patch knife's blade.

I picked up my Colt and reholstered it before going over to check on the saloon owner. He was dead. I was pretty sure he had been before he hit the ground. Straightening, Jenny walked over and gathered up the coins Montgomery had tossed my way, then went to her bay and loosened its reins.

"What are you doing?" I asked.

"I'm leaving," she replied. She gave me a hard look, as if daring me to ask her about the money, but I didn't have any intention of poking that hornet's nest.

"What about him?" I motioned toward Montgomery's body. "Are you just going to ride off and leave him for the coyotes?"

"You wanna bury him, go ahead and do it." She stepped up into the saddle and pulled the bay around. "I'll leave your horse on the Flat. It won't be hard to find."

I watched her go, thinking she'd probably stop and come back once she thought about it, but she never did. I don't hold it against her that she didn't want to waste any effort burying the saloon owner, but I wasn't yet that hardened. Finally accepting that Jenny was going her own way, I went looking for a gully where I could lay Montgomery's corpse, then pushed some dirt in on top of it. It wouldn't be much of a burial, but as with Tell, it was the best I could manage without implements for digging.

It took half the morning to get Montgomery underground, then find his horse and bring it back to where I'd left my buckskin. I took the bridle off and fastened a lead rope to the halter, then climbed into my own saddle and reined toward Fort Griffin.

Chapter Twenty-Seven

Even though I kept my horse moving along at a good clip, I never caught up with Jenny, and I never saw her again. I was afraid I'd missed her somewhere along the trail, but when I arrived on the Flat several days later, I learned she'd beaten me there by twenty-four hours, leaving the bay at the local stage station lathered and still under saddle. The agent was irate about being tasked with the animal's care. I didn't blame him, but I appreciated him doing it. Too many people in that rough frontier community wouldn't have gone to the trouble.

I asked if she was still around and he said she'd bought a ticket to Jacksboro on the stage that had pulled out that morning at seven. I also asked if she'd left me any kind of message, but he said her only instructions had been that if I didn't show up in a couple of days, the company could keep the horse with her blessing.

"I told her we wouldn't do that," he huffed. "Hell, as far as I knew, that animal could've been stolen, but she didn't act like she cared."

I explained that the horse belonged to me, and produced the bill of sale with its description — right down to the question-mark-shaped star under its forelock — then paid the agent a dollar for the animal's keep.

With the two extra horses in tow, I rode over to Tolliver's Emporium and tied up out front. Uncle Abran was behind the counter when I walked in. He gave me a brief but disinterested glance, then returned his attention to a catalog he was perusing, sliding a finger slowly down the page. Then his head jerked up and his eyes widened.

"Gage!"

I smiled and nodded.

"Damn me, young buck," he exclaimed, striding swiftly around the end of the counter. "I didn't recognize you." When he got close he grabbed a handful of my beard and gave it an affectionate tug. Then his gaze turned thoughtful as he regarded me more closely. "You have changed, you."

"I reckon I have," I acknowledged.

Having caught a glimpse of my reflection in the stage office's front window, I could appreciate Abran not recognizing me. It was

more than just my physical appearance, too
— the wind-burnished flesh and sinewy
muscle, the long hair of a hider hanging
below my collar in back, my beard thick and
curly, reaching the second button of my
shirt. Nor did I feel like a lump of un-
molded clay, gangling and unsure of myself.
I think that showed in my stride, as well,
and I thought that's what Uncle Abran
meant, but it turned out there was something else.

"I see it in your eyes," he said quietly. "As
I have seen it in the eyes of others who have
traveled far. Sometimes these trips, they do
not cover miles so much as something in
here." He tapped my chest lightly with a
closed fist. "No?"

"Maybe," I said, then smiled and slapped
his shoulder in an effort to change the
subject. "How have you been, old man?"

"Old man!" His head reared back in loud
laughter. "Now the young buck wants to
challenge the old bull, is that it?"

"Actually, this young buck would be satisfied with a warm meal and a place to spread
his blankets for the night."

"That I can make happen," he assured
me, then shouted into the dimness at the
rear of the store. "Lester, I will be gone

awhile. Tell the boss I be back soon, you hear?"

"I hear," came faintly from the store's interior.

Abran spun me around and marched me outside. "Grab your horse," he said. "I want to see the look on Rita's face when I bring you home."

I grabbed all three, leading them with the reins in one hand, my Spencer in the other. I know the local law wasn't supposed to be looking for me anymore, but I'd already endured one bad experience on the Flat, and didn't intend to be taken unaware again. Although Abran gave me an odd look when I joined him with my small cavvy in tow, he didn't comment on it.

Rita was out back whacking on a rug with a wire beater. She looked around when we cornered the house, her gaze as suspicious as ever until she recognized me. Then she dropped the beater in the dirt and ran over to give me an honest to God hug, something I sure wasn't expecting. Apparently, her reservations about me had eased up considerably during my time away.

"I wouldn't have known you," she confessed, stepping back with a brilliant smile.

"I reckon you did, Boo, or have you started hugging up on any stranger I bring around?"

"You," she scolded. "Hush yourself." Then, as Abran had done earlier, she reached up to tug on my beard, although gentler than he had done. "You have grown up, Gage," she said softly, her eyes boring into mine as if trying to read more there than I wanted to reveal. "I think your journey has been hard, too."

I shrugged and, not knowing what else to do or say, made a comment about looking forward to her cooking. I think she must have sensed my reticence, because her expression immediately lightened.

"See to your horses," she told me. "I am going to finish this rug, and when I'm done, I will fix you something good." She smiled. "But not buffalo."

"No," I agreed. "Not buffalo."

Abran helped me unsaddle the horses and carry the tack inside. Then, instead of having me take them to the corral behind Tolliver's as he'd had me to do with Dusty last fall, he took the lead ropes himself.

"Go inside and talk to Rita," he said. "She has been worried about you."

"Rita?"

He grinned. "Her bite is worse than her bark, but she has softened her opinion of you after learning the whole story of your troubles. Your mama's letters helped her see you were not born a troublemaker, only a foolish youth trying to mend his sister's honor." He gave me a light shove toward the rear door, where I could hear Rita kindling a fire in the stove inside. "I will be back before you finish your first cup of coffee."

The meal Rita fixed that night was the best I'd had in months. There was tomato soup and peas and cornbread and stewed apples, and she'd roasted a haunch of goat to near perfection. The coffee was good, and there was cream to pour over a dried cherry pie for dessert. I was in danger of popping the buttons on my trousers by the time I finished, but they were good Levis, and took the strain of overeating better than I did. Afterward, Uncle Abran and I retreated to the parlor while Rita cleared away the dishes. It wasn't quite full dark, but the light was ducking out the windows like thieves as I stretched my feet in front of me, crossed my ankles, and loosened the top button of my pants. Abran filled a pipe with tobacco, studying me silently as he did.

"You want to tell me, young buck?"

"About what?" I replied vaguely.

He jerked his chin up, probably not even an inch, but enough for me to know he wasn't in a mood to dally around a subject. If I wanted to talk, he was ready to listen. If I didn't, we could either move on to less weighty subjects or sit in silence while the darkness closed in around us like a comfortable shawl.

Taking a deep breath, I started talking, and I didn't stop for nearly two hours. It was well past full dark when I stopped, and Rita had lit a candle in the kitchen whose light barely reached the parlor. I hadn't heard anything from her in a while, and figured she was sitting at the table listening in without interrupting. When I was finished, I said, "I guess that's pretty much all of it."

"But maybe not." His head dipped, and I knew he meant my hand. "You going to tell me about that?"

"One of the wounds I got in Amos's," I said.

"One?"

I'd already told them I was shot by a couple of men I suspected were bounty hunters hired by Linus Kalb. Now I elaborated on the injuries, how my shoulder was tender but not bothersome, and how my rib was still sore enough that I couldn't lie on my left side at night. I figured the thumb spoke for itself, and Abran didn't push it.

"Why did you come back, Gage?"

"I'm going home."

"Even after what your mama say?"

"What does Ma say?"

Abran frowned. "You have not seen her letter?"

"The last letter I got from her, or you, for that matter, was late last fall."

Abran cursed softly in Créole, then smiled ruefully. "Your mama, Gage, she write you regular. The letters she send to me, I send on through Jolley."

"I never saw anything after those first two from her and that one from you."

"Damn Jolley," he said softly. "I did not read your mama's letters, so I do not know what she said to you, but she wrote to me from time to time, too, and in those letters she says nothing has changed in Milam County. She say you should stay here until it does. She say your papa writes to Austin often, but that nothing comes of it. She thinks maybe Kalb has a spy at the post office in Shelburn, and that when the rains quit and the roads dry out, your papa will maybe go to Austin and try to get your case moved there."

"It wouldn't do any good," I said. "I'd be better off standing trial in Shelburn, where folks know me, and they know the Kalbs,

427

too. Anywhere else and a jury probably wouldn't believe me."

Shrugging, Abran said, "Maybe you are right, I don't know."

A shadow appeared in the door to the kitchen.

"You know he is right," Rita chided Abran. "I know this boy now, through his mother's letters, but no one who doesn't know him would believe Henry Kalb put his pistol back in its holster."

Abran sighed, but he didn't disagree with her.

"All right, Gage will go back." He looked at me. "What are you going to do with your horses?"

"That fancy bay ain't mine, and I don't want it, but the other two are." I shrugged. "I guess I'll keep them." After a moment, I asked, "What's the name of that livery where Max Jennison sold my dun?"

"That horse you called Dusty?"

"Yeah."

"He sold it to Charlie Hill, south side of town."

"That the one with the big sign painted across the top of the barn door?"

"One and the same, that, but Charlie, he already sold that horse to someone else."

I swore softly and looked away.

"You ain't got you no mischief in mind, have you, Gage? They dropped those murder charges against you last year, but that won't cut no bread if they catch you stealing a horse."

"Tell me something, did Charlie Hill know Jennison stole my horse?"

"No, Charlie is a good man, him. He didn't know."

"Why do you want to be so mean to this boy, Abran?" Rita asked.

Uncle Abran laughed at that. "Because it makes the good news that much better, Boo." He looked at me, smiling broadly. "I got your horse, young buck. Bought him off Hill last fall, after you left for the buffalo ranges. I might consider selling him, too, if the price is right."

I felt anger, but only for a second. Then I laughed with relief. "I might buy him, if the price is right. Or I might steal him myself, rather than take a skinning from a hide trader."

"Gilson made Jennison return the money to Hill, and Hill returned the money Abran paid. You don't owe anyone anything," Rita said.

"What about board?"

"Bah, that was nothing, young buck. A little hay forked in with the other horses

Tolliver keeps behind his store. We won't worry about that. Especially not after your mama and papa fed me for so long, back when you was still a runt."

I was smiling big and wanted to get up right away and go say hello to Dusty, but it was dark, and I was feeling wrung out after my long ride in from Jolley Town, so when Rita suggested we all turn in a few minutes later, I didn't protest.

Dawn rose the next morning like some gray-fleshed beast pushing the night out of its way. Although the rain had stopped, what passed for the Flat's main street was dappled with puddles reflecting the scattered clouds and patches of blue sky. Tolliver's opened at six. I walked down to the store with Abran to check on my horses and see that they were fed and watered. But mostly I went to see Dusty, feeling like a kid on Christmas morning as we walked around back to the small stable and corrals where Tolliver kept a few head of horses and mules he occasionally took in on trade. I spotted Dusty, and damned if he didn't see me, too. He raised his head and nickered and starting toward me, causing Abran to chuckle as he propped his arms over the top rail.

"I believe that rascal is as glad to see you as you are to see him."

430

I didn't try to explain the kinship I felt for the horse. I doubted if my uncle would have understood, although I suspect Rita might have. I crawled through the railings and walked out to meet my old pal, and Dusty came right up and pressed his forehead into my chest as if he'd known all along that I would be back someday. I rubbed the dun's neck and scratched across his bridle path, grown out over the winter. He was mud up to his hocks and shaggy all over, but I figured he'd clean up just fine. I had. I kept Abran behind me as I said my hellos, not wanting him to see the expression on my face or the moisture in my eyes as I fussed over the horse. While I was doing that, the buckskin and bay I'd purchased in Jolley wandered over as if wanting their fair share of attention.

Montgomery's horse hung back suspiciously, which I thought spoke more about Amos's relationship with the horse than mine. I still didn't know what I was going to do with it. Although determined not to keep it, by the same token I couldn't sell it. I couldn't even palm it off on somebody and expect them to care for it, and knowing Bob Jolley as I did, I doubted I could send it back with his next supply caravan.

After a while, Abran disappeared into the

store to begin his day. I stayed at the corral. After finding a brush and a set of small shears in a box nailed to the inside wall of the stable, I cleaned Dusty up as best I could, then went to work on the buckskin and bay. Amos's horse stayed away, and I didn't try to catch it.

Around midmorning I went back to the house to look for something to do. There was a pile of deadwood out back waiting to be split to stove-length, so I started there. Hearing the steady thunk of the ax soon brought Rita to the back door. She stood there watching me work for a few minutes. When I stopped to wipe the sweat from my brow with a sleeve, she said, "You're going to tear open that wound in your side if you aren't careful."

"I'm not worried about my side, but it's a chore to hang onto this ax without a thumb on my left hand."

She nodded to the remaining firewood. "When you finish that, come on in and I'll fix you something to eat."

I nodded and got back to work. Although slowed by my injuries, I kept at it and was able to complete the task by the time the sun reached its apex. After washing up at a tin basin next to the back door, I went inside, where Rita had some warm goat and cornbread waiting on the table. Back home we generally had our big meal of the day in early afternoon — more to give the livestock a break than to satisfy our own needs — and ate only a light supper in the evening. That wasn't as feasible for townsmen like Uncle Abran, who worked from early morning to well into the evening tending store.

That afternoon and on into the next day I patched the outer walls of Abran and Rita's little picket-post house, hauling mud up from the river that I mixed with straw to rechink the cracks. In doing so I discovered the frame of the kitchen window in the north wall had come loose over the winter, and fixed that as well. Rita seemed amused by my need to keep busy. Abran appeared mostly to appreciate my help, no doubt relieved that he wouldn't have to tackle them himself.

Early evening a few days later, I walked down to the Bee Hive Saloon and ordered a beer. Although not a big drinker, I have to admit it tasted good that night. It was nice to be among others, too, and I soon struck up a conversation with a traveling minister named Samuels. We talked about horses for a while — always a safe subject in that part of the country — then about my impressions of Jolley Town, and if I thought the citizenry there would be amicable to a man of the cloth offering a few sermons. Before I could reply, Preacher Samuels went on to explain how he would only stay a few days, a week at the most.

"The need for my services are widespread, Mr. Pardell," Samuels explained earnestly. "From the countless small burgs to outlying ranches and the occasional wayfarer encountered along the trail. I offer them peace for their soul, and a chance to confess their sins, if they are so inclined. Of course, not all men are ready to receive the Savior's blessings, even though it is often those who need it most who resist with the greatest vigor.

"For instance, a shepherd of a flock whose carnality is an abomination within the Lord's eyes actually ran me out of his camp with an ax. Or the gentleman I came across last month, leading his mules to eastern markets. There was a soul urgently in need of salvation. His fear was manifest in his eyes, a man haunted by some former indiscretion only he and the Lord know the truth of. Yet would he allow me even a prayer for his comfort —"

"You said a man leading a string of mules," I interrupted.

He looked at me with a rapid blinking of

his eyes, as if brought unexpectedly to the reality of the Bee Hive, while his mind lingered along his back trail.

"Mules," I repeated. "You said he had a string of mules?"

"Yes, nice ones, too. I suspect he will find a ready market for them upon arrival at his destination."

"Did he say what his destination was?"

"Jacksboro. Are you in search of a sturdy team? I daresay they would serve you well."

"Was this man riding a mule, or a horse?"

"A horse," Samuels replied, his enthusiasm starting to wane. "Why do you ask, friend?"

"A steel dust gray and a double-rigged saddle."

"I paid little heed to horse or tack, Mr. Pardell. It was the man's soul I attempt to solace."

"But you noticed it was a horse, not a mule. Was it a steel dust gray?"

After some hesitation, Samuels admitted that it was.

"A fine animal, too," he added.

"Then I'm going to assume he was leading, what? Six mules?"

"Six was the number, yes."

I nodded with mixed emotions. It seemed a long time ago that I'd made up my mind to find Roy Potter and Andy Brenner and see that justice was served in the deaths of Jim Scurlock and Ralph Tellis. I'd been in possession of both my thumbs then, and more determination than I felt there in the Bee Hive.

"Was there just one man?" I asked after a minute.

"There was."

I described him in some detail, including his dress.

"Is he a friend of yours?" Samuels asked when I'd finished, acknowledging Potter's identity by his question.

"No, he isn't."

"Then is it vengeance you seek?"

"If it's who I think it is, he killed a friend of mine, and I want to see him turned over to the law."

"To the law, or dealt with to your own satisfaction?"

"A fair trial would be satisfaction enough," I said.

"I pray you speak the truth, Mr. Pardell. I would hate to think my assistance helped perpetrate a murder."

"Where was he headed, Mr. Samuels? After Jacksboro, I mean."

"Jacksboro is my own assumption, friend, though based upon both the road and direction he followed. If he had an objective beyond that, it was not shared with me."

Having originally approached Fort Griffin from the southeast, I'd missed Jacksboro last fall, which laid just a shade north of due east from the military outpost, but I knew the road between the two communities was the main route into Griffin, and the quickest and most popular way out. It was how the stage line ran, and how the hides from farther west were transported to eastern markets. It made sense to me that Potter would use that route in his flight from the buffalo range. I wondered about Andy Brenner, too. Had the two men parted company along the way? Or was Andy lying somewhere behind me, his body hidden where only scavengers could find it?

I motioned the bartender over and bought another beer for Preacher Samuels, then said my goodbyes and left the saloon. Uncle Abran wasn't around when I entered Tolliver's Emporium, but a clerk named Lester was behind the counter. I borrowed a gunny sack from him and quickly made my way up and down the aisles until I had what supplies I figured I'd need for the trail. Abran returned as Lester and I finished totaling my bill.

"You are leaving us, Gage?"

I said that I was, and after Lester went off to fetch my change, I told Abran what I'd learned about Roy Potter. A scowl began to form across his brow almost as soon as I began speaking. It deepened as I continued.

"Not many would consider it your duty to go after this man," Abran said when I finished.

"Would you?" I asked, and after a moment he sighed and nodded.

"Foolishly, perhaps, but yes, probably I would."

"Jacksboro is on the way home, more or less."

"Be careful with this one, Gage. A bushwhacker is a dangerous man to follow."

"I'll watch myself," I promised, but I could see the concern in my uncle's eyes.

"I will ask Rita to pray for you, as well, young buck," he said. "I think against this man Potter, you will need all the help you can get."

CHAPTER TWENTY-EIGHT

My last evening meal with Abran and Rita was a solemn affair. Although each of us in turn tried to keep the conversation light, it was interspersed with long minutes of brooding silence. Bedded down on the parlor floor afterward, I heard them arguing in their bedroom. It didn't take much effort to realize I was the subject of their dispute. From the tones, I could tell Rita was wanting Abran to intervene, but he was holding strong. At one point I heard him say, "He is a man grown now, Boo, there is nothing I can do."

If supper had been sedate, breakfast was downright gloomy. Rita served up eggs and bacon and fried potatoes, and fixed a fresh pot of coffee even though there was cold left from the night before that could have easily been warmed. She fixed food for the trail, as well, but seldom spoke or even acknowledged my presence. It felt almost as it had on my arrival, although her anger had different roots. Afterward, Abran went to fetch my horse while I furled my blankets. When Abran returned, it was with Dusty alone.

"Are you sure about the others?" he asked.

"I'm sure. Sell them, take a commission, and send the money home to Ma and Pa."

He nodded. "As you wish. And I will see that Montgomery's horse is returned to Jolley Town. They can decide there what to do with him."

"I appreciate you doing this," I said. "Hell, I appreciate everything you and Rita have done for me."

"It was nothing, young buck. Now go talk to Rita, tell her what you have told me about your appreciation."

I glanced at the house, where the banging of pots and pans from the kitchen sounded like there was a brawl taking place.

"Go on," he said, grinning. "If you healed from bullets, you will heal from Rita's scolding, though it may take a little longer."

I grinned weakly and went inside. Rita stood at the stove with tears streaming down her dusky cheeks. She looked at me as if I were some kind of wormy beast that had snuck into her house, and I thought for a minute she might throw a knife or skillet at me. Then she came over and wrapped her arms around my shoulders, and her tears came faster. Uncertainly, I put one arm around her waist and held her without speaking. We stood that way nearly a full minute. Then she pushed back and sniffed and swiped a knuckle angrily under her eyes.

"Don't get yourself killed," she said fiercely.

"I ain't planning on it."

"Cemeteries are full of fools who didn't plan on it." She shook her head and looked away. "Your uncle is a good man, Gage, but it gets lonely here with no family. Then you showed up and put a face to what had only been a name before. Family, you know?"

I nodded that I did, but I didn't. It would be a long time before I realized what she was really saying. I think she understood that herself, but was saying it for that future day when I finally figured out what she was talking about.

Jutting her chin toward the door, she said, "You had better go."

I nodded but still hesitated, struggling to find the words I wanted to say, to let her know how much she and Abran had come to mean to me. But in the end, all I could do was mutter a pathetic, "Thank you for everything," and turned away.

The sun was already pulling free of the horizon by the time I reined away from Uncle Abran's small house there on the Flat, but I didn't regret my late start. At the time I was afraid I'd never see either of them again, and the ache was like losing your best friend.

It was right at seventy-five miles from Fort Griffin to Jacksboro. Pushing hard, I could have made it in a day, but there was no reason to hurry. If Potter was the man Preacher Samuels had spoken to, he was probably long gone before I ever left Jolley. The most I was hoping for at that point was to pick up his trail.

With those thoughts in mind, it became an easy three-day journey to Jacksboro, across Keechi Creek's west fork from Fort Richardson. The town was a going concern by anyone's standards. Probably six or seven hundred souls by that time, with brick buildings lining its main street, at least two banks that I saw, and a newspaper office near the center of town called *The Frontier Echo.* I saw church steeples on the horizon and mills offering a variety of services along the town's perimeter.

I stopped at Olsen's Stables on the west side of town because I liked the looks of the paddocks that I could see from the road —

fences in good repair, water troughs in every pen — and I rented a stall for Dusty. Such accommodations farther west would have cost me a dollar a day minimum on the Flat, and twice that in Jolley. Olsen charged fifty cents a night, and fed my choice of oats or corn for an additional ten cents a gallon. A room at Hannah Mitchell's Boarding House less than a block away was another seventy-five cents, and included two meals a day and clean linens on a bed I didn't have to share with other travelers — well worth the money in my opinion. With myself and my horse secured for the night, I went out in search of information.

Olsen had claimed he hadn't seen anyone fitting Roy Potter's description passing through town, and insisted he would have remembered a string of mules even if he couldn't recall the man. I got similar responses at the town's three other liveries, but ran into a bit of luck at a blacksmith's shop on the town's east side.

"Yeah, I saw 'im," the smithy grunted as he strained to lower a nearly red-hot rim over the felloes of a wagon wheel, six of its twelve spokes recently replaced. I waited until he had the iron rim in place, then handed him a bucket of water that he began pouring carefully over the steaming, hissing iron, shrinking the metal to a tight fit, although now and again having to tap it with a six-pound hammer where additional nudging was needed. When he was satisfied with the results, he came over to where I was standing, using a piece of burlap to wipe the sweat from his brow.

"You say this man is a friend of yours?"

"No, sir, he's just someone I'm looking for."

The blacksmith eyed me thoughtfully for a moment, then shrugged indifferently. "Go talk to Mark Sutton, at the Stockman's Tavern."

"Where is that?"

"On the square in town, two doors down from the *Echo.*"

I nodded. I hadn't noticed the name of the pub, but I'd spotted the newspaper office earlier.

"If it's the guy I'm thinking of, Mark will be able to tell you more than I can."

I thanked the smith and walked back into town. The Stockman's was smaller and a whole lot quieter than the Bee Hive on the Flat or Amos's place in Jolley Town. It was cool and dark inside, and there were stools lining the bar where a hard-working man looking for a quiet drink before heading home could get off his feet for a few minutes. I took the stool nearest the front door and waited until a middle-aged man with slick hair parted in the middle and bright green garters on his sleeves came over.

"What'll you have, friend?"

"A beer sounds good."

He chuckled good-naturedly. "A beer always sounds good about this time of day," he agreed.

I glanced around for a clock, but the walls were bare save for lithographs of horses and cattle, all standing stiff and proud as if in a show arena. Wanting to get my questions out of the way before the evening crowd showed up, I told the bartender who I was, then described the blacksmith who had sent me there.

"Alan Jones," he said, nodding.

"Mr. Jones suggested I talk to Mark, at the Stockman's. Is that you?"

"It was the last time I checked," he replied with a grin.

There was no suspicion in Sutton's manner when I asked him about Roy Potter, which reflected the differences between a settled community and one of those still raw and uncooked farther west. He also knew who I was talking about, although he wasn't much help beyond that.

"I didn't get a name," he admitted. "The

guy was only in here that one time, but he was the kind to make an impression, if you know what I mean."

I thought I did, but asked anyway.

"Like he thought I was trying to cheat him on everything I did, or lying about anything I said. I told him to talk to a farmer up north of here along Lost Creek about selling his mules, and dogged if the guy didn't act like I was in cahoots with the farmer."

"Do you know if he sold the mules?"

"I know he didn't, is what I know. Oh, he talked to the farmer all right, but he wanted too much for what he had, and he wasn't willing to dicker." He shook his head. "The guy said he came from farther west, out past Fort Griffin. I told him he should have sold his mules there. He would've gotten a better price for them. Of course, that made him mad, too."

"What happened to him?"

"He hung around town the next day, still trying to sell his mules, but nobody would buy them. By that time, we were all becoming a little suspicious. Finally, someone told him he was going to talk to the sheriff and see what he knew about any missing mules, and after that the guy saddled up and rode away." He chuckled. "It was a bluff. If the mules weren't stolen in Jack County, the

446

sheriff couldn't have done anything even if he wanted to."

"Did he take the mules with him?"

"Oh, sure. He wasn't in that big of a hurry."

"Which way did he go?"

"On east, although I couldn't tell you where." Then his brows furrowed thoughtfully. "Maybe I can. He mentioned Fort Worth at one point, saying it was a cattle town, and that folks there would appreciate quality animals. He might be right. Fort Worth is on the Chisholm Trail. He'd likely have better luck selling his mules there than around here."

"Fort Worth," I repeated quietly. I'd heard about it, of course. What Texas farm boy hadn't? Fort Worth and Hell's Half Acre, where just about any kind of sin could be accommodated — for a price. "Thanks," I said. "I'll try there next."

Although grateful for the information, I was no longer optimistic about finding Potter. Not in a boom town like Fort Worth, with so many avenues in and out of the place. Still, even though I knew it was a long shot, I rode on into Fort Worth to have a look around. But it was as I'd feared. It was as if Roy Potter and his mules had vanished down a badger's hole. After two days pok-

ing around the numerous liveries and stockyards, I saddled up and headed for home.

Chapter Twenty-Nine

The closer I got to home, the more nervous I became. It wasn't the mess I'd left behind in Shelburn with the Kalbs that gnawed at me, nor even my impending arrest for Henry's death. It was Ma, and wondering how she'd react to my return, and what it would all mean before it was settled. I knew she'd be happy to see me, but how was she going to feel when I told her why I'd come back, and that I intended to set things straight with Linus Kalb?

I wasn't as worried about Pa, who I suspected would support my decision whether or not he agreed with it. With Pa there was always a basic right and wrong to a thing, but generally with quite a bit of leeway in between. I expected him to argue against me staying, but that he wouldn't come unglued if I did.

It was a cool April morning when I came down the road past our farm, although from the west, so I was able to avoid Shelburn. I figured I owed my family that much, to stop in and visit awhile before riding on into town. I'd been jogging along at an easy clip, but slowed to a walk when I turned into our lane.

I spotted Beau first. He was splitting shakes beside the barn, and I remembered how Pa had been wanting a new roof on the henhouse even last summer. Beau stopped what he was doing as soon as he saw me, and after a moment's hesitation he set his froe and mallet to one side and picked up a rifle. I eased back on Dusty's reins, bringing him to a halt. Beau called into the barn and Pa appeared soon after. He was also carrying a rifle, and my jaw tightened in outrage. I'd thought often of my family in the time I'd been away, and regretted the heartache I knew I'd caused them, but it hadn't occurred to me — despite the tone of Ma's two letters — that their own lives might be in peril.

Pa looked close, and I raised my right hand in a half salute. When I did, the expression on his face changed from one of distrust to astonishment. He slammed his rifle into Beau's chest, and was already running toward me before Beau could register what was going on. Smiling with relief, I swung down and walked forward to meet him. He skidded to a stop in front of me, his grin nearly consuming the lower half of his face as he thrust a grubby paw my way. We shook hands like old friends, with words tumbling from his lips faster than he could get them in order. Finally he just shut up and shook his head.

"By *God,* Gage, it's good to see you again."

"It's good to see you, too." I looked past him to where Beau was coming up with a rifle in each hand, his grin nearly the size of Pa's. "Look who found his way home," he said.

"It's been a while," I admitted.

Beau handed Pa his rifle, then used his free hand to punch me on the shoulder. "How've you been, big brother?"

"Fair to middling," I replied, but I could see that Pa had already noticed my mangled left hand holding Dusty's reins. Feeling self-conscious, I twisted partway around to hide the angry red flesh where my thumb had once wiggled.

"Your ma's going to have a fit, Gage," Pa said quietly.

"Is she still mad at me?"

"Hell, no," he exclaimed, then laughed. "This is going to be a good fit, although I suspect she'll be hard to rein for a while."

"Shoot, when ain't Ma hard to rein?" Beau said, and we all laughed.

Then I heard a scream from the house and here she came, skirts flapping like a mad hen's wings, her tears already started. She didn't stop when she got close like Pa did, and she didn't shake hands or slug me on the shoulder or welcome me back. She did nearly squeeze the wind right out of me, spilling probably a quart of tears over my shoulder before Pa finally peeled her off.

I'm not sure there's any reason to dwell too much on the next twenty-four hours. It was about what you'd expect of any homecoming where the shadow of a noose hangs over the head of the wayward son.

Everyone was happy to see me, of course, even though Ma and Ester would every so often break into tears for no apparent reason, and whenever I was within reach they would both hover over me like doting aunts, asking if I needed my coffee warmed or another helping of whatever food we were eating, and there was no shortage of that. Ester fixed a blueberry cobbler that was the equal of any I've had before or since, and Ma killed a laying hen because she felt the meat would taste better than a rooster's.

There were fresh-pulled onions and greens and fried crawfish already made, along with a wheel of yellow cheese strong enough to arm wrestle with.

With an almost frenzied effort, Ma soon added helpings of bell peppers stuffed with boudins, fried rice, and pork cracklings served with cane syrup. Lord a'mighty it was good, but it was also too much. It was as if she was trying to smother her fears for me through her cooking, creating an illusion of well-being with the production of a feast. It is, I've often thought, a farmer's tenet — a reward for past labors, a sign of prosperous times to come, and above all, hope for the future.

Early the next morning, sitting in Pa's rocker in the dogtrot while my breakfast digested, Ma showed up with scissors, a comb, and Pa's razor shoved down in her apron pocket. I had to laugh, seeing it. Back on the Flat I'd considered keeping my long hair and thick beard as the mark of a frontiersman, but it seemed the farther east I rode, the more out of place I felt. So, noting the determined thrust of Ma's jaw, I didn't make a fuss when she draped a towel over my shoulders and started pruning. I'll admit I felt kind of skinned afterward, but cooler, too.

I helped around the house that day, sharpening the plow's chisel first, then going ahead and touching up the various ax, saw, shovel, and spade bits that afternoon. Beau continued splitting shakes for the henhouse roof, while Pa worked on getting the rest of the equipment ready for spring planting. It was time to start, but the ground was still too wet from recent rains. Meanwhile Ester and Bess toiled in the garden and Luke — I was still calling him Baby Luke, although I soon picked up that the others had dropped the *baby* appellation, him being three and already charged with some of the smaller responsibilities around the place — helped his sisters by gathering the smaller stones they tilled from the soil and dumping them in a pile to the side. Ma stayed inside fixing another big meal and, I'd find out later, mending the clothes I'd brought back with me from the buffalo range. She set up the big washtub in the summer kitchen and scrubbed them as best she could first, although most of the stains proved too stubborn to remove entirely.

From time to time I'd pause in my work to watch Ester in the garden. She worried me, acting happy and upbeat for a while, then her mood sinking and her eyes growing weepy. Pa said she'd been that way ever since the day of Henry Kalb's trial last October, but he didn't speculate on whether it was my killing Henry or Ann Dunford's betrayal that weighed heaviest on her. My guess, even then, was that it was a combination of both those things, and even more, her own feelings of guilt. Ester blamed her naïvety the night of the Harvest Festival dance for all the tribulations that had befallen the family since then. My heart ached for her, but I didn't know what I could say to ease her burden. In looking back, I realize her troubles were beyond my ability to help, beyond any of our abilities.

After supper that second night, Pa and Beau and I walked down to the barn. Beau lit a lantern and set it on the floor in the central aisle, while Pa took a seat in the tack room door and I climbed up on the anvil like I used to do as a kid, tucking my heels tight against its base atop the oak block it was spiked to, perching there like a stuffed crow.

"What happened out there, Gage?" Pa asked quietly.

I'd told the family some of it already, of course, but I'd held a lot back, too, for fear of how Ma and Ester would react. I hadn't said anything about the wound in my side or the deep graze across my shoulder from

Thornton's bullets, or the one across my back from that ambush at Clark's store on my journey west. As far as my missing digit, I told them I'd lost it when my knife slipped while skinning a buffalo. I'm not sure Ma believed that, but I know for damn certain that Pa didn't, although thankfully he didn't pursue it at the supper table.

Taking a slow breath to gather my thoughts, I decided I'd tell him everything — good and bad — and if he decided he didn't want Beau hearing what I had to say, he could shoo him off to the house himself.

It took a while, and sometimes I'd remember a little detail and have to go back and fit it in like a piece to a picture puzzle. Pa listened attentively, while Beau displayed an expression of equal parts awe and envy. He didn't say anything when I finished, though, but looked at Pa and waited for him to speak.

"What are your plans?" Pa asked.

"Tomorrow's Saturday," I replied, stating a fact I'd only become aware of that afternoon, the days of the week having little value on the range. "If Linus Kalb holds true to habit, he'll be in town around noon. I'm going into Shelburn to see him."

I expected Pa to object, but he remained unexpectedly quiet for a couple of minutes, as if absorbing my intentions and searching for flaws. Finally he said, "Would you do me a favor?"

"What's that?"

"Don't brace the Kalbs tomorrow." He held a hand up palm out to stop my protest. "Hear me out, son."

I closed my mouth and nodded for him to continue.

"What's been going on between the Kalbs and the Pardells isn't going to change. Linus Kalb isn't going to change, no matter what you say to him. The only way you'll ever stop him face to face is to kill him, and if you do that, they'll hang you for sure."

I could feel my temperature rising and my nostrils beginning to flare, but I remained still.

"Talk to Judge Wetzel first, see what he says," Pa continued. "He'll be limited in what action or advice he can offer, but he won't stick a knife in your back, either. As long as you were on the scout, a fugitive from justice in the eyes of the law is how he put it, he couldn't do much to help, but he also said if you ever came back, he'd do what he could to see that you got a fair trial. I believe him, Gage. Wetzel's a good man. I'd trust him a long time before I would Hunnicutt."

Robert Wetzel was our local judge, and he was a good man by most accounts. Eugene Hunnicutt was Shelburn's city marshal, a man of waffling fidelity and venal integrity, the kind of politician men like Linus Kalb loved to pocket.

"Hunnicutt," I grunted, then shook my head.

"He's . . . malleable," Pa said, trying to be kind, I suppose.

"He's as crooked as the hind leg of a crippled dog," Beau declared, which pretty much echoed my own opinion of the man. Then he added, "No better than Baggs."

Randolph Baggs was our local postmaster.

"What's Baggs got to do with this?" I asked.

"Pa figures that's how Kalb found out you was headed to Fort Griffin," Beau said.

"That's speculation only," Pa said, "and it has nothing to do with facing down Linus Kalb tomorrow. Just think about what I'm saying, Gage. Let the law settle the matter of Henry's death."

"By law, you mean Judge Wetzel?"

"Yeah, Wetzel. Going at it that way would give you a lot more credibility in the long run, and might kick the chocks out from under Linus Kalb's wheels."

"All right," I said, sliding my boots off the

anvil's block and dropping to the ground. "I'll think about it."

But the truth was, there wasn't all that much to think about. After shoving my anger out of the equation, it just seemed wiser to talk with Judge Wetzel first, and find out from him what my options were. We'd have to hire an attorney, but I still had the money from Scurlock's outfit, and would soon have what Uncle Abran would send after selling the two horses I'd left with him on the Flat.

I told Pa of my plans the next day at breakfast, and he nodded with obvious relief. Ma looked surprised by the news, and Ester looked stricken, as if someone had plunged a knife through her heart. Beau's eyes brightened, and he immediately volunteered to saddle our horses.

"Just Gage's Dusty and my Sally."

"What about Brownie?" he asked, meaning Pa's seal brown gelding.

"Just those two, Beau. You're staying home."

Oh, he wanted to protest, and probably would have liked to complain about how he never got to do this or go there — typical laments from most youngsters his age — but with Pa there was always a time to speak up and a time to keep your mouth shut, and there was seldom any mistaking which mood he was in.

"Yes, sir," Beau said cheerlessly.

"Orrin?" Ma said hesitantly.

"It can't be put off forever, Molly."

"A few more days wouldn't hurt, would it?"

"It might, if word reached town that Gage was back. It's best we get this settled as soon as possible."

Her face seemed to crumble with worry and disappointment, but she didn't push the matter. It made for a glum breakfast, though, and a deep silence as Pa and I walked outside afterward, both of us weighed down with rifles and revolvers. Beau had Dusty and Sally hitched to a porch railing, and I grimly shoved the Spencer into its scabbard before stepping into the saddle and reining away from the house. I tried to smile reassuringly at Ma and Ester and Bess — Luke was still abed — standing in a tight cluster on the porch, but it didn't seem to help much.

"We should be back before dark," Pa told Ma, "but don't get your feathers ruffled if we ain't. I aim to do Wetzel's bidding, and see Gage gets the footing he needs for a fair trial."

"You do what you have to do, Orrin

Pardell," Ma said, then looked at me. "Promise you won't do nothing rash, Gage?"

"I promise, Ma."

She nodded, but had to struggle to keep her lower lip from trembling, tears from spilling down her weathered cheeks. Ester was already crying softly. I winked and smiled at Bess to ease her confusion at an adult world she couldn't possibly comprehend, then turned Dusty toward the road. Pa fell in beside me and we lifted our horses to a slow lope, as much to get out of sight and ease Ma and Ester's anguish as anything, I think.

We didn't talk much on the way into town, and were nearly there before I said to Pa, "I know I've put the family through a lot of hell these past months, but I don't think I've asked for much otherwise."

"You've never asked for anything," Pa replied without hesitation. He gave me an inquisitive glance. "Why?"

"Because I'm going to ask for something now. If . . . no matter what happens today, please don't sell Dusty. I know things —"

Pa's hand darted with the swiftness of a cottonmouth across the space separating us, latching onto my bicep hard enough to make me wonder if he was angry.

461

"No matter what happens, no matter when you come home, if it's today or a year from now, Dusty will be here waiting for you, Gage. I promise you that."

I nodded gratefully, afraid to speak for the way my throat seemed to tighten down on the things I wanted to say. I kept my gaze fixed on the road ahead, no matter that it seemed unaccountably blurry all of a sudden. I was aware of Pa keeping pace beside me, his own expression looking like something carved from rock.

It was midmorning before we reached Shelburn. Judge Wetzel's home was on the town's west side, so we stopped there first, looping our reins through the iron rings of a couple of fancy metal hitching posts before entering the yard through the low gate of a white picket fence. Mrs. Wetzel's love of gardening was well-known throughout that part of Milam County, and her knowledge of it showed everywhere you looked. The lawn was a brilliant green and recently mowed, the flagstone walk lined with primroses, daylilies, and bluebonnets; hollyhocks and irises grew close to the house's foundation, and a pair of towering oak trees shaded the south and west sides of the property.

Mrs. Wetzel — I don't think I ever heard her Christian name; even Ma always referred to her as *Mrs.* — opened the door at my knock, and I immediately removed my hat, as did Pa, standing behind me.

"Good morning, ma'am," I said. "I hope I'm not disturbing you, but I'd like to speak to your husband if he's available."

"Are you friends of my husband?"

"No, ma'am, this is strictly business."

"Then I'm afraid I can't help you. Robert doesn't normally accept business appointments at home or on the weekend, but your request is doubly impossible today. He's gone to Cameron to see an old acquaintance, and isn't expected back until Wednesday."

My heart sank a little at that. We'd been spotted on our ride into town, and I knew word would spread quickly that Gage Pardell was back.

"Is there anyone else we can talk to?" Pa asked. "Maybe an attorney your husband trusts."

"In matters of the law, my husband trusts all attorneys, sir. There are several listed in the town's directory, or perhaps you would prefer to speak with our Marshal, Mr. Hunnicutt."

"No, ma'am," Pa said, his voice unconsciously hardening at this unexpected set-back.

"We won't bother you any longer, Mrs. Wetzel," I hastened to add, not wanting to alarm her and knowing Pa wouldn't, either.

"May I tell my husband who called . . . when he returns?"

"That won't be necessary," I replied. "When he gets back, we'll stop by his office in town, and not bother him at home. We only stopped today because it's Saturday, and we didn't think he'd be at the court-house."

"Very well, then," she said. "Good day, gentlemen."

She closed the door, gently but firmly, in our faces, and I glanced at Pa and tipped my head toward our waiting horses. Back outside the gate, gathering our reins, I said, "We can't go home, not now."

"I wish I'd have thought to ride into town myself and make sure the judge was here," Pa replied. "It never even crossed my mind he might not be."

"Well, what's done is done, and there's no turning back now." I slid my foot into the stirrup and hauled up into the saddle. Pa mounted his chestnut and reined over beside me, straight-lipped and worried look-ing.

"I reckon we'd better go on in," he said after a bit.

"Where to?"

"The marshal's office. We need to get it on record that you came back on your own accord. That way, if someone comes after you before Wetzel returns, we'll have proof you weren't captured while trying to hide out at home."

We rode on into the central part of town and turned north where our road — what the locals called the West Road — junctioned with Main Street, which ran parallel to the Brazos River. Although it had been wet and chilly in recent weeks, the past couple of days had turned hot, and Main Street was already drying out and turning to dust. The business district was crowded with farmers in town for supplies and housewives doing their weekly shopping. Wagons and buckboards jammed the street, and the boardwalks teemed with people. The marshal's office was two blocks north of the intersection, on the west side of the street. It was a square brick structure with a flat roof, looking more like a pale red box than a government office. A couple of sugar maples provided some skimpy afternoon shade.

Pa and I dismounted out front and hitched

our horses to the wooden rail and climbed the steps to the front door. My heart was galloping along at a good clip by then, and I was second-guessing just about every decision I'd made since making up my mind to return to Milam County and hobble this thing between me and the Kalbs before it got further out of hand. I paused in front of the jail and Pa gave me a look to let me know the final decision was mine to make. Flashing a crooked grin that in no way reflected what I was really feeling, I twisted the knob and shoved the door inward.

Hunnicutt wasn't there, which was a relief, but his deputy was, and that quickly negated any feelings of reprieve. Neil Jepson was only a couple of years older than I was, with a long neck that kind of wobbled when he walked and ears sticking out from either side of his head like handles on a jug. He was sitting in the marshal's chair when Pa and I walked in, leaning back with his heels on the desk. He brought them down in a hurried, furtive manner and jackknifed into a more upright position when he heard us, and from the sheen of drool he quickly wiped from the lower corner of his mouth, I suspected he'd been dozing. Neil and I knew one another from years back, had played mumblety-peg together in the schoolyard with our folding knives during the noon break from classes, and he recognized me immediately. He gulped loudly and his eyes flitted from me to Pa, then back again. Saving him the effort, I spoke first.

"We're looking for Gene Hunnicutt."

"He ain't here."

"Do you know where he is?"

Neil's head bobbed a few times. "Yeah, yeah, he went home."

"Do you think you could run and fetch him?" Pa asked without much patience.

"Uh-huh." His gaze did that darting thing again, filled with uncertainty.

"Go get him," I said, figuring someone needed to take charge, since it didn't seem like Jepson was going to.

"Sure," Neil said, edging around the desk. Pa and I moved out of his way. "Don't you two go anywhere," he added. "Marshal Hunnicutt has been wanting to talk to you for a long time." He said this last to me.

"Just go get him," I said.

When the deputy was gone, Pa closed the door and walked to the window, staring out at the street. Over his shoulder I saw Jepson moving away at a swift walk, his head looking like it might come loose at any moment.

"I don't like this," Pa said softly.

"Not much we can do about it at this point."

"I don't trust Hunnicutt."

"All we've got to do is make sure he knows I'm back, and that we plan to talk to Judge Wetzel as soon as he returns from Cameron."

"What if he wants to lock you up until Wetzel gets back?"

I thought about that for a moment, then said, "We just won't let him."

Pa looked at me and smiled. "That simple, huh?"

"I don't know if it'll be simple, but I'm not going to let a Kalb man take away my gun, then lock me in a cage." My gaze fell on a narrow, wood-framed building across the street with the words *Dexter's Diner* painted across the large, single window next to the door. "How about a cup of coffee while we wait?" I asked Pa.

"I'm not sure coming into town was such a good idea, but some coffee would be. Maybe a piece of pie to go with it, if he's got any."

We left our horses at the jail and ambled across the street, trying to appear nonchalant despite the multitude of eyes following us. I doubted if many of them were feeling overly hostile. The Kalbs weren't well thought of by most folks in that part of Milam County, while the Pardells largely were, save for those whose negative views of Catholicism colored their opinions. But I suspect everyone was feeling wary, maybe fearing the trouble we, meaning me, might bring into their lives when word of my presence reached Linus Kalb and his boys.

Dexter Hamblin was standing behind the counter when Pa and I walked in. He usually was, the diner being a two-person affair, with his wife in back manning the stoves while Dex handled the customers up front. Although his usual welcoming smile was absent when we walked in, he did nod to one of the booths near the front of the restaurant for our use.

"What kind of pie have you got, Dex?" Pa asked as we seated ourselves, me facing the street while he kept an eye on the rear of the restaurant.

"Cherry, peach, apple, and rhubarb," Dexter replied. "The rhubarb is this year's crop, just picked."

Pa ordered the rhubarb while I took peach with cream poured over the top. We both drank our coffee black. Dexter brought the coffee first, then the pies, his movements hurried, almost clumsy.

"How have you been, Gage?" he asked.

"Middlin'," I replied, and he nodded and quickly walked away as if to contemplate my answer.

"He's nervous," Pa said under his breath. Glancing around at the other customers — a man and woman in the rearmost booth, a farmer with his wife and two children at a table, a couple of lone men in work clothes sitting separately — he added, "They all are." Then he sighed, his expression troubled. "I guess we shouldn't have come here, either."

"They'll live," I replied shortly, and carved off a corner of pie with my spoon.

The truth is, I couldn't blame the others for their feelings. Despite my conviction that I was doing the right thing in returning to Shelburn, my own nervousness was increasing steadily as I wolfed down my pie and coffee. So much so that afterward I couldn't have told you how it tasted. Good, I'd guess, knowing Dex and his wife, but I likely could as easily have consumed one of Bess's mud pies and not realized the difference. The problem was that I knew where Marshal Hunnicutt lived, and if he was home when his deputy arrived, as Jepson had stated, then they both should have been back by now. That they weren't was troubling. I could tell it was bothering Pa, as well.

When we finished, Pa dropped a fifty-cent piece on the table and we walked outside without speaking. Dexter watched silently, without wishing us a good day, and that told me a lot, too. We were about halfway across Main when a trio of men stepped out from the alley beside the Shelburn Hotel, two buildings down from the marshal's office, and started toward us. I recognized all three men immediately — Seth Henning, who had been in the Alamo the night I killed Henry, and the Lapwin boys, Don and Jay. Pa touched my shoulder and we stopped.

"Over your left shoulder, Gage."

I looked cautiously, without fully removing my gaze from Seth and the Lapwins. Seth's brothers, Burt and Frank, were standing at the arched entrance to the First Bank of Shelburn, thumbs hooked behind the buckles of their gun belts, shoulders propped against the brick wall. Their stance was casual, but an aura of tension emanated off them like the stench of a frightened skunk. I also noticed that folks along the street were scurrying inside nearby buildings as if sensing what was to come. Then Pa cursed softly and I followed his gaze to my right, where Linus Kalb and his sons, Jacob and Paul, were striding determinedly down the middle of the street toward us.

CHAPTER THIRTY

My throat tightened as if it already had a noose around it. "It had to be Jepson," I said.

"That'd be my guess," Pa agreed. "Probably him and Hunnicutt both, the cowardly bastards."

"Linus would be a fool to try something out here in the open with the whole town watching."

"Take a real good look," Pa replied. "Do any of these birds look overly enlightened to you?"

I had to admit they didn't, although I wasn't ready to give up hope just yet. "Linus should know better, even if the others don't."

"Yeah, he should. They all should. But Linus Kalb's heart is pumping venom right now, and he ain't thinking square. And the others, they're too callow to buck the old man."

"What do you want to do?"

As if hearing my nearly whispered question to Pa, Linus shouted, "Hold it right there, Pardells."

Linus and his sons were still some forty yards away, though closing the gap fast.

"Stay back, Linus," Pa returned. "We're here to see the marshal, since Judge Wetzel ain't around."

"Neither Wetzel nor Hunnicutt has anything to do with this, Orrin. This is between me and your boy."

"Is that why you have all these guns backing you?"

"You damned right it is. He ain't gettin' away this time."

"I didn't come back to get away," I hollered louder than I needed to, but wanting folks along the street to hear what I had to say. "I came to turn myself in to Judge Wetzel."

"You're shit outta luck on that account, boy," Linus fired back, stopping twenty or so yards away with Jacob and Paul flanking him. Pointing his finger at me like it was the barrel of a pistol, he added, "Drop your guns, Pardells. I won't tell you twice."

"Walk away, Pa," I said as firmly as I knew how.

He gave me a nettled look, and didn't

bother to reply. Down the street, Kalb was spitting words out of his mouth like they were hot biscuits burning his tongue, mostly about Henry and what a good son he'd been.

"All right," I conceded. "Then when the shooting starts, we'll make a break for that alley next to Dexter's. You shoot at the Lapwins and Hennings. I'll take Linus if I can."

"We don't want a gunfight here, Gage," Pa replied tersely.

"I don't think it matters what we want. You take a close look this time. Look at Linus. He didn't come here to lock us up. He wants me dead. He'd lynch me if he could, or he'll try to shoot me down in the street if I don't give myself up, but he ain't going to walk away. Fighting's our only chance now."

"Okay, but we won't wait for them to start shooting. As soon as Linus stops talking, we'll make our play."

I nodded consent without taking my eyes off Kalb. By now his rant had moved on to how Henry had been misled by Ester's wiles, and how someone had to pay for his death. It was the usual bullshit, and I didn't pay it much heed. When he finally paused to suck in a breath, Pa said, "Now!" and bolted for the alley. I was right behind him, drawing my gun and sprinting low.

Oh, they were ready for it, don't think they weren't. I'd barely gotten turned around when Jacob went for his pistol, and Paul was barely a beat behind. Linus was the slowest of the three, but that's not saying much.

I beat Jacob to the punch by a hair, my shot catching his holster and knocking it halfway around his waist. Too bad his revolver wasn't still in it. He snapped off a shot, then Paul, both bullets coming close enough for me to hear the fizz of their passage. My second shot and Linus's first came as one solid roar, the gun smoke already raising a sulfuric fog between us. I heard Pa's revolver blazing away behind me and others returning his fire until the air around us seemed thick with swarming wasps. I kept firing as I ran. So did Pa. Jacob had started running for the west side of the street, toward the jail, before letting go of his second round, while Paul was ducking and firing without even trying to aim.

Only Linus maintained any semblance of composure. He stood with his feet braced wide, firing methodically with a nickeled revolver that caught the sun's glare and threw it back at me. His first shot missed. So did his second, but the third took the hat off my head as neat as if it had been yanked off with a lariat. Pa and I were less than ten feet from the alley's entrance when I heard Pa cry out. I skidded to a stop and felt the tug of a bullet at my sleeve. Pa had stumbled to one knee, but lunged to his feet before I could turn back. He caught me around the waist as he plunged forward and nearly carried me into the temporary shelter of the alley.

He fell and I went down with him but quickly scrambled to my feet. I grabbed him by the arm and hauled him up and gave him a push toward the rear of the alley, the steep bank of the Brazos beyond, River Street below. Had I been in the lead, I would have plunged over the bank to seek shelter somewhere along the river, but Pa had other plans. After exiting the rear of the alley, he spun hard to his right, hobbling badly but still making good speed.

"Pa!" I hissed, but he just hollered for me to keep running. Didn't even look around. I glanced behind me as Seth Henning appeared at the alley's mouth and snapped off a shot that caught the younger man in the hip, twisting him around and dumping him to the ground. Then I was gone, racing after Pa and hoping he knew where he was going.

We passed behind old man Bailey's saddle

shop and the law offices of Atkins and King. The next building was Sullivan's Hardware. Pa tried the knob to the back door but it was locked, being so close to the riffraff that hung out along River Street, but he didn't let that stop him. Hell, it barely slowed him down. Taking a couple of steps back, he plunged into the door like a maddened bull, and the wood around the bolt gave with a loud pop. Pa fell inside and I jumped in after him just as a bullet pinged off the bricks at my side.

"Shut the door," Pa gasped as he squirmed out of the way, and I did as ordered. Still on his back, Pa pointed to a pair of crates with the words *Horse Shoes* stenciled across the sides. "Block the door."

I did the best I could, wedging the second crate between the first and a pallet of nails that probably weighed close to five hundred pounds. With the door secured, I knelt at Pa's side. Although a spreading stain of blood darkened the fabric of his trousers below his left hip, he slapped my hand away when I tried to examine it.

"Reload, boy," he grated, then hitched himself around and started punching the empties from his own revolver.

All this happened in . . . what? Two minutes? Certainly no more than that. Then figure another minute to reload. I heard footfalls outside the rear door and urgent whispering, but knew no one was going to come in after us that way. The problem was a pair of windows up high in the wall, not to mention the front door. I guess that was what worried Pa the most, because he gave me a small shove toward the store area and said, "Get up front, Gage."

"How bad are you hurt?" I asked.

"Not bad enough to kill me, but that son of a bitch Kalb might if he gets inside. Go!"

I went, staying low with the Colt thrust before me like the sniffing nose of a hunting dog. When I got into the store proper I saw Penrod Sullivan on his knees behind the counter, his expression terrified. He didn't say a word as I slipped behind the counter with him, and only moved out of the way when I reached for a couple of boxes of .45s on the shelf behind him. Pa had shuffled in from the back room and I tossed one of the boxes to him and thumbed the second box open for myself, dumping them across the counter and scooping a handful into my pocket. A shadow stopped in front of the window and Burt Henning pressed his face close to the glass to peer inside. It was as pretty a target as you'd ever want, but neither me nor Pa took it. We both aimed our revolvers at him, though, and as soon as he saw us he yelped and dived belly-first to the boardwalk, his toes rattling the planks as he scooted from sight.

Things slowed down after that. Pa limped over to a couple of chairs where, on a normal day, loafers could while away some time. He plopped into the nearest one and set his Colt on top of a small checkers table at his side. Drawing a folding knife from his pocket, he sliced delicately through the fabric over his wound. I stayed where I was, watching as he exposed the wound but mostly keeping an eye on the street. Not a soul moved out there. Nor were they likely to until everyone was satisfied the shooting had stopped.

After a couple of minutes, Pa said, "Sully?"

"Yeah, Orrin?"

"You got any bandages over there?"

"No, but I've got some mechanic's rags on a shelf in that last aisle."

"Fetch me a few, would you?"

"I'd rather not, if it's all the same to you," Sullivan replied, still crouched behind the counter.

I pointed my Colt at him and thumbed the hammer to full cock.

"Go get him some rags, goddamnit. He's

bleeding."

"All right," Sullivan nearly stuttered. "Just, j . . . just don't shoot me."

"Ain't nobody going to shoot you," Pa said, but you could tell the storekeeper didn't believe him by the way he kept his eyes on the muzzle of my Colt as he made his way on bent knees around the counter to disappear into the deeper recesses of the store.

"How bad is it?" I asked Pa.

"It ain't as bad as it looks. The artery ain't cut, and that's good, but the bullet is still in there. I can feel it, like a damn boil."

"If we had the time I could cut it out."

"Well, we ain't got the time now. I'll wrap it up with some of Sully's shop rags. That'll have to do until we can find a way out of this fracas."

Sullivan returned with a handful of rags that he handed to Pa. He started to hurry away, until I barked, "Help him, damnit."

He came back and took the rags from Pa's hands, and I swear after that he seemed to calm down, as if having something to do, to occupy his mind, lowered the flames of fear. It took only a couple of minutes to wrap Pa's wound and tie it off. Rocking back on his heels, Sullivan said, "That's about the best I can do for you, Orrin."

"It's enough," Pa said, then gave the shopkeeper a sympathetic smile. "I am surely sorry we brought this kettle of trouble down on top of you, Sully. Had I a choice, I wouldn't have done it."

The storekeeper glanced over to where I was keeping watch from behind the counter. "I heard Gage was back. I guess we all expected trouble once Linus Kalb found out about it."

As if on cue, a shout came from the street, although muffled through the hardware store's front wall and closed door.

"Pardell!"

Moving around from behind the counter, I dropped into a crouch to stay below the store's window sills and approached the door.

"Careful, son," Pa admonished.

"I just want to hear what he has to say."

Pa started to reply, then abruptly closed his mouth. He had both hands clutching his leg firmly above the wound, and his face paled as the first tentative waves of shock set in.

"Gage Pardell! You hear me?"

Coming up from the side, I gently turned the knob, then yanked the door open. A shot rang out from across the street, slamming into a barrel containing an assortment of replacement handles for axes, picks, shovels, and such. I swore and ducked back. Outside, Linus Kalb was cussing a blue streak, apparently chewing out whoever had taken that shot at me. Staying low, out of view of the men hiding across the street, I shouted, "Kalb, don't shoot. Pen Sullivan is in here."

"The hell with you, Pardell, and the hell with him. Come out here where I can see you, and leave your gun behind."

"Let Sully come out."

"No, it's you I want. Sullivan can stay where he is until this is over."

"Damnit, Kalb, Sully ain't a part of this. Let him come out before he gets hurt."

"That's tough luck for Sullivan, but no concern of mine. If you care about him, come out here and give yourself up. Otherwise, if anybody other than you pokes his nose out that door, I'm gonna shoot the bastard. And if you don't show yourself damn quick, I'm gonna fire the place."

"You'd risk Sully's life?" I yelled incredulously.

"It ain't me riskin' it, boy, it's you."

Kalb's motive in refusing to let the storekeeper leave suddenly made sense. He saw Sullivan as a hostage, but wanted to pin the blame, the responsibility for his safety, on me. I glanced at Pa. He'd moved from the

483

chair to the floor behind a metal bin filled with bolts, nuts, and screws. His face looked even more ashen in the store's shadowy interior, his features drawn tight with pain. His wound, I noticed, was still bleeding through the rags Sullivan had tied around it.

"You've got five minutes, Pardell," Linus shouted.

I raised my head high enough to peek out the dusty window. Linus Kalb was holed up directly across the street in a small wooden structure next to the hotel. Once upon a time the place had belonged to a tinsmith named Foster — his name still hung from a sign above the door — but it had been deserted for several years by then, the former owner having moved to Houston and the building being too small for any kind of businesses with a steady clientele, in addition to sitting on a lot too narrow to accommodate anything larger. If they ever tore it down, most people who didn't know better would probably assume it was just an overly wide alley.

"What are they doing?" Pa asked.

"Nothing that I can see. They're in Foster's old place. I can see several of them moving around through the window."

Sullivan snorted. "There's a place that'd

burn down easy. Or you could just blow it out of there like a stump." He got a funny look on his face then, and looked at Pa.

"Sully," Pa said, meeting the storekeeper's eyes levelly. "You still sell dynamite here?"

"Aw, hell, Orrin. If you was to miscalculate, you'd blow a hole in the side of the hotel big enough to drive a wagon through."

"Better a hole in a brick wall than my son hanging from a rope."

I knew what they were talking about. Back in the day, most hardware stores carried a case or two of dynamite for those who might need it. I'd bought a couple of sticks myself some years earlier when Pa sent me in to fetch it. We'd been struggling with a deep-rooted oak stump for nearly a week by then, trying to pry it out of a field he wanted to plant in sorghum. Two sticks had been just enough to heave it free. Sully hadn't hesitated to sell it to me, either.

"Gage," Pa said. "You reckon you could hit that place with a stick of dynamite?"

"Not from in here, but maybe from the roof, where I could get some loft to it."

"Pen," Pa said, making sure Sullivan knew he was dead serious by addressing him by his first name. "Go get a couple of sticks of dynamite, and about two inches of fuse for each of them."

I think Sullivan was going to protest the dynamite at first, until Pa mentioned such short fuses.

"Gawda'mighty, Orrin," he squawked. "Those are five-second fuses."

Meaning they burned at an approximate rate of one inch per five seconds, or ten seconds from the time I lit one until it blew.

"Two'll be enough," Pa said. "I don't want Kalb and his boys slipping out the back while that fuse is sputtering at the front."

Sullivan gave me a pleading look, but I was backing Pa on this one. We were trapped fair — Kalb's eight against just the two of us — and we needed something to even the odds. I figured a well-placed stick of dynamite would do that with powder to spare.

"Go get the dynamite," I told Sullivan, and he made a sound of exasperation before disappearing into the back room.

"What else can you see out there, Gage?"

"That's about it."

"Anyone anywhere else?"

"Not that I can tell. Judging from what little I can make out through the window, it looks like Kalb's got several men in there with him."

"He'll have one or two out back to watch the rear door, but if we're lucky, the rest of them will be in Foster's with Linus."

"What'll we do afterward?"

"We'll take that as it comes, but I'm betting a single stick will take the fight out of most of them."

Kalb's voice drifted across the street, shrill with impatience. "Thirty seconds, Pardell. Best give yourself up before we come in after you."

"There's no reason for this, Kalb," I yelled back. "I came to Shelburn to turn myself in to Judge Wetzel, and I'll do it as soon as he —"

Kalb's voice was like a train whistle shrieking in the distance. "I don't wanna hear it, boy! I don't wanna hear it! I want your ass out here now!"

"No, sir," I replied. "I won't —"

That was as far as I got before a hail of gunfire came slamming through the store. It shattered the glass in the windows and rattled the door in its frame; it knocked merchandise off the shelves and spilled liquids — including a good amount of coal oil — over the floor. I curled up behind several boxes of ax heads stacked under the front window while Pa scuttled farther back behind the bolt and nail bins. Neither of us tried to return fire. Poking our heads up in the middle of that fusillade would have been akin to suicide, and neither of us were ready to go just yet.

After several minutes the shooting tapered off, then died away completely. Out front, gun smoke swirled in the torpid breeze like slowly twirling wraiths.

"Gage," Pa called softly.

"I'm all right. Were you hit?"

"No. Sully?"

"I'm here." He came squirming into the front room on his elbows and knees, two bright red sticks of dynamite jutting from his arms like Christmas decorations. Pushing away from my shelter under the front window, I crawled over to meet him. He handed me the dynamite, then pulled a box of matches from his pocket and shoved it into my hand. "There's a trapdoor to the roof in the storeroom," he said. "You'll have to use the ladder to reach it. It's right behind the door."

"I'll find it," I promised, then continued on into the back room before standing. I could hear Kalb out front calling my name, but didn't linger to hear what he had to say.

The ladder to the roof was bolted permanently to the wall, directly under the trapdoor. I tucked the dynamite inside my shirt and pocketed the matches, then started climbing. A simple latch opened with a flip of my thumb, and I clambered onto a tar-papered roof with a gentle slope to either side. The store's false front hid me from view from the street, although I figured that would change the second I stuck my head above the parapet. That was something I couldn't risk, not with the thin planks of the façade as my only protection. But then I realized that I wouldn't have to. Foster's was directly across the street from me, no more than thirty yards away. I could lob a stick of dynamite to the front door from memory.

My heart was thumping along at a hard gallop as I withdrew the two sticks of dynamite from my shirt. I set one of them aside, braced against the inside of the façade, and dug the box of matches from my pocket. Out front, Kalb was still shouting threats — what he'd do next, what would happen if he had to send his men in after me, things like that. I didn't pay him any heed. I was dealing with my own problems at the time, trying to figure out how to hold a stick of dynamite in my right hand while striking a match with my thumbless left. It took some adjustments but I finally got it solved. When I was ready, I moved away from the façade so that I'd have room to maneuver, took a deep breath, then lit the fuse. It stuttered instantly to life and I leaned back, then heaved forward.

I didn't see the explosion, but Pa did from inside the store. He said it landed about as true as a man could hope for, bouncing up against the front wall of Foster's dilapidated old tin shop barely a second before it detonated with a roar that shook the town. I did see foot-long splinters and broken boards above the parapet, and watched a cloud of smoke and dust shoot deep into the sky. Drawing my revolver, I cautiously poked my head above the coping cap to have a look.

The building was a shambles, its front wall all but gone, roof sagging. Linus was just then lurching into the street, his head bent in a racking cough. Jacob and Paul Kalb and all three of the Henning boys followed along like ducklings after their mother. That meant the Lapwin brothers were around back, and I cat-footed in that direction to peer over the rear of the hardware store in time to see the two of them skedaddling down the steep bank toward River Street. If I hadn't been so weary, I might have laughed. Instead I walked back to the front of the building to retrieve the remaining stick of dynamite, then climbed down and went through the store to where Pa was sitting on a crate on the boardwalk out front, pointing a shotgun I assumed he'd borrowed from Sullivan — I never did ask to be sure — to where Kalb and his defeated army were circling aimlessly in the middle of the street.

With Colt in hand, I walked out to meet them. Oddly, no one spoke or made any kind of threatening gesture at my approach. It was as if they'd all been struck dumb by the blast, dazed and staggered and barely able to comprehend my command to drop their weapons. I walked them to the jail and ordered them inside. The keys to the cells — there were four of them, with two bunks apiece — hung from a peg beside the entrance to the back room. I snagged them on the way in, and after the Kalbs and Hennings entered their cells, I locked the doors and left them to regain their senses on their own.

When I got back outside, I saw Gene Hunnicutt and Neil Jepson hurrying my way with expressions of great importance stamped upon their faces. Hunnicutt demanded to know what was going on and I told him Linus Kalb had blown up the old Foster shop. He knew better, of course. I'd find out later that he and Jepson had watched the whole thing from behind a parked wagon two blocks down the street, no doubt staying out of the way until the Kalbs had finished their dirty work. I don't think Gene had anticipated the eventual outcome, though. I don't think any of us had. Hunnicutt was still blustering about when Pa limped over still carrying that shotgun and told the city marshal that his services were no longer required, and that he should go home and not come back again until Judge Wetzel returned from Cameron.

Hunnicutt protested, of course, but Pa stood firm and several of the local citizens and storeowners who'd witnessed the event up close sided with Pa. Finally a couple of members of the town board showed up and repeated Pa's instructions that Hunnicutt make himself scarce, which he eventually did. I'd also find out later that the two council members had also witnessed Hunnicutt's actions. Later on, they would prove instrumental in having him removed from office.

CHAPTER THIRTY-ONE

The next few days were possibly the most chaotic of my life. There's no doubt Pa and I had bit off an awfully big chunk of responsibility when Pa told Hunnicutt to vamoose. After the marshal and his deputy took off, I noticed those two city council members huddling together on the street in front of what was left of Foster's tin shop — mostly just smoking rubble, surrounded by a crowd of goose-necking citizens jockeying for a better view. After a while the councilmen came over to where Pa was sitting on a chair in front of the jail to ease the weight from his injured limb. He was smoking a cigar someone had given him, his lips clamped tight around it. He was hurting bad. I could see that because I knew him; I'm not sure if anyone else noticed.

"Mr. Pardell," the taller of the two said. "My name is Simon Jones, and this is Mark Matheson."

"I know you," Pa replied curtly.

"Very well, then you also know we serve on the Shelburn City Council."

"I do."

Jones looked oddly pleased by this recognition, but his expression quickly sobered. "Then I hope you can appreciate the difficulty your conduct has placed on us."

Pa's eyes flashed a warning. "That bunch locked up in there stays locked up."

"Yes, yes, I quite agree about that. The situation I'm speaking of is your dismissal of our marshal."

"Your marshal is a coward, Mr. Jones, and he was derelict in his duty as a lawman in allowing this attack upon my son and I to escalate to the point that it did. Had he been true to his oath, he would have stopped it before the first shot was fired."

Pa was glaring now, and I think it's fair to say his response surprised everyone within hearing with its substance and vigor. I know he sure as hell caught me off guard.

"I won't argue Marshal Hunnicutt's merits, but your action leaves us without a peace officer," Jones continued.

"You've been without a peace officer ever since you elected that apple polisher."

"He was adequate, Mr. Pardell," Matheson said, seemingly chagrined by Pa's assessment of their lawman. "Certainly, he is more adequate than his deputy."

Pa laughed crudely. "And I won't argue that. But I won't let this bunch," he jerked a thumb over his shoulder, toward the jail, "go free until Wetzel gets back."

"We'll take care of them," I said, stepping forward to inject myself into the conversation.

"I would say that's somewhat like asking the fox to guard the henhouse, isn't it?" Matheson replied.

"Except we won't haul them out of their cells in the middle of the night and let some lynch mob string them up," Pa stated flatly.

"Very well then," Jones said, shooting Matheson a cautionary glance. "It seems we find ourselves in a difficult position, with only one viable option." He paused, his gaze lingering on Matheson. "It is your call, Mark."

"I don't see where we have much of a choice," the shorter of the two replied.

"Then if you are so insistent upon accepting the responsibility for these wards, young man, so be it," Jones said to me. "Acting on behalf of the council at large, Mr. Matheson and I accept your offer. We'll need to make it official, of course."

Pa's eyes narrowed. I think mine might

have, as well.

"Just what does that mean?" Pa asked.

"It means we are going to deputize you and your son, Mr. Pardell, at least until Judge Wetzel returns from Cameron. The two of you will be assigned sole obligation for the care and safety of the men locked within these cells."

"And that the city of Shelburn will be absolved of all liabilities in regard to their incarceration," Matheson was quick to add.

Pa and I both laughed at the same time. "Don't worry," Pa said. "They'll be here when Wetzel shows up."

The two councilmen hung around a while longer to talk with Pa, but I'd run out of patience and went back inside the jail to check on the prisoners. Linus Kalb gave me a look that spelled hatred in capital letters, but the others appeared more subdued, and more than a little bewildered yet. Noticing blood staining the coarse fabric of Seth Henning's trousers, I asked if he needed a doctor. He gave me a puzzled look and I had to repeat myself twice more, nearly shouting, before he understood what I was asking and told me to go to hell.

When I went back outside, Jones and Matheson had disappeared, and the local doctor was binding the wound in Pa's thigh.

After he'd finished that, I escorted him into the cells to examine Seth's leg. Several of the others had small injuries, but the bullet — mine, if you recall — that had carved a trough through Seth's flesh was the worst of the bunch.

It was late afternoon before the crowd began to disperse from around the destroyed tinsmith's shop. I'd already gotten Pa inside and made him as comfortable as possible, then took our horses to the Shelburn Livery for the night. I'd also sent a man out to the farm to tell Ma what had happened, and she and Beau and Ester showed up in the buggy shortly before dusk. After some debate, Pa consented to let them drive him home, as long as Beau stayed behind to help me keep tabs on the prisoners.

A lot of the local citizens helped out more than I would have anticipated, bringing us food and cool drinks like lemonade, and coffee every morning, along with our breakfast. Someone must have sent word to Cameron, because Judge Wetzel showed up early Monday afternoon and immediately took charge of the jail. That suited me fine, although I think Beau would have liked to have stayed.

Because of the scope and seriousness of the various offenses, Wetzel took it upon himself to charge me with the killing of Henry Kalb, then immediately released me on what he called *personal recognizance,* meaning he trusted me to show up in court when my case was brought to trial. I appreciated his trust, and was damn glad to get out of town. Beau and I rode home immediately, where we found Pa sitting in his rocker in the dogtrot mending some old harness that we seldom used anymore.

Because the city attorney recused himself from the proceedings by citing conflict of interest, Wetzel brought in the county prosecutor from Cameron to help sort it all out. After charges were filed against Linus Kalb and his sons and the Henning boys, the prisoners were released on a five-hundred-dollar bail apiece, the money for all six put up by the Kalb family. The prosecutor also assigned a temporary officer to the city marshal's post until a special election could be held in June. The Kalbs and Hennings were given strict orders to stay away from the Pardell farm, and surprisingly, they did as they were told.

Don and Jay Lapwin couldn't be found. They apparently fled Milam County without even passing by home to tell their folks goodbye. About five years later I heard that Don Lapwin had been shot up in the Indian

Nations when federal marshals out of Fort Smith tried to arrest him for selling whiskey to some Choctaws. Jay was captured, and, since two of the marshals were wounded in the fight that resulted in the older Lapwin's death, Jay spend the next twenty years in the federal prison in Detroit, Michigan. I suppose he eventually got out. Or maybe he died there. To my knowledge, he never returned to Milam County.

The Hennings were charged with attempted murder for their ambush of Pa and me in Shelburn, and sentenced to three years apiece at the state prison in Huntsville. After their release in early 1881, Frank and Burt fell in with a rough crowd and were eventually captured after robbing a bank in a little town outside of Alexandria, Louisiana. When a teller shot during the holdup passed away several days later, a masked mob stormed the jail, hauled the two boys and another accomplice outside, and hung them from a magnolia tree on the town square. Then they shot them numerous times and finally splashed coal oil onto the bodies and set them afire. Sure as hell, they picked the wrong bank teller to shoot that day.

Seth Henning surprised us all by returning home and settling down on the family farm. He proved to be a hard worker, and when he married some years later, most folks figured he'd found the path of righteousness. Others weren't as ready to forget the past, but in time Seth proved them wrong. He grew the farm to nearly two hundred acres, and he and his wife raised six fine children to take over when they got too old to continue. Over the years, Seth and I would meet from time to time and talk about whatever it is men talk about in passing, but we never mentioned those wild, early days of our youth. Truth to tell, I think Seth was kind of embarrassed by what he'd once been, although as far as I was concerned, what he'd become more than made amends for that.

Linus, Jacob, and Paul Kalb were also charged with attempted murder and sent to Huntsville. Linus died there in 1880 from some type of congestion of the bowels. They say it was a horribly painful death.

Jacob and Paul were given early releases, and Jacob returned to the family farm and took over as patriarch, while Paul went to Arizona and started a cattle ranch. Jacob was a good farmer — he never was as wild as his younger brothers — and did well. I'm told Paul was also successful in life. He never came back to Milam County, though, and they say he held a grudge against Pa and me until his death from natural causes in 1901.

There were some around Shelburn who mourned Linus Kalb's death, but I don't think it was many. I know I didn't, and neither did Pa, who gained a limp out of that bullet wound and a dull ache that never completely went away.

Not long after the Kalbs were sentenced to Huntsville, Ester and Ann Dunford reunited to become best friends once more. Ester was a bridesmaid at Ann's wedding the following year, and Ann — although she couldn't participate in Ester's marriage to her brother, Carl, because she was expecting her first child at any time — did manage to attend the service. Ann gave birth to a girl the very next day and named her Ester Marie. Carl and Ester eventually had three children themselves. They lived in Shelburn for the first ten years of their marriage, until Carl bought a feed store in Rockdale and they moved there.

Bob Jolley died less than two weeks after I left the ranges. From what I heard, he was on his way to the Flat to put together another supply train, and his saddle mule stumbled coming up out of a creek and fell back on top of him. Jolley's spine was broken, his chest crushed on one side. The men with him said he breathed his last within thirty minutes of the fall. The mule was muddied but unhurt.

With Jolley gone, his business soon collapsed. A hide hunter named Pete Snyder bought out his stock and freighted it north to where he'd built a similar trading post that same year. Harry Brooks and Pedro Morales helped freight the supplies. With a capriciousness unique to expansionism, Jolley Town failed and faded from memory, while the community of Snyder, Texas, thrives to this day.

When I left the Flat below Fort Gibson in the spring of 1878, I was afraid I'd never see Uncle Abran or Rita again, but fate shines in your direction sometimes. It sure did for me with those two, and I was lucky enough to see them often over the years. After the buffalo were shot out in Texas, Abran and Rita moved to Santa Fe, New Mexico Territory, where they were married in the Catholic Church, and where Abran started working as a wood contractor. Early on, that meant taking a pack string of mules up into the mountains east of town and bringing back firewood that he'd sell to various businesses and well-to-do families around town. In time, he became a full-fledged timber speculator, buying entire sections of forest that he'd have crews cut down, then haul to his sawmill north of Santa Fe. There, he'd let the wood dry, then cut it into planks and beams that he sold throughout northern New Mexico and southern Colorado. Maybe you've heard of Foret Lumber. They've got yards in Santa Fe, Albuquerque, and Alamosa, Colorado.

Although the child taken from Aunt Rita by the Comanches was never recovered, she and Uncle Abran did raise seven children of their own, all of them adopted, and made it a point to visit our family on a regular basis. These joyous events were highly anticipated by everyone involved, including my own wife and daughters, when they came along.

I can't offer much firsthand information about Jenny Heflin, as I never saw or heard from her again. I did, however, do a little research on the name after finally receiving tenure, which granted me the free time and a staff of students to pursue my other interests. It seems Jennifer Delores Heflin, *née* Kline, was born in 1857 in Knox County, Tennessee. She married John Heflin in 1874, the two of them moving to Denton County, Texas, that same year. John Heflin died under mysterious circumstances in August of 1876 — strangulation, although the county coroner was unable to determine whether it was murder or suicide. No mention of Jennifer Heflin could be found in the following two years, but records indicate she married a Maxwell Stephens of San Antonio, Texas, in November, 1878. The two resided there until their deaths in 1926, when an automobile they were riding in was caught in the floodwaters of the San Antonio River.

I never saw Roy Potter again, either, but I did run across Andy Brenner quite a few years later, in Fort Worth of all places, the same city where I lost Potter's trail all those years before. Andy was working for the stockyards there, and had come into a small pub where I'd stopped off on my way home from visiting a colleague who'd been taken ill with a cancer of the esophagus. Saddened for my friend's prognosis, I barely took notice when a middle-aged gentleman in work clothes slipped onto the stool next to mine. Even after speaking my name in a hesitant tone, it took a moment to recognize him.

"I thought it was you," Andy said after confirming his own identity. He thrust a hand out and we shook warmly.

I won't bore you with the entire conversation, which included baseball scores, the price per pound for beef, and the threat of an impending war with Cuba. Suffice it to say, we spent several hours reminiscing about our time on the buffalo ranges of West Texas.

On the matter of Roy Potter, Andy had this to say: "He was a double-crosser, Gage. I'll admit I was suspicious of him from the moment he told me Scurlock and Tell had been killed by Indians, but I was scared, too. Hell, even without Indians, I was feeling desperate to get out of Scurlock's range. I'd swear that s.o.b. had ice water running through his veins. Roy and me discussed more than once the odds of him shooting us on the way back to Jolley Town so he could keep the money he owed us for peeling them shaggies.

"But once we pulled out of camp and left you behind, Roy changed for the worse. After we went a few miles, he stopped and said he needed to go back and get something. Right then is when I knew he'd been lying to me. I told him we didn't need anything from camp, but he said what he wanted wasn't at the camp, it was out there where we'd left Scurlock."

"Did he say what it was?"

"No, he didn't. I kinda figured he was going to see if he could find those two mules he'd cut loose from the wagon, but when he got back, he didn't have 'em, and he didn't say anything about where he'd been, either. If I hadn't been so worried about my own skin, I'd have asked what he was up to, but the way he was acting, I was half afraid he'd shoot me if I started to show any distrust.

"Anyway, I was anxious to get back to Jolley and see what the word was about Comanche raiders, but Roy only stopped long enough for us to buy a few supplies from one of those little stores north of the big post. He said we wasn't going to take time to talk to anyone, and it didn't sound like I was going to have any choice in that decision, either. Hell, we probably wasn't in town more than twenty minutes before Roy struck out for the Flat. I went with him because I was scared not to, but right before we got there, I slipped off in the middle of the night."

"Did you take any of the mules with you?"

"Nope, I didn't. I still had Tell's horse, and that was theft enough for my gullet. I headed east, and managed to stay ahead of Potter the whole way, although I saw him come through here some days later."

"Here?"

"Here is where I lit, and here is where I've stayed, one job or another."

I told him about my experiences after he and Roy left me out there on the range, and about afterward, too. He said he hadn't known I'd come through Fort Worth or he would have looked me up.

"Did you ever hear what happened to Potter?" I asked, and Andy immediately nodded.

"I did, although I ain't sure I believe it."

Now, there's a statement to get your attention, and I didn't need to tell him to go on.

"The Comanches got him."

"Comanches!"

"God's honest truth, at least as far as what I heard. Roy was heading north with those mules when a hunting party off the reservation caught him somewhere above the Red River and shot him dead. If they'd have left those mules alone, nobody likely would have ever known, but they took 'em back to the reservation and one of the agents there started asking questions."

"What happened?"

"Nothing that I know of. The agency confiscated the mules, but them Comanches said they found 'em wandering, and no one could prove otherwise. By the time they located Roy, he was too far gone to bring in, what with the wolves and other scavengers. They buried him where they found him, and let it drop after that."

I remember saying, "I'll be damned." Then the conversation moved on to other Indian issues and we never got back to the subject of Roy Potter. I always said I was going to look into it and see if I could confirm Andy's story, since he wasn't certain himself how much of what he'd heard was true, but I never got around to it. It would have been poetic justice if it happened that way, though.

I guess that leaves only one individual unaccounted for.

I said I was released on my own recognizance. That was in April of '78. On May 3rd, my case was brought before the court in Shelburn. Although I believe the jury was sympathetic to my cause, the defense that Henry Kalb had first drawn his weapon, then reholstered it *after* being mortally wounded, was too much for them to accept. I was found guilty of manslaughter and sentenced to seven to ten years. Because of my history with the Kalbs and Hennings, and because Judge Wetzel had taken a personal interest in my case, a trade was worked out where I served my time at the Arkansas State Penitentiary in Little Rock. It was hard labor and brutal conditions, but

I kept my nose clean, and Wetzel quietly commuted my sentence to five years. I was set free on May 19th, 1883, and never spent another night behind bars in my life.

Before the trial, I'd sent letters to newspapers in central New York and Manchester, England, but if anyone from those locations knew Jim Scurlock, they apparently didn't care enough to respond to my inquiries. After my release, I discovered Pa and Ma hadn't spent a nickel of the money Bob Jolley paid me for Scurlock's wagons and supplies. They said I'd earned it, and I reckon I did.

They did accept the cash Ma had sent along in that little clasp purse of hers when I first left home. To this day I don't know how much money they'd squeezed into that tiny, green-dyed pouch, but I appreciated every hard-earned dollar of it.

Oh, and Dusty . . . you might be interested to know he was as glad to see me when I returned from Arkansas as he had been when we reunited at Fort Gibson in the spring of '78. I sure did like that ol' horse.

Letter from Gage Foret to Rita Martinez Foret, Dallas, Texas July 8, 1951

Dear Mother:

I hope this message finds you in better health than when I left Santa Fe last week. Although I had my doubts of the necessity of attending your nephew's funeral, I am convinced now it was the right decision. Trust you to make it, and to "encourage" your children to find the correct path. And I agree that, as Gage's namesake, it was my duty to honor his place within our family. I think my presence pleased his siblings greatly.

Be assured that I conveyed to his immediate family that only a broken hip from your fall in the garden last May prevented you from being here, and that if Father were still alive, he would have "moved heaven and earth" to attend.

Cousin Gage's funeral was the largest I have ever attended. There must have been six hundred mourners in attendance at St. Anthony's alone, and at least two hundred souls graveside. Afterward, at a nearby community hall, I counted sixty-two individuals who approached the podium to speak of their admiration for Gage, or to relate their favorite memories of him. Surprisingly, an old acquaintance from his winter as a buffalo hunter, a Mr. Andrew Brenner, spoke briefly of that period of Gage's life. I think many within the audience were surprised to learn their staid old comrade and college professor had once exhibited a wilder side. Most, naturally, were more familiar with his numerous academic successes, and the accolades in that arena were generous.

I spoke only briefly with Gage's wife and children. Wilma sends her love and promises to write soon. The "kids," all grown now with children of their own, recalled your and father's visits to the Pardell family home with much fondness. Wilma mentioned that she and Gage had been married sixty-four years last March, and still lived in the same small house they had purchased after moving to Dallas all those years ago.

I will add within this note a Holy Card from St. Anthony's Church, and bring another that you may place in your Bible. I also accepted a snippet of satin ribbon from the flower arrangement you ordered. The array was striking and well

ABOUT THE AUTHOR

Michael Zimmer is the author of seventeen previous novels. His work has been praised by *Library Journal, Publishers Weekly, Booklist, Historical Novel Society,* and others. *The Poacher's Daughter* was the recipient of the 2015 Wrangler Award for Outstanding Western Novel from the National Cowboy and Western Heritage Museum; it received a Starred Review from *Booklist,* was included in True West Magazine's *Best of the West* (January 2015), and was a Spur Finalist from the Western Writers of America. *City of Rocks* was chosen by *Booklist* as one of the top ten Western novels of 2012. *Rio Tinto* and *Leaving Yuma* have also won awards. Zimmer resides in Utah with his wife, Vanessa, and two dogs. His website is www.michael-zimmer.com.

The employees of Thorndike Press hope you have enjoyed this Large Print book. All our Thorndike, Wheeler, and Kennebec Large Print titles are designed for easy reading, and all our books are made to last. Other Thorndike Press Large Print books are available at your library, through selected bookstores, or directly from us.

For information about titles, please call:
(800) 223-1244

or visit our Web site at:
http://gale.com/thorndike

To share your comments, please write:
Publisher
Thorndike Press
10 Water St., Suite 310
Waterville, ME 04901